A Village Tale

Donald McDonald. Drawing by Enrico Fornaini, Pisa, Italy.

Donald McDonald has been writing and telling stories all his life; his imagination being fired by Saturday morning cinema in Worthing and his first hero Black Bob in *The Dandy* during the fifties.

After the Suez crisis the family moved to Malta where he attended the Royal Naval School, Verdala.

Donald became a schoolmaster after graduating from Birmingham University School of Education though he has had a variety of jobs including advertising copywriter, assistant cinema manager and scaffolder's mate.

While his novels *Ignatius-Tagg* and its sequel *Sunshine for the Righteous* were published by *The Daily Mail* as one, titled *Ignatius Tagg – Dark Horse* and critically acclaimed by Amazon book reviewers his American novel – *9/12 Another Day* – was published by Harper Collins (New York) on their authonomy site.

He has a canon of work including screenplays, stage and radio plays and having written the definitive sequel to the original *The Italian Job* film, he hopes Columbia Pictures will consider it.

A Village Tale is Donald's third novel published by Brewin Books; his previous two *The Bridge* and *For The Glory of Stevenson* also garnered five star reviews on Amazon. He is currently penning *Someone*, a story set in New York during the fifties.

His passion for film, sport, books and art remains intact and he has travelled extensively in Europe and America; no trip to New York is complete without a visit to Madison Square Garden (and he still believes Stanley Ketchel was, pound for pound, the greatest fighter).

He now lives in Lincolnshire and supports Birmingham City FC and Widnes RLFC.

A Village Tale

A NOVEL BY
Donald McDonald

BREWIN BOOKS

BREWIN BOOKS
56 Alcester Road,
Studley,
Warwickshire,
B80 7LG

www.brewinbooks.com

Published by Brewin Books 2015

ISBN: 978-1-85858-535-2

Printed and bound
in Great Britain by 4edge Ltd.

Contents

A memory never far away...
Eileen Carter
1913-2004

There is no such thing as an unwounded soldier or an unwounded civilian in war.

Many of us are now tired.

Field Marshal Sir Douglas Haig
Commander in Chief, British Army in France, 1918.

Chapter I

The Roman philosopher Cicero wrote that a man with a garden and a library has all he needs. Donald Reid recalled his aged schoolmaster's words and the image of bloated cheeks, split veins and watery eyes built up in his mind. He mumbled "What Whistler failed to add was and also a view like this with Black Bob by my side." On hearing his name the Collie instinctively moved his jaw onto the young shepherd's lap. Even a spurr of rain couldn't encroach on master and dog's well being. In fact it personified an ideal Hogarth composition.

The view over the Wolds was majestic, no matter what time of year on the calendar. The man from Tunby Hill took a small dog-eared book from inside his thick tweed jacket and started reading as the sun had finally aroused itself after two hours of hanging low behind the horizon. The shooting rays illuminated Black Bob's body and if he could have spoken his pleasure he would have done, instead he arched his back and stretched the last vestiges of tiredness out of his frame with a yawn which if it could be spelt would probably appear written as "Rooo"!

Donald was studying a sepia print of a farmer cutting hay with a long scythe, in the background were fields of haystacks and beyond that a church. The subject's clothes suggested nineteenth century and the longer Donald studied the idealised representation of rural England, the picture almost seemed to come to life before Donald read aloud the inscription "From a different line of work my colleagues, I bring you an idea. You smirk! It's in the line of duty. Wipe off that smile and as our grandfathers used to say: GO ASK THE FELLOWS WHO CUT THE HAY." The young man took out his pocket watch and announced to his faithful friend it was time to return home for breakfast.

Half an hour later they were strolling toward the village and Donald wondered why a cart with a broken wheel slumped half-way down a track had not been repaired, after all it had been abandoned for months. At the top end of Tunby Hill, Black Bob paid fleeting interest to moorhens and herons busying themselves in a pond, while cows in an adjacent field merely looked on. The oldest son of a tenant farmer grinned when he recognised a bicycle slumped up against the wall of the local inn The Red Lion. Minutes later they were passing a row of thatched cottages whose white walls were glistening in the sun. Beyond that and already opened were two shops - Eric V. Snipe Butcher and Arthur E. Buckingham Baker and General Stores. Both man and dog followed the winding road and into view came cottages constructed of brick and pan tiled roofs, some larger than others, spotting the landscape at irregular intervals. One hundred years later the same irregular images would appear worldwide under the written headline 'England's Golden Sunset'.

Pale morning light kept rising like a thick fog and spreading softly over the land. "Two strong bursts of sunshine will filter it," Donald said to his Collie as his own home came into view and the prospect of fried eggs, bacon and black pudding brought a cabaret smile to his face. Exaggerated. He slowly tilted his head, a gesture of politeness when he passed three older women in a tight huddle of intense conversation, which dried up until he was out of earshot. He smiled as he often did at the mysteries of women.

The back door to the cottage creaked as he shut it behind him before removing his heavy waterproof coat, which wasn't as rain resistant as the manufacturers had boasted in their sales literature. He collapsed into a high backed oak chair and despite the fire having fallen low it still threw out a deep glow his feet immediately felt once he'd kicked off his hobnail boots. Black Bob took his customary place on the hearth rug and didn't resist sleep despite the distant shout of a cock-crow.

"Good morning son," his small framed mother offered him proffering a large mug of tea, "I've put two sugars in," she said as an afterthought. Donald thanked her and immediately took a large mouthful which put life back into him.

"You have a quiet nap and I'll have your breakfast ready in half an hour." Before she could continue her son was asleep and almost in a state of jubilation while steam could still be seen rising out the mug. Before leaving the room she looked at her eldest son safe in the knowledge she thought, that whatever lay ahead whether it was a life of hardship, he might be beaten from time to time but never broken. Perceptive.

"These eggs are good mother. I must thank Johnboy," he said before puncturing the yoke of his second. Donald smiled when his father, John, commented as he did about the food every breakfast and Peter, his younger brother, tapped his brother's leg, under the table with his boot. The teapot was filled up with scolding water from a metal saucepan bubbling on the range. While mother cleared the plates away the men took their mugs with them outside and rolled up cigarettes while eagerly looking at the sky which told them the degree of toil they would undertake over the next few hours. Father, lighting his sons' fags, was almost a ritual as was scrutinising his pocket watch when only seconds of life were left in his roll up. Then came that lull working men returned to, fleetingly, before stirring themselves and permitting themselves the luxury of being amiable to passers-by, also on their way to work, with a genuine bonhomie and avuncular enquiry.

"The sky will be clear in half an hour Bert, you'll see right across the Wolds." The latter short, snub nosed but oozing vitality replied,

"Long day... but the fair's arriving at the weekend... if it's anything like last year..." He didn't finish the sentence instead he smiled and nodded approvingly. The Reids stood up and father rasped to his wife tidying the kitchen,

"Make sure you treat those pheasants hanging in the back shed with respect... I don't want them complaining when we sit down to them on Sunday!" The two sons laughed in a disciplined manner and their father slyly winked in their direction.

Across the thicket and coming into view stood an imposing building, the intervals of silence heard earlier had disappeared and been replaced by what seemed metallic percussion. Fifteen year old David Croft rattled the milking pails as he gave them to the cowman.

"Lovely day?" queried the teenager.

"Isn't it," was the immediate reply followed by, "back on my rounds late morning," and with that he was off.

David retreated indoors, full of industry. He made up the copper fire having dutifully undertaken preparatory work at six o'clock that morning. In an hour that would provide hot water for the master and his family to wash. On to the black stocks – the open barrel fire grates which he lit in readiness for the family cook.

"Aren't we methodical?" teased Mary, the slightly older maid who looked a picture in her pinafore and apron. Neither had quite grasped the art of flirting but she was more practised at it than David.

"All ready," Mary glanced down at the master's and his family's footwear.

"A cup of tea would be champion while I tend to these?" asked David dolefully collecting the shoes before moving to a corner of the kitchen where he laid down paper on the stone floor and retrieved polish and brushes from a small cupboard attached to the wall.

"And don't forget the master likes to see himself in them and don't put too much shine on Miss Lucy's... she says it makes her feel on parade." Despite having his back to her he couldn't resist grinning. As an afterthought Mary piped up again,

"Don't let Maud catch you doing those in here..." The sudden silence was deafening and David swung his neck round,

"Morning Miss Maud… I was just about to take these outside." Stern faced but with a twinkle in her eye Maud stood with hands on hips; she was neither patriarch nor matriarch – somewhere in between,

"Outside indeed… off with you." David scooped the assorted shoes up in the paper and crammed them against his chest with both hands and deliberately struggled to the door as though the weight was unbearable. Mary didn't dare laugh until given permission to by Maud's wink.

"Right… Mary you can grind the coffee seeing as David's busy, then I want all the knives cleaned and make sure you use bath brick and board, that's what it's kept for." The young maid never needed to be told when to start. An interval of silence fell on the kitchen before Maud made a cursory inspection of the kitchen and once again stood with hands on hips.

"I think the master would like herrings and salt pork for his breakfast… Yes, he'll appreciate that on a day like today." She was meticulous in the manner in which she took down a few herrings strung up on a line across two corners of the kitchen.

As the morning wore on David feeding the fowls was interrupted by the chimes of the church clock; those same chimes that had serenaded generation after generation for centuries. He threw what was left of the feed for the fowls and went back inside the house, picking up the footwear outside the back door, while half a mile away the Revered Mitchell gripped the handlebars of his bicycle with arthritic hands and slowly pedalled through the village, wearing his cleric's uniform and a permanent smile. He slowed when David Baumber, the blacksmith working in his forge came into sight,

"Morning, David, beautiful morning."

"That it sure is Vicar," he said crashing his hammer down on a horseshoe, each stroke delivered with patience and increasing in strength and sharpness.

"Don't forget – bell ringing." David smiled, "Don't worry I'll be there." Suddenly he was immersed in his job and whistling loudly as he always did.

Breakfast was over in the Prior household and as Mary collected the dishes Mr Prior was patting his stomach; his hooked nose was emphasised by shining black hair worn with vigorous sideboards that ended up level with the bottom of his ears. He looked capable of throwing two tantrums at once, nasty even, but he wasn't – quite the reverse.

"Mary."

"Yes sir," Mary responded.

"Tell Maud before she passes away I want to know exactly how she manages to make those smoked herrings so good." When his daughters tittered he looked in their direction, tilting his head back,

"Did you enjoy your breakfast Ann?"

She nodded.

"Lucy?"

"Yes, thank you, father."

Suddenly Ann called to Mary and the maid waited expectantly,

"Thank Maud for the pork and oatmeal porridge... I don't think I shall want to eat again."

Lucy laughed to herself as Mary, faintly amused, offered,

"I'll tell her rightly, Miss Ann." A minute later Mr Prior jumped to his feet,

"I shall expect everyone in the drawing room for prayers in five minutes."

Mary carried the dishes into the kitchen where David was sat eating porridge.

"Hurry up, we've got prayers in five minutes," she continued as David began scoffing as his food, "and the master wants everyone there."

"I'll have to get into the garden after and start digging up potatoes, cabbages and other vegetables for dinner."

"Then," said Mary, "you'll have to chop up some more wood and fill up the coal scuttles." He smiled because he considered he had a good life and later that day warmed to this thought that after feeding the fowls he would be collecting the cows from the marshes; it was in this environment he felt, rather than could articulate, his place in rural England's new twentieth century albeit over a decade old.

Despite the slowness of change the working day always passed swiftly and late in the afternoon Mr Prior was sat at the mahogany desk in his study, exceptionally masculine in appearance, writing letters and reading correspondence. David looked whacked and this elicited a smile from Maud who poured piping hot tea into a large mug intending for him to put in his own sugar before buttering a warm scone and noting his warm expression, smiled to herself, "Master wants me to take the letters to the post office." Looking at Maud's breast pocket he enquired,

"What time is it?"

Maud retrieved her watch from the pocket of her dress,

"It's all right... you've plenty of time, it's not struck six yet, as long as you're there by 6.15 p.m."

David finished his tea, "Thank you but I think I'll go now." Catching Maud by surprise.

"My, we are hardworking today my lad," she said smiling with genuine affection.

"Yes, well I'm done for today. I shall stay up in the village and see my friends. Master says further digging in the garden I don't have to do until Friday."

Maud's expression changed,

"Well don't forget I shall need you to churn the butter tomorrow night, so don't get planning to do anything tomorrow evening will you?" David was about to take his leave but paused,

"All right... did I tell you I found a hen's nest in the hedge last Tuesday, should get me another three pence for all the eggs I've collected. That, plus my money for plucking the fowl the master sold to Wilson – I've got it all entered in me book. I'll be rich like the master if I continues to save."

Maud shook her head for she couldn't believe his innocence, "Go on with you and make sure you're tucked up in bed before 9.30 p.m. and don't get drinking ale with the older boys. They'll never make proper men – gentlemen." Just when she thought she'd had the last word, watching David raise the latch to open the door he swiftly turned around.

"I want to be a shepherd Maud, not a gentleman. Next year I'll be about ready to be a shepherd's page. I've stayed out several nights before now and them queer noises don't bother me anymore. I know the master lets the shepherd get on by himself, trusts him to do a good job and respects him for it." Throughout this final conversation piece Maud deliberately kept her decorative mug of tea against her lips, looking up with simple eyes.

Chapter 2

The lambing sales in the Tunby Hill market were a bustling affair when each village shepherd came to see what was on offer; there was unanimity in them when they got together and an erratic discipline. Their uniform was simple sleeved waistcoats and breeches and during the sales some became excited, some unfriendly, but no one exactly hostile. When bidding began to reach fever pitch one shepherd from a distant market town was known to exhibit petulant anger as if the frayed skin of his patience had been punctured.

Donald leaned over the iron railings which penned in the lambs and was joined by Sid Hardy, the younger brother of Harry, a most unpleasant man. There had, for as long as anyone could remember, been an air of suspicion and mistrust between their families.

"Hello Donald," Sid said and gesturing towards the animals continued, "like anything today?" Donald deliberately took time to reply, "Can't make me mind up Sid, but I tell these can do with some lambing money." As he looked around recognising faces, affable words were exchanged and half vocalised pleasantries filled the air. Donald knew Sid wanted his undivided attention but had always thought of him as resembling a musician out of a cheap dance hall rather than a farmer, playing notes that were very dull and colourless.

"I hear you're fighting Michael Jeffries at the fair?" Sid waited impatiently for an answer, releasing an air of contempt.

"Michael's a good boy, make no mistake..."

Sid couldn't wait to respond, "Harry says he wants you in the square next fair... reckons he's got the measure of you." His tone was designed to provoke Donald but the latter knew Sid was uncomfortable and hesitant – the classic sign that he'd been put up to it. Donald gave himself time to think, he almost felt sorry for the younger brother knowing if the little rat had had any brains it might be worse.

"What do you think of Michael?" asked Sid.

Donald replied, "I think Michael's a good 'un talk is he's after courting one of those Prior girls." Sid's face suddenly lit up as though he was freed from his prepared script, "Sure are pretty them two." Donald chuckled, "Sid, don't listen to idle gossip and worry about your own love life an' no one else's 'cause they aren't worried about you." The sudden change of direction had inadvertently wrong footed Sid, diminishing his earlier confidence and slight annoyance registered in his small eyes.

"Harry says he wants to court the young one, Lucy. Yeah that's it, Lucy is her name. I reckon he could if he put his mind to it... do you?" The last two words seemed to offer a threat. Donald, tired of the younger man's presence walked to another side of the pen deliberately acknowledging other farmers knowing Sid's eyes would be stabbing him repeatedly. If their conversation had been in letter form it would have been badly written with a scratchy nib on cheap paper.

When the sales were finally over everyone returned to the thatched pub whose interior charm lay in the exposed beams and stone fireplace with inglenook. The landlord a retired, be-whiskered gent joyfully pulled pints into straight glasses and pewter mugs. The starched white tea towel over his shoulder gave him a certain charm. It was just as well Donald had declined a drink on this occasion as louder than usual Harry Hardy oafish, arrogant and slightly drunk was among friends including his two brothers Arthur and Sid. The older customers tended to give the party as wide a berth as was possible in the packed inn.

"I want to know when Mr Prior is going to let his two daughters come to the village dance," Harry said. His friends laughed and David Croft, sat discretely out of sight, was startled by the rasping voice as it continued following his brother's query as to why either of them girls should look at him?

"They likes a man when they sees one, just haven't seen one yet. Those business people of Mr Prior who invite them out... they ain't men, not one of them knows the meaning of hard work." Arthur winking at the group chipped in, "Well any more of this ale, Harry, and you won't know the meaning of work today or tomorrow or next week... that's for sure." Everyone laughed while Harry stumbled to the bar and slammed his glass down on the counter. It was reluctantly filled up by the landlord, who kept his thoughts to himself...

Three miles away after attending the sales, Donald could feel the April chill on his face as he sat on the heath watching his flock scattered among the whin bushes. He stood up, his shepherd's smock flowing behind him, crook on shoulder and Black Bob at heel walking in front of his sheep at a steady pace, but longing to release his energies. If it was a long day, the evening would be longer where men's work was involved and the women said nothing; his mother knew what the men got up to and subsequently produced a rich dumpling stew and apple pie topped with custard. It was this that Donald's nostrils tuned to when he entered the family home just after seven o'clock. His father and brother, Peter had already scrubbed their hands having had their sleeves rolled up by mother. "Come on son, let me help you off with that," his brother said as Donald was momentarily overcome with tiredness. With his top removed he sauntered to the kitchen sink and put his head under the tap already flowing with cold water. He grabbed a small towel lying on the draining board and wrapped it round his head before washing his hands, with carbolic soap, vigorously.

He joined the rest of the family at the table having put on a clean shirt hanging on a string line near the range. Four large soup bowls were now full of stew and Mr Reid clicked his hob nailed boots together before taking a mouthful of dumpling. Little was said as a baked loaf, fresh out the oven, was cut up by mother and passed around her boys. In the background the range blazed a fire that crackled like a million insect eggs being crushed. Finally the apple pie was gone and the men retreated to easy chairs facing the range while Mrs Reid made a pot of tea. They dozed, each with their own memories brought alive with vivid colouring; later they would be out for the night but for now they could luxuriate in the smell of flour, characteristic of the kitchen because it usually overcame the other smells which at this time of year were numerous and sometimes strong. Only the flies springing from a decaying corner of the wall were a nuisance, despite Mrs Reid's daily assault on them.

From the outside the cottage seemed derelict; all light had been extinguished and John Reid's wife was sound asleep in bed, it was approaching midnight. A few miles away Donald was marching his sheep to an inlet on the Lincolnshire coast where contraband goods were being loaded from a boat by his father and brother onto a wagon. He strained his eyes but visibility was so poor that eager customs men could be less than twenty yards away. Only once had his father nearly been caught when the look-out had fallen asleep on a balmy night. "This job," his father had once told him, "was like a ship to be sailed in all weathers despite sea sickness or uncertain winds." He thought he now understood what his father had meant. The whole operation was down to meticulous timing and once over, Donald guided his sheep to cover up the tracks of the wagon, particularly at their derelict barn where the contraband was unloaded.

Later that morning Donald was listening to shots in an adjoining thicket before scampering over to find two dead hares which he quickly put into pockets sewn into his smock; he allowed himself an impish smile before disappearing into the shadows.

Unfortunately, buckets of rain commenced falling from the sky as the church clock announced six o'clock but Donald was too far away to hear it. Huddled by some large boulders with a canvas wrap over himself, he drank from a wooden keg strapped across his shoulder with Black Bob his only companion. When daylight replaced the rain Donald gave his Collie the nod and he began rounding up the stragglers and all followed the shepherd after he had used a stick to break up turnips into pieces for the animals to eat. He attached a sheep bell to the chosen leader of the flock and as a mist descended the others followed guided only by the sound of the bell.

Later that day his father John and brother Peter were by a river bank filling a large square tub with water and before long the sheep were being washed individually under breast before being turned over on the bank and then lifted out of the tub and onto a platform of straw. Laughter broke out when a sheep weighed down with water was unable to stand until it had shaken itself free of excess water, "Hooray!" shouted Peter as it drifted away to join the others.

The following day was put aside for the sheep shearers at the Reid farm when mother would go overboard with hospitality for those skilled workers whom it seemed to Mr Reid had a balletic approach to their work. Finally the sheep would be 'dipped' to kill off lice and ticks. A tortuous, thirty-six hours that none ever complained about for the Reids had an incipient dignity and Donald in particular, a certain 'presence'. From afar the boys understood their father's rather silent attitude, his gentlemanly reserve and both admired his intelligence while their mother always saw a halo of mystery about her husband and it was enough to fire her constant cheeriness. When this punishing work week was over no wonder the boys looked forward to the fair arriving on Saturday morning. On Friday night just before ten o'clock Donald lay spread-eagled on his bed and with a sigh blew out the candle fixed into a holder and sank into sleep. He knew he would handle himself well the next day.

Chapter 3

The roar was deafening as the older Reid son walked into a straight right; he fell to the ground and the cheering continued. This was one of the main attractions each year: a makeshift ring and men eagerly betting on the outcome of the fight. The other fighter, Michael, also the son of a tenant farmer looked battered and bruised and kept going by sheer willpower.

"Have you had enough?"

"No, I don't think so" and with that Donald rose to his feet. The referee was happy and as Michael advanced believing this his greatest opportunity he was floored by a mighty blow which sent him reeling around the ring, as more money changed hands. He hit the canvas deck. Despite his seconds beseeching him to get up, it was over.

Both referee and Donald crouched down, gently sitting up the dazed fighter who had blood flowing out of his mouth like the River Nile. Gradually he was raised to his feet and a chair found and he acknowledged the gesture. Within minutes both contestants were sat in one corner. "Donald I think that makes it two all... I hope they get two different men next year?" This elicited a smile from his opponent whose gloves had also been removed. "Yeah, come on let's go and have a drink and see if my sister can't patch these cuts up." When the fighters left the ring those spectators remaining clapped in a civilised manner – gone was the former chimpanzee excitement.

As the two walked towards one of several makeshift bars so they were followed by some admirers. Michael whispered, "Play our cards right and we won't have to pay for any beer today!" Donald tired, tried to laugh but could still feel his friend and opponent pounding away at his solar plexus. They watched rich in anticipation, as Lincolnshire's sole brewery and supporter of the fair poured slowly, deliberately, Batemans bitter into a straight glass. The head was inviting without being over elaborate and a cheer went up as both fighters chinked glasses and drank most of the beer without pause.

"That tastes good Michael."

"Bitter and blood," responded the defeated man and they chuckled while the brewer aware of the value of publicity drew two fresh pint glasses and began filling them up in a stylish manner, deliberately pausing to hold the glass up to check for sediment, knowing damn well there wouldn't be any! Another couple of pints were drunk but this time sat at hastily arranged wooden tables and chairs and both men were happy to let the early afternoon sunshine beat down on their heads. Michael became slightly tipsy and began talking with all the enthusiasm of a month's worth of Friday evenings in the pub. Donald slowed him down. It was a gallant gesture and Michael was his friend and not his erstwhile adversary or an acquaintance. He dispatched a young boy to get them some bread and pork "with crackling" from one of the spits dotted around the field. As the money changed hands his last instruction was for two large mugs of sugary tea "then I'll give you a tip". What boy wouldn't acquiesce having witnessed two older boys in the ring?

While the men slurped their tea, Flora, Donald's teenage sister wiped down their faces as she'd done earlier and rubbed cream into cuts that no longer seeped blood, she had dressed up for this important day in the social calendar. Both men thanked her and she left arm in arm with her girlfriend each confiding their secrets to one another as they waltzed towards one of the attractions. Watching them Donald shook his head. Had words dropped from his mouth they would have roughly translated to "Ain't life grand". The annual fair brought joy into the lives of these rural communities; apart from the singing it was something they loved and looked forward to and for some it might have taken the place of the sun in their hearts.

In one corner of the field numbers were increasing and both fighters decided to investigate. As they approached they noticed the audience was mainly children, whose eyes were bright with excitement. Having shuffled their way to a corner near the front, Donald pointed out a poster pinned to the tree and read aloud, "H. Andrews Dentist – service to include extractions and fillings, artificial teeth supplied – it is important to have healthy teeth." Michael read the final statement printed in bold capitals, "All teeth extracted – painless work guaranteed." The audience were mesmerised by the sight of a miserable looking man lying back in an unusual looking chair screaming with agony as a tooth was being pulled by a self-styled dentist. Most of the audience winced, though a couple of boys thought it was hilarious. The patient's fist was clenched tight as he fought against the pain while the dentist offered soothing comfort even if his manner was overall, one of cynical amusement, "Just a little more and I'll have this stubborn one out." His assistant who resembled a solemn grave digger took a bottle of whisky from a doctor's bag and poured a large measure down the patient's throat.

Looking at the assembled audience with a smile, the dentist offered hollow words of comfort to his patient, "Are you ready?" Suddenly an excruciating yell pierced the afternoon setting followed by the dentist proudly showing off the extracted molar, dripping blood, held between a pair of evil looking tongs, "There you are." The crowd winced, and looking at his patient still spitting blood into a bowl held by his assistant, the dentist continued, "There you are... you see a bit of pain but it is over. Anyone else ready?" The audience collectively retreated one step but he wasn't put off, "Don't think you can withstand the pain of toothache because you cannot... it hurts today but next week you will be in agony... not only that but during your working day..." he deliberately left the last sentence dangling knowing many would have food for thought. "Come on let's go," said Michael almost pulling Donald away. "Poor bloke looks like he needs to go to bed for a week," Donald said as they watched the patient being led away supported by two friends.

They were attracted to organ music and soon both men were laughing at the sight of an organ grinder's monkey wearing a pink dress with white trim and drinking from a bottle; once again the children found it hilarious. Not so funny though and Michael remarked about it was a rather mangy looking dancing bear held at bay by a chain and nearby a couple of hats for spectators to throw coins into. More pleasing though were expressions of childhood: excited boys playing marbles and girls using skipping ropes.

Eventually Michael and Donald walked towards a hastily constructed pavilion that had been assembled for the occasion where women sat on the veranda, while inside the men drank ale in robust fashion. Michael estimated that up to four hundred had attended but Donald wasn't so sure, nevertheless it was the parents who actively supported the notion of an annual fair because it promoted companionship for older boys other than that found in alleyways or public houses which were synonymous with unlawful activities. The expression "hope, would not go wrong" was always in the back of adults' minds. That evening Donald and Michael met up again, in the local inn.

The following week, a Tuesday to be exact, the morning sun burnt into the energy of Arthur Hardy as he guided two horses dragging a metal plough amidst a jangling of chains and leather straps; the soil was churned up in a ruthless fashion by metal spikes. The horses looked an odd pair, one lean, one overweight but both breathing heavily as their hooves sank into the soil before being pulled out. The same scenario inhabited an adjacent field where Jack Hardy drove his horses with guttural charm occasionally taking in the views seen through the dappled foliage of trees while seventy-five yards away a couple of jackdaws characteristically dropped their cries from the sky having circled in menacing fashion. When they caught sight of each other the older man motioned with his hand to a clump of trees separating the two fields; both had been working non-stop for three hours. Within ten minutes they had guided the ploughs towards this rendezvous where Jack had prepared four feed bags for the horses. Arthur was blowing hard, "I'll get our grub if you're going to feed the horses" and with that he undid a haversack leaning against a sturdy, misshapen Elm tree and took out a parcel and metal pot. Meanwhile his father was patting the horses' necks offering encouragement as he put their feed bags over their heads; immediately they were munching the oats and Arthur was munching a home-made meat pie,

"This is good father... I'm starved all right." He handed the other pie over to his father who sat down and unwrapped it, "Thank you son." He too tucked into it, "Man, it's good."

Nothing was said until Arthur unscrewed the top of the metal container and poured the contents into two unmatched cups, both chipped at the rim. Jack took one of the cups graciously from his son and sipped the first mouthful. Arthur slurped his mouthful.

"Your mother wouldn't like to hear you, would she?"

Arthur was bemused, "Out here it's different, no airs and graces."

Jack allowed himself a smile, "All the same, forget not your manners, you might find you need them one day," and with that he drank his tea quietly.

"Do you believe in all that stuff about being a gentleman?" Arthur was impatient for an answer so his father took his time in the hope that his younger son would absorb what he was saying.

"Having money doesn't make you a gentleman, no sir, but the older you get, the older Harry and Sid get, you'll all understand one day, hopefully." He deliberately stressed the last word and another pause ensued.

"Harry's getting more restless as the months go on, talking of going away last week," Arthur stopped to sip the remainder of his tea before continuing, "joining the army of all things." He expected a reaction from his father but didn't understand yet that often with age came guile. Nevertheless he was intrigued by how his father would respond.

"Well he might just find himself quicker in the army than even he reckons to be there!" Arthur adjusted his position and asked what his father meant before taking another bite of pie.

"Don't you ever look at the newspaper, son?"

"Well just the..." he was abruptly interrupted.

"There's going to be war in Europe before long." Arthur looked alarmed.

"That won't affect us will it?"

The conversation had ignited Arthur's imagination and troops of colourful images started peppering his imagination as his father continued.

"Not if we didn't have them silly alliances! What do we want to be friends with the French for? We fought them enough times." Arthur tilted his head back.

"Is France going to war then?"

Jack looked his son in the eye.

"No, but she could get dragged in, the Kaiser's getting too big for his boots, they say he can't stand the idea of France being a powerful country at Germany's expense. In the foreign part of Africa they say France, Germany and the Empire have all got a bit greedy." Not wishing to lose the thread yet wondering how his father was so knowledgeable he asked him the ultimate question "Do you think there will be war?" Jack almost took a final mouthful of tea. "Who knows, but one thing's for sure I won't be able to manage if you three go off to war. Break your mother's heart it will. She lost her only brother in the Boer War." Arthur rose to his feet walked over to the horses to renew their feed bags and put the animals at ease with his gentle approach before returning to the plough.

"Would they call you up?"

"No, not me," smiled Jack.

"No, I didn't mean you. I mean me, Harry and Sid." The response had reluctance attached to it.

"Well it would get to these parts eventually I suppose." Jack looked into the distance while Arthur asked him, "How do you mean?" Still looking away he answered his son's question.

"Well there'll be big fanfares in the towns first, everyone getting excitable, and young men, very impressionable trying to impress with stories about what they gonna do to win a Victoria Cross. It spreads like a ripple in a pond. One thing is," he paused before returning his gaze towards his son, "once the fighting gets underway it ain't no picnic – well certainly wasn't for me." Arthur was now sat bolt-upright his eyes eager for information.

"That's right you fought... where was it?"

Jack appeared reluctant to expand but because of his son's age he couldn't deny him, his inquisitive nature yet at first he tried to deny any emotional entanglement with what he said,

"Karee with Tuckers 7th Division. We had shrapnel burst over us and the Scottish Borderers. Five men were killed, five with a single shell. Wavell's Brigade of Cheshire, East Lancashires, North Staffords and I think South Wales Borderers came up in support." Arthur was transfixed.

"What happened?"

Jack took a bite of pie and small swig from his cup, which only increased his son's impatient curiosity.

"The ground was too open and the position too strong to push the attack home."

Jack looked around for a broken stick and immediately he saw one to his right side. He drew a map in the dusty soil that sheltered under the shade afforded by a long bough.

"The French with their horses began to make an impact because the Boers fled but they still got their guns away safely."

"Were, are, the French good horsemen?" All thoughts of getting back to the grind of work had disappeared for Arthur and Jack knew it.

"They say the Irish are natural horsemen... the cavalry who charged at the head of the Eighth Hussars, into the valley of death at Balaclava in the Crimea were the Royal Irish... we were told they were a 'swashbuckling regiment' well trained in tactics and the care and use of weapons. With the sabre they learned the cuts and guards, how to use the point and how to 'slash' to lop off arms, legs and hands. Those cavalrymen loved their horses and the latter would work their socks off for anyone who showed them some affection."

"They sound like an improvement on people." His son's remark brought a smile to Jack's weather-beaten face and he took out his pocket watch to scrutinise the time. Arthur wasn't ready to resume work.

"I've never heard you talk of that war before today." He looked for an explanation and his father obliged in a thoughtful manner.

"That's because I saw good men have the life ripped out of them... only in war do you realise how precious life is." Arthur was eager for more.

"Where else did you fight... please... I'd like to know." His father reluctantly acquiesced, "I'll tell thee then no more will be said on the matter nor will you say anything to your brothers... don't ask why." Arthur nodded.

"Okay father."

Jack inhaled, "We came under fierce attack at a place called Vitrals Deck that was only twenty miles from the capital. We weren't really part of the support line, more a link. The gunner was attacked." Once again he started drawing with his stick before continuing.

"We were waiting for reinforcements all day. By night we had run out of ammunition, lost a third of our men and the only option left was surrender," he paused to look at his son,

"you know I never really understood why I was there or what I was fighting for. A soldier obeys orders and does his duty."

Suddenly he rose to his feet and threw the remains of his tea out of the cup. As they prepared the ploughs Arthur said, "Father, don't tell Harry all that, he'll make you out to be everyone's hero. He's already winning everything that's going." Before they parted for their respective fields Jack smiled at his son before concluding with "Harry's gonna get a rude awakening one of these days. I've heard all his bragging, it gets back and if someone don't give him a pasting soon, I will." The sun was by now high in the sky and another five hours of strength sapping toil lay ahead for the men and horses.

Chapter 4

The farmhouse nestled on the brow of a small hill looked solid and dependable with outbuildings surrounding it on two sides. Three hours earlier Helen Clements had awakened from a deep sleep and though she found no energy sufficient to stretch her arms in a yawn and make a fist, she couldn't stop gazing at the recently pruned Ash tree. It appeared to take on a physical form and for no particular reason she saw Marco Polo walking through history with the aid of a long stick, maybe the image had been created by the way the leaves had been clipped or it was the young lady's prolific imagination. She lay gazing, then smiled to herself and ten minutes later threw the blankets off her bed and yawned her way to the bathroom. The day ahead would be long.

It was almost seven o'clock when she joined her mother for breakfast, dressed accordingly. She looked at the bruised fruits jutting out of the top of a wooden bowl and began cutting a large slice from the cooling loaf her mother baked each morning at five-thirty leaving it in the oven until it was ready to be placed on the dining table.

"Let's hope this stops soon," her mother said watching the eddying raindrops throwing up little mists of spray on the outside window ledge. She returned to the range and moved pots to strategic positions with hands that were roughened with years of labour. Despite the warmth in her eyes she had a resolute chin that announced character and determination.

"This rain will be over soon," said Elizabeth making a cursory glance towards the window. When her mother retreated to the range she nearly lost her balance, for the floor was not only as shiny and hard as marble but as slippery as ice. "Careful mother!" gasped her daughter and at that precise moment the cuckoo sprang out the clock to announce seven o'clock. "And you can stop laughing!" Emily rattled deliberately pulling a stern expression which had her daughter smiling. There was a brave cheerfulness about Elizabeth's mother; she had the ability to turn most troubles into pleasantries until they vanished. She was, thought Elizabeth, as gallant as a ship in heaving seas plunging through any storm, riding over it, circling it but never going under it.

The table was cleared and Mrs Clements began the task of ham curing. She hummed a tune as she gave the meat a dry salt bath rubbing vigorously before putting it in a pot and covering it with more salt.

"That should stand for seven days," she said slapping her hands together repeatedly, "right Elizabeth bring the other pot." Elizabeth obeyed her mother's instruction but made an enquiry.

"This has only stood for six days... are you sure it really is ready?" Mrs Clements took hold of the pot and looked inside, "I don't think a day will hurt it." Her daughter began mixing black treacle and brown sugar, creasing the expression on her face as her hands got stickier and stickier; satisfied she then heated a quart of beer in a dark pot before pouring it over the mixture. The kitchen was heating up and Elizabeth continued to smile; her face had that charm of infinite variety and this endeared her to friends and strangers alike; her hair was the envy of other women – darker than most, curly, of true Saxon colour and full of life, health and energy.

Later that morning the daughter, her figure cast as a shadow by the sun onto a whitewashed shed, began collecting water from the adjacent well. Despite her slight appearance three pails were soon full to the brim and Elizabeth began washing clothes stacked in a bundle at her feet.

Mrs Clements, as meticulous as ever, had drained the ham of all salt and began smelling the aroma given off by the mixture "I think it's ready" she said quietly to herself before pouring another mixture over the meat then rubbing it in. As she did so Elizabeth appeared back in the kitchen carrying a large stone and placing it on the working table.

"I think it's my turn to turn it this week," she said to her mother who replied, "Well don't forget it must be done every day, flesh side up one day and skin side the next." Elizabeth paused to scratch a tickle on the end of her nose then continued, "Helen can take this to the wheelwright this time mother." Her mother scrutinised her before responding.

"Well, just make sure she tells him to dry them out good and proper." Elizabeth was quick with her reply.

"That's not fair, you know Mr Scotford had built himself a special drying house and all the villagers for miles send their bacons and hams to him." Her mother afforded herself a moment's relaxation before responding.

"Yes, well maybe I'm getting suspicious as I grow older... I remember my father telling me no one worked hard or did what he called a full day anymore." Silence entered the kitchen as both women began tidying up and washing the dishes. Mrs Clements began sweeping the floor, leaving no corner untouched; soon the bristles on the broom head were clogged up and she took it outside to rub it down against rough brick before coming back in and continuing her chores. Elizabeth was busy heating the water in order to make a fresh pot of tea.

"I hear from the parish that your sister is quite taken with that Donald Reid – that so?" Elizabeth pretended she hadn't heard until her mother almost barked "Well?"

"Oh mother, don't listen to gossip you'll be believing that Reverend Mitchell wants to marry them off." There was a deliberate pause then Elizabeth, adopting a casual stance, offered, "She likes Donald and why not, he's a fine upstanding young man. The family are good tenant farmers, honest and forthright." Her mother was quick on the uptake,

"They're good all right, better than the Hardy family but tenant farmers are all the same. We're not in the same class as the new Priors people, but your father and me started with little and worked all our time to arrive at this." She looked around with an air of satisfaction rather than smugness.

"I know you and Papa worked hard and I admire you for it."

Mrs Clements smiled and looking out the window saw Helen hanging up some clothes on a line fixed between two trees.

"Come here and look at your sister." It was a soft rather than authoritative command and soon both of them were looking at the younger daughter.

"Helen is really beautiful, isn't she mother?"

Emily Clements pondered this remark.

"I think both of you are angels of perfection," Elizabeth was stunned at her mother's eloquence, "I hope she doesn't marry an older man." Her daughter stood beside her and understood what she meant. She continued with, "It would be a pity and it's not quite right... she does remind me of my own mother." Elizabeth allowed her mother to luxuriate in this reminiscence and nothing more was said as they continued looking, however Elizabeth through her eyes, blue and frank as the sun, detected the momentary sadness in her mother's face; a sadness she surmised might only be lifted by a warbler and a willow wren singing.

Mrs Jeffries was one of those no nonsense women fired through with God, good order, loyalty, tradition and was thoroughly decent. She was outside her home with two old casks inserting an old piece of chain in the bung hole then shaking the cask before rolling it about. When she removed the chain her daughter, Ann, a lithe and attractive creature came into the kitchen carrying a pot of boiling water. Her mother addressed her in cautious fashion, "Mind what you're doing with that... I don't want you being scolded." Ann grimaced.

"It is heavy."

Her exasperated mother retorted, "Well, put it down child and give me a hand." For a third time the cask was rolled back and forth, back and forth.

"Well, that ought to loosen the mash. Right let's have the water." Her daughter called on Herculean strength to pick the pot up and pour the contents into the cask.

"I hope you gave these things a proper cleaning in piping hot water." Her look was firm and quizzical.

"Mother, I wish you wouldn't treat me like a child. I am nineteen years old." Mrs Jeffries ignored her indignant daughter.

"When I was your age it was traditional for the horseman to take charge of the brewing. There were hog stands in those days, great big barrels holding fifty gallons or more." She felt an air of satisfaction making that statement and looked for Ann's reply.

"Was them for the harvest or Christmas?" she asked meekly.

"Both, see families took it in turns to make for each other. The barrel horse was made to scrape out the barrels with lime wash. Before he was lowered in," she gestured the movement with her hands before continuing, "the horseman would test the air with a candle, you know that same way a well is tested before a man is lowered in. If the flame continued to burn brightly then no foul air was present. It was a big event." She began nodding her head while her daughter remained motionless.

"Everything else went by the board, even children kept off schooling to do odd jobs about the house. I remember him writing to say his lad would not attend school because he was needed at home for brewing." The last remark surprised Ann.

"Shouldn't miss his schooling, that's not fair is it?" Her mother didn't reply merely stretched her frame up and down before looking at her daughter.

"Ready?"

They rolled the cask back into the kitchen where everything had been meticulously prepared for brewing. On a long table was a wooden tub banded with metal and a plain wooden barrel. Alongside was a horsehair sieve for straining, a funnel on a rack which the sieve would rest on during the straining process also a hand cup, wooden ladle, a witch, taps made of wood and a brass tap with key. Adjacent to this stood a brick wall built oven and beside it a six pail copper which added a certain characteristic to the kitchen. They enjoyed a mug of hot tea before operations began.

Mrs Jeffries lit the copper, sitting the brewing tub on the stool before placing the witch over the tap on the inside of the tub. Satisfied she looked to her daughter.

"Right Ann, pour the water in." This she did as delicately as possible. First two pails of cold water followed by one pail of boiling water, "Ok" muttered her mother before pouring some malt into the water. Some minutes passed before she started draining the malt from one side of the tub to the other repeatedly. Ann watched absorbing everything for she knew that one day this would be her job and she listened with undivided attention as her mother went through each step explained every procedure. Ann watched as her mother opened the tap and drew off a bucket of the liquid then putting it back in. She then poured a bucket of hot water to ensure no particle of malt was left dry. A rack was then placed across the tub and covered with cloths and sacks and left.

There was a break for another cup of tea before Mrs Jeffries indicated "time-up" and continued the brewing. Ann was instructed to take out five pails of boiling water from the copper and pour them onto the malt. Her mother stirred the resulting mash before covering it up and leaving it to stand. Four hours passed before both were back in the kitchen and Mrs Jeffries cleaned the witch in the previous manner before the liquid was drawn off into the other wooden barrel. Once again Ann filled the copper with four pails of water and as the water boiled it was poured into the mash left in the tub and once again left to stand for four hours while the women attended to other chores.

When the correct time had elapsed Mrs Jeffries poured the liquid from the first wooden barrel into the copper adding some hops to it. Once it had boiled up she drained it through the hair sieve back into the barrel. This operation was repeated for the second load.

"Yes, I think it's warm enough," she said to her daughter, dipping her finger in and adding yeast to the beer. She smiled broadly when she saw the yeast beginning to collect around a couple of corks she'd put in prior to pouring in the yeast. Ann couldn't think of anything to do or say so settled for nodding her head in an approving fashion. Finally Mrs Jeffries exhaled and gritted her teeth.

"Everything is all right now that the beer is smiling." Her last action was to spread a thick cloth over it. She wore the look of someone who understood her place in her community – forever cheerful, healthy looking with ruddy cheeks and no one would have known she was half crippled with rheumatism. Mrs Jeffries left the kitchen feeling keen and happy, her next chore was tending to the cabbages in the vegetable patch and taking care of the white caterpillars with soapy water. City dwellers visiting this slice of country life would probably have described it with one word – frugal.

That evening mother and daughter discussed Evensong at the church they attended on Friday evening with several other women, young and old, while the majority of men congregated at the local inn, The Red Lion.

Thursday was a mellow day; the sky registered not one cloud and a breath of warmth hit everyone working outside as though summer had forgotten it wasn't her season. The Reids and the Hardys toiled away even when the sunlight became harsh and began vibrating and their words jarred under it. As was tradition they dispensed with a lunch break preferring to eat while they worked knowing that they would finish earlier than on the previous days of the week. After three o'clock their spirits were on the way home and the uppermost questions in their minds were 'who would get in the tin bath first and enjoy the clean water?', 'Would hot tea with bread, butter and jam revitalise them and dispel any feeling of pessimism?' For now the sons had hearts as light and free as air, a cheery disposition and their conversation was about young women which was often checked by their respective fathers for the latter knew that village girls were a vision of youth and candid innocence and their behaviour, usually, sanctioned by the law of God and by their own hearts...

A glow of silence dropped out of the sky and blanketed the whole area except for one venue – the inn. Fortified by food and rest some men quickened their pace as the lights became brighter, the noise louder and the prospect of good ale, all consuming. The latch-key inner door made a welcoming distinctive sound each time it was opened and every denizen was welcomed as though they had been missing for a week. Men with similar pint pots and different style pipes were watching an arm wrestling contest between Harry Hardy and Michael Jeffries. The atmosphere in that corner was tense as first Harry gained the upper hand and then Michael. The cheers of the spectators lifted the fug of smoke up into the ceiling before returning in visible balls. Ten minutes had passed since the young men took their seats and now Michael was desperately trying to hold his own but he was racked with the continuous effort of it all; his opponent, a man of immense strength and often uncontrollable in his anger, knew victory was moments away.

Cheering could be heard outside the inn for fifty yards as Harry finally forced Michael's arm down before standing up, smug with satisfaction and shouldering his way to the bar.

"That was a good show, that was, Harry," said the landlord.

The response was terse, "Yeah, well I won't be content till I've beaten Donald Reid in here, in front of everyone." The landlord continued filling up Harry's mug.

"Ah that might be a different proposition." The response was immediate and with faintly concealed anger.

"Why? What's so special about him? This boy," he nodded his head in Michael's direction, "beat him all right in the boxing match."

The landlord paused placing the mug in front of Harry, "Did you see him when he won?"

Harry was abrupt, "No, why?"

"The men say Donald still had some to spare, never gave his all. Besides he put his opponent down just before it was over."

Harry took a large gulp of beer and couldn't wait to get the words out, scoffing,

"I thought there would be a reason why he couldn't accept defeat."

The landlord stood his ground, "No it wasn't Donald who said that, just an observation or two."

Harry was dismissive and took another mouthful before replying,

"Yeah from Donald's observation."

The landlord began wiping down the counter with a damp cloth and rearranging the sodden beer mats while Harry waited for his response.

"You don't wanna go getting bitter Harry, no point living your life that way. You're worse sometimes than a bear with a sore head." Harry picked up his pint mug and before walking back to join his group said, "You tell Donald what happened here tonight." The landlord now busy pulling another pint for an elderly man with mutton chop whiskers and a pantomime paunch muttered to himself "I'm sure he'll hear from someone."

Michael was occasionally revolving his arm in windmill fashion, trying to shake the numbness out. He took a drink before announcing to his friends, "Harry's stronger than I thought, he's got all that venom locked up him, you can feel it let alone see it." There was a moment's hesitation before one of his friends made the obvious statement "Him and Donald Reid don't get on, do they?" Michael paused before drawing his seat in closer to his friend.

"No, goes back to when they were both in school – Donald saw Harry stealing a ball from Peter's coat... didn't say anything for the rest of the day."

"What happened?" another friend asked eagerly. Michael continued,

"Donald took Peter home. You know how he always protected Peter." He waited, allowing this statement to be absorbed before continuing,

"Poor Peter cried all the way home because he'd had his ball taken." Another friend slurred his words.

"Come on Michael what happened when Donald saw Harry?" Again Michael drew his seat in closer.

"Well Harry denied it of course. This made Donald mad because he had seen him. He gave him every opportunity to come clean but you know Harry... I think he thought he could beat the stuffing out of Donald." The assembled crew laughed knowingly yet softly and Michael acknowledged this.

"Yeah, sure as hell Donald gave Harry a pasting and he," Michael moved his eyes to the right where Harry and his group were sitting, "has never forgotten it. You know not many people found out. Donald's not one to boast about anything. He's strange like that; almost everyone would have been shouting it from the roof tops." The friends were quiet before one chipped in with "I reckon half the village folk would have thanked Donald had they known, especially in view of how Harry's turning out." Michael winked and a large smile ran across his face.

"Well, now that the Prior family have moved into the locality and that them two girls of his seem to be the biggest catch around these parts, it might be that Harry and Donald's paths are going to meet up again." When he'd finished his speculation he muttered "Yep".

"Why's that?" asked someone to his left who like the others had been listening intently.

"Talk is," whispered Michael, "one of the girls has taken a liking to Donald."

"That's impossible, the girls haven't even been to the local dance yet."

Michael was adamant, "No, but you've seen them at church each Sunday with their father all eyes they are."

"So?" queried another. Michael was enjoying the role of a magistrate, manipulating his audience.

"And of course, Donald and Peter are at church on Sunday."

"Have they spoken?" was the immediate repartee.

"How do I know?" was Michael's nonchalant reply. His friends remained persistent for on the horizon they could see the inevitable yet eagerly anticipated clash though not one of them could remotely imagine the circumstances… One of them said "You know Donald the best of all of us." They waited for Michael's reply and whilst they did so he took a slow drink.

"Donald's already spoken for, but Ann thinks that one of the Prior girls can't take her eyes off him," he paused for another slow drink before continuing, "you know… what women call their own intuition." Another mouthful and Michael put his mug down on the table.

"Come on whose turn is it to buy the drinks?" Fortunately there was no dispute as most had already had their fill and while they waited for the beer to arrive the conversation commenced again.

"Where does Harry fit into all this?" the young man opposite Michael whispered.

"Harry thinks that he is going to court the girl when she decides to come to the village dance."

"When is the next dance?" the former enquired with mischief in his eyes. Michael was by now watching the landlord filling up six pint mugs and smiling; still he was pressed for an answer.

"Not for a couple of months. Anyway as I said Donald's spoken for." Finally the beer arrived and as the men took their mugs off the tray, the singing grew louder and louder and Harry Hardy's voice could be heard above the impromptu choir. Michael's table collapsed in laughter when they overheard someone on the table next to them playing cards, scrutinising his hand before saying to his three friends "I wish he'd bought a bloody ticket for the Titanic's maiden voyage!"

Very early the following Monday morning Mrs Jeffries was in her kitchen straining off the yeast into an earthenware bowl. After this was complete she picked up a hand cup and ladled the beer into casks leaving them uncorked. Ann, her daughter, and a picture of innocence emerged into the kitchen and seeing what her mother had done enquired "Well, is it fine?" Mrs Jeffries was quick with her answer, "Yes just a little yeast has worked its way out of the bung hole. I'll skim them off over the next few days and then we can bang down these corks." Her smiling daughter caught her mother's eye before saying, "The men will be pleased mother, don't know what they'd do without that." Ever the industrious, Mrs Jeffries began straightening out her kitchen.

"Another week and your father can have his first drink."

Despite the hour Ann was eager, "I suppose we had better begin to think about making the cheese and bread, mother?" The response was forthright, "Yes, the devil makes work for idle hands and no one can accuse us of that, no sir."

Less than half a mile away the clock resting on the mantelpiece in the Hardys cottage revealed the time – 5.40 a.m. Upstairs Arthur, Harry and Sid were getting dressed and pulling their boots on, with bleary eyes. Jack Hardy was pouring hot soup into four large mugs. He waited a couple of minutes before banging the ceiling three times with the handle of a broom. "Lazy buggers" he muttered to himself. Another two minutes elapsed before the boys strolled into the kitchen and sat down, eyeing the mugs of soup.

"Come on boys, get this inside you it's going to be another long day."

Harry grunted, "Isn't it just". Arthur yawned and kept his mouth open for over a minute much to the disgust of his father.

"Didn't your mother teach you any manners?"

His son ignored the remark and when he closed his mouth, opened it again to say,

"This month will be the death of me, father,"

Sid was folded over tying his boots into a double bow, "My back won't stop aching."

His father began laughing, "It won't if you keep moaning, you bugger. None of you," he pointed at Arthur and Sid, "works as hard as he does," he looked at Harry before continuing, "if you did we might get the lot over and done with before the four weeks, then we could start earning more money on the other jobs as we're on a fixed rate for the harvest."

Harry put his mug down and looked at his father, "Just pray it don't rain because I'd certainly not be happy about working a fifth week in the harvest and not being paid for it."

Sid, looked quizzical, "How do mean, Harry?"

The rather gruff response was in contrast to the soft sobbing of the flame on the hearth, "All that farmers gets paid for in the harvest is a month's work, right?" He glanced at his father who nodded and then continued, "so if we get done under a month we can start work somewhere else, but if we go over our month that's just tough." Harry finished his soup, he stood up, his upright carriage as strong as his pride, "So the sooner we get out of there the better." When he left the room Sid and Arthur hurriedly checked the lacing of their boots. Within two hours four horses were each pulling a wagon loaded with corn.

Harry was working at a furious pace, like a schoolboy cycling to school knowing he might be late and the consequences for such a crime… "Ignore them" he'd bark at the carthorse vainly flicking his tail at flies as he began loading the corn manually, on to one of the wagons. He was sweating profusely and expending great energy throwing the bulk up to his father busily stacking them up. His hands, eyes and body moved together in the spontaneous harmony of an athlete. Occasionally Mr Hardy stole a view over the Wolds for with the mellowing of middle age there was no more pleasant place to be than open countryside for the ripening of his thoughts. At this time of year to see trees rising in the background and the ebb and flow of light when leaves fluttered pleased him in a way the passions in a young woman's eyes had done three decades earlier.

He glanced down at Harry, "No wonder you're so bloody strong," he paused and steering his son's eyes to where his brothers were loading in another part of the field, said, "Not within a foot of us." Harry only half heard and threw another load up.

"That's the Reverend's lot for this year." He took a breather much to the relief of his father and looked scornfully across at his brothers. Jack noticed but said nothing, he became preoccupied with the blackthorn in the hedge flanking either side of the tree where the men rested. He noticed the blossom had begun to fade but further along he looked initially at the tight buds of reddened bronze and even further along he admired a golden head, almost sculptured, shining and looking up toward heaven. His eldest boy thought his father's love of nature amusing and broke the impasse with a derisory "Here come the workers!" His brothers were too far away to hear him and soon all four were sat using the trunk of the Oak tree as a back rest. The tea they drank was barely warm but it was drunk if only to whet their whistle.

Sid groaned in a deliberate manner as he stretched both arms out.

"Reverend Mitchell does well out of it all, doesn't he Harry?"

The reply was sarcastic, "Specially as the only thing he ever lifts up is that prayer book of his." His brothers roared with laughter but his father said nothing, almost pretending he hadn't heard his eldest son's uncharitable remark. When Sid regained his composure he continued, "Mother would scold you for saying that."

Harry was not amused, "Well, all I know is I don't intend to do this for all my life."

His brother mocked him, "And what are you gonna do?"

Harry's reply was immediate, "Something, I don't know what but something."

Sid thought for a moment while looking across at a copse in the distance, "Maybe you think you'll get your own farm one day, that's what the Reid boys say they're gonna do."

A measure of anger rolled off Harry's tongue, "They're talking cream talk Sid. Donald Reid is not going to be a farm owner before me that's for sure." He made a deliberate emphasis on the final three words.

"You really don't like Donald, do you?"

Harry didn't answer, instead he took a mouthful of tea before throwing the remainder into the grass.

Sid continued, "Father says they're good boys, he's known John Reid all his life, not what you'd call the best of friends but respectful of him – you know what I mean."

Harry shook his head like a wet dog and the men waited for him to say something.

"Me and Donald got something to sort out – goes back a long time, too far for you to remember, Sid, but I haven't forgotten," while he spoke he deliberately looked straight ahead with almost meditative slowness.

Eventually his brother broke the silence, "You're too straight to bear a grudge all your life – what for?" A gush of wind was suddenly heard and the farm labourers were almost overpowered by a powerful scent upon the breeze. Jack closed his eyes and inhaled.

Harry stood up, "Right, better get up you two and let's see you do some work for a change," he put his hand out and helped everyone to their feet. Sid grimaced and rubbed his back, Harry merely smirked.

They worked for another two hours plus the time father toiled with Arthur. When Jack thought they had done enough he spoke in his ordinary voice.

"Soon be time for grub, your mother should be on her way by now."

Arthur scanned all points of the compass, "Can't see her yet father, but I'm hungry all right." He could see the tiredness in his father's eyes which prompted him to say,

"You get on top here and let me load."

Jack still had his pride and attempted nonchalance, "A few more minutes and then we'll swap over," he hurled another load up, "phew, I'm not getting any younger."

Arthur pressed on with the conversation, "Harry had a lot to drink at the inn last night."

Jack Hardy gave his son a disapproving look, "Harry's always having too much to drink... something eats at him from time to time."

Arthur was slightly flippant in his response, "You know Harry, he wants to be the top man." There was a pause before his father, fortifying himself offered a deliberate moan.

"This feud he has with Donald Reid, plain stupid if you ask me. Donald is a likeable young man, no side to him, does his family credit. I think Harry's secretly jealous. I've said to him before, he's my son and I love him for it. That should be enough. Donald doesn't hold any grudge for whatever reason... it's all one sided." He placed a strong emphasis on the last two words and Arthur ballooned his cheeks before blowing out.

"It will probably blow over, father."

Jack looked his son in the eyes, "I don't know, Harry's so bloody pig headed when he wants to be. But," there was a long sigh, "let's hope so before long at any roads."

"Hooray!" Arthur exclaimed as he caught a glimpse of his mother in the distance. He put four fingers in his mouth, just as he had been taught as a six year old and whistled loudly. Jack looked up and waved and it was reciprocated.

"Ah, good, here comes my maid."

The other two sons sauntered over and within minutes the family were sitting in the shade, under the Oak tree, smoking, laughing and talking effervescently.

Harry took a large chunk out of his meat pie and waited while chewing before opening up the next conversation.

"Father, this is hard work just us on each wagon. Gosh days gone by we'd have a gaveller with his stack fork feeding the corn to me and Sid and then another two on top arranging it evening."

Sid slurped his tea which garnered disapproving looks from all so he quickly continued his brother's conversation, "We would have cleared a mighty few harvests that way."

His father butted in, "And a few more pounds to pay, don't forget that. No, we got a good deal, believe you me. Probably better than the Reids got this year." The food changed any mournful feelings the workers might have secretly felt. Their mother's presence often changed the family mood; maybe it was the bright friendliness of age or maybe it was the way she charmed them with her grace and courtesy. Whatever it was one absolute was always present: she never allowed herself to be downcast for it would clash with her romantic tenderness.

She joined in the conversation, "Don't forget Jack, they haven't got the men folk we have with only Donald and Peter to accomplish their harvesting."

Harry seemed to have put away his animosity, maybe it was his mother's presence.

"But we do more than Donald and Peter even if I have to carry the loafer," and with that he slapped his brother's back.

Sid retorted, "I may not be as strong as you Harry but I pay me way."

Now it was their mother's turn, "Yes, don't be unfair Harry. You're a big strapping lad... it doesn't take half as much out of you as it does a little 'un."

Sid grinned and was encouraged to say something, "That's right mother," he paused for effect, "anyway who wants to be a big ugly brute?"

Harry's response was predictable; he rolled over and locked his brother's head in his arm, "Now say that again." He could barely stifle his guffawing.

Sid began struggling for breath, "Ahh, I can't breathe!"

Harry tightened his grip, "Just you be careful little 'un." He released his brother and dusted him down.

"No need for that Harry... only a joke? Many men are gonna have a joke on you as you will on them believe me."

Harry was dismissive, "We'll see about that."

By way of retaliation Sid seized his moment, "You won't get to courting the Prior girl with that sort of behaviour – all unrefined." Those assembled didn't know whether to laugh at the remark but all were smiling. A large belch was suddenly heard – it was Harry playing the pantomime villain for effect but it displeased his mother.

"Harry, I've told you about your manners, you listen to me," she waved her finger at her eldest son before continuing, "one day you are gonna leave the village..." before she could say anymore Harry intervened with a cursory "Am I?"

His mother remained undaunted, "Yes, you are and I hope it is as a Christian and a gentleman that you carry our name with you. You may be big and strong and think you're tough but there's bigger and tougher and what's more you may not find out 'till it's too late."

Harry like the other sons present was impressed by their mother's calmness even if Harry fell into his caricatured self, "And why's that?"

His mother remained unabashed, "Because gentlemen don't look for trouble they behaves accordingly but when trouble starts they will stand up."

Harry was one step away from goading his mother and his eyes made a conspiratorial sweep over the men, "Come on mother tell me who's a gentleman round these parts?"

Mrs Hardy felt a jolt but she remained demure, "Don't be cheeky, your father for a start and yes those Reid boys."

Now Harry dispensed with the early playfulness; his movement kept him apart from the others and began to fuel new rage.

"I thought you'd get round to that, telling me about Donald and Peter. Don't you wish they were your sons?"

His father leapt to his feet, anger swirling in his eyes, "That'll do, don't speak to your mother like that, don't upset her." Silence could be felt everywhere as he caressed his wife, visibly upset by her eldest son's callous remark.

Harry was unrepentant and it was obvious to his brothers who looked at him spare and hard, "I'm fed up with hearing about the Reids in this village. Anyone would think they were God Almighty."

Sid got up, "That's enough."

Arthur also pulled his wiry frame up from his seated position. They looked at their father who said,

"Come on it's time to get back to work, Harry apologise to your mother... I will not have you or anyone talk to her like that."

Harry remained quiet for seconds before allowing himself a self-conscious smile "Sorry mother." Three sparrows suddenly flew out the bough above camouflaged with leaves as though they didn't want to intrude on the private conversation anymore and this simple action galvanised everyone's attention and offered a balm of sorts.

Carrie was the first to speak and she looked at Harry, "That's all right, son, I know you get carried away and say things you don't really mean, but please will you do one thing for me?"

"What's that?" Harry enquired with sudden humility.

"Try not to have hate in your heart. It just eats all the goodness away. Don't be jealous, be proud of who you are and you'll find people will like you for it. You don't really hate Donald Reid – not really."

Mrs Hardy gently walked off leaving her boys behind and half an hour later the toil was back in full flow. Sid noticed the clouds beginning to move with more grey entering them but said nothing. Three and a half hours later the horse drawn carts were pulling up outside the Hardys barn. The men looked distinctly tired and their movements from carriage to ground could best be described as rickety with the accompanying groan of fatigue. Before Jack started walking towards the farmhouse he turned to his sons.

"Right," he looked up at the sky, "no point trusting the rain to stay away."

Harry's reply was shot through with exasperation, "But it's bright enough. Let's have something to eat first, I'm famished."

Sid joined in, "Come on father, we're all in."

Jack remained adamant, "No start unloading. I'll be back to give you a helping hand in a few minutes. No sense in not finishing the job completely now is there?" He turned and walked away, leaving his sons too tired to respond.

Before they completed the task Sid and Arthur walked over to the corner of the garden which was where the compost stood in a rectangular heap. It was rotting and giving a distinct odour, the mixture of grass cuttings, hedge clippings, weeds, nettles and vegetable waste provided by their mother was thoroughly congealed and Sid couldn't resist commenting.

"Do you think that's what's inside Harry's head?" They laughed quietly as they didn't want to arouse their brother's curiosity nor a fierce vindictive look coming their way at speed.

Inside the cottage, Jack Hardy's energies collapsed as he sat down by his wife's side.

Chapter 5

Life proceeded much as it always did, days turned into weeks, weeks into months and the cycle of work was never complete but no one ever considered it unjust. Sunday provided a change, it was the cleric's day and another half century would pass before it was challenged by intellectuals and commoners alike. Not even Reverend Mitchell could contemplate such a thing even when he fished among his own nightmares. Despite his years and with the veins in his hands permanently on show he talked with a certain spice of determination yet when he saw his parishioners sad he became humble again and with a deep-drawn painful breath he would sigh before looking up to the sky and asking for divine intervention. One or two saw it as an act that couldn't be bettered, even on a London stage but said nothing lest their Reverend revert to an angry powerful voice with words that might condemn them to perpetual darkness.

The church had been built in Norman times and a committee of ladies drawn from all social classes in the area drew up a rota for cleaning, polishing and in the summer flooding the altar with an array of fresh flowers. Inevitably a bazaar was held in July and again the ladies sold homemade jam, cakes, scones and bread besides a raffle for chocolates and a bottle of whisky. Every last penny went to the church's upkeep even if dampness could never be expunged; generations had avoided the two pews which shone when rays of light threw themselves through the North West stained glass window. Nevertheless it had a homely feel and most villagers made the effort to present themselves as clean and tidy; it was noticeable that a little subtle competition was present amongst the women but distinctly absent amongst the men.

Reverend Mitchell walked towards the pulpit and it was a sign for the congregation to sit down and clear their throats all in one movement. Today the Reverend looked gentle and his manner was engaging as he looked about his flock but he was troubled by events outside his control, events in the people's world not God's world.

"Today, I want to talk to you and your praises to the Lord. The harvest has been collected for another year and you, my brethren, God's own creatures, have worked hard and toiled with an unyielding spirit. It is this spirit which is a part of God in you that will preserve the smaller communities scattered about the length and breadth of the country. The peace and idyll that we have treasured, which our forefathers also treasured, may even come under threat," he paused and looked melancholic but kept tearful emotion at bay.

"My brethren let us not begin to think that we can ever match God. The changes that have begun in the earliest part of this century I fear are for the worse. Some men are turning away from God toward the pursuit of material gain but let me remind you of what Jesus said 'whoever he that gained the whole world and lost his soul gained nothing'."

Harry Hardy sat at the end of the pew for a quick getaway, rolled his eyes and started measuring in his mind the amount of glass in the church, oblivious to the sermon continuing.

"God's wrath should not be tampered with, we have already witnessed the unsinkable ship that sank on her maiden voyage. Some of you I know have not heard me speak of this before. I am a patriotic man despite the cloth, proud of King and Empire but I owe my allegiance, as all of you do, first to God's will. I pray and I hope that you will join me in prayer that war, which may be just around the corner will be averted, that the politicians who ask for sacrifice in war will be guided by God in deliberation that will turn against war... that we may continue to live our simple yet peaceful lives, happy in the knowledge that God is guiding us." The silence in the church was deafening as though time had been frozen. Half a moment elapsed before Reverend Mitchell asked the congregation to stand, "that we may sing Hymn number seventeen 'The Lord is My Shepherd'."

Back in the village only a few inhabitants could be seen; the impression was one of a wake. Outside the church the vicar was shaking hands with various people and offering them good wishes. Many congratulated him on a fine sermon. To the right of the entrance Lucy Prior was looking in the direction of Donald Reid despite being in conversation with her sister. When Donald turned and saw her, the eye contact was barely registered for she turned and began conversing again with her sister, while Donald continued talking with his family. Harry Hardy had witnessed the faintest of exchanges between them and turned to his brother.

"I'm gonna have a drink, coming?" It felt more like a command than a question and Arthur was keen not to upset his brother.

"Sounds like a good idea." Both walked in the direction of the inn but Harry's eyes lingered long enough on the Reid family for Donald to notice. Harry grinned to himself and nodded. Peter noticed his brother watching the Hardy boys quicken their steps.

"You obviously saw the look Harry gave you?"

Resplendent in a grey charcoal suit and highly polished black boots Donald chuckled.

"Even a blind man would have seen that."

Peter wanted to laugh but checked himself, "You know sooner or later..."

Donald interrupted him, "Yes, I know," there was a slight pause as he watched his would be nemesis disappear behind a clump of laurel bushes, "come on, let's get back and take the horse out."

Both moved away from the church eagerly. Unbeknown to them Helen Clements had been watching Lucy Prior looking at the Reid boys and again as they walked off. When she thought Lucy Prior was about to look at her she directed her eyes towards the crumbling tower on the west side. Soon the grounds of the church were empty and the Reverend Mitchell had God to himself.

While Donald and Peter were laughing like drains as the horse they shared cantered across the field with Donald holding the bridle and Peter holding on to his brother for dear life, Harry was relaxing his large frame into the largest wicker seat in The Red Lion. Despite having already drunk a pint he looked morose. Even a game of skittles along the side wall failed to grab his interest. Instead he opened a conversation with 'Dan the Duck'.

"What have you got to tell me Dan?"

The latter was known to have a dishevelled appearance, dishevelled digs and dishevelled conversation but today he was surprisingly articulate, "War's coming Harry. You'll get a chance to show what you're made of." Harry, who'd removed his sports jacket which was now wrapped around the back of his seat and loosened his tie, was taken aback but chose to be sarcastic.

"How do you know that, been looking in a crystal ball?"

Dan had already supped two pints and wasn't about to be affected by the person sat across from him, despite his reputation. In fact the older man was quite determined.

"You may mock me but I tell you war with Germany ain't far off, from what I've read... the Empire and Germany are on a collision course." Those eavesdropping on the conversation laughed out loud and when it died down he continued.

"You'll see, no room for two at the top."

Harry nodded in the manner of a wise sage before drinking his beer in one go and standing up.

"Come on Arthur better get home for lunch, no point upsetting the old boy again." As he put his jacket on Arthur hurriedly swallowed the remainder of his beer.

"OK, I'm coming." He turned to the landlord who acknowledged him, "Cheers, all the best." After they'd closed the door Bert moved among the tables collecting the empty glasses; he frowned when he noticed half his customers still had near full glasses as he enjoyed the afternoon snooze following his Sunday lunch before re-opening at seven o'clock. His regulars knew he dropped hints each Sunday and also knew that their custom provided him with his livelihood.

Time was often left astern and forgotten because the pattern of life in this and other villages in rural England seldom faltered or changed. Often the smell of flour characterised the interior of homes and when summer approached old women sat next to decaying walls some with a forbidding countenance yet everyone knew they had stories to tell; the problem was no one particularly wanted to listen to them so they repeated them among themselves each time they congregated. Their one redeeming feature was among the villagers they were the most generous lovers of animals and their understanding of each other was as easy and pleasant as laughter. Similarly the old men enjoyed talking with each other yet they garnered respect and their conversation remained unhurried like that of a spring. Each was pleased to give of himself and that is why some would talk to their dog about the wonders of a wandering track and be as guileless as morning light. In the early twentieth century they were still as usual in the world as hedgerows and grass despite the youngsters often seeing them as a nuisance.

The church clock rotated enough times for another barn dance to be on the schedule of the Parish notice board. The Priors' farmhouse, large and imposing with several outbuildings stood out as the superior dwelling for miles around. In the upstairs bedroom two young ladies, soberly dressed as befitting daughters of a fairly well off farmer were getting ready. Ann was combing her sister Lucy's hair. Lucy was fascinated with butterflies and her sketch book was a myriad of colour and notes. Unfortunately for her no one else shared her passion. Out of sisterly love Ann was always prepared to comment on the quality of the sketches and listen while her sister talked of the colours of butterflies. Lucy would talk about colour aided by shape which was capable of bringing about a general harmonising with surroundings. This evening Ann was informed that the Kallima, a tropical leaf butterfly could settle on twigs, fold up its wings and look precisely like withered leaves.

Before she could continue talking about the beautiful and artistic combination of tints on butterfly wings being examples of courtship colouration Ann stepped in.

"I think I will die if George Hawkins or worse Gordon Sharman asks me to dance with him." She waited wondering if the butterflies had been put back in the closed sketch book.

Her sister laughed, "Don't be silly Ann you may find he is a nice young man... just because he is not obviously handsome doesn't mean you won't like him." Lucy immediately stuck her tongue in her cheek and made sure her sister could see.

Ann tried to be serious but was unconvincing, "Oh listen to you. I shall remember that if some blacksmith or whatever asks you to dance and don't forget several villages will be represented."

Lucy took on a superior attitude instructing Ann to tie a white ribbon in her hair.

"You're sure... white?"

"Of course, it will match the pattern on my dress," she continued, "if I was asked to dance I would do so for isn't that what a young lady should do on such occasions? To embarrass a man would be both cruel and unfair."

Now it seemed butterflies had been forgotten Ann attempted to tease her sister.

"I bet you won't dance with..." she deliberately paused and let a sly grin sweep over her cheeks, "I shan't say his name because if I do and he asked you to dance you will do so, just so you can say – I told you so." The conversation though calm now boasted an element of competition.

Lucy eagerly asked her sister, "Will you dance with Donald Reid, should he ask you?"

There was a lull before Ann responded slowly and in a soft voice almost resembling a whisper, "And make you jealous?"

Lucy couldn't hide her self-consciousness when she responded, "You won't make me jealous, whatever makes you think that?" As an aside she added, "I think Donald is spoken for."

Ann probed, "You mean Helen Clements?"

Lucy faltered when she tried to appear self-assured, "Yes, she is a fine girl and will make somebody a good wife, you'll see."

Ann couldn't resist taking the upper hand, "You don't fool me Lucy... I've seen the way you look at that young man."

Lucy stood up and walked over to the full length mirror attached to the oak wardrobe. She turned from side to side running her eyes in slide-rule fashion over her garment.

"Do you think this looks all right?"

Before any doubt could arise Ann said, "Yes, anyway you haven't time to change again. Father will be getting impatient if we don't appear soon." It was obvious the sparring was over when Lucy kissed her sister on the forehead.

"You look a picture Ann, so pretty. Many of the boys will want to dance with you."

Finally they crept downstairs and could see their father pacing up and down the sitting room because the door was half open. He looked impatient and when his daughters appeared deliberately took his watch from his waistcoat pocket and glanced at it in cursory fashion.

"Ah so you've decided to go to the dance then?"

The girls giggled and Lucy stepped forward, "I'm sorry we kept you waiting Father." The simple contribution disarmed him and he stood admiring his girls.

"I wish your mother could be here to see you both, she would have been immensely proud." He pursed his lips and nodded his head slowly.

Ann asked him, "Are you going to walk with us all the way?"

"Of course, and all the way back. Don't want you girls getting up to any mischief."

The stroll was a pleasant one. Inside the barn paraffin lamps glowed and a makeshift bar had been set up by The Red Lion proprietor, taking charge of the corner where crates of ale were stacked up and glasses neatly arranged in rows on a table. The main area had been cleared for dancing and one couple had an air of intimacy and relaxation about them, Donald Reid and Helen Clements. To their right and barely noticeable because of the lighting arrangement was the band consisting of an accordionist and two men playing fiddles. They had a complete repertoire and would run through it maybe changing the order depending on mood, but music sheets were unnecessary.

After refreshments Donald and Helen took to the dance floor and exchanged smiles with Arthur Hardy and his dance partner. When Donald swung Helen around in a showy twist he was able to see Bert and Michael Jeffries with their respective partners. Donald winked at both men who tried to conceal self consciousness.

When Helen looked up at him he said, "See Michael has a pretty girl." Helen craned her neck.

"Yes, she is pretty, comes from the village of Raby... it's a long way for her to come unless she's got some transport."

Donald smiled, "Maybe Michael is going to take her home."

Helen thought for a moment before commenting, "Michael's got to be up early for work tomorrow."

"Oh that won't stop Michael... yes she's very pretty." Helen stood on Donald's toe, deliberately.

"Donald you are a terrible flirt. I suppose you noticed those two daughters of Mr Prior have come to the dance?"

Donald smiled for he was brimming with confidence, "Do I detect a hint of jealousy?"

Helen suddenly flushed and gasped, "No... what makes you think that?"

Donald bided his time, spun his girl around before saying, "Oh nothing in particular. I wonder if Harry is going to chance his arm and ask one of them for a dance."

Helen suddenly regained her composure, "That would be amusing wouldn't it?" A minute later the dance finished, everybody applauded and the band dutifully bowed before taking a drink from recently arrived pint mugs on a tray.

Seeing them relax Donald turned to Helen.

"Phew, I could do with a drink, pretty maid. How about you?" Helen's eyes sparkled and she secretly hoped Donald had really noticed the outfit she'd spent days agonising about and re-cutting and stitching to hang on her slender body.

"Nothing too strong" she said smiling, "I don't want to get dizzy." Donald turned and throwing his shoulders back, paced toward the beer while Helen took a seat a couple of tables away where Peter Reid and companions Bert, Michael and Ann Jeffries had congregated. Pleasantries were exchanged and the party looked around as there were more visitors than locals at the hop. Donald returned and placed a pint of beer and glass of punch on the table as the appointed glass collector removed the empties into a hessian sack.

"Good evening everyone" could be heard before he took his seat alongside Helen.

A couple of notes were played on the fiddle after the fifteen minute break, just to let the audience know the band were ready to go again. Harry Hardy swallowed the last of his beer stood at the bar, before running the back of his hand over his mouth; his suit, collar and tie looked new if not expensive. Confidently he approached Lucy Prior.

"Excuse me Miss Lucy, may I have the next dance?"

Taken aback she mumbled before regaining the essential demure characteristics both she and her sister possessed, "Well, yes." Suddenly the music sprang to life and Harry ushered her away from the table. He was light on his feet, surprisingly, and looked proud while his partner looked self-conscious. He hoped everyone took notice and when Helen and Donald smiled at them Lucy returned it, Harry didn't.

Outside the dance hall light had faded whilst the revelries inside continued. A group of boys played marbles in a garden, enthusiastic as ever despite visibility being almost nil.

"Come on," said one of the boys having set up a large marble against a stone, "hit this in three and you can have it." From a few yards away another boy scoffed.

"I'll hit that easy Jim Brenton and it'll be mine."

"Come on get on with it," said another of the group in exasperation, "or it'll be too dark to even see it."

The fourth member of the group chipped in, "I bet you don't do it."

Immediately the fifth friend challenged him, "Wanna put a bet on it?"

Quick as a flash the other said, "You're on. My Kingfisher to your blue 'un."

The first boy who'd been waiting for these comments to fade stepped in, "Have you finished… right come on then big mouth?"

His challenger warmed his hands, "Don't try and put me off. It won't work." He took careful aim threw his marble hitting the other and leapt into the air, triumphantly.

"Yippee! I told you didn't I?"

Not wishing to lose any more face the defeated boy mumbled, "Right, put one of yours down and let me have a go." While another marble was set down against a stone the other two boys settled their debt. There was a lull and the sky cleared offering a subtle improvement in light.

"Come on then, hit it once and it's yours." They watched as the boy took aim and threw his marble. He missed but there was no whoop of derision or laughter instead his opponent, in a show of compassion, offered him a second chance.

"Just to show you I'm a good sport."

"Right, I'll get it this time."

He was successful and one of the friends remarked, "I have to admit it was a pretty good shot," before looking up to the sky and continuing, "come on then, one more go then I'm off home, my ma's gonna skin me for staying out this late." The party laughed and dispersed because the boy had changed his mind.

When at last the night sky dropped her cosy blanket over Tunby Hill she did so knowing that most beneath her slept peacefully for family and the presence of God were the cornerstones of their way of life, particularly among the women; for the men it was patriotism and a sense of duty whatever form the latter took. Soon it would be called upon. In 1913 things were hotting up and they continued into the following year when the Great Imperial powers who'd carved up Africa thought, misguidedly, that treaties with potential opponents would ease potential tensions were living in a fool's paradise. The point of no return required a mere trigger and that was provided by the assassination of Franz Ferdinand in Sarajevo in August 1914. The propagandist machine went into overdrive when governments confident of their military might told potential fighting men it would be over before the leaves had dropped of the trees. In Britain cartoonists and the columnist Jesse Pope referred to war as a game – better to come home on a crutch than miss the fun.

Before the carnage commenced John Reid took his son Donald, to the Assembly Rooms in Lincoln to listen to a fine speaker promoting journalism as a career; it was the quality of this presentation that impressed both father and son even if their own future livelihood had been decided at birth. John had been attending talks given by 'experts in their field' for many years, usually on Saturdays, often his day off and had always come away impressed; he wanted his son to have knowledge and possibly wisdom beyond the milieu life had already mapped out for him.

The hall was packed with men from all classes and the elderly journalist had the fury of an evangelist which reduced his audience to silence when he gripped the podium and bellowed.

"Journalism is the most truly democratic of all callings. It has been a greater power in the world than any mechanical force controlled by man, it has controlled those forces. In the history of mankind newspapers have been stronger than armies." He paused and threw his shoulders back and breathed in deeply and smiled, his starched white collar never moved but it seemed to glisten when he continued.

"Napoleon feared four hostile papers more than a thousand bayonets." The audience mumbled their acknowledgement and father whispered in his son's ear, "Reverend Mitchell might learn a thing or two from him." Donald smiled and both were ready for more.

"The power of the journalist cannot be exaggerated. If he cannot make laws, he makes the law makers. He is present, invisible in every government cabinet.

Not a prince upon his throne, not a draper behind his counter is beyond his range or outside his interest. No door is locked to him." Donald noticed a group of boys four rows ahead writing notes and smiled as he was aware that their clothing betrayed them as the new emerging middle class that lived outside towns but never regarded the land as a workplace, merely pleasant recreational space. It was the one time he thought how his life might have been different and whispered to himself "I suppose accident of birth".

The speaker invited the audience to have refreshments pointing to a large urn of tea and a middle-aged frumpy looking woman already pouring into several mugs. The conversation was all about the commitment and eloquence of the orator rather than unashamedly promoting his profession. The break was soon over and everyone took their seats and then once again the speaker employed the same modus operandi though this time his voice seemed louder.

"He can make wars and bring peace; he can make revolutions and destroy them. He has more power in the market than the Stock Exchange. Even the scales of legal justice may be subject to his will..." Suddenly a rumpus broke out and all eyes turned to the rear where two men, the worse for drink were being removed by three burly officials. When everything calmed down the journalist continued building up to a crescendo.

"He stands between light and darkness, between social peace and despotism between the freedom of the twentieth century and the inquisition of the Middle Ages. He is the guardian of the liberties of the human race." As he finished and before he could return to his seat thunderous applause shook the walls and uninhibited cheering could be heard out in the adjacent street.

"I've never heard anyone speak with such passion like him," offered Donald still handclapping, "I'd like to come again father."

John Reid smiled, "We will son". He too was also still applauding. When everything had died down and people began leaving John jostled to the front while Donald remained in his seat.

That evening Donald asked his father what the small conversation with the speaker had been about.

"I asked him if war was inevitable."

"What was his response?" asked Donald eagerly. John Reid paused and looked into the distance before turning his gaze towards his son.

"He said 'It's inevitable. The point of no return has been reached despite the mushy offerings of diplomats and politicians in the Foreign Office'." It was food for thought for neither man continued with the conversation.

The following day before they left their home for work John Reid told his son what the journalist had said to a motley group of men surrounding him.

"He said whatever your work, bring your mind and your soul because it is the latter that should engage the deepest feelings and enlist the warmest sympathies." The journalist was right, the carnage had begun.

Chapter 6

In England when a glittering moon shone out of heaven and appeared to be listening for nature's expression it was often obliged by a Nightingale singing, sometimes all night long. This was folklore passed down by generations of farming folk and no one wanted to be a kill joy and examine it or worse even test it. In France it was different: an excruciating volume of noise lasted hour after hour and yellow flashes punctuated the sky allowing soldiers to get a fleeting glance of the face next to theirs huddled down in a trench, sick with fear and when some of these soldiers, tough nuts in civilian life, looked at their officers for inspiration they saw boys with no power in their voices merely degrees of hopelessness. Only those men brought up in the countryside, living and working on farms had an understanding of nature's balance and now it was here in a foreign land – life and death.

When morning broke it was dull, damp and still. The only movement to the imaginative eye was air filling the craters caused by incessant shelling of the landscape; it brought a measure of comfort to the terrain that looked to be in the grip of permanent anxiety. Trees now resembled burnt stumps shot through with death. Mangled bodies lying beside tangled wires and abandoned artillery were as familiar as coloured postcards in a seaside town.

A sergeant looking through his field periscope chuckled and in an attempt to raise morale invited two soldiers either side 'to take a gander'. Both men grimaced, changing their position and when one looked out he smiled for he saw a crate up-ended and stamped on the side – *50 tons Ideal Sweetened Milk.* He encouraged his friend to look through, however this young soldier still in his teens was more interested in watching a solitary bird fly into the last battle area looking for scraps of foods. Momentarily it appeared to be trapped in the mud but managed to fly away, the soldier heard an extra beat in his heart...

In Britain the propagandists had got it wrong – 'Home before Christmas' would prove a cruel joke. In the centre of towns including Lincoln, Louth, Boston and Sleaford a bold poster with the command YOUR COUNTRY NEEDS YOU! was pinned up at chosen sites. Kitchener looked menacing and comical in equal degrees, nevertheless it had an effect even in the largest and least populated counties of the United Kingdom. Sometimes it seemed hypnotic and men most shabbily attired were applauded by passers-by as they waited in line outside hastily constructed recruiting offices.

Harry Hardy, bold, deliberately mean looking stood at the front. He was summoned by a robust Sergeant Major who looked him up and down, probably thinking he'd cut this type down to size on numerous occasions.

"Follow me and remove your cap the moment you step inside."

"Whatever you say," announced Harry.

The Sergeant stopped in his tracks and waited. Harry stood nonplussed.

"Laddie never speak to me without finishing your sentence with Sergeant."

Before Harry could utter anything out loud or under his breath he heard, "And get rid of that cockiness, the army doesn't like it."

"Yes Sergeant," said Harry suitably humbled but seething because it was him who usually did the humbling and he had walked very fast as though conscious of the impetus of youth driving him to serve King and Country. It was noticeable that as men moved up the line towards that meeting with regulars the shiny face of confidence lessened and if some lost their nerve none were brave enough to walk away. No one in any line the length and breadth of Britain could envisage the effect of chlorine gas inhalation or imagine the soldier next to them reduced in height, in a flash, from five foot eight to five foot because his head was missing. Three brothers joined the back of the queue biting their lips with a resolute half-combative air. For them to be subject to the torment of a long hidden but never to be healed wound in the future was preposterous.

Harry was pleased to be inside the building because although the wind had dropped it was still uncomfortably cold outside. Nevertheless the interior was in a state of dilapidation; the window sashes looked as if they would splinter at the merest touch and a thick coat of mildew covered some windows. The whole building was pervaded by a damp and disagreeable smell and despite most lights being on, dusk seemed to have been transported from outside to inside.

Two unsmiling soldiers, in full uniform, stood erect like notes of exclamation either side of an oak panelled door. Harry was walked inside. Ahead of him sat a large moustached officer in uniform looking every inch the veteran of numerous campaigns. Two hostile looking privates stood either side looking through and beyond the latest volunteer. A large log book, a bible and a wooden bowl full of shiny shillings rested on an imposing Oak table. The recruiting officer moved his head slowly and looked Harry in the eye without saying a word; his eyes had a fiery lustre enough to unnerve anyone seeing themselves as a future hero on a battlefield. The look lasted fifteen seconds, enough to turn the strongest heart cold.

Harry walked closer to the table and his escort left, it was the point of no return and the farm labourer held his nerve. Suddenly the recruiting officer having fiddled with official papers looked back up and smiled as did the two privates. It created a sense of togetherness though largely contrived.

"You look like what we are after," said the officer. Suddenly pride emanated from Harry though he was astute enough not to say anything.

"This country needs all the strong fit men it can get," the officer paused and deliberately tapped his index finger on the table before continuing, "I am looking for men with guts." He thumped the table with his fist but Harry remained composed and the officer warmed to him.

"Here is a real man not a pretend one." As if on cue both privates nodded and smiled. The officer stood up and it surprised Harry that although broad he was shorter than him. He continued with melodrama in his voice.

"Our cause is just – God and Empire. The war will be short, sweet and victorious." Harry looked at the gleaming coins and a smile lit up his face. The officer continued.

"When you take the King's shilling you do so with the knowledge that you will serve the Empire with unflagging loyalty and that you will have a generous pride in allegiance and dedication to the Empire." Harry had never heard patriotic talk like this from someone sober; he was stunned. To add a hint of danger, the officer slowly fingered the line of colourful ribbon on his tunic.

"These do not come easy." In his imagination Harry heard enemy machine gun fire which abruptly stopped when he shot dead the enemy; this sweetened his desire to get at 'The Hun'. Suddenly a Lance Corporal entered through a side door; a tall slightly stooped man with hanging cheekbones and a suppressed anger.

"That's four in this room I could beat at arm wrestling," the farm labourer muttered under his breath. King and Empire had another one in their ranks and wouldn't Kitchener have been pleased because at the outbreak of war the British Army was 450,000 strong and required a huge expansion of manpower to bring it into line with European armies.

The new Secretary of War wanted a million men. He had ideas of organising enlisted men into an army of service battalions named after the areas they were raised; these would then be attached to local regular units. Kitchener had his wish and before the end of 1914 a million men were in uniform – the creation of battalions formed from men of common background, occupations, professions and sporting associations. Three hundred and four of these battalions were finally created. The Pals; only the Grimsby contingent were known as chums. The town was also the recruiting centre. In early 1915 the 10th Lincolns moved to Ripon for musketry training and joined up with other units to form their brigade and their destination was France. Of the eight battalions of the Lincolnshire regiment the first and second would see action throughout the war while others were moved as support. Men may not have been from military stock but believed in England and Empire.

Word spread fast in Tunby and Harry Hardy could be seen walking through the village cock-a-hoop and spinning a shilling on his thumb. When he caught sight of 'Dan the Duck' he couldn't resist grabbing his attention shouting "You were right after all Dan!" The older man absorbed in his misery as usual, nodded and walked on. He wasn't out of earshot and heard the remainder of the younger man's conversation.

"My brothers are joining, so is David Baumber, no shortage of brave men here," he paused for what he said next he knew would travel, "mind you no sign of the Reids and Jeffries at the recruitment office unless they went to Louth." Harry smiled to himself. A couple of old women, who having heard his impromptu self-promotion, looked disdainfully.

"He'll wake from his delusion... a cruel and rueful time won't be far off. That's what Bill told me after his experience of war." The other woman looked inquisitively at her, so she continued, "He looked what he was, a spirit broken man... I could see it in his face and I'm sure it hurried him to his grave."

With his chest puffed out, Harry and a couple of friends from a nearby parish sought another watering hole that evening and pitched up at The Royal Oak in Mareham-Le-Fen where they were anonymous. The boys were intrigued by a group of men, dressed in their Sunday best playing poker at a table reserved for them; Harry watched the dealer slide two cards, with consummate ease to the players involved and for the first time heard the expressions 'all in', 'match' and 'fold'. He loved the mystery and secretiveness of it all and the way each player scrutinised his cards having dragged them up his chest before taking a peek. As the tension increased and pipe smoke filled the bar, Harry despite his ignorance, tried to pick the likely winner based on instinct and he was sure he was right when his chosen one having run out of money threw in his gold watch to the pot; he was wrong and he cursed before drinking more Batemans ale.

Just after ten o'clock the trio left and ventured into Fulsby Wood with the intention of poaching until they were seen off by the gamekeeper, a man with a crafty reputation who took pride in his work despite having been on the opposition side during his youth! It was a long walk home...

"We want some rain," said John Reid, "and I fancy it's on the way." He looked at a pack of white cumulus nimbus clouds moving slowly towards the east. The family worked like Trojans and by later afternoon they had finished and were putting farm implements in the store; they had been spared the downpour. When John had secured the barn door with a cross-over bolt he noticed how tired his sons looked.

"Sit down here for twenty minutes... you deserve it."

He offered hoping to raise their morale, "Another day over and I wouldn't want anyone but you boys out there with me." The sons smiled because they'd heard it all before but lacked the energy to indulge in any mimicry. Their father knew it.

That evening the dining room table was carefully laid. An oil lamp offered light to the room for outside it was fading. The men ambled into the room taking their places at the table as their mother carried a bowl of steaming potatoes following by a bowl of stew. The boys were impatient to get grace over with as Mrs Reid began taking her pinafore off. She nodded and her husband began.

"Blessed be the Lord for what we are about to receive."

Everyone replied "Amen" but it was out of synchronisation. As was usual John poured water into glasses while his wife began dishing up. "Thank you's" were heard and Peter took a mouthful of stew grimacing because it was too hot and he dare not spit it out; instead he took a mighty mouthful of water.

"This tastes good ma," he exclaimed.

"Thank you," his mother said in demure fashion.

Peter continued, "I hear Harry Hardy's enlisted and Arthur and Sid are going down tomorrow. Should be interesting."

A quick response shot across the table from his mother, "I don't know what their father's playing at letting the three sons go and do that. I could understand maybe one of them but three! Who is going to do the work on the farm?"

Her husband chipped in, "They'll manage, besides there's talk of this war being over before it's begun."

She fixed him with a withering look, "That's what they say about all wars."

Peter tried to appear nonchalant but knew there would be a backlash when he offered, "I've been thinking of enlisting myself, after all, someone's got to."

His mother shifted her weight letting her warm thigh press heavily against him. The second's silence could have cracked ice.

"You'll do no such thing," she said and turning to her husband continued, "You won't weather that will you? He's hardly out of his cradle!"

Peter was indignant. "I'm nearly eighteen – a man!"

Donald smirked but said nothing instead he tore off a slice from the home baked loaf that was still warm, while his mother berated her son.

"That don't mean anything."

Peter's stomach burned sourly and his eyelids felt gritty and he detached his leg from his mother's, "It does to me. I thought you'd be proud of me wanting to fight for King and Country," he couldn't hide his hurt, "and Empire. Aren't you going to say anything, father?" He looked as earnest as a vicar trying to save souls in far off Africa.

Mrs Reid had heard enough and took away some of the empty dishes to the kitchen; her husband watched and when she was out of sight he looked at Peter who was getting impatient now, "Well, are you going to give me your consent or not?" He said it in a matter of fact way that surprised the occupants of the dining table though Donald still kept his own counsel apart from asking his father to pass the bowl of stew over so he could help himself. He poured another ladle into his own bowl before indicating to the others who wanted more. "Go on then" his father said and then thanked him.

While Mrs Reid remained in the kitchen, melting with smothered tears, Peter relaxed and poured out his feelings.

"Bert Jeffries and me are going to see what all the fuss is about at the recruiting office in town." The other two men remained silent which Peter took as a good omen and gave him additional confidence to continue. "I'm not saying

I'm going to sign on the dotted line. I'm not that stupid." There began an element of cunning in his further discourse.

"No, Bert and me just felt it was our duty to go and get as much information as we could. They say the infantry get a magazine rifle capable of delivering fifteen shots a minute and a belt fed machine gun what pumps out bullets at the rate of ten a second... Just think." Only the wick in the oil lamp moved before Donald joined the conversation.

"Did you get this from one of the Hardys?" He asked trying not to appear sceptical. Before Peter could respond his mother returned carrying another bowl of steaming potatoes, she looked self-conscious for she had been shedding tears and her husband knew it. He attempted to put her at ease.

"Those look lovely mother, don't they boys?" Her sons answered in unison and Donald served his brother and father.

Mrs Reid who'd remained standing said, "If you'll excuse me I've got a couple of things I want to get on with."

Donald was alarmed, "But you've hardly touched your own meal." When everyone looked for an answer Mrs Reid composed herself.

"It's alright," she said cheerily, "I wasn't very hungry to start with." An hour earlier she had beamed like a rising sun, all friendliness and jocularity and proud of her family.

When she had departed a dulled atmosphere remained.

"I didn't mean to upset her" said Peter feeling a pang of guilt.

His father quickly intervened "That's all right Peter, just don't let's have any more talk about the war, particularly when she is in earshot."

Donald was dying to empty his bladder but remained at the table to offer his brother advice, "Find out some facts brother... I did and I tell you the French with all their gallantry lost three hundred thousand men in one battle called Frontiers and that in less than two weeks." Hearing the power in his brother's voice left Peter aghast. Donald rose and began walking to the door. Watching him his father asked, "Are you going back to the fields?" His son pulled his cap on at a jaunty angle and stretched his arms out and it was easy to see the strength stored in them.

"Yeah, there's some fencing I want to see," he then shrugged his powerful shoulders, "if it's left much longer the job will..."

His father interrupted, "But it's dark son!"

Donald smiled and shrugged, "It's a full moon tonight according to meteorology... be plenty of light to do it. Anyway it's a small repair, no sense in leaving it anymore." He closed the door gently behind him, now fifty percent of the family who started the meal remained.

John Reid adjusted the wick in the lamp as it was beginning to flicker in an irritating way cutting down the light. When he sat back down at the table, Peter was looking at him.

"How did Donald know about the battle in France?"

"Donald makes it his business to find out about whatever is going on, he maybe what three years older than you but it's a lifetime son."

Peter misjudged his father's remark and let his feelings be known, "Oh so I'm a disappointment then?"

His father smiled, "No of course not, you're my son how can you be a disappointment to me? But you may be grateful for having a brother like Donald especially if you both get conscripted into the war."

Peter assumed an air of defiance which he hoped concealed his real lack of confidence, "I don't want conscription. I want to volunteer. They say when you have enough volunteers, conscription won't be needed. Already in Louth some men have been given white feathers…"

His father interrupted him in a savage voice, "Those people who give white feathers are the very people who should receive them." It was obvious his son didn't understand and the conversation was effectively over.

The war progressed and it seemed to coarsen the country. Older women bemoaned what they saw as the decline of impeccable Victorian manners despite officers still holding themselves upright in smart uniform, some bespoke for those who could afford them. The distinction between city life and country life had never been more apparent.

In the early morning Donald Reid continued to toil in the fields, driving a stubborn oxen to pull a plough at an even pace despite the soil never being even, which required great physical effort which he demanded of them as well as himself. Alone he remained a picture of contentment for no adverse thoughts occurred to him and he could drink in life unlike a tame householder who might hesitate over a medicinal glass of wine. Jack Hardy had been watching Donald from the hedgerows; he liked him and never understood the animosity between his son and this young man whom he thought resembled a sunlit parody of high purpose even if he would never use those exact words. Jack carried a haversack over his shoulder and strolled slowly towards Donald, still engrossed with the oxen, he was almost within touching distance before the Donald noticed him and both men exchanged smiles though Donald was surprised to see him.

"Hello Donald."

"Hello Jack, surprised to see you here, thought you'd be on the farm with Arthur and Sid?" He allowed the oxen a break from duty and mopped his brow with a cloth that hung out of his back trouser pocket.

"Well, I would have but I called at your father's and your mother asked me if I would bring your lunch out." Donald smiled generously as Jack took off the haversack.

"Anyway, I wanted to talk with you," he patted the haversack and smiled, "enough in there to feed a horse!"

Donald was laughing and in light hearted vein took the haversack, "I'm still a growing boy."

Jack nodded approvingly, "That you are and a fair one too... Are you going to take a break? I can call back later if you want to finish the row."

Donald's laughter continued and took on an unexpected quality, its note gentle as it expressed amusement, "No don't go Jack... Come on let's get over to the tree. I'm ready for some grub."

When they plonked themselves down with their backs upright against the trunk a vagrant breeze dispelled some of the day's heat and Donald sighed with pleasure waiting for Jack to let go of his hesitation for he could see the discomfort, restraint and hidden alarm on his neighbour's face.

The breeze blew more strongly before Donald asked, "Whatever's on your mind? Come on... it can't be that terrible."

Jack's voice was harshly self-conscious, at odds with the aesthetic mood early afternoon in the countryside offered on a fine day, "I don't think it's fair to burden you – it probably isn't, but you are just about the most sensible young man in the village."

"Right then Jack lets have it," he said taking a small bite out of his meat pie.

"You know Harry's gone to France?"

Donald's response was immediate, "Have you heard – is he OK?"

The older man threw his head back in idiosyncratic fashion which wasn't lost on the younger man and continued, "Oh, Harry will always be OK he's a born survivor. I know there is no love lost between you and him." Jack looked for a response but nothing was forthcoming, "He seems to relish the war. We had a letter last week, he's not allowed to say where exactly but he's fighting in the trenches... they call it trench warfare and he reckons one of his officers is so impressed he might get a promotion."

Donald nodded in the affirmative, "You should be proud Jack."

The latter looked bashful and began talking again, "Oh I am. Harry would kill the whole bloody German army."

Donald smiled and it didn't go unnoticed, "And if he got himself into one of his rages probably half of the English army." He continued eating until he'd finished the pie and then took out a large apple which he brushed vigorously along his shirt sleeve arm. The crunching sound when he bit into it elicited a smile from both men.

As he took another bite Jack gave him a knowing look, "Your mother isn't going to let you go hungry is she?" Silence passed between them before Jack spoke with dry displeasure in his voice, "I'm a bit worried about Arthur and Sid, they've been down the city and been into the army offices, I know Peter wants to volunteer and it's not for me to question why you haven't done so." Donald remained silent.

"No, your father and I both did our turn out there in South Africa, no joy in that I can tell thee." A measure of hostility crept into his voice, "Jumped up men playing with others lives, often on no more than a whim or even a bet." Suddenly

Jack Hardy was flooded with melancholia and Donald could see the anguish in his eyes and the angular carriage in his body suddenly seemed more acute and he let him continue.

"Donald before long all the young men in the village and surrounding villages will have gone to France either called up or volunteered."

Donald interrupted, "You're worried about Arthur and Sid?"

Jack looked solemn and paused for thought. "Harry's headstrong."

"I know."

"Arthur and Sid aren't men they're still boys like your Peter. They've got caught up in this thing." Their attention was suddenly taken by a quartet of deer running across an open field adjacent to them.

"I tried telling my eldest son what my father told me about war." He paused and momentarily retreated inside himself before continuing. "He said no matter what happens when you return make sure you can enter your home justified, otherwise the rest of your life may be a nightmare." Jack Hardy then smiled to himself, "Of course Harry wasn't listening..."

"You never know," replied Donald shrugging his shoulders.

"Pig-headed arrogance... never liked it in anyone, young or old," he gritted his teeth.

Donald was gingerly feeling the inside of the haversack and taking out a metal container careful not to burn his fingers. He gave a mug to Jack to hold while he poured hot tea into it indicating for Jack to have a drink but the latter declined and when the mug was almost full and Donald had screwed back the cap on the container, held the mug out for him. Donald took a swig before continuing their conversation with understated fervour.

"The army should fight the wars. Generals and politicians they decide on war... let them sort it out. We have enough on our plates making our living here." He gestured with both hands and it was understood.

"I don't want to fight, I will if I have to or circumstances are such that I am obliged to go but I don't want to. Folks say I'm not patriotic but being patriotic doesn't mean fighting for your country in some other country. Not to me it doesn't...."

There was a refreshing air of liberty about what Donald had said, though Jack couldn't articulate it but he did feel it as Donald had used gestures to transmit shades of meaning and emotion. The older man looked into the distance where he saw a collapsed tree; it suggested the havoc of nature rather than the deliberate work of men.

Then he spoke "I think, Donald that you will end up in France."

"What makes you think that, Jack?"

"Peter. Every mother is distraught when her boy goes off to war. Carrie's been worried sick, first Harry now the prospect of Arthur and Sid. Your mother will be the same, you'll see." There was an extended pause while Donald sipped the cooled tea.

"She's already asked my father to stop Peter."

"And?"

"Nothing he can do. Anyway, if Peter is determined to go, let him go, trying to stop him will only make him more determined."

Jack turned to face Donald, "When he goes – so will you, eventually." A hoarse murmur fell out of his mouth as he shook the leaves out of his mug.

"Do you think so?"

"Yes you'll go to look after him." Donald looked at Jack in a questioning manner.

"I've seen it before, the youngster all full of glamour and heroism and the wiser older obliged to look after him. At the end of the day blood is thicker than water, can't interfere with that, it's just nature." Both looked across the Wolds as though enticed into a mild trance, for whatever time of year each season threw out her best characteristics and welcomed admiration even adoration and only the dullards could never respond. For a moment or two both men seemed lost before they continued conversing.

"I don't like to say this but within six months, Donald, you'll be there. They put all boys in the infantry and all the Pals. Chances are that most young men from this and surrounding villages will be herded together." Tears began to well-up in Jack's eyes as though his spirit had gone down to the place of the dead and returned with their wisdom which was superior to that of the living.

"This war is going to be like no other. I can feel it, the slaughter is too terrible for me to contemplate, modern weapons and all. When you go look after the boys in this village Donald, they respect you... you'll realise what I mean." He offered his hand and a handshake formed and despite Jack Hardy's attempted smile Donald could see it was forced.

Jack wended his way home and Donald went back to work but it was hard for him to concentrate for their conversation was swirling around in his head and he was wise enough to know that too long thinking about death would paralyse anyone with fear; emotions were to be controlled not abandoned. For four more hours he toiled and when the oxen dropped to their knees he was relieved; there were no clouds above the Wolds and the promise of the sky was a clear morning.

Chapter 7

The late spring of 1915 witnessed the first raid on London by a Zeppelin. On the evening of May 31st it hovered over the Woolwich Arsenal before dropping bombs and causing massive explosions. Fortunately for the Allies it was an extremely vulnerable war machine, despite the terror it inflicted on the population. On this occasion a plane got above the Zeppelin to drop bombs and suddenly the sky was lit up. To make the airship lighter the crew were instructed to throw everything over the side but the damage could not be repaired and eventually the Zeppelin crashed over Essex. Acres of print were devoted to the slaying of 'a vulnerable animal' and the German High Command suspended further raids on the South East of England deciding its effectiveness was limited.

Earlier in the month warfare had taken on a new meaning, the use of gas by the Germans at the second Battle of Ypres. The enemy had taken Hill 60 in Flanders, a strategic objective. The deadly poison had arrived so quietly that most of the British troops were unable to put on their improvised gas respirators as the Germans attacked from the flanks with bombing parties and artillery shelling the British approaches to the Hill. The British garrison were able to return fire until reinforcements arrived having pushed through gas clouds. Fortunately for the Allies nature intervened; the wind changed direction pushing the gas along rather than across the British defences allowing the alarm to be sounded. The gas hung like a deep fog and soldiers having re-dampened cotton respirators found it impossible to stay in the trenches. When two more battalions were released into battle the Germans released more gas. Attack and counter-attack happened hour after hour and both sides were near exhaustion and neither side able to claim victory.

Both sets of generals claimed the other had used gas first and both played down the casualty rates. Both armies set their engineers the task of digging deep tunnels and packing them with explosives and nobody was under the illusion 'home by Christmas' anymore. In casualty stations lungs showed symptoms of phthisis due to chlorine gas inhalation and heartbeats were irregular and these were the simple cases.

The attack at Aubers Ridge resulted in 11,000 British casualties, many killed within yards of their own front line trench; it proved to be one of the highest rates of loss during the entire war. The battle was an unmitigated disaster for the support battalions – The Notts and Derbys backing up the Lancashires. The trenches were full and chaotic as were the communication posts with German shelling adding to the confusion. The laceration of fire across No Mans' Land resembled Hell's madness yet the 25th Brigade, the 2/Lincolns was ordered forward, to cross by the craters; there was no heather for men to look at one last time or bells coming into colour they could admire before death tumbled them by the score.

Against this backdrop Lucy Prior was pestering her father to allow her to join the nursing auxiliaries at home as the first casualties arrived by train and ship. She had revealed an inner core not previously evident and after she read accounts, often sanitized, in the national newspapers she gained access to when in Lincoln, she announced. "With or without your consent I am going to do something to help." Mr Prior wasn't a snob but had an irrational fear of his daughters mixing with common girls and his tone though light, had a tinge of malice. When Lucy threatened to go and work in a munitions factory in Sheffield and return with a broad Yorkshire accent suddenly nursing didn't appear so awful. At least it was a great leveller and doctors were of a certain class he thought. He didn't give unqualified approval but there was no mistaking his eldest daughter was in defiant bloom and her colourful cheeks, blonde hair and blue eyes would beam at him defiantly, knowingly. He eventually decided it was better to support her and alone in the evening, he could read the Bible, without guilt before smoking his pipe and attempting a challenging crossword in one of the upmarket newspapers. He didn't appear to miss his late wife, or if he did he kept his sorrow locked up. They had been married for twenty years and throughout the union she had flattered all and sundry with kindness, enthusiasm and good advice whether anyone asked for it or not. Perhaps Mr Prior no longer felt claustrophobic. Perhaps.

So Lucy Prior's life changed dramatically. At first she was detached for home service only – staff auxiliary hospitals and rest stations. She worked feverishly towards gaining certificates in Home Nursing and first aid; it appeared she had suddenly found her vocation unlike other girls who saw it as 'a bit of fun'. Bandaging, dressing were easily mastered and her superiors arranged for her to go into Lincolnshire hospitals to gain insight into ward work including the transportation of the sick and wounded and stretcher cases because of the shortage of male recruits. "I have never known someone so dedicated," an experienced doctor told her one day, "we can never have enough nurses of high calibre if this war is going to go the way I think it might." There was a stern look creeping up his face despite his usual air of bluff cheeriness. Lucy liked him and his inner warmth for it contrasted perfectly with a couple of the younger doctors who had the air of righteous overseers.

Nothing was too much for the young lady from a sheltered upbringing who suddenly had her eyes opened. Besides carrying out duties a char lady would be doing in civilian life, for the first time she was alone, unchaperoned with the opposite sex many of whom were in immense pain and looked to nurses to give them comfort, strength and courage. "How terribly British," she said to a colleague one day, "all the regulations about how we should wear our uniform... aprons not to be longer than overalls and a spare apron for emergencies." The other nurse had laughed before quipping, "And no travelling to and from the hospital in clean aprons and sleeves." Lucy was shaking her head, "We also need a long night's rest, fresh air combined with moderate exercise." Their conversation gained vivacity but when they saw Sister their ebullient youth was suddenly checked by her cold authority for she viewed auxiliary nurses as augmenting the numbers of trained nurses.

Fifteen months into the war more and more hospitals were needed to cope with an ever increasing number of casualties and Lucy Prior knew it was only a matter of time before she started working in overseas hospitals, under the control of the War Office. She had been granted leave and took a train from Sheffield where she'd undertaken a three month secondment to Lincoln where her sister met her. Their celebrations were muted as they watched wounded soldiers, some on crutches being helped by other soldiers disembark from the train and mothers, many weeping because they didn't recognise the faces of their sons, in many instances. Grogginess packed the railway station.

When the sisters retired to a tea shop both were pleased to see each other.

"I must see you in your full uniform when we get home!" Ann exclaimed, followed by "isn't that suitcase rather heavy to carry?"

Lucy laughed, "Ann I've carried twelve stone men from A to B." Her sister gasped, it was the innocence in her eyes that forebade Lucy telling the younger girl some of the horrific sights she'd witnessed and no doubt would witness on a daily basis when she got to France.

"How is father?" Lucy asked.

"Oh, he's fighting the war like most who aren't involved." A smile lit up Ann's face – she saw her father with a contemptuous voice flicking like the tail end of a whip devouring the Germans and not caring if the hot fury in his mind threatened to explode. Ann paid the bill and they left. An hour and a half later they walked into their home and immediately drew seats up by the open fire while their father, dressed suitably for the evening, poured three Sherrys and brought them over. He shifted his weight in another chair with a nervous gesture. "I'm very proud of you Lucy," he said thinly and then clamped his mouth around a large cigar. The sisters knew not to say anything until he had lit it and taken a long drag.

Lucy talked about the friends she'd made – like minded young women who now saw themselves as essential to the war effort and her audience of two listened intently. She didn't mention that some nurses loved the shape their uniform gave them. "Damned noble isn't it father?" interrupted Ann as though rehearsed in readiness for Lucy to declare her intention of going abroad 'on active service'. In fact she announced it rather breezily and her father nodded which surprised the girls. Only the full horrors would be relived after the slaughter was finally over in 1918.

Lucy Prior quickly realised her work in the hospital trains had the power of life or death. It was no secret that they were vastly understaffed; maybe a dozen medical personnel including two doctors for four to five hundred patients, some critical and over half helpless. Many had been brought directly from the field of combat and of those some were determined to stay alive until they knew they were in England and were told or it was whispered to them when the train stopped in a French provincial station that they had arrived in England for it was a humane gesture designed to end unnecessary suffering.

Many of the soldiers' uniforms were in a shocking condition which made undressing them difficult. Lucy moved from carriage to carriage with a lamp and a bag containing dressings and medicaments as the train thundered through the day and night. As time went on most hospitals trains were completely stripped and redesigned as medical staff suggested – for lying cases and sitting cases.

After three months, exhausted and witness to a life time's suffering Lucy was given leave and travelled back to England with a nurse, Helen Hedger who possessed the face of youth and the friendliness of age. Both girls were fond of each other and having worked together on the team an 'esprit de corps' had grown between the whole group with Sarah Liddel, a native of Edinburgh, providing essential Celtic humour. Nurse Hedger was destined to resume work in Birmingham where she would meet a soldier recovering from wounds and fall madly in love only to be cruelly robbed when he returned to action and was killed. The nurse never recovered and practically lost the will to live. No one would have thought it watching the two laughing and screaming whoops of delight at the prospect of a hot bath and, at last, finally able to apply makeup.

"I think I've forgotten how to dance," guffawed Helen, "and I can't remember how one hits a tennis ball let alone scores." Neither ever forgot that train ride up from Portsmouth to Waterloo; the sky turned crimson and when the train stopped at Woking the full moon glowed out of heaven. "I bet you nightingales are singing tonight" said Lucy before sleep overtook both girls, who had to be woken by a train inspector half an hour after they'd arrived in London.

That night Lucy pondered if she and Helen's paths would cross again during the war as she lay in a London hotel bed used by the nursing profession courtesy of special arrangement. She dreamed of the private whose wounds she'd dressed telling her about the Battle of Mons and of the luminous angels he'd seen in the skies above the battlefield. When others also swore under oath of having seen similar there had been disquiet among the army's top brass who felt their grip might be loosened, nevertheless both they and the government were quick to see it as 'evidence', as the British public did, that Divine intervention was on the allies side and not the Hun, who represented evil. Ironically it had been a military retreat not the advance HQ had hoped for.

Chapter 8

The men met at the White Swan cafe. All were portly, dressed for the shoot and had smudge-red faces - a few were bad tempered. The same form of bad temper that possesses a man when he discovers his wife is sleeping with another man. Bloated on bacon, egg, sausage and black pudding the gentlemen farmers climbed, awkwardly, into the open wagon fixed to a tractor. An hour later the fun was in full cry: pheasants were dropping like dead flies and gun powder lit the nostrils. Across the Channel the gunfire was aimed at a different quarry.

A wailing, shrieking shell flew overhead and without invitation exploded scattering body parts in all directions. Those soldiers crouching down in recently formed craters kissed any religious artefact they had; the fear was tangible and many cried unashamedly while waiting for the word to advance. Each day it was only a matter of time before the German artillery found its range. Two direct hits in less than five minutes. The whistle of death carried, stopped and suddenly fifty men were wiped out.

Soldiers in the next crater knew their name was on the next one and they looked through anguished eyes at their officer, no older than twenty, who'd drawn his pistol fearful the men might panic and run. The previous evening along with two other junior officers he'd been looking at the Stock Exchange prices in an old copy of 'The Times'. However, his fear was greater and his hand trembled before the whistle was heard and his nerve deserted him and he fled only to catch the full force of the shell; those infantrymen who had abandoned the crater had also paid the ultimate price. Their regimental comrades sat frozen, uncomfortable and hesitant, glowering at the dead bodies in a sullen way; a vision of hell had been visited upon them and back in England it became obvious no politician could find solution to a problem he had never faced, even if some continued to try. They had no understanding of despair whereas those men who had been seduced by the perceived glamour of war had fallen into a rhythm and design of life which always concluded in an orgy of death. The torment of long hidden but never to be healed wounds would plague those survivors for the rest of their lives but they didn't know it yet.

Along swathes of countryside men barely advanced fifteen yards before being skittled down by machine guns. On one occasion an infantryman in the Lancashires having got further was beginning to thread his way through barbed wire; encouraging cheering suddenly broke out and rose to fever pitch as allied soldiers willed him to safety. His elated face told everyone a crater, seconds away, and at last safety was within his grasp. Suddenly a single shot was heard and the young man's eyes rolled and there was a deafening silence but it wasn't heard in the Lincolnshire countryside where an occasional staccato of gunfire was heard followed by gruff congratulatory words the most common of which were "Well done old fellow... rather good shot." And then a worker threw two pheasants into a hessian sack.

In another part of the country between green cushioned hills and far from the industrial cities which were fast filling up with men and young girls filthy with venereal disease and soldiers on leave with the blurred and angry eyes of the drunkard, sat the Clements girls under the swaying branches of a silver birch tree. Both wore expertly pressed cream blouses, dark skirts and leather boots though the younger of the two had polished hers as if she was on parade! Helen produced a letter and her sister watched expectantly as she read it to herself, her facial expression changing with each new paragraph. Elizabeth couldn't contain her patience. "Come on what does Donald say?"

Helen continued reading before looking up "Give me a chance... I haven't even read it through myself yet." Elizabeth was having none of this and began gesticulating.

"Liar, I bet you've read it to yourself at least ten times." The inquisition ceased for a moment as faint gunfire was heard in the distance causing both girls to look in a North West direction. When silence prevailed Elizabeth continued.

"I wish they didn't shoot those poor things, it's so unfair. They haven't hurt anyone so why should they be treated like that?"

Helen was too absorbed in her mail and had only half heard her sister, "What was that?"

"Oh nothing, come on tell me." The older of the two was about to say something when they were distracted by the sight of a squirrel bolting up another tree and out of sight. It elicited a warm glow from the sisters.

Helen inhaled. "Right, Donald says they are right in the thick of it and some of the others realise it's no Sunday afternoon picnic like most thought it was going to be. Here I'll read you a bit." Helen lifted the letter close to her eyes while Elizabeth's eyes never moved off her sister.

"Yesterday along with the Suffolks, Lancashires and men of the Essex Infantry we gained some ground. I am not allowed to say how much or mention any place names but I can tell you that the sights are none too pleasant, in fact I didn't realise the stench burning flesh gives. Some of us can't bear to look at even dead Germans when we advance not that you can tell them from us. I mean the uniforms are sometimes in shreds. I don't know if the censor will allow this bit but I'll try (maybe he's got too many to get through). Last week a group of Aussies advanced along the front and took the enemy by surprise, there was fierce hand to hand fighting with heavy losses on both sides and then when it was all over some of the men took watches and rings off the dead enemy. I hope this war never turns me in such a way, my discomfort is obvious but I try to force a grin and long for the day I will be home." Both girls were locked in reflection and as Helen held the letter to her bosom they were startled by more shots ringing out in the distance nevertheless she kept her lips loose with a smile.

Chapter 9

Only the blue sky offered refuge from the madness below and most infantrymen on both sides often looked up with a mixture of rage and jealousy at those crossing the skyline and joining 'the party' for a brief moment before retiring to the safety of their clubhouse where a rich coal fire was kept alight for eight months of the year and where food and even alcohol was never in short supply. The infantry even sang songs about it for their warmth came from genuine comradeship and a tacit understanding that happens when men are in great peril.

From the cockpit a German pilot surveyed the craters, puffs of smoke and miniature figures lacing the torn landscape. When he dropped lower everything grew larger and the noise increased before bullets riddled the landscape. Despite diving for cover the anguished cries of men could be heard everywhere as bombs caused a vibration in the earth and air.

Donald Reid in mud splattered uniform lay in a waterlogged trench having eased another soldier, barely recognisable because of the mud, into a more comfortable position. He cradled his head in his arms and began clearing the mud from his face. He stopped, stunned when he recognised David Baumber the village blacksmith a few years older than the other 'Pals'.

"Christ Donald, I feel so cold." Despite the arrival of another Fokker Triplane strafing the ground held by the Tommies, Donald could only hear an inner silence which life seldom reached.

"Just rest... just rest." It was difficult to hold back the tears. When he looked up into the sky clearing of greyness and enemy aircraft he began a soliloquy. "When we get home we'll drink the beer till it comes out of our ears and sweat like pigs in front of Bert's roaring fire. Don't let go, David, just keep that picture in your mind and in your heart. Remember those..." He paused, looked down at his friend before gently closing the dead man's eyes.

From the west rapid rain clouds suddenly blew in and within minutes it had begun to pour in biblical fashion. The whole of the battlefield resembled a swamp and the crater was waist deep in water. Donald made a resolution, considered unlucky, that he would survive no matter what and one day cherish the memory of David Baumber in The Red Lion back home. The effort of holding the blacksmith's body drew the last dregs of strength before he let it sink beneath him. When the water level rose another eight feet Donald was able to roll out and under cover of darkness crawled back, exhausted, to British occupied trenches where he was debriefed and given dry clothing, food and allowed to sleep.

The following day Private Reid was transported to a garrison in the nearby woods where guards stood on duty at the main gates and to the right restless horses shuffled in a pen. He didn't know it but soon he would be transferred again to join up with the boys he'd grown up with. For the time being it was a relief not to be on the front line. Here the wind seemed to fall and despite noise coming from the North West and East, the night was still and the full moon could be looked at...

Donald struck up a friendship with a Brummie, Richard Carter, whose accent could be cut in half and both men were self-effacing in the other's company. He enjoyed the way he was referred to as 'our kid' and the private, a native of the borough of Ladywood teased his new friend with mimicry of his rural accent - 'yissmate'.

Their officer actually cared for his men and instructed Donald that he was in no rush to move him on having listened to his war record to date.

"See this as unofficial leave, Private Reid." He said lighting up a cigarette and Donald looking at the young man's slightly bloodshot eyes wasn't about to query.

"C'mon you can help me prepare sir's horse," Private Carter said after the officer walked back to his tent. "First the brushes... she loves having her body stroked," the Brummie said winking in a sly manner that elicited a florid smile from Donald, the first he'd issued for what seemed ages.

"I suppose she loves flattery too... mind you they do look lovely animals and so healthy in this environment." Private Carter realised that having been brought up in rural England his new mate would probably know a lot more about horses than any city boy.

"Well I'll watch you our kid and I think I'll have a smoke as well." He produced a packet of ten Weights and offered one immediately to Donald who declined.

"Let's get the horse ready and then have a fag with a cup of char?"

"OK boss." Both men laughed and Private Carter went to the barn where the officer's blanket and saddle were kept while Private Reid climbed quietly into the pen and gently approached their officer's horse careful not to alarm the others.

He spoke words of comfort he'd seen blacksmiths do when shoeing a horse and the animal moved her head in his direction before standing motionless as he brushed her neck with a hairbrush talking at the same time. He didn't realise the boy from Ladywood had stood watching him, in awe, before coming into the paddock with blanket, saddle and reins.

Twenty minutes later they walked the horse towards the officer's tent as he appeared with another junior officer who was a caricature of what he was – a boy in man's uniform.

"Sir" and with that Richard Carter beckoned his officer to mount.

"Thank you Private.... old girl looks wonderful."

"Thank Private Reid Sir... after this war's over he could make a handsome living grooming horses..." A light hearted chuckle was transferred between the men as the officer mounted and rode south to where the senior officers, stationed in mansions, were 'preparing' the next phase of the war. The two Privates sauntered to the kitchen where they persuaded a flabby, permanently sweating cook to make them a pot of tea as duty had prevented them from taking a break.

"When it's all over come to Ladywood Donald... one of my older sisters has a spare room in her terrace and it's near a reservoir." Donald listened intently and could see the tenderness in his companion's eyes.

"Each Sunday I walk around there, sometimes twice looking at the birds buzzing in and out of bushes and trees... always know it's going to be a lucky day if I see two Widgeon sail by." Donald laughed and the effort was almost too much for his constricted chest because he hadn't laughed in a long while.

"Yeah the last hundred yards I usually decide whether I'm going to the Bricklayers Arms, The Wheatsheaf or the Monument... that will determine which entrance I leave by."

"Which is your favourite?"

The Brummie paused. "Good question either way I usually end up going to all three," he said in a matter of fact manner and both men laughed for their conversation that morning had been far removed from the infantryman's usual thoughts about fear, food, fornication and courage until the very end that would help them avoid death. Two months later Private Carter was killed when his regiment mounted a second assault to establish a foothold across a river. Donald Reid never found out.

Chapter 10

Lucy Prior had gained the respect of all her colleagues, particularly the senior doctors, with her sense of unflinching duty during the long hours of work. Her reward, if that's what it could be called, resulted in her being selected to the Nursing Staff of a Casualty Clearing Station. This promotion was based on Confidential Reports about her previous service and record of health. Once again Regulations about matters of discipline were to the fore such as off-duty time, uniform and keeping relatives informed including writing immediately after death and caring for the mortuary.

After the first gas attack her work was extremely testing, for large numbers were admitted. She put in some twenty hour days and the saddest outcome was that she could see little result borne of her efforts; she remained stoic despite tears welling up behind her eyes. The hospitals were full as were the grounds where soldiers lay on stretchers gasping for breath, unable to remain still and craving water.

"I don't think I can do this anymore" another nurse confided in her before breaking down and kneeling on the floor sobbing.

"You will because these men depend on us... just to see us is enough especially those about to die," Nurse Prior said. She was surprised because the woman she comforted was about to be promoted to sister and she had always worked in a calm manner often administering chloroform as a remedy for the suffering.

Soon Lucy, who had on the surface turned her back on a privileged life, was in the operating theatres mixing jugs of sterilised lotions and assisting the anaesthetists. For the war effort as a whole, great improvements had been made and by early 1916 some clearing stations were almost as well equipped as General Hospitals and the operating theatres were unrecognisable from those often makeshift, in the early part of the war. "We've even got a hot chamber for keeping blankets and clothes warm" Nurse Prior shrieked in amazement when showing new nurses around. She could see the nursing new recruits' starched uniforms matched only by the stark anxiety in their faces and she told them of her experiences and that the "essential requirement of remaining passionate, dispassionate and above all else always professional". As a reminder she followed up with "That way we save lives even if it's not apparent at the time".

In Lincolnshire her sister Ann, would always read her sister's letters from the Front after supper when her father was in a 'balanced' mood. Often there would be weeks between the letters. Ann always skipped the personal parts and her father would rattle "Come on girl... come on." In the spring of 1916 from somewhere near the Belgian border she read, "Two buildings have been requisitioned for our patients and one in a convent where Nurse Alison Frances is in the tiny room next door. We look out onto brown fields and the countryside is flat, more so than home. Some nights we hear continuous heavy artillery and the sky lights up or should I say is ablaze in angry yellow, sometimes red. This goes on until morning. Unfortunately we have serious casualties with chest and abdominal wounds and everyday amputations are carried out. Ambulance Convoys arrive mid morning and soldiers straight from the battlefield are carried in. The first thing we do is attend to their dressings and change their often sodden uniforms. Then ambulances arrive to take them to the Hospital train. The serious cases are taken in a ward and prepared for surgery." Ann paused and her father said nothing.

"Many are too brave and try to smile even if they know they will die shortly. For those that survive surgery they are kept as long as necessary before being evacuated. When there is a lull, which is rare, everyone scrubs the wards and the whole place stinks of disinfectant. Then we prepare dressings. We just never know what will happen next or if the Germans will bomb us from the sky. This happened at another clearing station and the medical staff were evacuated while shells exploded all around them. No one wanted to leave their patients but orders are orders I suppose. There is a wonderful spirit most of the time amongst us and I know I am making friends for life. Say a prayer for me as I do for you and father. One day this war will be over and the world will have peace for eternity."

Both father and daughter were reduced to stunned silence, they knew Lucy must be under terrifying gusts of invisible pressure and when Ann broke the silence she did so in a husky voice.

"I'm proud of her." Her father felt weaker than a dying plant but he was careful not to let his other daughter see the tears in his eyes.

"The whole village, the country can be proud of her and the like."

That night in bed he said softly to himself "You don't know anything" then he used the sleeve of his nightshirt to mop his tears. Fear of the apparition of death had left his subconscious and was in his thoughts, if he suspected his daughter might be in harm's way he had no illusions anymore. Ann read the letter many times by candlelight, before she finally succumbed to sleep.

Chapter 11

Faint sounds of revelry could be heard in the distance when a Lance Corporal in mud splattered uniform kicked over the dying embers of a small camp fire inside the Allies compound. He walked in the direction from which he could hear the sound of an old melodeon; he slowed when he approached a solitary Ash tree, its silhouette dark, mysterious and dramatically shadowed by the full moon and stood motionless as the trunk itself, his own outline defined against the sky beyond. It reminded Harry Hardy of home and he put his hand against it reasoning it to be sixty to seventy years old. "Your money or your life Lance Corporal Hardy" said a young voice suddenly appearing. Despite tiredness Harry immediately braced himself and saluted. The officer returned the salute before retrieving a silver cigarette case and offering a smoke to Harry. He hesitated but was encouraged by the similarly aged young man, stretching his legs before retiring for the night "Go on... we might both be dead this time tomorrow." It elicited a smile and Lance Corporal Hardy took the fourth cigarette in line from the packed case before striking a light for both of them from the pocket matches he always kept in the top pocket of his tunic. He was hardly recognizable, as the Army had turned the erstwhile boorish, surly bruiser and would-be bully into a responsible young man who was protective of his men.

It was hard for Harry to discern where the young officer was from as he had no regional accent that was instantly recognisable, unlike his own. What he did notice was how pristine the other's uniform was, particularly the leather belt and holster.

"Do you think it will ever be over Lance Corporal?"

There was a pause before Harry responded "Who knows sir... there are rumours that we are all building up to a big offensive but we've been hearing that now for fifteen months... you know off and on." He looked at the junior officer and took another drag on his cigarette.

The officer gazed up at the sky before declaring "Yes, HQ and I believe this goes up to the top, want us over the Somme... but these things take time not to mention the logistics of getting enough artillery and of the right calibre into place." He paused and inhaled slowly before pushing the smoke out through his nostrils, "Then there's the question of having sufficient shells to pierce their defences. Night patrols have come across deserted trenches that go much deeper than ours and if, as I suspect, they have turned the last line into fortified living quarters shelling may not be enough."

Harry always felt uncomfortable when conversation with officers elapsed for some minutes into silence then raising his head spoke firmly.

"Oh we'll win through Sir... we have to."

"Pray to God that we do... goodnight Lance Corporal." With that the officer stubbed out his cigarette under foot, turned and walked away leaving Harry pondering.

The singing was less boisterous as he approached the tent and pulled the flap over the opening to one side. The men sat on wooden boxes drinking tea from a large urn, acknowledged Harry and he picked up a scruffy looking mug and tilted the urn to get what tea was left.

The 'choir' struck up a chorus just for Harry and mighty chuffed he was. His smile could have been measured in feet and inches. When the singing died down he addressed the men.

"Boys, you'll be pleased to know that some of the Fens Pals will be joining us this week." Jubilation almost broke out because experience had told these men that death stared at them every day, the statistics had proved that, but Harry remained undeterred.

"We're gonna see the old faces. Captain told me that some battalions are being moved up nearer the enemy lines." He looked around at tired eyes before continuing. "Now, don't get asking me who's coming that's classified information but surely some old boys will be meeting up with us."

Harry winced when he took a mouthful of warm stewed tea and some of the soldiers chuckled. To his right he heard coughing and when he looked he saw one of the men cleaning his bayonet before sharpening it with stone.

"Are we taking anyone out tonight?"

The Lance Corporal's reply was swift and forthright "Yes, a few of us." He looked at his watch "About ten o'clock." While someone adjusted the wick in the oil lamp because the flame had started to flicker, Harry looked at Michael Jeffries and Peter Reid.

"You two and anyone else?" He looked around, deliberately smiling but no volunteers were forthcoming so he raised his voice, slightly "Us three are all from the same village. Let's have some more represented." Two men looked at each other before raising their hands.

Harry acknowledged them "Jim, Dave, cheers. Good. If everyone takes their fair share there'll be no need to put up a rota like the officers want, believe you me they are impressed with us from the Fens... let's keep it that way." The audience murmured an approval for it was nice to have a sense of worth in what one had described earlier in the day as "Hell's playground".

When the volunteers left the tent the singing returned but was more muted. The party reported to the designated tent for their orders but none were impressed by one of the officers lolling in his chair and throwing paper balls, already prepared, into a wicker basket. The senior officer realising the disdain of men about to risk their lives again asked the others to leave in such a voice that didn't merit any challenge. Then he apologised "He's new... doesn't understand... he will." Harry recognised the man's discomfort "Sir". While the officer poured small measures of rum the night patrollers removed all badges, letters, and any identifiable objects and placed them in a draw bag.

All studied the detailed map stretched across an easel and the senior officer now smoking his walnut pipe pointed out the operation.

"You will be taken by armed escort to the Front Line, as per usual... we have no reliable intelligence." He paused and tapped the particular area with his index finger. Before any questions were asked, the officer, aware that each of these missions was this side of suicide blurted out "I don't know how you chaps do it." The men warmed to this officer because any vestige of superiority, condescension and dismissal of class many officers retained had long been stripped bare, if it had ever been there in the first place. All the men shook hands and Harry piped up "Make sure you've removed everything, check again." The last two words were said in a whisper.

Out on the Front Line the moon was occasionally blotted out by moving clouds and as the men lay flat conversation and instruction barely audible as Harry took charge.

"Michael, Peter, you go out to the listening post beyond the second line of trenches and remember one pull on the wire when you arrive," Michael nodded, "two pulls mean we're coming out, four pulls means enemy and five return to the trench smartish."

Ten years earlier the two boys had slithered along mud flats, on their bellies in the hope that their traps had borne fruit. Now, this was a different kind of poaching yet they tried to retain that essential sense of naughtiness that had always characterised their earlier exploits.

Harry watched anxiously from a makeshift trench. Michael paused because a twisted wire stake was blocking his way and signalled to Peter before raising himself up, hoping to mount the object. Suddenly a flare light shot up over No Man's Land.

"Stay where you are" whispered Peter in trembling voice. Another flare went up and suddenly the whole area appeared under floodlight. Michael was trapped in the tangled wire attached at all angles to the leaning stake yet he still had the presence of mind to crane his neck round and whisper to Peter, "Stay where you are." In less than half a minute the light flickered and died and darkness resumed. Both men heaved a sigh of relief and within three minutes Michael had extricated himself from the wire and held it down while Peter crawled across. Both men crawled into a huge shell hole.

"I'm going to die of a heart attack, not bullets, in this war," Michael gasped in a palpitating voice, before allowing a grin to run over his face while Peter patted him on the back.

Harry with two others was getting impatient crouched down in his trench.

"Come on we're going out," and with that he tugged the wire twice. All three began crawling out. Michael pulled himself up to ground level and eventually ushered Harry in a straight line. At last all the boys were sat at the bottom of the crater which had begun oozing underground water. They huddled around Harry who produced a tattered small map and tapped a certain area before whispering, "We're here... one of the scouting parties in the Suffolks thinks there's a German listening post not far from here."

He tapped the map again "This is where they're certain movement was coming from."

Only when the clouds moved could each man see the facial features of his fellow soldiers and at that precise moment Michael looked at Harry and his eyes went watery with the gravity of their predicament yet his remark was light, almost casual.

"Harry, you're not trying to get us killed are you?" Everyone wanted to laugh but silence was essential. The men huddled closer and Harry spoke.

"Listen, if there are Germans there they're not going to expect us besides we're country boys, we don't announce our presence." One of the party broke wind and five rib cases moved up and down rapidly and silently - all must have wondered if they would ever live to tell this tale.

Peter tapped Harry's shoulder because a cloud obstructed the moon, "If this is just hearsay intelligence not an official report you're taking an awful risk. These Krauts have already lit the place up twice, suppose they do it a third time. We'll be sitting ducks."

Harry knew the odds and he too wanted to survive the war, "All right we'll just go so far... I'll go first. I'll give it ten minutes no more I promise you." Fortunately he couldn't see the reluctant acquiescent looks on his men's faces.

Thirty miles away muted gunfire erupted which Harry thought might be a pleasing distraction for the enemy as he crawled closer towards the German line. A huge crater hole lay fifteen yards in front and the men were instructed to remain still while Harry gestured that he was going to have a look. It was a relief for the men not to hear their joints cracking as was always the case on night sorties or their thoughts racing about in all directions when they were on the move. For all involved in nocturnal reconnaissance the fear above all fear was to be left dead, unnoticed and feasted on by slugs, insects and rats growing fatter than cats by the hour.

Harry had noticed a large hole in the side covered with planks of wood and he smiled to himself before turning back and beckoning Peter to take up position in a couple of bushes to his right, then he motioned to Michael to lie on top of what appeared to be the concealed entrance to a German trench.

Slowly, methodically, they took up their positions with the other two pals moving to a clump of bushes opposite the planks of wood. Everything was still, but recognisable was the sudden click of a rifle bolt. It startled Michael who looked to Harry who motioned his hand up and down in a calming way before drawing his revolver slowly and pushing it into a crack in the boards. He counted to three then fired several shots. Boards flew in all directions and a bayonet flashed by Harry's ear, he shot a German who all but collapsed on him. Pandemonium broke out as the British soldiers all armed with pistols fired shot after shot at the trench before scuttling away from the shell hole as gun fire was returned.

The men zigzagged their way into another shell hole, rolling into a foot of fetid water. They were emotionally spent and physically exhausted but silent until Harry, no longer gasping for air, spat out his words through clenched teeth.

"The bastards must have been waiting for us, why else would they have been so wary?" He paused and smiled at the others, "Still we got a few, now let's hope our route back to the trench hasn't been cut off."

Peter had struggled to regain a semblance of calm, "I don't mind saying I'm frightened stiff."

Harry looked intense and loosened his top button "We all are, even your brother wherever he is."

It wasn't a remark Peter, despite their position, would let go "Don't start, not here of all places." He could feel anger overtaking his fear and he moved his face closer to Harry so the Lance Corporal would be in no doubt of the offence he'd caused. "Besides you said you were looking forward to seeing some of the boys again didn't you?"

Harry tried to pull rank "Yeah well I wasn't thinking of your brother." He began loading his revolver before handing bullets to Peter, "Here make sure you load up." Jim pulled himself up to the top because despite being out of sight their position was obviously vulnerable. Satisfied it was clear he slid back down to the others, nodding his head.

Peter whispered, "They want to send all the men that were poachers in the villages out on these recces... they'd be home from home."

When the party looked to Harry he spoke softly, "Just remember we're capable of doing as good a scouting job as those Canadians. They think they've got a monopoly on No Man's Land."

Peter was quick with his response "Well they're welcome to it" he muttered more to himself than anyone else.

Harry gestured with hand signals indicating that they would crawl in line back to the top. "Ready?" Five silent shadows slithered on their bellies towards the British line – five yards pause then another five. The rats were already scavenging and it was a sickening sight. Harry suddenly raised his hand for he was leading the line, he'd spotted a German helmet sticking above a trench and glistening in the moonlight.

When he turned to face Michael he gestured with his right hand that the party would have to go round the other way because he could hear, very faintly, the sound of dull thuds in succession which indicated a German working party were repairing trenches not far away. They all knew the slightest loss of concentration through tiredness could prove fatal.

It was their longest hour to date and finally the recognition of British voices buoyed them as did steaming mugs of Bovril. All of them slept like dead men for the next seven hours and when they awoke they shook hands, lit roll-ups and drank copious amounts of warm stewed tea.

Debriefing was always held in the largest white tent, fronted by a sentry, in the top right hand corner of the military settlement. Harry, Peter, Michael, Jim and Dave stood to attention while a pallid faced Colonel Teale continued to scrutinise a map drawn across a utility table made of elm. An N.C.O. mute as marble stood at ease to their right. Finally the Colonel turned sideways to face the men who were astonished at how impeccable his officer's uniform was as though it had just been returned from the cleaners. Despite his complexion he had a firm mouth and moved easily in a measured way which suggested to Harry he was a deliberate person, a man with courage who never rushed at life haphazardly, like the Lance Corporal had once done.

The Colonel looked at his men and gave them a sudden, pleasant smile but it was the quality of his voice that surprised everyone.

"That was a fine piece of work you did last night gentlemen," he chuckled and in a self-effacing manner continued, "wouldn't have minded going along for the craic meself. You Fens Pals are becoming the talk of the regiment with these night time sorties into No Man's Land." He deliberately paused because he wanted to look at each of them, individually, so there would be no doubting his sincerity.

"It must be your background. Send some of these city types out and they would awaken half of France!" The men couldn't disguise their laughter and they were told to stand at ease. To make them feel ever more relaxed the Colonel walked over and perched himself on the front of his desk, a couple of yards in front of his night patrol. He lit his pipe and flattened some of the loose tobacco with his finger. The aroma was intoxicating and he continued.

"Even some of my officers are like bulls in china shops. I've been thinking that the longer this war continues in its present form the more important it is that we have a keen intelligence section combining the efforts of scouting soldiers, snipers and observers." He straightened up and the Fens Pals automatically stood to attention.

"Some of you fellows are about to join us and I want us to have the finest scouts. Honour and Duty goes without saying." Pride began to swell in the chests of the five soldiers and they had already forgiven the old man his previous silent attitude and air of gentlemanly reserve for he was a gentleman but unlike most senior officers he had an air of mystery above his intelligent forehead.

Lance Corporal Hardy waited to hear more "Sir?"

The colonel obliged, "An Intelligence Officer will give instructions to the unit separated from the rest of the battalion. A training programme will be devised when the battalion is resting." He looked at Harry for a query and wasn't disappointed.

"Sir, how many men will be in the unit?" There was eagerness in his voice that didn't go unnoticed and it was returned with the confidence associated with former public school pupils.

"Who knows what the eventual complement will be – twenty five, thirty." He straightened his shoulders up and inhaled deeply before resuming "This war's already gone on much longer than anyone supposed. Both us and the Hun know it's stalemate so progress has got to come from somewhere. The unit will be billeted together and instructions will take place in the following: map reading, use of prismatic compass by day and night, marking of compass bearings, signalling, semaphore and Morse and then combat skills such as crawling, bomb throwing and revolver practice."

Harry looked hesitant and bit his lip "Sir."

"What is it?" asked the Colonel who suddenly put his hands up and turned his head towards the N.C.O., "Could you rustle up some tea and biscuits if we've got any?"

"Sir," was the immediate reply and he left. Again the Colonel turned to the men.

"Let's ditch protocol for a moment, draw that table up and lean on it and I'll sit on mine," and it was said without a shred of self-consciousness. All of the men had noticed the Colonel's ribbons and knew he was neither a desk jockey nor a stranger to combat.

Suddenly the N.C.O. announced his return, carrying a large tray he placed a brown teapot, milk jug, barrel of biscuits and cups and saucers on the Colonel's desk. He was about to start pouring when the senior officer suggested he took a cigarette break and began pouring the tea into cups himself, followed by milk.

"No bloody sugar I'm afraid, still..." The men grinned and soon all of them were enjoying hot freshly brewed tea, something of a treat for them. The Colonel scratched the back of his head and rubbed his fingers up and down his throat, gurning at the same time, he invited Harry to continue.

"This training sounds all right but surely the first thing there needs to be is a lot of reconnaissance to familiarise ourselves with all the routes in every area. No good having all these skills without knowing where you are heading." As an afterthought he said "With respect Sir."

Colonel Teale paused, "You have a very good point Lance Corporal. I have consulted with my fellow officers and we are all of the opinion that you are more than equipped to..." he left the sentence dangling in mid air, "well your record of night patrols speaks for itself." The pals were trying to come to terms with the familiarity with which they were conversing though they covered it well.

"Hardy I want you to be, what you might call, Scout Officer to be promoted to Corporal once the paperwork is done." Harry was astonished and lost for words because most officers had only ever seen the uncouth vigour of his exterior.

Colonel Teale tapped the barrel of his pipe on the desk and began relighting it, once again puffs of smoke formed a haze and he continued.

"I like you rural types. The Air Force can provide aerial reconnaissance but at ground level is where the real work is done." The men exchanged smiles and nearly broke into laughter when he quipped, "Tell that to the Air Force and it gets their backs up."

He looked at Dave "What part of the shire are you from Private?"

"Astergy Fen, Sir."

"Do much fishing, hunting?"

In a relaxed manner he answered, "Well Sir, fishing in the season when work allows it and hunting, if I'm honest Sir, it's more like poaching." He grinned and Teale broke into a hearty laugh for which he was renowned.

"Gosh you're so honest do you know ninety-five per cent of men tell lies as a matter of course. Some can't even distinguish between reality and unreality."

He turned to Jim "And are you from the same village?"

"Yes Sir," was the immediate reply.

"So you two are friends?"

"I suppose so," acknowledged Jim.

The Colonel looked satisfied.

"Keep hold of it no matter what happens in this war, keep it."

Turning to Harry, Peter and Michael he asked, "And you three are from what you would say, over yonder."

Harry, the obvious spokesman replied, "That's correct Sir."

"Any of you thought of staying on after this thing is over?"

Again it was Harry who stepped forward, "No Sir, we are not professional soldiers like you."

"Nonsense. You are as good soldiers as regulars." This was followed by slow nodding and the Colonel took another sip of tea whilst waiting for one of the men to respond.

Harry piped up, "We haven't really discussed it amongst ourselves. Most of us have responsibilities back home with the farming."

The Colonel looked pensive, "Yes, quite."

Harry continued, "I have thought whether or not I might stay in when the war's over but I don't even know if I'll still be alive, no one does." He said it with no degree of awkwardness.

His Colonel smiled, "I hope so." He then looked at the rest of the men, "That goes for all of you... you're fine men." The Colonel turned away, the men stood to attention, saluted and marched out of the tent past the N.C.O. who'd returned from his break and was straightening his tie.

Outside there was an eerie silence. The din of German batteries could always be heard even faintly and was something all soldiers were used to by 1916. Stories were rife amongst the ranks as news of military executions began to filter along the front and the disturbing fact that often the condemned were found guilty after obscenely brief trials for desertion with little or no experienced defence, and were shot by a firing squad selected from their own regiment. It was unsettling to think that a man mentioned in dispatches and with two years on the Western Front was called a deserter because he was found wandering, aimlessly in No Man's Land without his rifle and at the mercy of both British and German snipers because his own uniform was barely recognisable under the accumulated mud.

Only at night did the men huddle to whisper what they had heard. Some of the stories were dripping in gallows humour, two in particular. The first concerned a soldier who had reached his limits and in order to be sent home shot himself in the foot following a skirmish with the Boche. When he reported to the casualty station, using a crutch, for support he was confronted by an unfeeling Scottish Sergeant Major who told him that "to get a bed in here laddie you'll need to be shot in both feet". Two hours later the soldier shot himself in the other foot but was careful not to report until the unfeeling Scotsman had completed his shift.

The best one though and all the Fens Pals loved it was the canny Devonian who wanted to get back to his farm outside Barnstaple; he even had a bet with his friend that he could do it within three weeks. One day he took to crawling on his hands and knees examining every piece of paper he could find. At first everyone laughed but after two days of this and him sleeping wherever he crawled to, a senior officer ordered him to be taken to hospital. Once there he had crawled out of bed and stayed on his hands and knees examining every piece of paper he could see; the less injured even tore up bits of newspaper and scattered them. The medical staff were baffled and after three days declared that this soldier had gone insane but was harmless. A senior officer signed his discharge papers. What had made the men roar was that the Devonian marched upright past the guard home, his discharge papers in hand and informed the sentries on duty that "I've found the paper I was looking for".

Harry Hardy climbed the observation tower followed by Peter Reid. The sight was like no other they had ever seen, the countryside was dotted with villages some still burning, field hospitals and dense columns of smoke the result of retreating forces burning anything they considered might be useful to the enemy. In the distance they saw heavy guns positioned ominously awaiting their orders.

When Peter had looked through the telescope he saw a column in single file suddenly appear against the Eastern skyline. At first he wasn't sure if they were German or British; bursts of machine gun fire were suddenly heard and men fell dead. When he made out the distinctive German helmet emerge from a copse to see the damage, he understood he'd witnessed his own comrades being killed and he was helpless to do anything. He realised it had affected him because he'd let his own defences down that morning, knowing he was relatively safe in the compound, free from any gnawing anxiety that gripped infantrymen most of the time even in their sleep which many resisted, fearful of the nightmares that lay in wait. Especially the recurring one where they saw themselves stiff as a statue, lying dead for a month in No Man's Land.

Both he and Harry walked over to a makeshift corral so they could look at the officers' horses and turn their backs on war for a fleeting second. The Lance Corporal was approached by a junior officer wearing a battle ribbon above the top pocket of his uniform. Salutes were exchanged before the officer, smiling, said the Colonel had asked him to "talk to you chaps" and that evening they could "drink tea and rum after the evening meal".

"Yes Sir, I'll bring the Fenlanders over... It's that tent?" He pointed with his finger.

"Yes that's right Lance Corporal... say eight o'clock?"

When he'd walked away Peter Reid hadn't been able to resist commenting.

"Maybe we're not the lowest of the low on God's earth after all."

Harry laughed, "Well we aren't crawling to that tent on our bellies!"

Before they returned to clean themselves, shave and put on clean shirts and socks they couldn't resist eavesdropping on a drill Sergeant's conversation with a hapless looking soldier.

"Did you ever learn to hold a bayonet the right way?" he barked.

Back came a timid response "No... never did."

The Sergeant bristled "Do you qualify to shoot a rifle then?"

"Never could do it accurately Sarge" came the soft reply.

With bulging eyes and the veins standing up on his neck the Sergeant enquired,

"What about grenades... can you throw them?"

"Well if I'm honest Sarge no better than I could in training camp." There was a fraction of a pause before the sergeant bellowed "Hasn't anyone killed you yet?"

The private still looking bemused replied "Well, not yet." Both Fenlanders were still chuckling when they entered the crowded tent.

"May I offer you gentlemen a drink?" asked the officer still in complete bespoke uniform.

"Thank you Sir," a chorus replied and large measures of rum were poured in glass tumblers and piping hot tea was poured into mugs.

"Oh I hope you don't mind... I've always put the milk in last... don't know why really." The boys were aghast and the toast went to King and Country. Once the officer had told them about his war record to date with action at Mons and Verdun, the sickening sight of unrecognisable bodies and the fear he felt always after the bloodshed, rather than before, when he reflected, the Fens Pals gave him their respect for there was nothing of the braggart in this youthful lieutenant perhaps a decade older than themselves.

"I hope we all get to go home, in one piece, some day." Sensing that his mood was becoming melancholic he poured some rum and produced a journal from a wooden crate, it galvanised the men's attention.

"It's a diary of sorts not just the battles and tactics but of the human side because when the war is over history, I fear, may recount the battles, the strategies and the counter attacks but somehow along the way, the soldiers will be forgotten... I would love to know your personal thoughts. I guarantee anonymity, no names will be recorded, that you have my word for." The Fens Pals didn't know the officer was an only child and as such was naturally both meticulous and secretive; what they saw was a man burdened by what he'd seen yet remaining stoical lest the men under his leadership lost confidence.

Each of the men was invited to speak freely about how he saw war and how he had adjusted to it. It was a revelation to each of them and it wasn't fuelled by the alcohol. Despite the early reticence all spoke from the heart as their recollections to date were summarised by the Lieutenant writing furiously on lined paper, attached to the front of his flat ledger.

Dave's story was poignant. "I was frozen and wet to the skin, shivering like, and I don't mind admitting I was trembling. The trench was shallow and taking in water and I kept my rifle proud against me worrying if in all the rain it would fire." He paused as a tear filled his left eye. "Dead bodies were everywhere, some in the most awful state of decay and despite the cold night time air the smell was overpowering. Then I saw a shimmering figure and my fear raged within and then I recognised Christ. I saw the tears in his eyes and the fear deserted me. The following day a relief party found me but I didn't say anything because I thought I would be ridiculed just the same way that I laughed when I'd read about the Angels of Mons." The whole tent was stunned into silence... no one could absorb what they'd just heard. More tea was poured then Michael Jeffries volunteered his story.

He began hesitantly but when he saw no judgement in the eyes watching him he told it exactly as it was. "After being at war for a year I came off watch, I was sodden and going down with flu. I could feel vermin running over my body probably because I hadn't had a bath for weeks and my feet were blistered. I wanted to vomit because the smell everywhere was horrific. I lit a candle and when I looked in the mirror I was appalled at what I saw. I resolved that night I would walk into No Man's Land and pray for a bullet. Just then I noticed some playing cards lying on a crate and instinctively picked one up and flipped it over. There looking back at me was a lady naked from the waist upward with the most beautiful milky complexion and eyes that just seemed to be looking at me. I squinted because I couldn't believe what I was seeing. I ran my finger over her cheeks and found myself talking to her... I've kept that card and each morning and each night I talk to her when no one is around. I will carry it everywhere till my dying day."

No one made a comment and Jim said, "OK mine is brief. Three months ago we were camped near a town, the name of which I've forgotten, but having been months at the front line it was leave of sorts. We were ordered to attend the delousing plant which was in an area to the side of the wood, half a mile out of town. Everyone stripped naked outside the building and an attendant put the clothes in an oven. We were told it would take about forty minutes. So we stood around naked in the adjacent fields. Several women sat on the perimeter grass watching unconcerned even an old lady who was sewing, I walked over to her and informed her that delousing was going to take place for hours thinking they would move somewhere else. I said hundreds but to no effect so I said it again HUNDREDS! Then the old lady smiled and said 'Comment?'" Everyone collapsed in laughter and the Lieutenant put his ledger down and was laughing that much that the tea pot was shaking in his hand.

"Come on Lance Corporal Hardy what have you got to say?" the officer asked. Harry hesitated but was encouraged by the others including the officer who again reminded them all of his promise of anonymity. "OK," said Harry and he started, "I had crawled up into a fox hole where Corporal Fraser Parkinson had been hit, a bullet had gone through his eye, through his skull and out the back. When all was quiet me and Swifty carried him back to where the stretcher bearers were waiting. Later that day after yet again no side had made any progress we retreated back while other troops took over our position. I was telling the boys all about how Corporal Parkinson had got hit, he just fell back no sound. I thought he was dead but he was breathing when the exhausted stretcher bearers took over. Christ this must be real magic I gasped. When I'd turned him over a teaspoons worth of brain just ran out his head from the hole. A couple of the men stopped me saying it couldn't have been Corporal Parkinson, but when I insisted it was one of them said 'Nah, that amount of brain... it couldn't have been him!'." Again bellicose laughter could be heard puncturing the night. "The bastard lived as well," was the Lance Corporal's final sentence.

Another man spoke up, "I haven't stopped thinking of this incident since it happened and I wonder if I ever will. I was trapped in a small shell hole with a soldier from the Lancers said his name was Alfred. The town was being shelled repeatedly by German artillery and the only other sign of life was a crazed dog, his coat erect and running aimlessly, the sound of his voice drowned out by the shelling. All around was destruction except for a wall painted with a religious picture depicting the crucifixion, I couldn't stop looking at it. When the shelling stopped dust and silence was everywhere. Alfred and me stood up and looked at this wall and the painting with no damage done to it. Then the dog started howling when Alfred walked closer to the wall to examine the picture. We were both thinking, or at least I was, why this wall alone was still standing while most of the small town had been reduced to rubble. The dog barked and moved back and I did. Alfred turned to face us and suddenly the wall collapsed crushing him to death."

Everyone in the tent suddenly possessed a thoughtful face and no one forgot that evening. The ledger would eventually be exhausted with soldiers' tales, the most horrific tales of man's inhumanity.

Chapter 12

Grave concern at how the Boche could get through the British battle zones so easily was the latest talk in London. The simmering rivalry between Douglas Haig and Lloyd George continued and was no secret to anyone in British High Command or the Government. Many generals saw their Chief of Staff as a 'remarkably stupid, narrow prejudiced insular person'. Under the strain of military crisis this personality clash between the Prime Minister and his overall Commander in Chief exacerbated the situation between London and the Field Generals.

It dawned bitter cold and fog, once more, covered the battlefield while the big guns in the north east were pounding, causing the sky to flicker incessantly. Flocks of startled birds erupted out of distant buildings suddenly reduced to dusty caverns while grim looking soldiers near the front line marched in step, resolute and shivering with pride.

Donald Reid waited with the other soldiers lined in the trenches. Each man had one eye on his creator and the other on the officer standing on a slightly elevated position, whistle in hand. Suddenly it was raised to his lips and a short blast was heard. Young men, teeth clenched went over the top many falling dead before they had covered twenty yards. When smoke engulfed the battlefield, pandemonium broke out. Amid the mayhem and unbearable noise the eldest Reid boy flung himself into a crater to shield himself from the rattling Spandau machine guns. Petrified men spilled in on top of him and two dead infantrymen driven back by the gunfire also toppled backwards onto the congregation.

The survivors looked in unison at Donald for guidance, for many privates after two and a half years of slaughter looked to a man they thought they could trust for leadership rather than at an officer's uniform, despite strict military code. The last soldier to throw himself into the makeshift cover was a Lancastrian who looked like he'd had to dig himself out of a collapsed fox-hole so heavy was the mud attached to him. He gulped in air heaving his chest up and down, up and down.... Two of the men, their faces etched with dirt, despair and disillusion started a conversation.

"Bloody madness, why do they keep doing it?"

"We're no more than lambs to the slaughter. Some of the officers seem to think that gallantry is getting more of your men killed than anyone else."

Another soldier having gathered his senses looked at them "That's treason talk, make sure you're among friends when you talk like that."

The second soldier looked thoroughly beaten, his sense of worth long ago diminished.

"If I'm going to die in the war I'd sooner it was now rather than have to endure this any longer... Every day I wake up and it... it... it..." Once the sobbing had begun everyone looked at him with compassion for in an age when men didn't cry, all were crying even if it was only on the inside.

"The noise..." he continued. Two soldiers moved nearer to huddle him and provide words of comfort "It's OK you're with Pals."

Arthur Hardy sidled up to Donald, "You know you are the only man who can get us out of this mess, back to our trenches."

Donald thought before replying, "What about our officer?"

"He went down."

Donald wasn't convinced but listened as Arthur explained "A couple of the boys say he went down about thirty yards or so to the right."

"Did they see him?" He searched the other infantryman's face for a clear answer.

"No, but there was a shell exploding and when the air cleared they couldn't see him anymore. I reckon he's blown to Kingdom come."

Donald looked quizzical, "Why do you think I can lead you back?" More shell whizzed over the terrain as everyone tensed and the sounds of war died down a little.

Arthur continued, "We trust you. We've been in similar situations, I admit not so bad as this one, surrounded by the enemy and cut off but we've always looked to you when there's been no officer around."

Donald despite the circumstances managed a smile, "Do you know what Arthur?"

"Yes?"

"What are you going to do when I'm not around. I could," he breathed in and looked at the sky before continuing, "stick my head up there and it might come down in your arms." The other man adjusted his helmet from a jaunty angle to a damp angle as if the inclement weather had confused his inner drizzle. He looked depressed and his mood clouded the crater weighing it down like smog because he suddenly realised the unfair burden he was placing on his neighbour.

Nevertheless he continued "I don't know why but the Pals look to you, there's only me who comes from the same village but most of the others are from the same area, same as us. There are very few officers we like, even fewer we respect. They are not like us, they don't know our kind..."

Donald had a shrewdness that belied his upbringing and his years, "It's not their fault, they inhabit a different world, no better no worse."

Arthur's face dropped "They're gentlemen I suppose."

Donald didn't respond because artillery noise was suddenly scratching at everyone's ear drums.

For forty-five minutes the shire men moved closer in together resembling a ball and each one of them closed his eyes, held motionless by fear while their individual minds were taunted by that old stern commodity called sin. Another lull occurred and someone whispered "What's happening?" The stillness was broken by the cry of a wounded man. The soldiers looked up and Donald said "Shut up, listen, can you hear it?" The Lancastrian having finally gained his second wind crawled over to the group "Yeah, sounds like someone's wounded."

Both Donald and Arthur gingerly moved to the top of the crater.

"What you gonna do?" asked Arthur while his friend retrieved a pair of field binoculars from his coat pocket.

"We can't stay here forever."

"Can you see anything... where are our boys?" Arthur's voice was now full of desperation. "Ssshhh" Donald rebuked him as he scanned the horizon like a vulture. He'd taken the binoculars away and rubbed his tired eyes several times before looking back through them. It was this second scanning that provided him with a semblance of joy for he could see a man moving but couldn't recognise him until he saw the distinctive leather boots

"It's Captain Johns."

Arthur was quick with his reply "How can you tell?"

"I know he's the only man out there wearing those fancy leather boots." There was conviction in his voice but Arthur was dismayed.

"You're not thinking of going out there are you?"

The rebuke was quick "Just leave him?"

Arthur's riposte was just as quick "He wouldn't go out for you, Donald." With the field binoculars still up at his eyes Donald continued to look around for it was a well known ruse of the enemy to plant wounded British soldiers, especially those moving in and out of consciousness and then wait fully armed for a rescue party to arrive.

"Maybe not."

Arthur waited a few seconds "Then why bother? He got us into this mess, let him sort himself out for once." These callous words, thought Donald, were the result of war, not the natural character of the Arthur Hardy he'd known in Tunby Hill.

"He's alive all right and like it or not he's just as much a victim as us. He gets his orders or hasn't that crossed your mind?"

"I'd leave it to him were it up to me."

Donald took the binoculars away and both slid a couple of yards down from the rim.

Then he looked up at the sky.

"It'll be dark in two or three hours... are you coming? Might be difficult dragging him back alone."

Arthur thought long and hard, he was desperately thirsty so the words were croaked rather than spoken "Promise me one thing?"

"What?"

"If the Huns open up fire then we leave him and scarper?"

Donald gave a reluctant "OK" and they joined the others who had been looking up at them in expectant fashion. What water was left in individual flasks was shared out before Donald said everyone needed to spread out and remain vigilant especially when darkness began dropping from the sky. No one had objected to his rescue plan.

It was mid evening when Donald and Arthur set out on their mission; Arthur looked petrified, his eyes darting from side to side. When they approached the Captain, having passed many mutilated corpses, they could see the officer's eyes flickering and hear his laboured breathing. When the Captain thought he heard someone he instinctively moved his shaking hand towards the Webley pistol encased in his leather holster but he was too weak; he appeared resigned to his fate. When he recognised the men he tried to smile. Donald freed the Captain's water bottle and poured small drops into his parted lips.

"It's all right Sir... slowly." The water seemed to momentarily revive him.

"Sorry-about-this-bloody-mess-ol'-boy-Pilgrim-at-HQ-needs-shooting-for-for..."

He was interrupted by Donald "Don't try to talk Sir." As he spoke he felt the Captain's side and it elicited a savage groan and when he withdrew his hand it was saturated with blood.

"Quick bandages."

Arthur responded with the makeshift first aid kit they'd cobbled together from the men and began tucking the bandages inside the Captain's uniform and against his side to stem the flow of blood. Throughout he groaned.

"Sorry about that Sir but you can't afford to lose anymore."

Johns nodded in appreciation.

"Look what we are going to do..." Suddenly the sound of a twig snapping was heard. Both soldiers lay flat on their stomachs not daring to look while Captain Johns had turned his head to the side but his vision was blurred, yet instinct told him it was the enemy – a night patrol maybe half a dozen or less. He heard voices and because he had more than a passing knowledge of the German language he understood the conversation.

"How much longer are we going to spend out here, I'm freezing."

"Shut up Hans."

"You afraid I might wake the dead?" They had moved away in a westerly direction placing them about twenty yards away from their enemy. Finally their leader said "Come on, we've done our bit. Let's get the report made out for headquarters."

Not one of the three allies moved for another two minutes and it occurred to Donald that Captain Johns not having cried out in pain had probably saved their lives. When Arthur asked what they might have been saying Johns interpreted.

"Like all soldiers, they were moaning." All three suddenly smiled. Arthur lifted the wounded man onto Donald's back and he began crawling while Arthur, also on his stomach, held the officer from time to time as they slid along. It was a slow process, fraught with danger because no battlefield had a straight line that marked out the opposing forces.

The survivors from the earlier battle had dragged themselves up to the rim trying in vain, to see through the darkness. All conversation was in a whisper.

"Can you see anything?"

"No this mist."

"Well let's keep alert, the boys may need some cover from us if they are spotted."

"If they get spotted it's curtains for them."

Donald sensed they were nearly home and dry and so did Arthur who whispered "Not far now Donald." They paused for yet another rest aware that Captain Johns had uttered nothing including muted groaning for an hour.

"Don't do anything stupid, just continue as before."

Arthur was not about to disobey anything he heard and twenty minutes passed before one of the infantrymen turned to his mates barely able to contain his excitement.

"I can see them."

He was rebuked. "Ssshhh. Keep your voice down you'll have the whole German army on top of us."

The three of them reached the rim and lay utterly spent, physically and emotionally.

Arthur whispered "Gently now, he's badly injured." The men seeing the state of their Captain was in handled him with the utmost care; gone was what may have been previous animosity as Arthur pulled Donald into the relative safety of the crater. Both rescuers allowed themselves one indulgence, a final sip of water from the near empty flask.

Arthur felt relief coursing through his veins, "That was a brave thing you did Donald, we're not the greatest of friends but you will always have, as you already had, my respect." A new mood had swept over the men; ecstasy had almost replaced despondency and despair. When Captain Johns regained consciousness his eyes had met Donald's and both men knew – it was a tacit understanding. Despite the onslaught of another barrage the men crouched down though this time the fear had been greatly diminished.

At dawn every one of the Englishmen had looked up at the new day; they didn't care a jot because they, including Captain Johns, were alive if not well. An eagle-eyed observer up in the look-out tower with a powerful field glass had spotted them and was scuttling down the extended ladder and running towards an officer's tent where he was checked by a guard on duty who informed him he couldn't go in.

"But it's urgent... I must see..." The guard had remained unmoved but fortunately two young gentlemen officers emerged from the tent, both having lit cigarettes, to see what the commotion was all about. The scout burst toward them.

"Sir I've just come from the observation tower," and he pointed excitedly, "Over there, there is..." The younger of the officers who had taken his cigarette away from his lips intervened.

"Calm down, now just calm down. Better come inside." The sentry stood to one side and allowed the scout into the tent.

Inside the Major was surprised to see them back in and looked for an explanation which the older officer offered.

"Sir thought we had better ask you to listen to the scout."

Despite seeing a brusque, outwardly unfeeling senior officer sat before him the scout burst out, "Sir, there are some of our men behind the enemy's first line." The major leapt to his feet, eyes bulging with surprise "What!"

The scout gathered himself but this time spoke in a deliberate tone, "It's one of the patrols that got trapped. We didn't think there were many survivors. None of the scout patrols that went out last night reported anyone left alive. They couldn't have gone beyond the first line of No Man's Land. Are you going to call on the artillery fire Sir?"

The Major having assimilated the information had looked at both his officers who had acknowledged the dilemma before looking back at the scout.

"That's fine observation. I want you to go back to your post and continue duty."

Once the scout had left he spoke with his officers, "This is a sticky situation, gentlemen." His expression had turned forlorn for he had never been in a war quite like this one. He had experienced two damp winters when leafless tree-filled woods and the incessant rain had rendered even the carefully constructed trenches into shapeless quagmires because the clay underfoot retained the water and men were soaked night and day wearing great coats now double their weight.

After each downpour a ghostly mist had spread over the countryside like an eiderdown. Whoever looked through binoculars over No Man's Land saw dead cattle, dead soldiers, in grotesque poses and what seemed the death of humanity's soul. These tempests followed by the misery of cold and damp stayed long in the memory of the eventual survivors. Only the braziers, with their crackling flames glowing brightly in the woods offered any cheer. After nearly two years of stalemate, the propaganda in the British and German press was still demonising each other and reporting imaginary progresss. Most front line soldiers felt weak and grey and the sight of ice gleaming on all craters did not illicit the feeling it would have done in England especially around Yuletide. Hot, sugary tea, a cigarette and forever bully-beef were small comforts.

The Major walked outside his tent with both young officers and one of them, who may have thought he had flair but in reality had a fragile chin and everyone knew it but him, spoke up.

"You're not going to call off the offensive, Sir? Isn't it just the fortunes of war that some of our chaps have been caught on the wrong side?"

For a second his senior officer's eyes had looked heavy with speechless pain as though the junior officer's words had struck him like an arrow. He retained his composure then looked savagely at both of them.

"How long have you been at the Front?"

The first officer looked startled, for the Major's words had seemed more of a threat than a question, before blurting out, "Three months Sir... why?"

The major deliberately let his face drop, "Some of these men have been at the Front, in harm's way, everyday for two years." He watched the embarrassment of both officers, but they were well schooled in the art of civilised debate.

"I fully appreciate that we have some splendid men... second to none in fact." His colleague offered tacit support and when the Major glanced at him he spoke.

"Sir, what are the chances of getting these men back in one piece and what casualties might we sustain if we hold up the artillery offensive?"

The Major had not been fooled and he bit his lip with that resolute half-combative air he was famed for, "I want you, Lieutenant Ponsford, to find the exact position of these men... go up into the observation post and when you have the information, I want you back here. The offensive will continue as planned but I don't want any shells landing anywhere near that group of men. Do I make myself clear?"

The junior officers were left in no doubt and it had been uncertain whether this Major had any thoughts of self-preservation should an enquiry be convened as to why the patrol had been expendable for an enquiry would not have taken place. With both officers gone he lit his mahogany wood pipe and pored over the battlefield map with concerned eyes.

Three miles in reserve the British artillery was being dragged by horses to the Front. The thundering of hooves sounded like drums in a constant sequence – no note of vanity but ever increasing urgency. The German intelligence, often unrivalled, made for preparation and in a forest behind their lines trenches had been hastily dug under the guidance of their officers; shells were stacked and guns checked in readiness before sufficient camouflage was removed. No one had a smile on their face; it was ironic that in mythology it had been suggested that the day a soldier smiled, unknowingly, in battle was the day he met his maker.

Some of the trenches were always given names such as 'Der Berliner' but not this time. The British horses had approached in uniform gallop despite the unevenness of the ground beneath them.

Suddenly a deafening explosion far greater than the thunder of hooves was heard as a horse, rider and field gun were blown into oblivion; seconds later puddles of blood hit the ground. The battery continued and some of the horses appeared insane with fear and broke from their reins and scattered in all directions. Two officers suddenly devoid of all poise took out their pistols and began shooting in all directions wounding and killing their animals – sheer madness.

Fortunately for the reconnaissance party this ferocity was happening about a mile or so away.

Yet strong shells were exploding nearby carrying shrapnel in all directions. The popping sound of machine gun fire and its whitish light became repetitive and grew into an ear-piercing stutter. The men felt unsafe waiting for a stream of bullets to pour into their crater; they were exposed not only to enemy shell fire but trench mortars from either side. They had been told of these during training; big bulbous bombs that went up almost in a straight line before arcing and exploding on impact. What soldiers feared most was that they made no sound as they travelled other than a gentle puffing. Both sets of troops had engaged in vicious hand to hand fighting; men found animal strength they didn't think existed let alone in themselves and no pity was given nor asked for. When a British Mark 5 tank advancing on the Germans had hit a crater and toppled over into a trench ten soldiers were crushed to death.

Again the rain had fallen in sheets and when carriages carrying shells, became bogged down horses were beaten sadistically in the vain hope that they would drag them free if made to suffer enough. When the rain stopped there appeared a cessation in hostilities not dissimilar to a stage being altered for Act Two – Sunshine replacing rain and the ground resembling moon craters with sodden soil absorbing blood.

The patrol had huddled together and the Lancastrian throughout had nervously recited five decades of the Rosary, clenching his beads. Donald was shattered physically and mentally, everywhere he looked there was carnage. He held his arm around Arthur who was motionless. Captain Johns, whose uniform now looked like theirs, lay beside Donald with his hand lying hopelessly on his leg. When Donald whispered to the Lancastrian there was no response; he was wide eyed but dead. Donald tried to speak but no words were forthcoming, the tears falling from his eyes spoke volumes.

Yards away he watched rats nibbling at dead bodies. He didn't know it but the Germans had retreated under the onslaught even though both sides had sustained casualties. Stretcher bearers, many of whom had been vilified for being conscientious objectors, began searching for the wounded. It was extremely dangerous because German snipers often shot these men the moment they lifted a wounded soldier onto a stretcher, exposing themselves as easy targets.

Arthur, despite bleeding profusely from a shrapnel wound, had raised his arm to gain the relief party's attention "Quick medic down here!" They looked at them before the stretcher bearer whispered, "OK boys we'll be with you soon."

A minute later two bearers, one opening a portable case of medicines waited for instructions as the medic examined Donald, "Quick bandages, morphine." When the medic had unceremoniously pulled Captain Johns away onto his back he was greeted with staring eyes.

"There's nothing we can do for him, he's been dead some hours... I don't know how many." Both survivors were numb and Donald was lifted onto a stretcher. The medic put a reassuring hand on the injured man, "Be careful this one has lost a lot of blood."

When he turned to Arthur his face dropped some of its anxiety "You don't seem in such a bad way." When he touched the man's ribcage Arthur grimaced before groaning.

"OK, I'll give you something for the pain. Both you two are going to hospital – you're out of it for now."

Chapter 13

Inside the walls, late at night, the atmosphere was musty as nurses in starched uniforms tended the sick and wounded; occasionally screams of men in great pain pierced the senses and could often be heard outside.

Donald had been put in a bed next to Arthur yet he – despite overwhelming fatigue couldn't sleep unlike his friend. He watched as a group of men in striped pyjamas, with bandaged eyes, walked in a line, each man with his left hand on the shoulder of the soldier in front. The front man trailed a stick left to right, feeling his way but movement was slow. Two nurses walked them, individually, into the latrines helping the victims of mustard gas retain some dignity.

On the third day of hospitalisation a Colonel and his aide arrived at the hospital in a staff car. It was an organised visit as the Matron had lined up some of her nurses to be introduced to the Colonel who walked briskly into the building and along the corridor where the reception waited.

"Good morning Matron, nurses." All the women curtsied and the Colonel glanced at his watch then at the ward, "Right, shall we get on with this?" They entered the dimly lit ward where blinds were deliberately closed. Two nurses had already propped up the pillows of the two patients on the left hand side of Donald, who watched as the Colonel's aide opened up a small case to reveal medals with ribbons. The aide whispered, "Infantryman Harold Leech, Norfolks." The Colonel nodded and approached the side of the bed; his manner was brusque and devoid of emotion which turned Donald's stomach as he watched the medal being pinned to the pillow. No words of comfort, no physical contact instead the Colonel had stood back while Leech didn't move. It was repeated at the next bed, "Jones, Hayden Corporal Welsh Fusiliers." When the Colonel had pinned the medal to the pillow the Corporal suddenly grabbed his arm eliciting a shocked expression on the Colonel's face. Donald watched as Matron stepped forward and gently released the patient's hand.

"There's no need to be frightened, it's all right. Just the Colonel come to see how his men are." When Donald Reid looked into Jones' face he couldn't see any expression but his flickering eyes, now free from bandages screamed in pain.

The matron turned to the Colonel almost apologetically, "Sorry sir, but some of these men – you know what they have been through."

She was hastily interrupted by the aide, "Thank you Matron and thank you nurses for the gallant service you are doing in looking after such brave men."

He deliberately paused allowing the nurses to smile contentedly before continuing, "It makes one think…" He coughed self-consciously then both walked out in identical fashion to how they had walked in.

Donald inhaled deeply, disgusted at this charade and told himself, "I will live through this and I'll make sure you do Arthur." With casualty rates increasing it was a bold prediction to make. No one, not even nursing auxiliaries, could guarantee survival.

In April 1916 Lucy Prior had found herself in Abbeville at a clearing station for the Third Army. The work was demanding but she now saw herself as a veteran. She'd heard tales about the Military Nursing Club, a private venture which had opened in Boulogne the previous year where a night's stay with food was affordable and intended for nurses about to go on leave or having just arrived in France. In true British fashion a committee had been set up to run it. "How civilised… in the midst of such an ugly war" Lucy muttered to herself having heard another nurse regale her with stories about her two night stay and "the glorious bath I had each morning and night."

In less than two years great steps had been made from turning Clearing Stations, essentially first aid posts into well-equipped hospitals. The operating theatres which had begun with the barest of necessities were now equipped with most modern conveniences. Great improvement in the organisation facilitated the nurses' work as though an unseen civil service had taken over the running on a daily basis. Reception departments were where cases were sorted – special pre-operative wards with resuscitation wards attached – different wards for chest and abdominal and operating wards with eight to twelve tables. Most of the patients fell in love with the nurses and Lucy had proposals of marriage on a fortnightly basis and back in Lincolnshire her sister had wanted to know about the most eligible officers so she went along with it making most of them out to be demi-gods in military uniform. She wrote little about the amputations and those unfortunates who died in the operating theatre, for these preyed on her mind as it did with doctors and other nurses who constantly asked themselves "Could I have done more?"

Tragedy stuck and it brought the war home to Tunby Hill and left the village in an emotional fog. Fortunately Mr Prior had been attending a meeting of corn merchants in London when a dispatch rider had slowed as he approached the large house on the hill. Ann Prior had watched his progress up the track from the kitchen window and still remained baffled when the rider, having straightened his uniform, knocked firmly on the door. When she answered, the young man's eyelids drooped slightly before he handed her the brown envelope – a telegram from the War Office – and quickly departed. Ann stood, stunned and her mind scrambled for sense and reasoning as the noise from the motorbike's engine receded. She whispered the contents *"We regret to inform you that your sister, Lucy Prior, has been killed following a German bombing raid on a hospital in Western France. His Majesty's government offer you their sincere condolences."*

Ann remained in her room all day sobbing until there were no tears left. She felt fearful of the effect it would have on her father who in recent years had not enjoyed the best of health even if he had kept up appearances. He was due back in two days.

The following day Ann assembled the staff before breakfast and with Maud, in whom she had already confided, at her side she broke the news. Hushed silence followed and eyes welled up including her own although she managed to regain sufficient composure to inform them that her father would be returning and "would you keep a distance until I have told him this tragic news". Then she dismissed everyone of their duties for the day and returned to the kitchen with Maud and broke down in floods of tears, highlighting the red in her eyes and nose.

Mr Prior returned on a slow train and got frustrated at how crowded the compartment was as he struggled for breath. The weather had been extremely cold but when the sun came out the afternoon was muggy and no one wanted to open the carriage window, subsequently the atmosphere was clogged up with warm bodies and tobacco smoke. He had closed his eyes, gritted his teeth and thought of the hot bath and glass of brandy he would have immediately he stepped into his home.

"Father, come into the study... I've already poured you a brandy." Ann retained a scintilla of poise and grace. Maud had deliberately packed the fire with coal and drawn the curtains. Mr Prior took a gulp of brandy and collapsed into his chair without taking his coat off. He was about to talk about corn prices when his daughter blurted out, "Lucy's been killed." It didn't register for her father hadn't heard her words. She waited until he had taken another drink then moved closer to him taking his hand while kneeling at the side of the chair.

Outside Maud pressed her ear to the door waiting... knowing....

Inside the study Mr Prior sat in stunned silence, his face ashen and his whole body in a state of collapse. For the next four hours his eyes, unblinking like a dead man's, stared at the fire. In such a short time he was a changed man and for the rest of his shortened life he ached every day; gone forever was the often ebullient, assertive nature hidden behind the icy exterior he presented in public. Once, Mr Prior had admired the colour changing countryside with warm sentiment, now when he stood looking out of the study casement window at the changing seasons he resembled a model dressed in clothes and his wide open eyes stared into the beyond and his younger daughter was obliged to take over the daily running of his business. Years later a local historian pieced together Lucy Prior's working life and found that following a period at Abbeville she had suddenly been transferred to Rouen where medical staff had quietly prepared themselves for the onslaught of casualties following action in Fromelles in the north and Pozieres. Despite large red crosses marked out on the buildings the German aircraft had attacked dropping whistling bombs.

The loss of life was greeted with shock followed by disbelief...

Perhaps what was the most difficult fact to come to terms with and which devastated morale further, was the loss of Matron: a no-nonsense battle-axe about whom even the surgeons whispered their saucy remarks, even when they were on leave such was their trepidation. She was considered indestructible and respected by everyone and now she was gone. No one seemed to have known her name and when it was announced at a memorial service it was a shock that she could be the possessor of such a sweet name – Jenny. Tears were shed...

Chapter 14

Conditions worsened for the soldiers and despair, some officers reasoned, was the biggest threat to morale but they were powerless to ameliorate the situation. Being up to four feet in mud and water and surviving on cold bacon, bread and jam slung together in a sack hanging from a dripping dugout roof was hardly appetising nor was the prospect of being buried alive if a dugout collapsed under artillery barrage.

Soldiers had often endured five days in a trench and collapsed with sheer exhaustion having survived on an hour's sleep, only to be woken by squealing rats on their shoulders. When the communication trenches were flooded, rations often failed to arrive and when they did ravenous men ate with filthy hands causing several outbreaks of acute dysentery.

Desperate vigilance was required just before dawn and sunset when the Germans had a habit of attacking, thinking these were the hours when their enemy was at his most vulnerable. Sometimes a joker among the men had given them a laugh with his antics – a common practice had been to fix a small piece of cheese on the end of a bayonet and wait for a 'greedy rat'. It never took longer than three minutes and once the rat had tucked in the trigger was pulled and everyone cheered. The Fenlanders were used to working outside and coped with the conditions or maybe they were more resilient and could appreciate a brilliantly sunny day in winter. All of the men loved a bet and looked on excitedly as one of the scouts, having peered through his binoculars from an observation post, called to those below "Can't say how far…"

Below, the men feverishly exchanged money laying bets as to whether a British sniper could hit a German periscope from the distance.

"Make sure you don't miss, I've got a oner riding on you," said a thickset Lancastrian rolling his vowels.

His friend piped up, "Yeah otherwise I'm gonna starve for a week… I'm putting my rations on you hitting something."

The sniper had checked his rifle, which looked in mint condition and bellowed "Don't worry boys."

The Lancastrian with the rosy cheeks, despite being undernourished, called back "Yeah well go on or you might not get another chance today."

The sniper full of confidence yet with dispassionate grey eyes climbed the tower. He went up four rungs before pausing and turning to the group of soldiers waiting impatiently below, "Which one of you has bet against me? I'm going to be rich by the time this war's over."

In the tower the scout kept bobbing up and down like a float, occasionally pointing to the German trenches. Now he marked them for the sniper who asked, "Is he visible himself?"

"No the Huns aren't that stupid. Just his periscope."

He removed his binoculars and gave them to the marksman "Here take a look."

The countryside was scanned quickly but forensically and then the sniper began laughing.

"I wish I could know what Fritz has to say when he sees a bullet coming down his periscope." The over excited scout gave those below the thumbs up and a solitary silence set in. The sights on the rifle were adjusted a fraction and no one dared move; each man could hear his own heartbeat. A distinct sound, like a sudden crack was heard and the scout looking through his binoculars cheered loudly on seeing the German periscope disintegrate.

"Hold on... Fritz is shaking a fist at us." Ribald laughter took over, which gave way to cheering which attracted the attention of others including Harry who was walking across the compound toward three soldiers one of whom was Peter Reid.

He spoke confidently "We're going out again tonight. Intelligence want us to find out if the Germans are getting up to anything on the right flank. Major says can't have anything interfering with the artillery that's being driven up on the side for another assault."

When he looked for questions Jim responded, "But Corp we've been out twice this week already."

Harry was unmoved, his gait had taken on a military bearing reducing the previous swagger to a forgotten memory, "Why do you think you have undergone the training you have for the last couple of months or so?"

Dave stepped in "Suppose it's just a job."

Harry was firm in his response "It's so you can do the job and stay alive at the same time no matter how many times we're called."

Now it was Peter's chance to say something and he seized the opportunity "Don't get carried away Harry, some officer's been filling your head with glory but just remember it's our lives that are at stake every time we go into that No Man's Land."

Harry could scarcely contain his annoyance "What are you saying Peter?"

The younger Reid had learned not to be brow beaten in Harry's presence. "I think you know... Look what happened to Donald and Arthur. I just got a letter from him and he tells me 'SURVIVE THE MADNESS' that's all, survive."

Harry deliberately paused because he had an ace up his sleeve. "Well, I've got news for him when he arrives which is sometime this month, depending on recovery, and it'll be interesting to hear how he takes it."

Peter's face lit up and he couldn't contain his excitement "Donald's coming here?"

Harry continued, "When he and a couple more arrive, they're being commissioned or whatever you want to call it, into the intelligence work."

Jim screwed his face up "It's scouting not intelligence, intelligence is what officers do back at headquarters."

Harry was eager not to diminish the importance of the Fens Pals role, "And who do you think provides them with the intelligence reports or the enemy position in the first place so they can plan according to whatever military strength is necessary?"

His smug face wasn't appreciated by the others, least of all Peter, "Harry you're beginning to get carried away with all this, just remember who you are." The words had an effect and they waited for the inevitable response and they didn't have to wait long.

"I've never pulled rank on any of the Pals but that's not to say I won't or aren't entitled to so..." He seemed lost for words for he had never been schooled, unlike his superiors, on how to manage a conversation or an argument. Nevertheless he had the last word, "We go out at nine o'clock and I expect all the necessary items to be on you: cutters, wires and make sure revolvers are loaded and all personal items left behind." He walked off quickly and behind him the others watched until he was out of sight.

"You gotta hand it to Harry, he's brave all right," stated Jim.

"Brave or foolish," muttered Dave.

Peter's mind was elsewhere and he smiled at the other two, "Still, that's great news about Donald joining us with some more of our boys. I thought I wasn't going to see him till after the war, had I survived, and he had. I wonder what it's been like for him and the others?" The last sentence he had spoken in a quiet, melancholic way because he knew it was rhetorical.

That evening another silence dropped over the military compound; there was little noticeable activity as though the war had taken a well deserved rest. From outside huts and tents only quiet conversation could be heard including that coming from behind a hut door painted in white, with the words "Fens Pals".

Corporal Hardy was looking over the party who all wore one piece suits and black balaclavas. All insignia had been removed and revolvers and respirators had been carefully laid out on a table. Peter was given a small tin of polish by Harry who now scrutinising each man.

"Here, get some more on your face."

Peter swivelled the lid off and added more polish before passing the tin around. Before anything else was said the men shook hands with each other; it had become a tradition before they left for each man knew his life might soon be taken from him, within hours.

"Right boys, everyone happy?" Harry said the words with defiance and when he could see defiant faces looking back at him continued, "Let's go and see the officers then."

The party walked purposely across the gravel; despite the occasional pettiness and masculine rivalries, together they had learnt to stand firm against what they perceived was a dying world riddled with loneliness and on the Western Front, despair. Nevertheless they had resolved to do their duty for King and Country.

Inside the Major's hut was spartan, except for a couple of mementos of home including a passing out photo of officer cadets resplendent in their uniforms, crudely framed and nailed to the wall behind a small oak desk; it took everyone's attention as soon as they walked in. Major Phillips had an air of authority about him whereas, by contrast, Captain Keaveney looked as though he had just left school; fresh faced, eager and aware he lacked combat experience which made him nervous in the presence of fighting men.

"Come in!" the Major bellowed and in walked the Fens Pals; quickly they stood to attention and saluted the Major almost ignoring the youthful officer.

"At ease, gentlemen." Major Phillips picked up his cherry wood pipe and inspected the fading glow before sucking the mouth piece and watching a wave of smoke spill over the rim.

"Gentlemen, I would like you to come and have a look at the map." Everyone moved over to a large map pinned to the wall. Major Phillips pondered before speaking and more smoke filled the air.

"We're getting all sorts of reports in about a tunnel in No Man's Land."

Harry looked closely at the map before addressing the senior officer quizzically, "A tunnel Sir?"

"Yes, Corporal, it is one of the sections we've taken over." He used his pipe to tap on the exact area, "You see it's about half way between the German lines and our own. There is a possibility that with a tunnel such as this, troops could be assembled for a raid or a severe attack on our line." He paused and the men moved closer to the map.

Peter asked "Raid Sir?"

"Yes."

"You want us to destroy the tunnel?"

The patrol party were surprised that the Major didn't immediately answer. This officer had a puckish intuition and in less intense moments he had been known to have a voice that could cross through a room like a river of laughter.

"Well," he said raising an eyebrow and reducing any tension, "we don't know for sure about it yet and we don't want to destroy something we might be able utilise. No point making unnecessary work for us, eh?"

Harry's response was quick. "Have any of the other patrols reported anything, Sir?"

Major Phillips kept his eyes on the map and scratched his chin with his index finger causing Peter to smile, "Yes, some of the Canadians approached it the other night and swore they could hear voices. They couldn't locate the entrance though. I'm sure if there is a tunnel, there will be some sort of store, possibly a camouflaged cabin or such like."

Throughout the discussion Captain Keaveney, with his sensitive mouth and finely cut features had said nothing but how he longed to be a gladiator was etched into him but first he would have to get shot of what looked liked beautifully manicured fingers.

Major Phillips did his utmost to allay any fear, "I know it's dangerous, however, I wouldn't ask you if it wasn't vital or I thought there was no chance of you getting back."

None doubted his sincerity and they all knew what was about to come.

"You won't find anyone here wanting Sir," Corporal Hardy said firmly, fiercely, fabulously, and his own desire was not without effect on both officers. There was something in Harry Hardy's eyes and his excited restraint which caused Captain Keaveney to blush.

"We may be simple folk, country boys in peace time but we understand the true meaning of King and Country... don't we boys?"

The men bellowed "Sir!" and the Major was visibly taken aback.

The minutiae of the operation was discussed further in a friendly rather than military manner even though the patrol members instinctively knew their lives would be on the line again as would Harry's, who had a different attitude seemingly borne of strength and innocence. For his part Major Phillips insisted on double rations for 'his boys' for the rest of the day and left them to conduct their own strategy in direct preparation. Once again the worse part of these reconnaissance 'jollies' was the waiting no matter how many times scouts went out at night.

Eventually a military vehicle pulled up and the driver sounded his horn twice, it had to be twice... superstition had decided so. The men sat in attitudes of thought as they were driven out of the compound. The sound of shells exploding began to sound ominously closer and each of the boys tried to disguise his anxiety, wondering if this time his number was up...

At an outpost two sentries approached the vehicle shining torches in the driver's eyes and one demanded his papers in an officious voice before asking, "What brings you here?"

The driver nodded his head towards the back, "Reconnaissance patrol in the back, going out tonight." The second guard walked to the back and raised the canvas flap shining his torch on the men much to their annoyance.

"Come on turn that bloody thing off will you?"

The guard walked back to the front.

"Well?"

"Six of them patrol all right" he said in a quiet voice as the driver was given back his papers. The engine stalled then fired enthusiastically and the crunching sound of first gear being rammed into place was at odds with the dark, quiet sky.

At the last observation post, Harry jumped out of the back and approached a couple of soldiers, "We're going out and need a couple of bombs, can you spare any?"

The first soldier responded immediately in a sardonic manner, "Not for me to say, you'll have to see the Sergeant about that." He tilted his head to the right in the direction of a hut, "Over there, should be planning the strategy for tomorrow along with others."

Harry paused then asked "What's it like up here?"

The other soldier answered in a blunt tone. "Hell, that's the only word for it."

As Harry walked in the direction of the hut the others jumped out of the back and began slapping each other's backs in an attempt to keep warm.

The guard noticing this piped up, "Rather you than me mate – it's bad enough having to go out there in daylight but now – they should pin a ruddy medal on all of you."

Peter forced a laugh. "Fat chance of that. This medal caper is sometimes a lottery."

A third soldier had joined the other two sentries and was sympathetic to the scouts and also scornful of others, "He's right. Some days they give out medals and other days nothing. Blokes like you doing one of the most dangerous jobs the whole time – you deserve recognition."

Peter couldn't resist a bit of humour, "I'd rather have myself in one piece."

The others smiled and attention was turned to another soldier walking in their direction. He looked at the party, "Here, your Corporal wants you." The men looked towards the hut and saw Harry waving them towards him. Within moments they had loaded a couple of bombs into each of their rucksacks.

The sentries watched them disappear into the darkness. Three hours later the patrol was climbing over a deserted wire and making their way down an embankment. Every movement was characterised by urgency and hesitancy especially when they saw human distortion in various stages of decompouse.

Harry gestured for his men to crouch down, Peter whispered, "What we stopped for?"

"Look yonder to the right, see it?"

Peter looked hard, "Can't make head nor tail of it."

Harry tried to conceal his impatience, "It might be the hut or whatever those others reported."

Peter's reply was swift. "We'll need to get closer Harry."

Their leader pondered while the group closed in around him, "We'll move single file up another thirty yards then split up. Peter and me will go close to whatever it is we can see. You two," he tapped Jim and Dave on their left shoulders, "stay in one of the shell holes OK, and you two," he looked to Bert and Alfred, "stay down and keep your eyes peeled. God knows what we're letting ourselves in for."

They waited for a couple of minutes, digesting what each of them had to do. Harry's thoughts turned to how the Hun had mounted a night time raid killing a Lewis gun team and making off with the machine gun only to be chased across No Man's Land. He bristled when he recalled how three Germans in British uniforms had taken a Sergeant off his guard by speaking to him in English in a trench that had all but been evacuated before knocking him unconscious and taking him prisoner.

Unknown to the others Major Phillips had taken Harry to one side and whispered in his ear, "The temerity of the Hun... I think retaliation might be in order," before nodding solemnly and leaving Corporal Hardy to interpret.

The men were waiting for the inevitable – machine gun fire strafing No Man's Land and bullets whizzing two feet off the ground. It was more a deterrent than anything else and they weren't disappointed even though they were relieved to know it wasn't directly near the ground they lay flat on.

Harry and Peter approached steadily and stopped when they heard a rustle.

"Can you hear movement?" Harry whispered in Peter's ear.

"Yes."

"It's too risky to go any further, we'll report back, come out with a larger unit." When Harry turned to go Peter grabbed him by the arm, "Don't you want to off load some of these bombs?" He tapped his rucksack.

Harry looked startled "And wake everybody up?" Both grinned but their expression turned to horror when they heard a German soldier talking to himself and it sounded like he was yards away. Then they heard the unmistakeable sound of urinating and both Englishmen creased their faces in laughter but remained mute. Then the slapping of hands on shoulders and the stomping of feet on the ground could be heard and still they remained motionless.

The German climbed up onto the same level as the scouts, then inexplicably sat down cross-legged and began smoking a cigarette careful to hide the glow behind his gloved hand. He closed his eyes.

Harry had made up his mind and the rumbling of distant gun fire in the North East presented him with the best opportunity. Using it as cover he crept up on the German and hit him with a thunderous left hook that rendered his enemy unconscious. Having delivered that blow Harry was shaking his hand as though he'd been caught by a demon delivery at Lords. Peter wanted to laugh and would have done if his own stomach wasn't turning over with apprehension.

"Quick" said Harry gritting his teeth. "Chloroform bottle in my rucksack and rag... give him a horse size measure... we're taking him back."

Peter's face dropped. "It'll take us beyond midnight."

Harry ignored the plea, "Quick before the bastard wakes up."

The scout acquiesced and five minutes later with the German on his back Harry bold and defiant was leading a hasty retreat, albeit on his stomach. Peter offered to share the burden knowing Harry would insist on carrying their prisoner over the British defence line.

The other four were astonished yet each agreed to do his fair share.

Fortunately the blazing sky, a result of increased artillery fire remained in the North East. It seemed an eternity before they got back and heard a soldier cry, "Halt who goes there?" Peter had become entangled in some wire as he made for the direction of the voice which sounded again this time with more menace, "HALT WHO GOES THERE!"

Peter responded, "It's all right it's us – the boys coming back from patrol."

"HALT! PASSWORD?" the voice boomed.

The patrol were huddled together desperately trying to free Peter who looked distinctly worried, "Come on chaps, names quick."

They were exhausted and Harry stumbled "Er, Labrador... Collie?"

"LABRADOR!" Peter shouted.

There was no response and the men looked anxiously around.

"COLLIE!" Peter shouted.

Again there was no response.

"BULLDOG!" he shouted barely able to disguise his fear.

When a voice responded, "OK come in." relief sped through the scouts. At last they were able to stand up and it was noticeable that two machine gun posts were at the ready as was a soldier with bomb in hand ready to throw it. Harry, with the German prisoner in a fireman's lift, looked at the soldiers, "Men you scared the very daylight out of us."

An officer rapidly approached, "God men! Are you trying to get yourselves killed?"

"Sorry Sir" was Corporal Hardy's brusque reply.

The officer continued, "We've had further reports of Huns dressed as our chaps infiltrating the lines for intelligence purposes."

"Well here's a present for Major Phillips," and with that Harry dropped the unconscious German at the feet of the officer who now looked flabbergasted.

The aroma of cooking was wafting through the air.

"Excuse me," said Dave, "but that smells good."

The officer responded knowing how valuable the cargo was, "Yes, you look as though you could do with something hot inside you." He nodded approvingly before shouting "Sergeant!" who came running over.

"Sir."

"Make sure these men get something to eat."

"Right away sir."

The officer turned back towards the group. "Go with my Sergeant and good luck. Probably see you up here some time again... well done men."

Corporal Hardy saluted, "Thank you Sir."

Having lit up their cigarettes the men walked with the Sergeant and all seemed to sink into the landscape. The excitement, albeit temporary, was over and the Fenlanders would see the next sunrise and that would be nourishment of another kind.

Despite their devil's advocate image and outward bravado all patrols felt fear when they thought about their escapades later on; it's what happened to brave men. Journals and diaries were treasured by these men and a combination of entries reveal a surprisingly common format. Usually four to six men reported at headquarters and having been given instructions via a map were transported to the front line where sentries were warned that a patrol was going out. The wire in front of the front line trench was always exceedingly thick and once this had been cut through the men often felt naked for they were in No Man's Land lying motionless and listening. Only the occasional shell whistling overhead broke the intimidating silence. Often three hundred yards had to be covered by crawling about looking for gaps in the enemy wire which suggested an inevitable raid.

On two occasions Harry's men had been tangled up in old wire and suddenly lights went up followed by artillery fire and the party were in the midst of bursting shells.

"Remember, we had to beat a hasty retreat so we were out of the Huns range," the Corporal said before laughing quietly and continuing, "and the battalion on our right thought the enemy were readying themselves for an attack and set its own artillery fire..."

Peter pulled an astonished expression and said, "Shells in front of us, shells behind us, shells all around us... that deafening din... the sky was a blaze of light and we scampered into a crater... yes sir all that blazing away because Dave got his foot tangled in some wire which set the cans rattling."

Some infantrymen had gathered to listen to the rural boys and they weren't disappointed.

"We couldn't move," said Corporal Hardy, "we ducked figuratively speaking." Before he continued, the soldiers had laughed and warmed to their fellow men.

"You die fifteen times out there because each shell seems to be getting lower and lower until they are screaming in your lug hole." Peter continued plaintively. "Sometimes we are surprised we get back in one piece and then HQ want a report so they can concentrate the artillery on to specific areas of enemy wire."

One of the soldiers chipped in, "Then you go back out through the newly created gaps... blimey rather you than me mate." Everyone laughed.

Harry was keen to keep the conversation light and relayed the story of one incident when his party had gone out to examine weaknesses in the enemy's defence, "I had almost got through pushing heavy wire to one side but my foot caught in it and a rattling noise could be heard." His audience learned forward.

"Six yards away I could see the parapet of a German trench. I moved slightly closer into a shell hole praying I hadn't been heard. The suspense was awful," his voice died to a whisper, "then the head and shoulders of a German appeared. He was carrying a pistol and straining to listen. He fired a flare and white light was everywhere. He looked around apprehensively, a big, fat round face he had. I was tempted to say 'Boo!' 'cause I was sure he'd have fainted." Everyone laughed including the patrol members even though they'd heard their leader recount this episode before. "Fortunately when the light flickered he returned to his trench. We crawled back and when we thought it was safe stood up and walked our side of No Man's Land. We were frozen and shivering."

"Then you had to write your report?" asked one of the infantrymen.

"Yeah, the following night we cut gaps in our wire and led a patrol in zigzag fashion. Fortunately the Germans hadn't repaired the gaps and the thick mist overhead was to our advantage. The raiders entered the German trenches unopposed, taking the enemy by surprise... took ten prisoners."

Peter Reid concluded the reminiscence, "We received special mention in orders for the work we'd done. Yep we'd taught the Hun a lesson or two." The mood of the party changed when a fat, sallow beast of a man joined the group emitting gulps of obscene humour. Harry thought about flooring the great sodden thing but was too tired to get beyond imagining it.

Chapter 15

Corporal Hardy's prisoner wore a withered, woebegone face. Despite his youth his cheeks were hollow and his forlorn expression highlighted his eyebrows. He believed he was going to be executed and therefore not have the opportunity to right past sorrows. A junior officer had given him a cigarette and a mug of hot tea, laced with sugar, for which he was grateful. When a Major had suddenly appeared in the small annexe attached to the officers' hut and now an interrogation room, fear shook the prisoner from head to toe as he accepted his fate, whenever that may be, resignedly. He watched as his captors spoke in a foreign language before the Major looking long and hard at the prisoner, deserted the room.

It was a shock when the junior officer removed his cap, smiled and began talking in almost fluent German. The prisoner gasped before offering his enemy a German cigarette and lighting it with two matches torn from a book. The Englishman had asked to look at the book and read aloud the information.

The interrogation which lasted almost two hours was a civilised affair and both men ate chicken sandwiches and drank several mugs of tea. The outcome, as was suspected, didn't yield much that wasn't already known by British Intelligence and the officer almost felt sorry for the other man, similar in age and not possessing the steeliness of a regular. Only when they spoke on common ground was there a relaxing of the situation.

"He looked yellow, his leg had been amputated and the lines on his face, suffering lines were engraved. He was a popular man but even his voice has lost favour."

The English officer was taken aback by how articulate the prisoner was at relaying his first glimpses of seeing severely injured men, many of whom knew that death was working out from within.

"They looked like ghosts inside their own bodies." The German called Hans nodded and it was obvious, in peace time, he had conversation rich in humour for he said, "When the men who declare war suddenly retreat they should be brought forward out on a stage and four from each team should fight one another and whoever wins... well that country has won the war. That would be just."

"That's one way of looking at it," said the officer in an even tone.

The German detected an element of doubt and felt confident enough to open up. "When I lay wounded, a year ago, in No Man's Land I noticed the bodies nearby turning pale and green and blood was no longer red but black. Hours went by, attack, counter attack, more bodies and more sounds of dying men who knew the stretcher bearers wouldn't reach them in time. I listened for thirty-six hours to two men within hearing distance of me trying to encourage each other to stay awake and listening to their voices grow hoarser, it's something I will never forget. The despair I felt made me want to die. Eventually I lost consciousness and when I awoke a nurse said they had just got to me in time. I thought I was in heaven until an unfeeling Sergeant told me I would be back on the front line within five weeks." He paused and the Englishman allowed him to continue by remaining silent. "If I could force myself to get used to seeing dead and dying men I could never get used to those repulsive rats... we called them corpse-rats and if we caught one inside the trench well..." He didn't elaborate because he didn't want to offend the young officer's sensibilities.

The officer asked Hans how the Germans dealt with lice, the bane of every front line soldier and was surprised by the response he got.

"We strip to the waist, with our hands at work and we hear the everlasting cracking with one's fingernails. But better one of the men rigged up the lid of a boot polish tin with a piece of wire over the lighted stump of a candle. The lice are thrown into this pan – crack – they're dead." Both young men smiled and then it was the German's turn to ask the officer what he thought when or if he got leave. At first reticent but realising he wasn't about to reveal any military secrets he said that on his first leave he sat in a train carriage and he was warmed when he saw familiar landscape followed by villages with white-washed half-timbered houses and thatched cottages and then cornfields and even derelict barns.

Hans responded, "When I travelled home to my town before the station was reached the train goes in an arcing formation and suddenly there was rows and rows and rows of Poplar trees swaying and the crisp noise as the train slowed sounded like bees shuttling and I knew I was home. As a boy I used to sit on the platform and watch steam trains enter and leave, it seemed so exciting and the smell was unique. On my first leave in May 1915 I sat on the station for two hours remembering and wondering if I would ever enjoy this simple experience again."

It was hard not to like Hans and the Englishman's thoughts went to his own father once a disciplinarian who, with advancing middle age had mellowed, becoming a garden lover. He had told his son that there was no better place than a garden for ripening a man's thoughts. Now that son having witnessed, albeit for a short time, the brutality of war and the brutalising of man could see his father admiring ancient trees, watching the shifting pattern of shadows when wind caressed the leaves forcing pockets of light through the gaps. Momentarily, he felt disorientated almost at odds with himself for his business was the business of killing and never more so when Hans talked of the day peace would come.

"Those lucky to survive will be wary and broken men and who knows what will happen later in this century because man doesn't learn, it will be repeated... what do you think?"

There was no reply and fortunately for the Englishman he was rescued by a Sergeant knocking on the door followed by a brusque entry. He saluted.

"Sir, Major would like to see you in his tent... I'll take the prisoner to the compound." The young men exchanged glances and the officer was gone.

Inside the tent he revealed that the prisoner had co-operated but knew nothing of the enemy's strategy or battle plans but was conscripted and really wanted it to be over so he could go home.

The Major deliberated, "Yes, pity we hadn't bagged one of their officers... Oh well," and with that he re-lit his pipe. Beside him stood another officer, a Lieutenant eager to demonstrate the more primitive part of himself, who saw the German speaking officer as the complete representation of all he disliked and these prejudices were always bristling.

"If I had my way I'd walk the prisoner round the back and shoot him... one less Boche to worry about." No one responded, which disappointed the known braggart always striving after vainglorious effect.

In the distance a soft swishing sound passed overhead towards a village then a crash and smoke and debris filled the air. "Trench mortars" someone uttered and then they were continuous, the noise and detonation rented the air, metal fragments flew everywhere and trees fell as the volley continued. The expected attack didn't happen and later dusk crept over the landscape and the air cooled. Troops and villagers willed the night to arrive because it provided a certain protection. The next day the troops in the trenches mused that the attack would happen and pandemonium would be the order of the day with shells shrieking, incessantly everywhere and bodies rising high into the sky. The battle weary never got used to the screams of agony because it was unlike anything they had ever heard. No matter how often, it was always the first time and never deadened by one, two or three rum rations.

Chapter 16

"Business as Usual" was the message crudely painted in white on a wooden board fixed to a post at the south entrance to the trench and evoked a wry smile from Harry and his band of merry men. They slowly made their way into the covered area which was faintly lit with candles and placed their rucksacks in a corner before enjoying a bowl of stew and fresh crusty bread; everyone had a second helping before the Corporal inspected the open rucksacks.

He looked at Dave, alarmed. "Where's your respirator?"

Realising he'd forgotten to include it Dave looked shocked, "Oh sod it! If they put over gas tonight…"

The others were stunned something so obvious had been forgotten and Peter shook his head. "Dave, that could be fatal, you ought to make sure you have one especially if we get the green light to go out later on."

Harry inhaled deeply and through gritted teeth said, "Never do this again. Your forgetfulness could put all of us in a difficult situation."

Looking self-conscious, Dave meekly offered, "Sorry boys."

Movement could be heard outside and the men's attention was taken away from themselves as Lieutenant Scott eagerly joined them. Immediately they stood.

"At ease gentlemen," was the officer's response and then he pulled an empty crate across and joined them.

"OK men," he said trying to get as comfortable as possible in the cramped space, "I've seen your commanding officer. Fine work I know you chaps have been doing recently."

The men nodded and the young officer devoid of facile pomposity or any sense of arbitrary patronage continued. "We might be on a sticky wicket with this hut or whatever it is out there."

Harry chipped in. "We thought, Sir, with a bigger patrol we could…"

The Lieutenant, smiling, interrupted. "I think Corporal that might cost us the element of surprise. We don't know for certain what the Hun has on offer, troops or garden implements." As though to make it all light hearted he laughed but it only elicited a smile from the patrol because they realised they were going back to the previous scene, though this time the odds at getting back in one piece would be shortened.

The officer sensed this and the chuckling ceased. "I think what I am going to ask you to do is fraught with danger." He waited for a response and Harry provided it.

"I'll say it is... why don't the artillery blow it to smithereens?"

The reply was quick. "It's not quite that simple."

Peter could see the retinal redness in the young officer's sensitive eyes but let his own emotional state expand saying, "Well Sir, it would seem the simple solution to me."

The Lieutenant blushed for he was beginning to experience one of those dramatic clashes that cannot be planned for and despite having huge respect for the assembled men he too had his orders from above so he continued, "If this hut or whatever, is housing anything it could be of strategic importance when we undertake our next offensive, particularly, if we repeat the same success as before and gain more ground."

Now it was Dave's turn and he asked in a sarcastic voice, "And casualties?"

Harry looked at him as in admonishment and invited the officer to continue which he did sensing the Corporal always held sway with his men.

"I want you to investigate the chances of blowing up the entrance to the tunnel. All the outposts will be notified that you are going out."

"Thank you, Sir." Harry paused while his men looked at him. "Damn well nearly got shot by our men earlier. They're getting trigger happy because of bogus patrols."

Lieutenant Scott altered the position of his head then said, "Bogus patrols?"

"Yes Sir. Huns dressed as our chaps crossing our lines."

"I must confess I had heard a rumour... but this damned war is full of rumours."

To ease the tension Harry offered, "Well maybe we'll bring another prisoner back for you, again."

An honest smile fell upon the officer's face. "Gentlemen get some rest and I'll return in a couple of hours."

Nothing was said until he had taken his leave.

Then Peter spoke for all of them. "God, Harry we're not going to survive much longer if this caper continues."

Harry looked thoughtful and tried to reassure the boys, "Don't worry we've been there once before." For the next hour they lay on the canvas covered floor with woollen blankets pulled over them but no one slept despite the silence.

When Captain Keaveney entered the trench the men rose swiftly but were told to remain as they were.

"Lieutenant Scott's seen you?"

The men nodded.

"Good, I'll see you later now get some well deserved rest."

In unison they responded, "Thank you, Sir."

No sooner had the men returned to their thoughts, than they were interrupted this time by a fair haired, boyish looking Captain Henderson who'd groped his way down the steps into the trench. His expression was one of bewilderment and his bespoke uniform only enhanced his lack of experience. Harry looked up and met the officer's eyes.

"You haven't seen Captain Keaveney by any chance?"

Harry stifled a yawn before replying. "You just missed him Sir not gone ten minutes. If you hurry you will catch him before he gets to his hut."

Henderson rapidly turned on his heel saying, "Thanks awfully."

Harry waited a minute before lying back. "Now he makes Keaveney positively an old man." Everyone chuckled which lessened their anxiety.

Inside the officers' hut Major Robertson, Captain Lamerton, Captain Keaveney, Lieutenant Moorcroft and the young fresh faced Captain Henderson were about to enjoy a meal of meat stew served by a private, who having completed his duty was given permission to leave.

"OK Johnson, that'll do no need to stay. I'll see to the wine."

The private saluted. "Very well Sir," and he marched out the hut leaving the officers to put their linen napkins on their knees.

"Sorry it's not the regimental silver but you never know when the Hun will make an unexpected entry." The Major's words had the desired effect and everyone laughed and looked pleased with themselves.

The senior officer then poured wine into the gleaming assembled glasses before speaking again. "I don't think we'll stand on ceremony, pass these around will you Captain Henderson?" Major Robertson had a reputation amongst the officers and non-officers alike; he got results, he was reliable and he never let people down or demanded his pound of flesh. He had a personality.

Soon they were tucking into their stew and three minutes later conversation initiated by the Major, broke out. "Tell me Lamerton, where did you school?"

The latter quickly swallowed a large piece of meat. "Winchester, Sir. My father and his before him," he paused to glance at the others before continuing, "and probably my own children will go there if I'm lucky enough to have boys."

There was a murmur of approval before the Major asked him, "Keen on rugger and cricket then?"

Lamerton's response was doused with pride. "That's right Sir, particularly cricket. The school boasts men who have represented England on more than one occasion."

The Major then diverted his eyes to Captain Keaveney. "Do you have the same sporting pedigree?"

When Captain Lamerton glanced toward Keaveney in supercilious fashion it was not lost on the Major; he invited Keaveney, masking his embarrassment to continue.

"My pleasure is the piano. I just seemed to have a natural talent for it Sir."

The Major deliberated adding more levity to the occasion. "Well now that we know it we must get hold of one from somewhere... I'm sure a rousing sing-song from time to time will do wonders for us all." He then rose to his feet and moved around the table filling up the officers' glasses, each said "Thank you, Sir."

Despite his inexperience, Henderson, emboldened by the wine coughed up, "Sir?"

"Yes, Captain Henderson."

"How long have you been over here?" His mouth dried up but he pushed the next sentence out. "I mean have you seen any action in the major battles?"

Everyone waited for the Major's response and they weren't disappointed with his reminiscence. First though he allowed his face an expression of thoughtfulness.

"I came over with the original Expeditionary Force that re-crossed the Marne. Like so much in this war, it makes grim reading. I don't go with this attrition," he paused and the officers were quickly surprised that their superior might be criticising the military. "Do you know I have heard it said in a briefing that the army which has the most men left will be the eventual victor."

Captain Lamerton desperate to announce his imaginary pedigree spoke with an undercurrent of challenge. "But Sir, hasn't that always been the case? Even going back to the Romans."

The Major's response was quick. "In theory yes, but who is the real victor when the spoils of war far exceed those left to enjoy it?"

Captain Keaveney attempted to join in the conversation. "Sir, surely the instances reported at the Marne can be regarded."

He was interrupted forcefully by Lamerton, "Captain Keaveney what were the instances at the Marne?"

Keaveney remained undeterred. "Well, the offensive was ambitious to say the least, the military had no mechanised transport nor air cover to take the load off the infantry."

This time Major Robertson, who had listened with increasing interest, aware of the minor spat raised his voice, "That's right!"

It commanded everyone's attention and he continued, "Everything was being tried for the first time - Generals commanding armies by telephone instead of by telescope and notepad and the cavalry officers, they learnt too." His eyes had travelled in an upwards direction but were quickly brought down when Lamerton asked dryly, "Learnt what Sir?"

"That their troops had a very short life against the machine gun." It was said pointedly and all knew it.

Captain Keaveney asked, "What happened Sir, when the Germans fell back from the Marne?"

There was no denying Robertson's sheer force of character in the way he answered. "The allies prevented a German formation of a front along the Aisne.

Both sides edged off to the north and west, each trying to find a way around the other's flank and eventually ending up on the channel coast."

The officers were captivated and Keaveney eagerly asked, "Then what Sir?"

Robertson continued with the same authority in his voice, "It was the end movement in the open country and since then this," he looked around the room and threw his hands up before continuing, "trench warfare. French losses are almost incalculable… into tens of thousands not hundreds." He had deliberately paused because he wanted everyone to understand fully, what he was about to say. "Gentlemen, men are going to pass through your hands like sand, most of them you won't even know but if I can give you the most surest advice it is this – try to treat each soldier as an individual, not as being regarded by some, mere corpuscles in this huge body of war."

Captain Keaveney pushed his meal to one side while the others looked stunned, except that is for Captain Lamerton who spoke up.

"Sir, do you agree with the use of chloride gas? I mean it was the Germans who began using it a couple of years ago." Before he could look self-satisfied he was ambushed by the Major, "Where was it first used Lamerton?"

Lamerton struggled and the Major quickly calculated that he didn't know.

Once again he had his audience in the palm of his hand, "Ypres, when they opened their attack on the Ypres salient and for a while it worked. They forced a gap in the line but were hesitant about advancing through that gap even though the breach was large enough." Suddenly he turned his eyes directly to Lamerton, "But back to your query, Captain Lamerton. The British offensive that followed resulted in a loss of around 300,000 men for a gain of eight square miles of shell shocked wild land." He nodded his head before continuing, "I haven't really thought about the morality of using gas."

Silence entered the room and the stillness matched the stillness in the sky outside which harboured silver stars, some ghosting their way to infinity, others crying for what they watched going on below, with no end in sight. The Fens Pals, fortified by hot food, sugary tea and some hours rest were good to go again under the star lit night.

The manner with which the patrol crawled along on their stomachs, making suitable progress revealed they were no longer novices. Harry Hardy in particular ploughed on like a frontiersman blazing a trail, aware only of the immediate obstacles and general lie of the land. The war had matured him and he had learnt to place the officers who issued instruction with a shrewdness shorn of sentimental illusions. The majority were of particular types and he could tell false faces from true one. He decided the very worst were those who concealed a bullying uxoriousness beneath a layer of sentimentality and out here in the early hours only his men's safety really mattered so he kept his head clear.

Harry and Peter moved quietly down an embankment while Dave and Jim remained at the top. Nothing could be heard and they looked for movement coming from the direction of the tunnel entrance. There was none and neither did it look that there had been any recent activity. When Harry suddenly kicked a piece of metal, alarm appeared on all their faces and they hastily looked around before the culprit cursed himself. It was the simple things, slight accidents that were often the difference between life and death for all patrols venturing into No Man's Land and further under cover of darkness.

When they approached the tunnel entrance Peter cocked an eyebrow at Harry who released a revolver from his holster; he indicated for Peter to do likewise and he complied but seeing Harry's silhouette thought what a thoroughly objectionable image it appeared, but this was no time for character observation. That could wait for discussion over a cigarette and more hot tea. Peter moved closer, his body curiously looking slack and boneless. He was ready.

Both men crept into the tunnel and began pointing out features of a makeshift hut inside made of logs and joined on three sides by wrought iron; only the full moon provided any light. Cautiously they walked down steps and stopped abruptly when they heard movement ahead; both hastily retreated but nothing was visible as clouds now fronted the moon. Once again they heard quiet voices and Harry licking his lips cocked the trigger of his revolver. Outside the duo took cover in shell holes either side of the entrance and waited for what seemed a long time.

Four Germans, quietly relaxed, emerged from the entrance and began speaking while Peter prepared to throw a bomb he'd retrieved from his rucksack. There was a lull before the younger man started firing and a cry of pain punctuated the air, then Harry shouted "Throw your bomb and let's go!"

The explosion was loud and fierce and destroyed the tunnel entrance. Again Harry shouted, "C'mon let's go!" and both scrambled up the embankment anticipating German retaliation and within half a moment the whole patrol was scrambling away on their bellies. Fortunately darkness now pervaded the sky above, providing a welcome camouflage. Before half an hour had elapsed they resumed a crawling position, thinking they were safe and then ran for safety.

Two minutes later flares lit up the sky and Harry barked out "Down!" Machine gun fire strafed the ground around them whilst the German pursuers lobbed bombs in their direction. The Englishmen lay still, their energies having collapsed. The assault stopped but no one dared to move.

Suddenly a single shot rang out and Harry cried out "I'm hit!"

Peter scampered in his direction only to find Harry holding his leg and grimacing with the pain. "OK don't panic" he said, tearing the scarf from his neck and tying it as tightly as possible around the wounded man's leg.

"God! My leg feels as if it's on fire," he said looking down and running his hand over it before realising that blood was pouring out. "Christ must have gone straight through... must get back."

"Don't worry we'll get you back," and with that Peter pulled him along but each movement witnessed the growing of severe pain.

Ahead Dave and Jim had stopped. Dave said, "Come on we can't leave Peter to drag Harry back in by himself." Jim's response was noble for he had surveyed the situation before responding, "No point both of us going back, you stay, I'll give Peter a hand."

Dave looked quizzical. "Sure?"

Before Jim started crawling back he said, "Keep your eyes skinned for those Huns... they'll be mad for sure."

The trio looked exhausted as they made towards the British line. Harry was distinctly pale having lost much blood despite the tourniquet. Yet he managed to mumble "Thanks Jim" aware that the latter was now pulling him along, by hand.

The fire power increased in No Man's Land - shells, machine gun fire and puffs of smoke prevented any lasting visibility.

A peculiar stillness suddenly rode over the terrain as the noise of gunfire abated followed by a dense atmosphere at once chilling and unnerving. Harry, Peter and Jim were overawed by the sudden silence which was broken by Peter seeing the mist descending in the darkness.

"Oh my God, gas! Quick the respirators!" Before they could fit Harry's on he was coughing and choking; it was a close thing.

Almost in unison Peter and Jim looked at each other, "Dave!" they shouted through their masks. Unfortunately he had waited for any sign of his friends returning but now his fixed expression turned to horror as he recognised approaching gas. A moment later his coughing and choking took on a relentless sound as he struggled to his feet and ran towards the British trenches pulling at his tunic as he did so; his voice had gone. The only sound heard was a guttural one "HALT!"

Dave, gasping for air, tried to cry out 'Gas!' but visibility was now exceedingly poor and again the guttural voice repeated itself "HALT!" though this time there was the ominous sound of a Lewis machine gun being loaded ready for use. When Dave caught sight of the British trench his attempts to shout 'Gas!' were useless, only the sound of the machine gun being chipped ready was audible.

Despite his discomfiture he smiled as he recognised the British troops in the trenches ahead and thanked the Lord before the sudden noise of machine gun fire rocked the stillness. He was stone dead before he hit the ground. The machine gunners, both wearing respirators, waited to greet the next form of human life before one of them put the safety chip back in position.

Harry, Peter and Jim had heard everything but seen nothing. They looked lost, almost too frightened to move and their situation wasn't helped by the fact that Harry was now drifting in and out of consciousness.

In the early morning the men wore ashen faces and gloom was writ large right through them; it seemed only their eyes were living as they waited for the sky to provide more than a tongue of light. Slowly the mist lifted and from a British

Observation Post a scout was looking through binoculars into No Man's Land. When he saw Dave's body he pulled the binoculars away. He resumed his observation before withdrawing the binoculars away again and noticing a sentry walking by shouted for him. "Can you get yourself up here?"

The sentry acknowledged his request and started climbing the ladder. When he stepped into the tower he was offered the binoculars. "Look out there, about forty yards to the left of that tree."

While the soldier looked intensely at the area pointed out the scout spoke, "Can you see – I thought I saw something move."

"You did see something and it looks like three of ours. How the hell…" before he could finish his sentence the scout asked for the binoculars.

"Here let me have another look." He witnessed the trio making feeble movements towards their own lines.

"Christ if the German snipers see them, they're dead."

The soldier turned to go back down the ladder. "I'm going to tell Sarge right away," and within seconds was running across the compound. The scout was looking back at the men muttering "Keep calm boys, help's on its way."

Two German snipers, positioned in a clump of trees just inside their own lines were also scanning the view in front with their binoculars though they were bored. They were about to break from their duty when one quickly diverted his gaze back over an area he had just scanned. "Hans I think we are in luck… to the left of that crater by the mangled wire." He handed his binoculars to his fellow sniper. "Here mine are better… see near the trees."

"Ah three of them… I must be going blind. I've looked over there a couple of times already."

The snipers smiled at each other before lifting their rifles and smiling at the prospect, "See how near you can get Hans then I will try." The second marksman slowly got into position adjusting the sights on his rifle before readjusting them again, having looked through them. "How much do you want to bet?" The words were delivered with disdain.

Peter pulled Harry a couple of feet before a shot was heard and mud flew up inches in front of Harry's respirator. The men looked about, nothing, and a second shot was fired and mud splattered up over Jim. The injured man was pulled along as fast as could be managed while a series of shots hit the ground inches away.

"The bastards are toying with us" said Jim before making the sign of the cross. Suddenly wholesale fire could be heard, a group of British soldiers including four snipers fired repeatedly into the trees where the enemy marksmen had been located while two stretcher bearers loaded Harry into a blood stained canvas and moved briskly back towards the trenches under cover of protective gunfire. Peter having taken his respirator off glanced for a second at Dave's body and an immeasurable sadness charged through him.

In Tunby Hill, the happiness that was once the usual hallmark of the village had momentarily gone. A black wreath hung in the window of 'Eric V. Snipe, Butcher' as it did in the shop two doors away 'Edwin Buckingham, Baker and General Stores'.

On the door of the blacksmith's forge a photograph covered in waterproof sheeting was nailed to the door and below a large wreath, in its centre a dedication written by lithograph pen – *Dave Baumber 1890-1916 Blacksmith. A fine craftsman born and bred in the village who lost his life serving King and Country on the battlefield of France. Though not your flower bloomed for long. The majesty touched all with but one glimpse.*

Chapter 17

Eager eyes, strongly marked eyebrows, square resolute chins that signified character and determination; reverenced physical strength in broad shoulders and muscular limbs, healthy cheeks – they stood principal figures in every picture of agricultural fields; and it was gone forever and only a memory of what had been would remain after the eleven o'clock chimes on the eleventh day of the eleventh month in 1918. Once the innocence had gone, no one would shirk the real truth and minds relieved by this ebullition would struggle for composure and no one would whistle a tune.

Inside his cottage John Reid drank his tea from a mug in a theatrical manner; accompanying him was Bert 'Jim' Jeffries who had called in for what was known as a social. Mr Reid put his mug down and waved a letter at his co-farmer "arrived the other day" he stated as he opened it, expectantly, not noticing the look of anxiousness on the other man's face.

"It's from Donald, says he and Arthur Hardy are in hospital and can't give the exact location mind – censorship – says they were caught while out on patrol." Before reading further and now picking up on his friend's worried expression he made light of everything.

"Bloody fools... they should have been more careful," and he released a chuckle which softened Jim Jeffries' facial expression. "He doesn't say how badly they were wounded just talks about the farm and all the jobs he's going to have to tackle when he gets back. Come on let's go outside you don't look well Jim."

They found themselves in the garden, walking by a thorn hedge. Their attention was taken with the flute song of a blackbird.

"Spring, what a time of year, Jim" said John Reid gazing at the lacework of buds, Lilacs, Chestnuts, Beeches, bronze to gold, the Oaks still dim and unburnished. He pointed out a thrush singing on the bough of an ageing Beech tree.

"You know them city dwellers never see this colour and those business men will never understand the mystery of life here... and they're the worse for it."

Still, Jim Jeffries was eager for John Reid to continue with the war news and offered a lame smile before asking, "Anything about my lads? I haven't heard anything for months." He wanted to unburden himself but John Reid had always been canny and he did it for him.

"Well this letter's taken six weeks to arrive so don't worry Jim. Donald says the last he heard of Michael was he was being seconded to some scouting patrol. Apparently they're training the boys to go out on recce near to enemy lines."

The other tenant farmer froze and a long stare filled his eyes which John Reid was quick to assuage, "They're learning map reading and training them how to take compass readings as well as arms training and tactical manoeuvring... Everything will have been planned and the officers won't send them into harm's way just for the sake of it." John Reid paused after the last sentence because he knew how manipulative those holding rank could be.

Jim's expression was one of pleading. "Hepzibah's worried sick about the boys, more Bert than Michael, says he can't even dress himself, properly."

John spontaneously put his arm around Jim's shoulders and squeezed him. "Don't worry, Bert will be OK... if anyone of the boys is going to have his head down it will be Bert."

The other man was far from convinced; he had long left the impetus of his own youth. They walked some more and John decided that he would not be affected by his friend's quivering confusion less his problem became his own; it would be all too easy to be engulfed in a moon of melancholy. "Look Jim, we got our own boys over there. I know it's a trying time but spare a thought for Mrs Baumber, he only..."

Jim's face dropped at the mention of the widow's name "Yes, you're right. God has been cruel there. Mrs Baumber looks so ill... she'll never get over this."

There was a delicate pause and both men stopped walking before John Reid spoke. "We have a duty to see that she and any of us that..." his words almost failed him but he inhaled deeply then continued. "One day the war is going to end. Life won't be the same because there's never been a war like this one, but we have to go on. All of us are going to suffer. If we don't how can we offer respect to those who eventually survive and what of those that perish? Jim do you think they'd be any happier thinking everything was in vain?"

Both men were deep in thoughts as they walked a circular route back to the Reid's cottage. Before Mr Jeffries bid good day and took his leave he tried to be upbeat "If I get any news from my boys I'll let you know." He declined another mug of tea.

Within an hour John Reid was toiling in the fields and he stayed there until late afternoon. Before returning home for his meal he sat under an oak tree and smoked a roll up slowly, visualising his sons post war, catching up on all those jobs they were determined to do and he knew that if all three survived it would equate with being on the threshold of heaven; and he couldn't bear to consider the alternative...

Everyone had thoroughly washed themselves before taking their places at the dining table. Mrs Clements, in masterly form, had put dishes of hot meat, vegetables and potatoes on the table and watching the steam rise everyone looked approvingly and waited for Mr Clements to say something.

"Thank you, Mother." He looked at his daughters and hands were joined. "Lord, for what we are about to receive make us truly thankful, Amen."

Immediately everyone repeated "Amen."

Mr Clements, as was his tradition, began serving the food onto plates which Mrs Clements passed to her daughters.

"Get this inside you. Both of you look as pale as ghosts." Mr Clements paused before continuing, "I know you've heard from Donald."

Helen suddenly looked startled.

His smile in Helen's direction was of the quiet sensitive type. "Surprises you doesn't it? Well, I too have a heart and know what you might be feeling but poking at your food is not going to improve this now."

Everyone took a mouthful of food before Mrs Clements, straightening her blouse spoke, "We've heard those Germans have been using gas against our boys, how terrifying – it's not right."

Mr Clements was quick in his response despite chewing a gristled piece of meat.

"Ain't no war ever been right Mother and we shall go on fighting them. Some of them politicians in London say it's going to be the war to end all wars but I doubt it. This village has given its share over the years."

No one quarrelled with his seriousness especially when it was a smiling seriousness and now the girls, including his wife, were keen not to offer him a platform when he might pontificate as though his life depended on it.

Mrs Clements had quickly stepped in. "Well Helen, are you going to tell us what Donald says?"

Elizabeth the younger daughter responded in playful mood. "Mother, you shouldn't be so nosey."

Suddenly the lady of the house was taken aback, but no one could be sure if she was joking, "Now less of that Elizabeth, just remember to whom you are speaking."

Her youngest daughter's gaze seemed to sink, but she was rescued by her sister.

"Just says he's out of hospital... he'll be away from the convalescent home by now I imagine... I think he was trying to say what it was like seeing row upon row of men blinded by the gas but it's hard to put together its..."

Mr Clements had his mouth full of food but it didn't inhibit him. "That be censorship, don't allow anything back that might harm morale."

His wife looked disdainful at her husband's lack of manners, which wasn't lost on anyone, before saying "Dick do you have to speak with your mouth full?"

In peacetime the girls might have erupted in laughter inwardly and save the outward expression until they were together later.

Mr Clements managed to swallow the mouthful before pulling a straight face.

"Apologies Mother... See while we're doing all right, the boys can write what they like, give or take, but when the goings rough the military get frightened that all them peace protestors and families of them that have fallen will call for a halt to all hostilities."

Elizabeth, belying her years, took her father up on that. "Isn't that a big against, father?"

"It may be against but that's right I tell thee."

Mrs Clements didn't want any arguments developing and having spooned more food onto her husband's plate, which elicited a nod of approval, addressed her eldest daughter.

"Has Donald said any more about the boys?"

Helen responded quickly. "No, he just says what the countryside is like and I think he tries to paint it much better than it actually is. I know he would have been very upset at David's death."

Mrs Clements face dropped on hearing these words and she spoke in a quieter manner. "The whole village is upset about David. Fine young man; he had time for everyone, couldn't have wished to meet a finer young man. God rest his soul."

Elizabeth sensing her father might help himself to more food offered her plate to him, "May I have some more?"

Mr Clements smiled. "That's what I like to see."

"It must be all the fresh air I'm getting" she said breezily.

"It won't do you any harm lass, it's much better than working in those factories making bolts and nuts."

Mrs Clements smiled. "I'm sure it's not that bad Dick."

Now her husband looked exasperated. "Mother, I wish you could look outside the village just once in a while. They may have brought in Parliamentary Acts to stop children working in factories and mines and reduced the number of working hours but these factory managers still get their pound of flesh."

A flash of anger stiffened Mrs Clements facial features. "Dick do you have to be so... so..."

Before she could find the right expression her husband bulldozed the table. "I speak my mind and so should you now and again."

In an instant Elizabeth joined in. "Father's right, mother. Some of the girls in Wragtoft Hill told Helen and I about one of the girls going to work in a factory in Nottingham."

"And what did they say?" asked her mother pointedly.

"That the poor girl was working fourteen hours a day and only had one day off. When she came back she looked as though she'd been through the wringer, all thin and pale." It was obvious Elizabeth had enjoyed saying this as a faint look of self-righteousness flickered across her face and her mother became conciliatory.

"Well, if that isn't an example to the other girls then nothing will be. The wages may be lower here but the quality of life..."

Helen suddenly interrupted her mother with a giggle and waited for the immediate admonishment.

"Ah, you may laugh my girl but I tell thee here is better than there or probably anywhere for that." The rest of the meal was conducted in silence and as always Mr Clements was the first to finish. Before standing up he inhaled and patted his substantial girth with both hands.

"Well if you will excuse me, Mother, while I get my pipe and go and sit down." His senses were alert and he wanted to leave the ladies to gossip among themselves. They remained seated and all three watched him leave the dining room quietly closing the door behind him.

"Try not to worry," Mrs Clements said looking at Helen. "Don't pay too much attention to father. He can be a bit brusque but I know he's worried about Donald, in fact all the boys from Tunby Hill."

Elizabeth immediately offered her sister a rallying cry. "Well if anyone's going to see this show out it will be Donald. He knows what is waiting for him when it's all over."

Helen said nothing as though she felt a sense of conflict within herself; as though she had begun wrestling with the silence. Maybe it was a shield, nevertheless tears started falling from her eyes which surprised the other two. Mrs Clements moved next to her daughter, putting an arm around her, "There now it's alright child... let it out." And with that she indicated for Elizabeth to leave the dining room. What was said and felt in the next hour stayed in that room, forever.

Chapter 18

The Great War, over twenty months old, had settled into uniformity. Sometimes it seemed time had been left astern almost forgotten. In peacetime uniformity was the abortion of creation and here an invisible factory kept churning out stereotypes: handsome officers with foppish ways and haughty manners – handsome officers with boyish faces and melodious laughs who couldn't conceal their fear and those tall, slender built with hopefully winning ways. All in bespoke uniforms which contrasted with those of the men under their command, however no one had expected that this war would rob mankind of its centuries old treasures and everyone now believed that the Devil lurked on the Western Front.

The gradual sound of marching could be heard in the distance. Slowly it got louder until a full view revealed soldiers flanked by others on horseback; far back occasional flashes of fire brightened up the day sky.

Donald Reid and Arthur Hardy marched at the head of a column making its way to the front line; the singing that had accompanied the men when they started out had dried up; it had been a gradual process.

All looked veterans and previous enthusiasm had been wiped out due mainly to what they had witnessed and experienced. Suddenly the sound of horns was heard and the column instinctively moved aside to allow three ambulances to speed ahead. Donald watched the ambulances before turning to Arthur.

"Funny, the first time I saw an ambulance it filled me with concern. I hoped that whoever it was going to would be all right. Now you don't know if they're taking them up or bringing them back."

Arthur's expression didn't change. "I no longer care... who cares anymore?"

To the soldiers right was a British military compound and they stopped adjacent to it; most slumped down wearily and lit cigarettes. The scouts in the observation posts jutting out of the ground at various intervals offered the thumbs up to them and then to despatch riders about to leave, each with a box containing carrier pigeons strapped to his back.

The columns were marched into the compound which seemed disorganised and assembled outside a wooden hut doubling as the military HQ. Besides this a smaller fenced off area contained dogs used as messengers; in attendance was a military veterinary surgeon examining them. Within minutes one of the Alsatians with a satchel attached to its back was led away by a soldier.

The door to the hut was flung open, obviously for dramatic effect and a starched looking Major walked outside smiling in the men's direction. He paused by the top step before addressing them in a well worn patronising manner.

"Good to have you alongside." He smiled, concealed his disappointment because the response from the soldiers was nil. "The Hun's been causing all sorts of problems for us recently but we've got a surprise in store for him, mark my words." He deliberately raised his voice possibly mimicking his old headmaster at prep school. "The German has made the mistake of underestimating us British, he has the audacity, yes the audacity..." Again the men looked at him with blank eyes which galvanised Major Fry even more, "to question our resolve. Well our friends over there are going to get a little surprise. Plans are afoot to mount an offensive the likes of which has never been seen in military history before and may never be seen again. It is a moment you will tell your grandchildren about, I promise. No one will be forgotten whatever the outcome."

The soldiers tired, drained and now disengaged looked in several directions getting their bearings and it became obvious to Fry they did not share his optimism. His voice became officious. "You will be billeted in the low side of the compound. N.C.O.'s will distribute divisions accordingly. I hope you are going to be reunited with familiar faces. That is all."

He promptly turned and walked into the hut closing the door behind him. If he had hoped his words would sound like explosive pugilistic utterances then he had failed and he knew it. Within minutes N.C.O.'s had dispersed the men. Fry had been right on one score, familiar faces did appear in the compound over a couple of days despite the often incessant shelling, particularly at night of enemy positions miles and miles away.

The gathering of Fens Pals was one of the biggest since hostilities had begun. Inside their hut they drank tea, smoked each other's cigarettes and exchanged pleasantries.

Arthur waited for a lull. "So Harry's been given a medal, er, in the hospital."

"That's what the Sergeant said," offered Peter with enthusiasm.

Jim beaming with an impish smile, long recognised by his friends couldn't resist the opportunity to say, "Well how come we didn't get one – we were all out there. In fact Harry won't go unless we keep him company."

Michael drew on his roll up before responding. "They can't give medals to everyone can they?"

Jim laughed and so did the other men when he said, "I suppose they need most of the metal to make guns. Christ, now conscription's come in they're gonna be very choosy, I reckon, who gets a medal and who don't."

Arthur, eager to keep everything light and optimistic, pulled a smiling face. "Still when Harry gets here at least it will be all the village together."

Before anyone could respond the mood suddenly altered when from the back of the hut they heard Donald, "Except for David."

Everyone nodded and returned to their own thoughts but the stillness was broken by Sid.

"We're still sorry about David. Only thing that can be said is that there are places worse off than us. One village lost eleven of their men folk, one deserted and only five are left. Everyone thinks they are jinxed or something."

Bert had been looking at Bertie and Alfred while Sid spoke and when they returned his look he spoke. "Bet you two wish you were back in Fenderby?"

Alfred smiled before speaking without a trace of bitterness. "Be a might sight quieter than here." Everyone laughed and a couple clapped their hands together and then they waited for Alfred to continue.

"Only me and Bertie from the Hill. The other boys from Woodside been taken up with the Lincolns, though I believe some may have joined after the Sherwoods."

Bertie joined in. "Word has it they haven't had it easy, lost a lot of men fighting at a place called Verdun some while back."

More tea was poured from an urn and the men huddled together before Sid spoke.

"We see several regiments have sustained heavy losses – Norfolks, Suffolks, East Lancs."

Donald who'd been blowing rapid smoke circles and watching them disintegrate told them, "And there's going to be a lot more before this war is over – if it ever finishes that is."

Alarm registered on Sid's face and he could barely get his words out until he had inwardly calmed down. "Don't you think it's gonna end soon? We've been fighting nearly two years now."

Donald was matter of fact in his response. "Have you seen any progress made... by either side besides the slaughter going on everywhere?"

Peter, whom the war had revealed to be a man of courage, a deliberate man who occasionally rushed at life haphazard, was determined the atmosphere would not be weighed down with melancholy. He stood up and this immediately garnered everyone's attention. He closed his eyes and held his hands out level, "What I wouldn't give to be in The Red Lion now... Ah that's all right Peter you can have this one on the house... Thank you landlord, that's mighty decent of you." They watched as he picked up an imaginary glass and began drinking slowly. The release the men felt from their present predicament was like being hit by a lightening conductor named Joy. All were living the moment. "Beautiful," Peter put his imaginary glass down. "Landlord I hear there were a couple of ladies asking after me, is that so? Yes, indeed pretty little maids mind you they can't come in here but you must be popular for they beckoned me from behind the bar to go and talk with them." Peter picked up the imaginary glass and closing his eyes took another drink before putting the glass back down and the Pals followed his every movement with eyes and mouth wide open. "Let me fill your glass up Peter. Well, as I was saying one of the girls said she thought you were the most upright young man she's seen in these parts and would I persuade you to take her to one of the village dances... By the way this ale is on the house tonight all right. I think you deserve it."

Once again Peter who had kept his eyes shut during the soliloquy put the glass back down. No one said anything until he opened them.

Arthur was nodding his head slowly. "Oh Peter you don't know the agony you've caused us all."

Everyone laughed especially Bertie. "I could feel that ale slipping down a real treat."

"And I!" burst out Sid.

"We want to know who the maids are!"

"I'm keeping that secret for my next instalment."

"Ah now we're going to be subjected to a raging thirst again. My throat is burning. I can even smell the hops!"

"Patience Sid, just concentration that's all and I promise you, you will drink from the glass you put up," and with that Peter smiled.

Arthur was shaking his head. "That would be something, if we could close our eyes, open them and find ourselves in The Lion, just the boys."

Bertie pulled his friends back. "We will, let's make a pact that when this is all over, the first night back we will get drunk – all of us as one." He looked about for approbation.

Alfred coughed up, "Yes, that's all right by me."

Both men shook hands and the others responded warmly.

"I'll be there" said Peter quickly followed by Sid, "Count me in."

Despite stretching his tired limbs Arthur remained buoyant. "I'll look forward to that night, it will be special."

Not to be outdone Jim made a noble gesture. "I'll buy the first round."

Donald who'd felt a warm glow listening to the spirited tirade had the final words as the men huddled even closer together. "I'll buy the last." Then all the Fens Pals placed their hands on top of each others for no more words were necessary and everyone knew it might never be a reunion with one hundred per cent attendance.

The intimacy of the moment was interrupted when Captain Keaveney resplendent in his officer's uniform ironed by angels, soldiered into the hut with a smile on his face.

"Men you'll be pleased to know that Corporal Hardy is being discharged from hospital tomorrow and we should have him back here the following day. Meanwhile, Private Reid," he turned his head and looked straight at Peter, "I want you to take out a group tonight for a general recce. I'll send for you later and we will go over the area on the OS map together."

Peter responded in a subdued manner, "Yes Sir," which left the junior officer slightly self-conscious.

"Fine, well I knew you'd be pleased about Corporal Hardy."

The men replied in unison. "Thank you Sir."

Keaveney retreated with indecent haste not noticing that Peter was looking at his brother who reluctantly smiled as he knew it was him who would be saddled with leadership and he never really understood why.

The Pals occupied themselves for the next couple of hours playing cards and drinking more tea. The shabby room suggested loneliness but this was the characteristic it seemed to take on before the patrol went out each time. Donald had declined the card school instead he lay down with eyes half closed meditating in a pleasant way occasionally watching the card players knowing each one had taken hard knocks but never whimpered; he felt proud to be one of them.

It was a brisk walk to the officers' hut and from the outside raucous laughter could be heard; that changed when the Yellow bellies joined the officers. Three of them stood with their backs to the door watching something on the floor while Captain Keaveney looking uneasy sat alone not really part of his fellow officers' activity.

Everyone watched two drunken rats fighting each other in a make shift ring formed by four pieces of wood. Rats were nobody's friend especially soldiers lying wounded in No Man's Land yet the Reid boys found the spectacle repulsive as eventually did two of the officers. But not Captain Lamerton who concealed a bullying disposition beneath a waistline riddled with fat. He took great delight in picking up one of the exhausted combatants.

"What you need is another tot to see him off." He held the rat's head back and inserted a tiny rubber tube attached to a small bottle containing whisky and tilted it up. He laughed and gloated while watching Keaveney's squeamishness.

"What's the matter Keaveney?" It was easy to see he had a mind of facetious envies that tied a sneer to the lapels of any jacket he wore and he disliked people whom he thought tickled life. He was detestable.

Keaveney couldn't hide his distaste. "I just don't think it's necessary." He had a vein of simplicity that the scouts warmed to. Lamerton felt a spasm of exultation and became even more detestable, if that was possible.

"If you've no steel man then what the devil are you doing here or come to that, why the hell did you join the army?" He may have looked combative but real combat had eluded him so far in this war yet he continued to look as black as thunder.

Fortunately one of the other officers intervened trying to diffuse the mounting tension. "Come on Keaveney, after all it's only a rat and you know what these blighters do." Lamerton had returned to the ring and dropped the rat into the arena and suddenly terrifying squealing echoed all around.

The Fens Pals remained silent observing Keaveney's anguished face while Lamerton watched the fight to the finish. The other two officers began straightening their uniforms occasionally glancing at the fighting rats. The situation changed when a sudden determined knock was heard on the door and a voice called out "Sir." It galvanised Lamerton into action and he picked up what was left of both rats put them in separate small boxes in the corner of the room before straightening himself up. When Keaveney opened the door he was relieved to see it was the last member of the patrol and beckoned him in with a friendly manner which didn't go unnoticed by the other officers.

Now that the entertainment was over there was an uneasiness in the room and Donald could see the disdain and insincerity in a couple of these officers by the way they glanced at each other. He knew Keaveney was out on a limb, nevertheless he was relieved to turn his back on the upper class and concentrate on the map now rolled out for the scouting patrol.

Keaveney pointed, "Here, I want you to go out as far as this, further if possible, but crikey be careful. We have had a few skirmishes with the German patrols in this particular area. They seem mightily determined to keep secret whatever it is they've got there."

Donald responded, "Sir, what about aerial reconnaissance, what do they report?"

The officer looked slightly crestfallen. "To be honest with you, I don't really know." Now it was the boys turn to look with disdain and they did hope the other officers might think they were being sneered at, apart from Keaveney, who continued, "There is a rumour that the Germans are prepared for a huge offensive on our part and have planned accordingly," once again he tapped the map with a ruler before continuing. "We've heard they have dug trenches in the chalk hills and devised a new system of them. We know surrounding villages and woods have been connected into strong posts for defensive purposes. We also have news of concrete pill boxes being built."

Donald moved even closer to the map and crouched down to scrutinise the area. As though to offer reassurance Captain Keaveney slowly nodded his head up and down. "But don't worry, very little will survive our offensive."

In the background the other officers had begun to take notice of the conversation and Lamerton, having lit his cherry wood pipe, bustled over and began tapping the map with it.

"Going out here are you?" He asked in a brusque manner.

"Yes Sir," was Donald's swift, polite reply.

"Never know you might bag a thing or two," said Keaveney in a light hearted, off the cuff manner. The Pals smiled but that didn't last long when another officer said, "Damned lucky, I wish I could join you out there on patrol." The fact that the officer had a pink, crumpled mouth didn't help and Peter was about to reply but Donald fully aware of the flippancy of such a remark put his hand on his brother's wrist to stop him.

Donald spoke in a quiet tone. "Excuse me Sir but why are the Generals so confident that this assault will smash right through the German lines when it's been stalemate for so long?"

Lamerton's intervention was fierce and his body swung forward at the hips, "Good God, such a thing is not taken lightly. Already elaborate calculations have been done, which have almost proved, in fact, that seven days torrent of high explosive shells will give the infantry a straight walk through to Berlin if they want to go there." He laughed and was joined by the other two officers. But despite the bluster he didn't sound convincing and he was aware of Donald, a fighting soldier, looking at him with an aggressive curiosity and it pricked Lamerton who offered in more bluster, looking pointedly at the scout. "Do you think that this followed by fourteen British, five French divisions – a total of 400,000 men spread across a twenty five mile or so front... I ask you..."

Donald remained steadfast and looked at Lamerton as if everything he'd just said sounded platitudinous. The third officer didn't take kindly to Donald's attitude, possibly because he didn't appear subservient or overwhelmed in the presence of a gentleman officer.

Peter looked admiringly at his brother even though he was feeling uneasy at the unspoken friction. He quickly came up with a question, "When is that offensive going to happen Sir?"

Lamerton still looked annoyed but nevertheless responded. "Soon... nothing can or will go wrong."

Donald was more interested in the map and studied the various arrows and pointers marked in green ink and the names of battalions, regiments and artillery deployed. He said in a quiet voice "The Somme."

Lamerton boomed. "Yes Private, the Battle of the Somme 1916!" Then an extraordinary thing happened - the door suddenly blew open and a lighted candle in a bottle on the table flickered and went out, taking everyone by surprise.

"Good God!" shouted Lamerton before slamming it shut.

Finally Keaveney wrapped the meeting up as well as the OS maps and carrying the night time map under his arm escorted the patrol back to their hut, though little conversation passed between them.

It was late and the only visible sign of life were sentries on guard duty and the full moon which had risen and was shining.

Chapter 19

Despite the time of year a blue grey, overcast sky hung over the French countryside and the breathless calm of a nearby river. The day had a melancholy stillness about it and when evening arrived the empty countryside lay vacant under a moody sky and superstitions the rank and file in any army developed were easier to understand. For the patrol it was business as usual.

Inside their tent Donald, Peter, Michael, Jim, Bertie and Alfred were preparing themselves. The light was provided by three candles upright on a wooden crate. The men dressed in one-piece suits and balaclavas, checked their revolvers while Peter checked his compass. They gathered round the crate and the Peter spread out a small map.

"Right you all know the password – Piccadilly."

Everyone nodded and Peter assumed a serious tone. "Don't forget it, too many of our boys are getting trigger happy."

He looked at the men and Bertie chipped in. "Are we going to try and bag one tonight?"

"Bag what?" replied Donald.

"A Fritz."

Peter half smiled. "Some of the patrols are taking bets now on who can bring back a live German."

Alfred, not known for his conversation but highly regarded by the others, offered, "We almost did a couple of patrols back."

"What happened?" asked Donald.

"Just as we were getting near to the gap the artillery made in the wire when we were spotted."

Bertie joined in the conversation. "All hell broke loose. Fritz started throwing bombs and there was machine gunning everywhere. We were lucky on that occasion." There was an unspoken foreboding forever hanging over the Fens Pals that they were on borrowed time so they tricked themselves with the promise of seeing pale sunlight when at last the sortie was over and they had recaptured much needed sleep. They encouraged each other almost subliminally to adopt this stance.

They sipped hot tea as Peter spoke. "Despite what the officers say, they are not fools these Germans. You cannot blast out a gap in the wire without giving the game away and even if you do get through the line it's near impossible to get into his trench because of the complexity of his second line of defence."

Bertie scratched his cheek before adding, "No good looking at the line from the observation post because when you get out there it's mighty different."

Peter nodded his head vigorously in agreement. "Right everyone good luck." He blew out the candles and they left. Outside it was almost pitch blackness as they steered their way along broken, creaking duckboards towards the trenches. When they passed soldiers they were encouraged with remarks of "Good luck!" and "bag us the Kaiser!".

Peter reminded his men "Don't forget – Piccadilly."

When they approached the communication trench he took out his prismatic compass and took a reading before informing the soldiers on duty, "Out now midnight in north east direction, back approximately two/three hours. There are six in the patrol, password Piccadilly." The sentries acknowledged and he repeated the word "Piccadilly". One of the sentries a tired, gaunt looking man in a filthy uniform raised a smile, "Good luck and keep your heads down."

A sudden sense of power had come to Peter, staying power, and he prayed inwardly that it would be untiring, callous if necessary.

The patrol assumed its customary V formation making cautious progress into the unknown.

The latest map of No Man's Land had arrived from Brigade earlier in the day and Peter reminded himself that the objective was to get to the German listening post that had been identified and to find out if it was possible to get through enemy wire and cut the post – not to venture in themselves. The high command wanted to do something in retaliation for what the Germans had done to the Battalion which had been to seize two prisoners on one of their raids.

Unfortunately rain began to fall out the sky with sheer abandon and the ground became saturated and muddy and immense weariness began to exert its influence over the patrol. What a piquant little tale it would make when they drank their beer having been invited to stay after closing hours in the Red Lion. The weather had unnerved the Germans and flares into the night sky increased joined by active machine guns spraying the area and never more than a foot above the Pals heads.

The patrol lay motionless in a shell hole, they were almost annoyed by what they regarded as an act of bad tempered petulance from the enemy. This contrasted with the soldiers back behind their own lines and in trenches who regarded looking out into No Man's Land an act of courage that these scouts were actually in the war not dressed up in a military uniform but facing the enemy sometimes twenty yards away.

The Pals senses were razor sharp obfuscating fatigue, despite their experience this area of mystery seemed to be peopled with shadowy forms and too much imagination could be a dangerous cocktail. Just one mistake. Just one...

The earliest patrols had gone out with long wire attached to a post in their trenches and a series of pulls conveyed different messages but under artillery fire those messages had been unanswered and often wire rustling against obstacles could give away a patrol's position to the enemy. The Fens Pals had long eschewed taking lengths of wire with them. No Man's Land held a fascination for many patrols – it was seductive, a place of adventure despite being a gamble with life and death.

The patrol had lain motionless for half an hour during the fire and remained so while stillness resumed its familiar position once again. Michael momentarily lost concentration and began to raise himself, looking around. Alarmed, Donald grabbed him but too late, a burst of gunfire and Michael slumped back into Donald's arms. A myriad of lights went up followed by a fusillade of bombs and machine gun fire yet the Donald remained oblivious for he stared stunned at the young man, his best friend, dying in his arms.

Peter sprang into action. "Come on Donald you can't do anything for him come on." Donald said nothing and Peter tugged at his arm. "Come on... do you want to end up the same?" Both men began climbing out the shell hole, one eagerly the other half-heartedly and both struggled with their footing as the landscape was sheeted in rain. Donald turned to look at his friend and he saw a smile descend before the eyes closed one last time.

The brothers scurried along trying to get out of the range of the bombs. Bertie and Alfred, minutes ahead, looked consciously in their direction but were reluctant to call out instead they mumbled words of encouragement. The guns gradually stopped and no more bombs were thrown.

An exhausted Peter spotted Bertie peering over the trench and was relieved when he and Donald were dragged into the trench by outstretched arms. They were still on the brink of a crisis and felt both giddy and bewildered. Donald sat rigid and buried his head in his hands; he began crying like a bird lost in the grey of an unsettled dawn. Then he bent his head between his knees and remained in that position.

Everyone knew before Peter spoke. "They got Michael, they got Michael."

With sad eyes Alfred mumbled, "What happened?"

Peter choked for words. "I... I don't know, we were right upon them when suddenly I heard a burst and..."

Bertie interrupted him in a near whisper. "But Michael was so cautious... he wouldn't have done anything stupid, not Michael." Their stricken faces looked unshaven and haggard, no longer present was the prodigious and chivalrous fence they had built round themselves.

All of them sat very still before Alfred spoke. "Fatigue, don't those officers realise the strain of coming out here... is it right, what's it all for? They say," large tears rolled effortlessly out of his eyes and he let them run, "it's vital information that could save lives but no one tells us it's our lives being exchanged in return." For once the men were no longer a mass of warning impulses and even the weather had ceased to be their enemy. They banded in as close as they could, arms wrapped around each other, for the impact of their friend's death began to exert a delayed stunned effect as the wind whipped up in hostile fashion.

In England whether in the cities, shires or market towns communities constantly endured great inward stress and were relieved by the enforced isolation from events in France. Everyone, from time to time had premonitions of disaster and unlike the following century when communication would be instant, it took a week for news to filter through. Nevertheless it was devastating particularly for village communities, each fatality felt like the first time. When the wounded returned home, discharged, a deep magic of gratitude for their salvation was felt but never spoken of.

The Pals stared into the mugs of hot tea they were given when they had finally reached the British trenches. While soldiers hurriedly carried tins of ammunition along the lines they sat numb.

Donald looked at Peter. "I'm going back."

His brother was lost for words. "I... er... don't," he remained incoherent but Donald was determined as always and knew he stood on his own ground when making bold decisions.

"I'm not leaving Michael out there."

Peter regained some composure. "There's nothing you can do for Michael nothing any of us can do."

Donald was adamant. "I'm bringing him back."

His brother was grasping for words, juggling the fingers on his hands. "I know it's the code of honour Donald but..."

He was interrupted. "I don't know about some codes of honour, I thought you," he looked around before continuing, "of all people would understand that."

The group were suddenly seized by a tenderness borne of what they'd seen for nearly two years – torn bodies in grotesque pose, healthy looking legs with no torso joined to them.

Peter sought to comfort his brother. "I know you and Michael were especially close but," he steered Donald's face towards him with a caressing hand, "there are no identification or insignia on Michael. There is nothing the German intelligence can use." Everywhere was suddenly silent, only the tongues of candle flames moved, the men stared at them with formless faces.

Peter was not finished. "The military won't sanction anyone going out there. Isn't that what the Huns want? They're probably waiting right now with two of their best snipers just waiting Donald."

A hard anguish grew within the older brother and everyone knew he had already made his mind up, for a sense of power had come to him and he knew he would fight a lone fight if necessary against bureaucratic indifference.

The lull was broken by Captain Keaveney's appearance, causing the flames to blow at acute angles before settling back. He took his cap off, which had the effect of emphasising his eyes, intelligent eyes seldom missing any detail.

"I'm sorry about your friend... he was a brave man." His face looked shocked but the war didn't stop and he looked to Peter who obliged, "Sir, you can't penetrate their network. It's more complicated than a maze, much more complex than ours."

Keaveney who'd lit a cigarette absorbed the information. "We know they've been planning for some time. Look I want you to get out of here and back to the compound and rest for a few hours. Corporal Hardy is back, I'm sure he's looking forward to meeting up with you."

"Sir?" asked Peter.

"Yes?" was the Captain's immediate response.

"We don't want to leave our friend out there."

Captain Keaveney knew he was on thin ice, knew the turmoil his men were feeling and was desperate that anything he said was inoffensive; he had a strong sense of duty towards the group who had never let him down.

"I know what you mean, but I'm afraid you can't bow to sentiment. It would be foolhardiness of the utmost to try and bring the body back even under the cover of darkness." He tried to remain composed without sounding callous, but he knew the men in front of him wouldn't take no for an answer and in his heart he secretly admired them for it.

Peter spoke in a considered tone. "But if the offensive isn't planned until a few days time, he's just going to, going to..." There was an uneasy pause.

"Say it Peter," Donald said before looking at the Captain who swallowed before he spoke, "Look I'll come and see you this afternoon, say four o'clock and we'll try and sort something out." He didn't sound nervous but felt it and looked around for a response.

"May I ask you something Sir?" said Donald.

"Go ahead," said Keaveney, quickly glancing at his watch and trying not to look like a swimmer doubtful if he will reach the shore.

"Supposing he's unconscious, what if the Germans take him in? I don't know what's of value to enemy intelligence at this exact moment. They probably have something afoot with all the artillery and movement like."

Maybe Keaveney was being given a lifeline. "I take your point but I think it's foolhardy... four o'clock... I'll discuss it with Corporal Hardy." His departure was prompt causing one of the candle's light to go out leaving a fizzle of smoke to disperse.

The men remained seated occasionally drinking their cooled tea and undoubtedly missing the music that sounded like the laughing wisdom of ages that united the generations late each Saturday night at the Red Lion Inn. One concertina and a few hardy voices linked the past with a rising future and that future might be no more than a continuing love affair with their garden, the following day. The Sabbath. The only day country men got to sleep after lunch.

Captain Lamerton stood looking with inattentive attention at some maps spread out on the table in the officers' hut. His hands were clammy and his movements jerky; he was thoroughly dislikeable and had an inability to disguise any eavesdropping and the other officers had learnt to tolerate his ugly interference and behind his back referred to him as an ugly attack of flu; and had he known, it would have appealed to his ego for all that might have been sensitive in him was forever ill.

Captain Keaveney was also present, smoking enthusiastically and seated with all that tense old fashioned chivalrous temperament to which the scouts had increasingly warmed to. He sprang to his feet when he heard three solid knocks on the door and swiftly moved across the room to open it.

"Come in Corporal Hardy I want to talk with you."

Harry strolled in and walked toward a table where two vacant chairs rested. Before indicating for the Corporal to be seated, Keaveney enquired about his health.

"Fine Sir," was the stout reply.

"You're looking especially fit I must say."

"Thank you Sir," beamed Harry.

Keaveney poured two generous measures of whisky into two elegant glasses much to the former's bemusement, "Here have a whisky."

Harry hesitated but his eyes beamed. "Thank you, Sir."

Captain Keaveney drank his in one go and Corporal Hardy followed suit.

"Let me refill."

Both men were aware of Lamerton's displeasure at what he considered over familiarity – a wretched disregard for protocol. Harry was deliberately grateful for the offer of a second whisky, "I don't mind if I do Sir." He smiled knowingly at the Captain and Keaveney, no fool, did not betray the Corporal's retaliation. In fact both men went one step further and clinked glasses.

"Well here's to having you back in one piece Corporal." After they had taken a drink Keaveney continued knowing interruption or not he wouldn't tumble on this occasion, in the other officer's presence.

"You know we've had a bit of trouble with one of the scout patrols recently?"

Harry decided to play a straight bat. "Trouble, Sir?" he asked in all innocence.

"Yes." The Captain took one final draw on his cigarette before crushing the nub in a glass ashtray positioned next to the whisky bottle. "This last week the Germans have been up to something... seem to know when and where we send our patrols out." He looked to Hardy for some explanation, any explanation, while watching the Corporal screw his face up and leaning forward.

"Sir, it's like game keeping and poaching, but here you see after a while there is a hint of stalemate. You know the gamekeeper will leave the poacher alone if he's not too greedy or brings anyone else along and the poacher won't receive a catch for the gentleman."

Keaveney scratched his head. "I've never thought about it like that." His face warmed and the smile that followed revealed private dental work.

Harry continued, "Those Germans know what we're up to the same as we know what they try and do. Only thing is trying to keep the balance right and sometimes it takes a while to even everything back out again." He had completely wrong footed both officers who looked at him incredulously.

The Corporal's life had taken a leap both in body and spirit and thus Keaveney spoke. "You know Corporal that is the most refreshing thing I've heard for months." He began shaking his head from side to side, slowly. Despite what appeared to be traces of soot around Harry's face he was enjoying himself like a child who neither understands nor gives a damn for social niceties nor has learnt to know his place.

"Don't get me wrong Sir, I know I've been decorated and that there are braver men than me who haven't but I will be pleased when this war is over." His manner was one of sudden maturity not that of a former youth whose teenage years had been wasted, rotted away with boredom.

Keaveney thought him strong, fresh and unhurried unlike many of the officer class, who appeared self-absorbed in their martyrdom. He smiled at Corporal Hardy.

"Are you thinking of staying in the army? I'm sure you could make a career out of it."

Harry was forthright. "That's what I thought Sir, staying on like."

Keaveney adopted a more erect posture before letting his shoulders slump forward once again. "You know Corporal you came into this war a ruffian and it's turned you into a soldier. From the intelligence report connecting with scouting, a fine one at that."

The remark caught Harry unprepared and he paused before answering. "Thank you Sir."

"You've seen all the ugliness but still possess that rural innocence."

When Harry smiled softly, the Captain was quick to take up the reins again.

"No, please I don't mean to be condescending. Some of us have seen things I hope we never have to... well, what I really wanted to talk about was your patrol."

Captain Lamerton who'd kept his back to them now turned round and perched on the table having moved the maps away. Keaveney now looked slightly self-conscious.

Harry spoke first. "I heard what happened Sir, there's a grapevine all the way to the hospital, everywhere in fact."

"No, I mean one of your men, Donald Reid." His expression changed to serious intent. "Do you know him?"

"Yes Sir." Harry waited, his head cocked.

"Well he's insistent on wanting to go and bring the dead chap back."

Inevitably the interruption arrived despite where the intimacy of the other two men's conversation was heading. Lamerton interrupted without caution and in a typical forceful manner, "We can't have the men saying what they intend to do without first consulting with their superiors." It was beyond Lamerton to even contemplate that the last word of his sentence might be offensive and thus he continued in his self-absorbed vein. "I mean we understand how he feels, it's only natural but it's bad for morale Corporal Hardy – a private being so insistent. Do you understand what I'm saying?"

There wasn't one shred of compassion in what Lamerton had said which embarrassed Captain Keaveney and that embarrassment was more acute when the officer looked at the Corporal for a sign of acquiescence.

"You want me to have a word...?" asked Harry Hardy deliberately playing, again, a straight bat.

Such was Lamerton's unattractive character he thought he'd got his own way and relaxed the tension in his upper body before speaking in a relaxed manner. "That sort of thing. Well I think," he looked across at his fellow officer, still annoyed at his intrusion, "Corporal Hardy understands the situation. Good, will you excuse me." He turned his back on the men and began poring over the maps he straightened out, once again.

Harry Hardy looked at him with ill-disguised contempt before turning his expression and face towards Captain Keaveney. "Right... er... I had better go now Sir."

While he walked across the compound pondering the situation his shadow stooped over his side like a huge quivering canopy. His pace slowed as he approached his tent; he was aware of much activity going on in the compound as preparations were in evidence for a giant offensive and this only served to increase his indecision.

Harry paused outside before pulling away the canvas wrap and walking into the tent. Everyone's eyes went in his direction and despite smiling he felt awkward and strangely distant even though he had already been reunited with the Fens men. This was possibly due to the presence of Donald Reid who looked anything but an itinerant flower seller; his was almost an air of critical and impertinent attention.

Harry stood back and noticing a large urn, he looked at Peter. "Is there a spare cuppa in there?"

Peter's response was quick. "Yes, help yourself."

He observed the men with a smile as he tilted the urn to pour himself half a mug full. "One thing I missed in hospital was a decent cup of tea." He felt self-conscious and stiffened while taking a sip, knowing he was the centre of attention. "That's better, right then I suppose I'd better tell you." He dug deep for his confidence and was helped by some of the smiling faces in the tent who also sipped tea from their mugs.

Bertie grew impatient. "Well?"

Harry let his rank do the talking. "The officers don't want us to go out and bring Michael's body back."

Silence engulfed the inside of the tent and each face appeared blank, expressionless. The tirade of abuse Harry expected remained on hold and he continued, confidence growing. "So that would appear to be that. If everyone was brought back..."

He was interrupted by Donald who had risen to his feet. "Michael isn't everyone, Harry. He's my friend and I thought he was yours too." Donald's eyes were bright and fearless and all the men could sense the age-old antagonism between these two beginning to simmer again. In the past Harry would have used his temperament to do his bidding for him but the army had changed him, given him a balance which had shaved off the excesses of his former boorish behaviour. He had matured and the change was evident to the Shire men.

"He was, but that doesn't alter the fact that we can't do anything for him. He's dead – dead." His words were delivered without emotion but they didn't seem cruel.

"I'm not satisfied with that," said Donald determined, yet remaining calm and collected. Silence filled the tent once again and the sense of conflict increased urging both men on against the silence. The Corporal and Private moved closer to one another and the disharmony in their thoughts bordered on indignation while respective rank was eschewed.

Harry spoke. " I knew something like this was bound to erupt sometime. You and me have been on a collision course for years, probably always will despite everything else." Both men looked into each other's eyes but because those eyes had seen horrific images over many months they somehow lacked the peacetime animosity.

"No, I'm not on a collision course with you or anybody else. But I'm not leaving my best friend out there."

Harry responded with urgency. "You attempt to go out there and you'll be court-martialled."

"Who by? You Harry?"

Peter rose to his feet stretching himself like some feline thing. "Shut up... shut up... shut up...! What makes you think you will find Michael's body, have you thought of that Donald? There's no markers out there are there? Just a mass of shell holes. Michael could be in any one of them couldn't he?"

Harry was careful to speak from the rank he held. "Besides why should everyone including you," he now viewed Donald through softer eyes, "be put at risk? You can't bring him back alone. I know what it's like out there you can hear a cork pop but you know there are Germans everywhere, machine guns just waiting... just waiting..."

Peter put his hand on his brother's shoulder. "He's right Donald."

Donald suddenly looked very tired as though a great deal of his vigour and impatience was dissipating against his conscious will. He felt flustered and he spoke softly. "It just doesn't seem right, Michael alone there with nothing but darkness and vermin." Instinctively the others built up images in their minds and said nothing for there was nothing more to be said. The images of whiskered gentlemen, hands streaming in full cry, the bear-baiting and coronations would never belong to Michael Jeffries again. All he would ever hear was silence.

Chapter 20

Late at night the military compounds often took on an eerie silence, only horses sneezing or muffled conversation between guards on duty broke the sound of sleep. Inside tents men groaned and snored and movement was the result of involuntary twitching.

Satisfied that his friends were asleep Donald quietly put his boots on, checked his compass under the light of a solitary candle and packed his revolver before standing up and tip-toeing out of the tent. He glanced back before pulling the flap shut, happy that no one had stirred.

He walked in a determined fashion in an eastern direction. He stopped to make small talk with a guard stood alone and looking more fed up than a boy dragged from a playing field to a church service by his parents. There was a restlessness about the two men as though some inward hunger was unappeased and likely to stay that way, nevertheless their conversation was simple.

"Good morning friend what a night, eh?" Donald said.

"What you doing out here?" the sentry asked in a brisk tone.

Donald looked up at the sky taking the sentry's gaze with him. "Word's come that a scout is needed up at the front line. You know the offensive that..." He shrugged his shoulders and tilted his head back in a gesture of exasperation.

The guard chuckled shaking the bored stiffness from his frame. "Bet you'll be pleased to get a ruddy night's sleep one of these days wont you?" He offered Donald a smoke which was accepted and turned his back while striking a match. Both men took a deep pull on their cigarettes.

"Yeah, it would be a welcome change" said Donald laconically. Three minutes passed before the guard stubbed out his nub-end under foot and unlocked the gate enabling the scout to disappear into the night.

Donald ran to warm himself up aware of occasional bombs ricocheting light across the sky in the far distance. Barely audible was the death rattle of machine guns and he was only too aware that a shell sent in the wrong direction might momentarily light him and his position up in a flash; it was a curse all scouts railed against on night time sorties.

His impatience grew. It gathered like blood on a bayonet and his restlessness grew when he saw a couple of stretcher bearers carrying the wounded towards improvised casualty stations. A few military vehicles scattered the landscape and dwarfed tired looking British soldiers lining the trenches in front of them.

Donald afforded himself a smile when he passed one trench with a wooden board nailed to its entrance proclaiming 'The Savoy – Gentlemen Only'. He smiled at the man waiting tentatively who returned his warm gesture; some didn't for all speculated whether this would be their final day. When he climbed down into the trench he was approached by a soldier he noticed had a tinge of yellow in his skin visible despite the dark.

"Hey matey, I want the shortest route to the observation trench... gotta go out tonight." He raised an eyebrow before he continued, "Sarge wants me to bring back some sausages from the other side."

The soldier found his remark amusing and chuckled. "Yeah, carry on through here," he began pointing, "then go left, remember left and follow that for fifty yards. Some of the boys will then direct you. It's not far from there. Good luck."

Donald assimilated the information. "Thank you." He began walking in the direction the soldier had suggested.

Strange, provoking semi-formless figures were scattered around the ground of the tent. All movement was characterised by involuntary jerks as the Fens men slowly arose from their slumbers. Long gone was the moonlight that had shone through a gap at the flap's entrance. Unlike other soldiers the scouts didn't view silence as painful or terrifying; it came easy to them because of the nature of their work. All that worried them on waking first thing was the rheumatic pain caused by dampness and anguished groans were plentiful, similar to those of people deprived of the sun. Nevertheless they felt good. They were alive and still in possession of their faculties. Bertie's eyes were now completely opening and he was blinking; a ritual he carried out each day for the purpose of clearing sleep out of them.

He turned towards Peter. "Morning Peter" and watched the latter sit up.

"Bertie."

Peter pulled his knees up to his chest wrapped his arms around them and held the position while he counted to ten before straightening them out and sitting up. Both men were yawning and stretching their arms when Peter noticed his brother wasn't there. "Where's Donald?" he said with just a scintilla of concern in his voice.

Bertie looked around. "God knows, probably gone for a walk."

Silence walked into their tent broken by Peter. "Christ!" Both realised the implications.

Peter leapt to his feet adjusting his uniform and tightening his braces. "Quick, I'll look around, you wake Harry up." He put on his boots and stepped outside the tent while Bertie jostled Harry's arm.

In No Man's Land a soldier was hanging over rusting barbed wire in grotesque form, it was a pose similar to that in modern art forty years later. The tattered uniform identified him as German. Donald crawled past slowly before looking at his compass and slightly changing direction. He could hear the wind blowing his own body and causing the barbed wire to creak. He looked back at his enemy and could see a photograph of a family held in the dead hand and pondered why the wind hadn't blown it away.

In the tent the Lincolnshire men were standing around the urn drinking hot tea and examining their pistols. There was an air of urgency.

"He could get court-martialled for this" said Harry in a strong voice. He had developed a certain presence and the men respected him for the army had changed him; at times the former braggart was unrecognisable and up to this moment had never pulled rank, something the men were silently surprised by.

Bertie was the first to reply. "Harry we don't know anything yet."

There was a degree of mocking in Harry's reply. "Oh I know." He checked his revolver and looked at the others. "Make sure we get what's necessary. Come on."

They abandoned the tent and began walking in earnest towards the front line trenches, their faces strained. Peter recalled what he'd overheard an officer say about war and whose side was God really on – the English Bishops had come out on the side of the Allies and the German Bishops on their own side. He mumbled to himself "Christianity must be corrupt."

They slowed as the front line trenches came into view.

Peter turned to Harry. "Well?"

Harry understood the nature of the younger brother's provocation but remained professional. "Your brother's ruined it for all of us you know."

In a slightly piqued tone Peter responded. "Are we going out or not?"

The others didn't have to wait for a response because there was no pause. "And all get court-martialled... that's if we get back. The unit could be disbanded for this."

Peter listened head cocked. "If you're worried about losing that rank say so but all the time we stand here it's my brother who is out there," he paused and deliberately pointed to No Man's Land, "alone."

Arthur came to his aid. "Peter's right Harry, I know it's against orders but..."

"But what?" rasped the Corporal tensing his face and pushing his chest out.

Arthur wasn't intimidated. "If it was one of us it wouldn't make no difference – Donald would still go."

Harry grimaced. "Except for me."

Arthur, often referred to as the quiet, one stepped outside his tranquil self, driven by an urgent spirit within him. "You're letting that niggle get at you again. I'll tell you something," he deliberately paused allowing all eyes to rest on Harry, "Donald tried to save an officer some while back. It was the bravest thing I've ever seen – no reason to do it, what would that officer have meant to Donald or any of us? I wouldn't have yet," he paused again before continuing, "he persuaded me. You don't know him Harry, never have. With Donald it's something in him, something he tries to preserve. He'd go back home today if he could."

A sense of helplessness almost bewilderment encased Harry as he struggled to regain his poise while rolling a cigarette. He was aware of the nausea of disagreement and he felt dulled. Nevertheless he struck a match from his pocket book and lit the roll up, inhaling deeply. As he blew the smoke out his lungs he spoke softly, "I don't want the glory but why shouldn't I feel proud that I got a medal for doing my job and to the best of my ability and hopefully saving lives because of the nature of the work." A mellowness seemed to wrap itself around him and the quiet was broken by Peter, "Harry, no one is saying you just want glory. You don't have to prove anything to anyone, least of all here, to us."

Harry sat down on a wooden box that was placed in a row of three, he looked confused as he once again tried to assess the situation. The men sat on the other boxes and while they pondered they heard, then saw, Captain Keaveney running towards them. It was an unusual sight for some officers thought that to be seen running lessened their dignified appearance among enlisted men; it was a peculiar English trait.

"Ah, good there you are," he said struggling to regain his breath followed by a laboured smile. While the men waited the Captain reached into his breast pocket and extracted his cigarette case. A more senior officer might have frowned at this repeated disregard for protocol but war and the stench of death on a daily basis had proved a great leveller for front line troops and their junior officers.

"I've been looking all over for you, you weren't in your tent and I know you weren't due out." His own voice surprised him for it was resonant and had a quality of bonhomie. "I'm lucky to have found you…Anyway, what are you doing out here?"

As the officer's eyes seemed to hold Harry in their gaze he responded. "We thought we'd come to the line, Sir, see if we could meet with any Canadian boys. Their patrols often go out round about now. We just want to compare notes, that sort of thing."

"Quite." The Captain looked about and was aware of Donald's absence. "Where's Private Reid, Corporal?"

All eyes ran to Harry and the men braced themselves.

With glacial calm he answered Keaveney. "Well he was here a few minutes ago," then he paused to look in another direction, "probably gone to have a cup of tea with some of the soldiers."

The Captain continued to turn his cigarette case between his fingers rhythmically. "Well don't let him stray too far. The reason I've come out for you is the Major wants a scout patrol to go pretty quickly and find out what, or if, the Germans have prepared over that," he pointed towards the horizon before continuing, "North easterly ridge. HQ doesn't want any surprises once the offensive begins. All units are sending patrols out for a final recce."

The sky was already promising a bright morning and clear visibility wasn't always the scout's friend.

"You're wanting us to go out Sir?" asked Harry feigning surprise.

The reply was swift. "That's right Corporal Hardy. Your patrol has become one of the most reliable here, I'm proud to say."

"Thank you Sir" said Harry beginning to use subtle expressive gestures knowing they gave life to what he said.

"How soon can you be ready?"

"As soon as you want, Sir."

Keaveney looked up at the sky. "Good. There's probably still a couple of hours before full light and you'll want to be on your way back before then." He knew every mission he sent the men out on was fraught with danger but it warmed him to know they took the same sort of satisfaction a steeplechase rider takes in a brave horse once the race is completed.

There was something wild and driven in the regularity of Donald's advance through 'Hell'. He ignored the exhaustion in his body as he rolled from one shell hole to another in a vain attempt to find Michael's body. Once again he looked at his compass then threw it away in despair.

Harry and boys had quickly assembled what they needed and all allowed themselves a knowing smile when they walked past a short, dome-headed officer with varnished boots looking impervious as he observed them.

"I wonder if he's a parlour maid in civvy street?" quipped Bertie and they chuckled before readying themselves as they approached the final Allies trenches. Two minutes later the Corporal paused and took another reading from his compass before indicating with his hand their direction.

They were unaware that a German patrol, four in all, were crawling about in No Man's Land with their leader indicating with his hand for the men to spread out. They were armed with jagged edged long knives and looked extremely purposeful.

Donald felt thwarted. He was weary and close to giving up as he lay on his back cold and hungry. Years of experience told him that light would soon be descending from the sky but he resolved to give it one last go. He inhaled deeply and began crawling about once more passing bodies in various stages of decomposition but remaining impassive to what was around him. Something drew him towards a shell hole and raised ground; utterly spent he stopped before peering over the ridge. "Michael" he whispered to himself and a soft smile registered on his face before he slithered into the crater.

Less than half a mile away Harry and Peter crawled across the terrain, fatigue sapping at their will. Harry rasped, "Not far now only about another forty or fifty yards by my reckoning."

Peter was blowing hard. "I hope your calculations are right... I'm feeling all in right now."

Harry was forceful in his response. "Don't lose concentration for one second." Though it was whispered it sounded louder than pub conversation. Peter nodded his head. "I know."

Harry craned his neck to look at the others behind him indicating he was going ahead and showing a vigorous thumbs up sign.

Donald had composed himself and sat upright opposite his best friend. Dawn was on the horizon and he knew the sun would accompany it once he had looked at the sky. For a moment he forgot his predicament "We'll feel the warmth soon Michael." He watched a few birds fly fleetingly overhead before continuing "there's no keeping them away no matter what, at first light they come over. I bet they're doing the same at Tunby Hill. Have you thought who has won the boxing match these last two years? Probably some foreigner from over the way. Remember how we used to say whatever happened the champion of the ring would always be a Tunby Hill man? I wonder what Ann makes of all this. I sometimes think what Helen, dear Helen, might be doing now." Donald paused to look at his watch "not quite five. Probably out in the cow sheds with her father. God she's a hardworking girl and a good sport at that. I suppose you are wondering whether we'll get wed... you're not the only one mate. A big step is marriage not a plough you can mend if it breaks, gotta be unbreakable from the beginning. Your father says the world's changing, all the old ways are going but the Empire will live on." He paused and rolled a cigarette effortlessly from the last strands of tobacco he kept in a leather pouch; he cupped his hands before striking a light and inhaled deeply. "The sun will never set on her. Once told me the sun hadn't even dipped behind the trees." With complete disregard for his safety Donald hauled himself to the top of the hold and looked out across the terrain watching the sun inching upwards from the distant horizon. The sight was worth the exposure to danger. "What a sight, Michael." Suddenly the bleakness and cruelty of No Man's Land was bathed by zigzags of warm light; it also shone on the Fens man's vulnerability before he slid down to pick up Michael and carry him out of the shell hole. The sunshine touched his body but he would never again feel its warmth.

Donald's whole frame sagged, even the newly formed pouches under his eyes, as he carried Michael in the traditional fireman's lift thus obscuring any vision over his right shoulder where a German scout, with the bright eyed glance of a fox, methodically took aim with his revolver. He cocked the catch back and the Englishman immediately recognised the sound and when he turned to face his enemy immediately, he started reliving again scenes of working in the fields surrounded by nature's beauty. He was feeling neither brave nor frightened looking up at the German; perhaps it was the right time for him to die with his friend, Michael.

The Hun's index finger moved to the trigger and he wrapped the top of it around. It seemed so melodramatic and in slow motion Donald's gaze went to his enemy's ropey moustache and it occurred to him that this was the image he would ride into eternity on. Five seconds flew by then another five before the German scout lowered his pistol and a white blaze of sympathy ran down his face.

Suddenly a single shot rang out, no cry was heard and the German fell head first into the shell hole. Donald stood stunned. He relaxed his grip on Michael and then Harry, revolver in hand, jumped into the crater looking contemptuously at the fallen enemy quickly followed by Peter whose pistol was still in its holster.

Donald lowered his best friend onto the ground, while Harry smiled in a gloating fashion at the man he'd shot. Peter watched his brother's reaction change colour but before he could intervene Donald landed a thunderous fist into his life-long rival's face. Harry reeled like a drunkard, bloodied and groggy before regaining composure and a determination to gain savage revenge.

Peter screamed "No! Harry can't you see he's..." but he was pushed away by Harry. Donald looked at his brother and his momentary distraction resulted in him taking a punch on the jaw which sent him reeling and drawing rattling breath. Harry Hardy was dressed in the expression of a man who had waited all his life for this moment. As Donald hauled himself up he was met by a boot in the face again thrusting him back into the semi circular wall of the crater. When his nemesis tried it again Donald caught his boot and pulled him off balance before hitting him with an almighty blow that sent Harry into temporary paralysis. However the fight was never going to be one advocated by the company boxing instructor who used patience when showing men how to avoid blows using the left arm extended and the right arm covering the chin and the correct posture.

Peter sat silently against the dead bodies as both men traded blows with terrifying ferocity. It wasn't quite 6.28 a.m. on the morning of July 1st, 1916 a date that had been penned into the diaries of high level ranking officers following Field Marshal Douglas Haig's decision to annihilate the enemy.

Chapter 21

On the 15th June that year the Kaiser had visited Bavaria's Sixth Army Headquarters at Douai where the Chief of Main General Headquarters had puzzled over why the British should attack on the Somme. Lieutenant-General von Falkenhayn had informed his superior that if successful, further fighting would take place in Belgium and Northern France which the Allies wouldn't want through fear of coal mines and iron industries being devastated.

Crown Prince Rupprecht informed the Kaiser that increased volume of railway traffic had been documented by intelligence which showed many artillery emplacements and assembly trenches behind British lines while camps had been built on both sides of the Roye-Montidier railway, south of Field Marshal Haig's back areas. General von Bülow suggested that if the attack on the Somme materialised, the British Forces should be let through into a large pocket and there be encircled by assaults driven into the flanks.

There was feverish speculation in the German High Command that though an offensive was imminent on what day and month would it be realised? The most reliable of German spy networks in The Hague suggested the end of June. This was contradicted by the German military attaché at Madrid who suggested July 1st.

Cat and mouse was an inevitability in all wars and fourteen British divisions waited in line north of the Somme but their guns were silent on the 27th June. There was speculation in German ranks that the British and French might be in disagreement despite for miles up and down the valley of the Ancre the countryside was dotted with little fires burning in the darkness. On the night of 29th June the weather cleared. The following night men rolled into their bivvies and slept their last sleep for they knew. In the morning the sun shone breaking up any congealed clouds in the sky. This was the smaller picture. More dramatic was the bigger one.

Along the front for more than twenty miles from the River Somme in the south to Fonqueisllers in the north fourteen British Infantry Divisions were moving. Shelling was spasmodic and the High Command congratulated themselves with the belief that the preliminary British bombardment had been effective, reducing the Germans retaliation to just so many Howitzer shells. The infamous phrase 'it will be a cake-walk' was born and watches were synchronised while infantrymen concentrated on anything or anyone to fortify themselves again the build up of fears hovering in their minds. Zero hour was 7.30 a.m. and thousands of soldiers would say farewell to life while feeling the slight breeze on their foreheads but the most intensive bombardment in history would start an hour earlier. At 6.29 a.m., the tension was unbearable. Meanwhile in a trench in No Man's Land, a fist fight was reaching new degrees of savagery. "FIRE!"

Chapter 22

Helen Clements had slept heavily that night and she woke startled; the blossom that filled her cheeks as she stretched her arms was missing. She hurriedly got out of bed and reached for her pale blue dressing gown crumpled over a chair. She put it on and hastily walked to the window and drew back the heavy curtains. The light momentarily blinded her and she squinted before slumping into a wooden chair positioned to the right. Helen trembled and in order to steady herself and regain control over her emotions she lifted the chair and herself to face towards the meadow she and her sister had been enchanted with during their childhood years. Momentarily she fondly remembered the lemon drink they took there and talks they had had about what they would do when they became women.

Suddenly a feeling of disaster invaded her psyche and she couldn't dismiss it and fearful it would translate into black depression, she made for her sister's bedroom, gently opened the door and tiptoed in. Elizabeth was asleep, nevertheless Helen climbed into her bed and lay there staring at the ceiling. She began to feel sleepy but her mind would not rest because it was working its way to the edge of frenzy.

Fifteen minutes passed before her sister stirred from her slumber; it was a gradual process. It was not unusual for the sisters to share each other's beds, particularly on wickedly cold winter nights. When Elizabeth became aware of her sister's presence she opened her eyes with a lazy "Good morning".

There was no response so she turned to her sister and noticed she looked weak and grey with tears in her eyes. "Don't say anything, let's get dressed and go outside."

Helen obeyed and within minutes Elizabeth was pulling the latch up on the back door and guiding her sister out with her arm wrapped around her.

The sun was shining, picking up strength the higher it rose in the sky and the only sound was that of a kestrel being pursued by other kestrels above the trees, familiar to both sisters.

"I know something's happened to Donald" said Helen finally getting out the words that had been lodged in her throat since she awoke.

Elizabeth was forthright. "Nonsense, it's your imagination you know. It was the same last month, remember, while we were out walking?"

Helen remained solemn. "No, this time it's real."

Elizabeth spoke stiffly. "How do you know real... all this imagining." She waved her long and intelligent hands; her sudden pleasant smile was in direct contrast to her words. "I don't think I'm going to want to come out here anymore if all you're going to do is to talk about this beastly war."

Helen composed herself as they walked in the direction of the meadow arm in arm. "Yes, I'm sorry Elizabeth... we should be thankful for beautiful days like these... I'm sorry."

Her sister felt a sense of remorse for her earlier words and attempted amelioration. "I know you are worried and all that and I don't mean to be selfish. You see, it's so strange now with so few of the young ones about the farms and villages – life doesn't seem real. This war has affected everyone."

They sat down looking at the blue sky and silence passed between them before Helen spoke in an extremely profound manner which surprised her elder sister. "For the soldiers there is no safety but in the acceptance of danger and for all of us well," she paused, "we can't bargain with life but just accept it and do our best." It was as though Helen's mind was instantly stilled and she stood up offering her hand to Elizabeth. "Come on let's go to the river." They strolled past birds perched on boughs and rabbits playing chase and stopped to allow Helen to take a caterpillar off a bush leaf and let it crawl up her bare arm which induced a squeamish response in Elizabeth.

They sat for fifteen minutes at the waters-edge occasionally throwing the tops of wild flowers they'd pulled up into the flow and watching them sail away gaining momentum as the current got stronger. When the girls' eyes travelled around ninety degrees they saw yellow cornfields and dark clumps of woodland dressing the environment in many colours including numerous shades of green. Everything was tinted with the tenderest English morning that never forgot to smile.

Chapter 23

No one laughed hoarsely despite the promise of a cake-walk. The iron gates of insanity had closed upon the men who were required, in their thousands, to walk through No Man's Land and relieve the dead Hun of their trenches, settlements, compounds especially as the army chaplains had insisted that 'God was on our side, not theirs'.

After nearly two years, Europe was close to moral bankruptcy. Millions had been maimed or killed whilst the rest of the population was suffering hunger and misery in different degrees. Each side still believed in the invincibility of its military strength and the fate of those men dying in Belgium, France, Italy and the Balkans, was dressed up in the phrase 'for the greater good'.

If the British High Command thought the only blood which might be spilled following the maniacal bombardment of German positions would be a rabbit shot by an eager Fusilier wanting something to do, they had been woefully uninformed. Padres had gleefully moved around the trenches in the early hours of July 1st giving communion and absolution to their flock. "Do your best boys" a dead Tommy's diary would later reveal the words of one cleric.

The air was still shaking and the rumbling under foot continued for minutes after the bombardment was silent. The men, many huddled in fear on the duckboards, some crying waited for the shrill blast from an officer's whistle, which, when it happened would signal the screeching noise of enemy machine gun fire once they were exposed in No Man's Land especially if the bombardment had failed to obliterate the Germans.

The offensive was a human disaster and arguably a military success, for the British and French advanced six miles on the Somme, on a front of sixteen miles. The German army was exhausted and the cumulative effects of attrition caused its eventual collapse in 1918, a process many historians would write, which began on the Somme.

The sixty thousand Allied casualties were mainly on the front between the Albert Bapaume Road and Gommecourt where the attack failed disastrously with few soldiers reaching the German front line. These were made up of a mixture of the remains of pre-war regulars, territorial forces and the debut of Kitchener's army composed of Pals battalions. The offensive was notable for the importance of air power and the beginning of tank warfare.

Confidence returned to many of the Shires men as they began, unopposed, their stroll across No Man's Land under a blue sky and a temperature in the seventies, the 1st, 8th and 10th Lincolns toward Fricourt. The Germans having survived the bombardment in deep underground shelters marshalled their forces and returned to the surface and waited.

The deadliest battle of the Great War lasted a further 141 days and threw up horrifying images of bodies littered everywhere, many contorted in grotesque fashion, most completely unrecognisable. Parties of stretcher bearers grossly inadequate in number piled up wounded bodies, three or four, on stretchers and under immense strain carried them back to hastily arranged surgery tents lit by hurricane lamps. Carnage.

Those wounded, with luck on their side, found themselves transported by ambulance to military hospitals behind the British lines where additional makeshift operating theatres were in vogue. Harassed surgeons worked around the clock, with nuns and nurses in attendance, trying to repair mutilated bodies. Words of comfort brought little relief to those soldiers in the death grip of pain and despite their training and professionalism many nurses broke down in tears when they realised many of the wounded didn't want another hour of life. In Lincolnshire the same blue sky and furious heat leaned over the Wolds during the early days of July but the environment below was characterised by emotional darkness. The murmur of sad voices could be heard throughout the county; carried under the smell of concealed despair and wretchedness.

Chapter 24

Bert 'Jim' Jeffries was a man liked, respected and known for his quiet demeanour and he had retreated into the Wolds to be alone. He was weary in body and soul and his eyes gazed through dull quietude; news of his son's death had arrived and his immediate concern had been for his family and how they would cope. It had been a punishing forty-eight hours and now away for the first time since the Despatch Rider had arrived he trembled within a hair's breadth of breaking down. His face was haggard and every sound caused a nervous reaction as he fought for self-control. He thought of Michael and how he had nurtured him in the Shire where children grew up while adults grew old, all under the providence of God's hand – where each season brought change, ripening all around the community which lived in unity and the two absolutes were warblers and willow wrens singing in the fields and woodlands and jackdaws circling above the towers of churches, their cries dropping from above onto lush green ground.

John Reid watched him from some distance; he had gone to the Jeffries' home to offer his condolences and had comforted Mrs Jeffries and her daughter though he had struggled with what to say for they resembled listless ghosts. Fortunately, he knew from conversation down the years where Bert Jeffries liked to go for peace and solitude. "Poor soul" he murmured as he made the decision to go and sit with his neighbour, having stood in the warm breeze and listening to the prattle of a stream singing along nearby.

If Bert Jeffries heard him approach he didn't show it until he stood beside him. John Reid thought his neighbour was showing extraordinary self-discipline as though he was attempting to rescue himself from the drug of bereavement. He sat down and put his right hand on the man's left shoulder which sagged at this show of intimacy. The men sat together for two hours and no words passed between them until John took out his tobacco tin from his Donegal Tweed Jacket and rolled two cigarettes.

A very human cry rifled through the operating room where a table covered in blood was washed down with a bucket of water thrown over it and another body put down. The cry was dead and the exhausted surgeon didn't bother to examine it. Instead he looked at the nurse and shook his head. All the surgeons had learnt how to be dispassionate in order to survive and do their job effectively, in the most trying of circumstances. Stress was a luxury they couldn't afford – it would have to wait for years if necessary. The nurses, too, learnt to put aside the sweet breezes and mockery of sunshine that summer of 1916.

Upstairs in the hospital characterised by its wide staircase and long corridors lay two large casement windows at the end, through which rays of sunlight shot for two hours each day covering the walls and floor. The room immediately to the right was numbered seven. Inside the room two beds almost joined together were partially lit up by a ray of light coming through a broken piece of the window shutter. Two bodies lay in the beds absolutely still and both were heavily bandaged from the waist up including part of the face. The only sound that could be heard was laboured breathing until a nurse entered in serene fashion.

Neither man stirred for they had been sedated. The nurse approached them and smiled with angelic eyes. The soldier whose face was partially bandaged tried to smile back, because the simple gesture had raised his spirits, but pain took over any movement whatsoever. The nurse gently lowered herself onto the edge of the bed frame and took hold of his hand while she read, softly, the name written on the card punched with a hole with string threaded through it and attached to the metal headboard. "Harry Hardy." It took an effort of will for Harry to make a small sign of the cross and pointing to the patient next to him. The nurse stood up without as much as a fidget and walked, silently, around to the other bed. She didn't sit, instead she leaned forward, her hands resting on the horizontal bed frame and kissed the bandaged face on the check. There was no response.

In the corner was a wooden chair and the young nurse, in her early twenties, with no hard features retired to it where she sat for twenty minutes for experience had taught her nature's own ordinance, that a nurse's influence over a badly injured man was often as strong as the most dedicated surgeon.

Her enthusiasm was not of the spluttering order nor did she cover up her sensitiveness unlike some other nurses who'd been instructed during training to 'lock it up in a safe'. Nurse Frances always let the patients see her heart when possible even when she had to appear dispassionate in some circumstances.

The only picture on the wall, inside a cheap wooden frame that did little to promote the colour, was that of a French peasant returning from a hayfield at dusk. "Tired, noble and dignified" she whispered to herself before averting her gaze to the two Tommies. The silence was broken by a small bird pecking at the crack in the shutter. When the nurse stood up, it flew away. She walked over to Harry and taking his hand leaned forward, this time the silver crucifix round her neck swung forward and rested on the white linen pillow as she whispered in his ear "God be with you." She felt his hand squeeze hers before he lapsed again into medicated sleep – that was the term given because unconsciousness was a word with harsh connotations.

The British compound was lacklustre; the virile ardour that the soldiers had strived for before the Somme offensive was gone. Unnerved men now walked about in uniforms made from low morale; even the stuffed jackets stopped looking absurd. Senior officers, previously displaying the qualities of well trained boxers, confident, strong and unafraid of the clock no longer read their newspapers or punched out the crossword with enviable steadiness while talking about cricket. In fact the whole army was struggling to find a punch in its fist after the number of casualties had been totted up and vast swathes of the French countryside was riddled with pickled carcases that had once been men eager to do their duty for King and Country.

Inside a threadbare tent Captain Keaveney sat, despairingly, on a rickety chair that, too, looked about to collapse. Another officer took a swig from a flagon of whisky, while a third pored studiously over hastily laid out maps that covered the table like a crumpled linen cloth. The Somme had challenged all their ambitions and Keaveney spoke with admirable honesty. "God, what a mess, what a pitiful mess." It appeared the impetus of his youth had gone, forever.

His statement, ploughed through with quivering confusion was greeted by surprising optimism from a second Lieutenant. "Steady on old chap, it's not over yet."

Keaveney hadn't really heard him for the idealism that he once relied upon to control the energy in his life was absent and he mused. "The waste, the total carnage and what for?"

The second Lieutenant, possessor of a shiny face and the near angry eyes of a drunk tried for pragmatism. "Everyone knew there was going to be casualties, even the best laid plans can sometimes go... go..."

The other Lieutenant butted in "Go awry!"

"No I wasn't going to say that" snapped the second Lieutenant glancing towards Keaveney who continued to stare at the ground. "But let's be positive about what effect the offensive by its sheer size and volume has had on the Huns." His voice sounded strange, hopeful even, but lacking conviction.

The silence that followed was the silence of sympathy and the three young men appeared motionless before the third Lieutenant spoke, unclogging the atmosphere. "Intelligence wasn't thorough enough. My men just walked into nests of machine gun fire... mowed down with the easiness of a scythe going through wheat."

Captain Keaveney looked up with a new air of defiant resignation. "Well my intelligence patrols did more than could have been asked."

The third lieutenant was quick to respond in an attitude of wise gentleness. "I don't mean the patrols, I mean HQ. They should have had greater aerial reconnaissance knowing that the enemy were dug in thirty feet down. I bet some of them just stayed there through it, with a titter." He suddenly looked strained. "Sixty thousand men, maybe more, lost in a single day. It's... it's just unbelievable." He looked away for he felt that cold understanding military men feel when disaster strikes and he was close to trembling.

Keaveney had felt cold, with the shock of the news for a few days and the image of torn Lincolnshire bodies constantly fed his imagination. "I didn't think I would feel for them the way I do but I can't help it."

The third lieutenant cast a sympathetic eye in Keaveney's direction before asking "Feel for whom?"

Keaveney looked up at his fellow officer. "My scout patrol... wiped out according to initial reports all but two and those two are now lying in hospital – who knows – never to recover."

The second Lieutenant who had been drawing pencil lines over the maps and a circle using a compass finally relit the candle that had gone out following two attempts and joined the conversation. "Yes, damned nuisance" he scraped dry dust off his breast pocket as he spoke. "You'll just have to train another unit."

When Keaveney and the third Lieutenant looked at him with faintly concealed anger they baulked at his cynical response. "For God's sake man, they were commoners after all."

The third Lieutenant walked out the tent in disgust and Keaveney stormed to his feet and walked up to the Lieutenant, barely restraining his anger. "I learnt so much from those countrymen in the short time it was my privilege to command them, something I think you could never understand."

The object of his vexation didn't have the maturity that would have permitted him to half laugh with insight, nevertheless he was aware that Keaveney's ire had emptied like a galloping wind in late autumn so he turned away to busy himself with more map calculations and kept his back to the other man as he spoke. "I believe the French fared better than our chaps. Germany must have thought them incapable of sustaining effort after their losses at Verdun. They seem to have captured some forward defences with their strategy. But it's meaningless as they haven't broken through," he tapped the map with his pipe for effect before lighting it. He still kept his back to the Captain who suddenly realised that within him was the ability to place men with a shrewdness shorn of any sentimental illusion. Never again would the rodent with his back to him make bullying inroads into his psyche. Now he could look with contempt and he did before, unannounced, he walked out of the tent feeling his heart shiver with hardness.

The battle hadn't ended; it threw up images of unrelenting exhaustion as much mental as physical. For the first time British Mark I tanks engaged the enemy but many got bogged down in waterlogged fields some collapsing trenches and crushing men fighting hand to hand in them. The infantrymen ploughed on like frontiersmen in several skirmishes capturing trenches and machine gun posts until the middle of October when the whole landscape, a shell torn battlefield had turned into a vast morass of deep mud. For many to survive they had to hide and imprison a part of themselves while retaining an easy dignity that no one would dare challenge even when war ended.

Chapter 25

Captain Keaveney had made an appointment to go and see his men in the hospital. The evening before he had sat, alone, in the officers' tent possessed by doubt and winced at what he knew he would see. Despite wearing his coat he shivered and his body was taut as he sipped hot, sugary tea – how he longed to be home, sat by the open fire, smoking and with his faithful collie 'Sea Nose' at his feet. During the course of the war he had written letters home and those to his parents had been matter of fact but to his sister they had been intimate and revealed his feelings while staying just inside the censors remit.

The following day he shaved meticulously, cleaned his boots and took longer than usual to dress. The quietness of journeying in a military vehicle to the hospital seemed strange to him. He looked in need of a good night's sleep but knew he had to give his best in the hospital ward.

When the car pulled up at the hospital entrance Captain Keaveney hesitated before assembling himself, instinctively straightening his cap and getting out of the rear seat. He instructed the driver to park by the adjacent wall pock marked by shelling and to stretch his legs, all done in a crisp friendly voice. Coming out of the entrance were two senior officers and he saluted them as vigorously as he could. It was returned but the two men looked pale, in need of whisky to avoid the increasing loneliness of life in this milieu where death might be seen to be a fit companion.

The Captain, carrying his briefcase as though it was a part of his uniform, inhaled and walked up the steps and into the long hallway. The monumental silence was deafening as he took the first flight of stairs. At the top he was met by a serene looking nun with a gentle smile and a gentler handshake.

"Excuse me sister, I've come to see two of my men. They are in room seven, have you visited them?" Both walked and aware that his heels were clipping the marble floors Keaveney resorted to walking on the front of his feet.

The nun smiled graciously before speaking. "Yes, every day. There is progress but it is slight. It will take a long, long time for the one to recover. Fortunately both are young and strong but one cannot tell whether they have the will anymore. They must have seen things that God did not intend them to see."

A sudden blast of wind rattled the tall windows and though it was seasonable the Captain resented its ugly interference but was incapable of combating it. The nun discerning his unease smiled. It was enough.

They walked in silence before the Captain spoke again. "I appreciate everything you and your sisters are doing. I don't expect you to understand about war." He was about to continue but she looked almost through him and he was lost for words.

"Come," she said taking his hand. "I will walk you to the room."

Through sad eyes he said "Thank you."

Outside the room the nun patted his arm and left. Captain Keaveney leaned his right ear against the door hoping he might hear something but nothing came back at him and he hesitated. He was in two minds whether to put his cap back on but decided against it before knocking gently on the door and walking in being as quiet as possible.

He noticed immediately how sparsely furnished the room was and the manner with which a single shaft of light coming through the cracked shutter offered hope of some kind. As he tiptoed towards Corporal Hardy's bed the wounded soldier stirred and half recognising the Captain attempted to move.

"Please Corporal," Keaveney whispered hoarsely, "Stay as you are."

Harry was struggling for words so Keaveney leaned forward.

"Sir."

The Captain quietly lifted the wooden chair in the corner and conscious not to disturb the other man gently placed it down beside Harry's bed. Momentarily the officer's gaze was transfixed by the crucifix nailed to the wall above the beds.

The conversation was in hushed tones. "Corporal Hardy I want to thank you and Private Reid."

Harry slowly tilted his head in Donald's direction which caught his Captain off guard. "You didn't know it was him?" Both looked at Donald who was propped up almost in a sitting position so as to prevent any blood running into his injured lung, before Harry asked "No Sir, but which one?"

Keaveney swallowed hard. "Donald – I wish I could tell you some good news but I can't." He watched as his Corporal writhed in pain before regaining his composure.

"What happened to the others?" The increasing glare of ordered confusion struck Keaveney for he said nothing until he felt a weak hand touch his. "I think everything had better wait until you've recovered." Again he felt the injured soldier's hand press his.

"Sir."

Keaveney looked at the warrior, heavily bandaged and prostrate in front of him yet still retaining that dignity and integrity he had come to admire so much and he felt tears saturate his eyes before they rolled away.

"Your brothers are all right. Peter Reid is dead. Bertie is missing presumed dead and Alfred is lying in a French hospital with both his legs amputated. Besides yourself and Donald the other man is Bert Jeffries also wounded." The words fell out his mouth with tumbling speed as if seeking in his voice a reflexion of the truth. Again he looked at the crucifix aware of the sounds of war somewhere in the distance. He remained still on the side of the bed listening to occasional laboured breathing wondering if the ghosts of the Somme would torment him till the end of his days. It was a bleak prospect, one he was almost resigned to and yet was able to master a scintilla of pride in the knowledge that his scouting patrol had always performed their duties bravely in wretched circumstances.

Before he left he took hold of Harry's hand and leaned forward whispering in his ear. "Harry look after him," before glancing towards Donald Reid. Harry said nothing, instead he nodded his head forward, slowly.

Captain Keaveney closed the door gently behind him and walked along the corridor; he appeared distressed but was neither flushed nor pale. Further along two other officers emerged from a room and one shook his head mournfully and neither took much notice as the other officer walked behind them. They were talking about a Sherwood Forester named Roy Dawson, a dedicated Sergeant, killed on his birthday the first day of the Somme. They said he had planned to start a building business after the war and move east into Lincolnshire; one of them commented, "the poor woman – a fiancée, a wife, a mother and now a widow all in less than a year." And, Captain Keaveney thought, how many other men never got to see their first born. The other officers then turned their conversation to the vicious fighting at Baupaume before Captain Keaveney walked down the steps and in the opposite direction. His driver opened the door of the staff car but no words were spoken on the journey back to camp for he was deep in thought as though he knew that if he was to marvel ever again at the scent of a flower, the shape of a tree and a white crocus in bloom he may have to be reborn.

When news filtered back to England about the disastrous casualties the whole country fell silent. The only conversation in Tunby Hill was that in hushed whispers with much wringing of hands, even in the Red Lion Inn. Clergymen through England gave up their vocation with no explanation to their Holy Order.

John Reid found solace of a kind sitting for hours under the apple tree in his garden once his work was over. He stared at the long rows of white-blossomed peas, wide cauliflowers and other vegetables easy of cultivation. He never let go of the image of his two sons as two young boys wrapped in his arms and the three of them counting the fruit on the celebrated Gooseberry bushes and wall fruit which their parents had boasted about. He recalled telling the boys that the best garden always remained half wild. He had often told them "fruits, flowers and vegetables live in comfortable equality and fraternity... let the natural profusion develop". The boys had grinned at each other for they often heard it but never understood the meaning of the words for years. Then their mother would appear with jugs of cold water into which she had crushed lemons and would regale 'the men' with "the old fashioned garden is the best... full of Sweet Williams and White Nancies, Larkspur and London Pride". She had always saved her favourites for last and even her husband had to interrupt her when she waxed lyrical about "evening primroses and hollyhocks reaching to the sky from yellow to purple".

This, then was where John Reid mourned his loss. Every inch of his garden provided memories of his boys and of his wife when she saw them together sat against the trunk her whole face would change – a brightness would suddenly appear like a meadow suddenly engulfed in sunshine. This would never happen again. Now it was the turn of Bert Jeffries to offer some form of comfort and he did his best even though his second son, Bert, had been injured during the offensive.

The two men sat together in an attitude of moods. Their conversation was full of reminiscences of their early days "the quiet days of poverty" when their whole world was bounded by work and their garden offered the perfect antidote. They talked often in croaked whispers of August nights when they were young marrieds who walked up and down their respective garden paths by star-light and because it was hot they were inclined to stay out half the night especially Fridays because the sweetness and haze seemingly melting the stars was something to be felt rather than seen.

Bert had carried two bottles of stout in each pocket of his jacket and he snapped them open offering one to his neighbour. They drank and paused and Bert allowed John to monopolise any conversation even though his voice sank when he spoke of his father and wondered if that austere figure had felt anything remotely similar to what he had felt when his sons were born following the build up and the hours spent on the garden bench just thinking about it; how he and Carrie his wife, would bring them up and the blessing they had been given.

He paused before looking at Bert. "Peter and Donald more than likely will never have that."

Minutes later his neighbour caught the dim outline of John Reid's face, half uplifted, looking towards the sky wondering if God really thought one human life was more precious than those myriad worlds he now gazed at. Bert put his hand on his friend's arm and neither spoke anymore because a friendly understanding between men who have lost a son in the same war was religion enough. Carrie Reid had wept buckets in private but remained stoic in public, unlike her husband she sought solace in the Reverend Mitchell whose own faith had been sorely tested but he knew he couldn't coach feelings nor was it his business to attempt to. Never in his life had he felt as rigid, as he had for the past two years, presiding over wounds and misfortune; he often shrank and an effort of will to keep going had taken its toll on him as he moved among the parishes that had given so much to the war effort.

The Reid's cottage now resembled a home without atmosphere, spiritually empty and full of shadows; the occupants were pale imitations of their former selves and understandably so. Flora, Donald's nine year old sister became the centre of attention in elementary school once the news of Peter's death had become common knowledge. The corridor of scurrying feet was dark which matched the young girl's mood day after day. The two school mistresses were as far apart as two characters could possibly be. The oldest had that strain of spinsterish chastity, occasionally volcanic, that terrified the children and openly announced that death in war was patriotic, even noble... It was the other teacher with friendliness of age despite youthful mannerism that Flora turned to and was greeted with warmth and compassion. Any slight reassurance she felt during the day evaporated when she lay motionless in her bed at night talking to her teddy bear as though it was her dead brother before crying herself to sleep. Often her mother would be listening outside the bedroom door before going in to sit with her daughter, holding back her own sorrow, just.

Chapter 26

A month passed and only one of the men in room seven sensed his strength returning. It was a triumph for the medical staff when Corporal Harry Hardy was able to walk again, albeit shakily on his own. Donald Reid continued to lie still, often semi-conscious. Though morphine dulled the pain the phosphorus burns were ever present and when the bandages were changed the stench was unbearable. He was almost blind and a bullet had torn away part of his lung which left it susceptible to infection despite constant treatment. His legs were shattered and Harry felt deep pangs of regret and guilt every time he looked at his fellow villager. It was a relief when the medical staff told the Corporal he was well enough to be transferred to another hospital closer to the front line and that a Ford ambulance would take him in four days time. He bitterly regretted that because of the injuries sustained no conversation had passed between him and Donald since the stretcher bearers had carried them, following surgery, into "that quiet room at the end of the upstairs corridor".

He insisted on not being helped downstairs and out into the mild autumn sun. He was aware that the deceased were laid in rows behind the hospital building and out of sight of visitors and new arrivals.

In a quiet compound shielded by bushes two nurses watched over dozens of men whose spirit had been completely broken yet their bodies remained intact. They resembled corpses with fidgety movement and they elicited sympathy from those soldiers with visible wounds even those in severe pain who knew that eventually they would be returned to hell or as they jokily referred to the front – 'hors de combat'.

When a fleet of ambulances arrived the wounded watched the stretchers being unloaded and placed on the ground. The gabble of conversation died down and they smoked watching a padre move amongst the new arrivals anointing the foreheads of those about to have the blanket pulled over their faces. One soldier concentrated their minds as he refused to be anointed and continuously shook his fist at the stretcher bearers, groaning as the effects of morphine were wearing off – it was obvious both his legs had been blown off below the knee and despite heavy bandaging blood saturated the bottom half of the stretcher. It was a relief to all when the padre acted as a stretcher bearer and the injured man was carried straight into the operating theatre.

The wounded, Harry included, spontaneously cheered but it was just audible. More ambulances arrived and stretchers were unloaded; bandages were of the colour red not white and the observers were grateful that life still possessed them and their own cries of unbearable pain belonged to yesterday for today it was just pain, though many talked through voices twisted with despair while flies searched for blood seeping through bandages. Harry counted five on his lower right leg which still had shell splinters.

On the penultimate day before his departure he was given a rigorous examination. The doctor told him that he would have fresh dressings but remarked that his burns were still oxidising and that he was going to soak them again in a solution of sodium bicarbonate and then apply it as a powder to stop the burns fizzing. An hour later and Harry was stretchered outside knowing that more phosphorus had been cleaned out. He was grateful for a mug of warm sugary tea and a roll up given by a Scottish Sergeant who had once been six foot three before having both legs amputated. There was absolutely no trace of self pity as he joked about how he was going to get up the Royal Mile the next New Year's Eve, he would spend in his native Edinburgh. "Strange isn't it that this hospital not only treats German wounded but has German orderlies supplementing the work of our own medical staff."

Harry could see he was in pain but admired his cheeriness, though that changed when both wounded men realised the Scotsman had messed himself and he looked thoroughly ashamed. Fortunately two orderlies were nearby and noticing his discreet gestures they wheeled him back inside.

Harry stayed outside and enjoyed another enamel mug of tea, this time containing more condensed milk which stirred his memories of pre-war Lincolnshire and peaceful workdays under a peaceful sun. His gaze held the sky and he realised he had changed and the irony was the savagery that had changed him; he had hated losing, could not play a losing game and the fierce self-regard he thought singled him out to be a man of some standing, substance devoid of humour which he associated with the easily bullied. His horizon had completely changed for sat as he'd been done for many days among injured soldiers far worse than himself he warmed to the river of human laughter that often brought tears and joy in equal measure and he realised that though the seasons came and went everything a man loved went on.

His departure was scheduled for 8 o'clock, after breakfast, and he paused at the door looking at Donald Reid before whispering "Get well". He looked for any sign of a response but there was none.

Downstairs he congregated with other soldiers waiting to be transported. Some appeared blissfully happy that they had survived surgery despite a loss of limb while others still had to be carried by stretcher. All tried to ignore the nervous apprehension that knitted them together and drank hot tea often licking their lips, theatrically.

Three stretchers were loaded in first followed by six infantrymen including Harry who occupied hastily arranged sitting spaces. The journey took roughly two hours and the men on stretchers despite having shots of morphine groaned every time the rear axle thudded against uneven roads and pot holes which were a feature of countryside tracks. The ambulance finally pulled into a courtyard and two stretcher bearers unloaded the injured and took them indoors where surgeons waited to assess whether or not they should return to England. Those in the courtyard who knew they were going home were full of 'Saturday night atmosphere' despite being in constant pain. Those who weren't going home were much quieter.

Harry was returned to a dormitory after his dressings had been changed; within hours he knew he was one of the more fortunate ones if only because he retained his mental faculties. It was dispiriting watching grown men trembling and huddling into balls under their beds when the sound of fifteen inch guns could be heard in the distance. Also distressing was the sight of regulars now emotionally emaciated staring through wild eyes and tearing at their dressings before being restrained by orderlies and heavily sedated. Whimpering cries greeted each new day and Harry caught up on sleep in the rest room during the day where two officers, in dressing gowns, whispered statistics to each other about the toll in France and the non-stop conveyor belt that began with the aid posts of battalion areas through dressing stations of brigade and casualty clearing stations of corps areas. They even spoken of base hospitals being cleared to take the wounded from battlefields being transported by barges on canals. It was the figure of half a million wounded that astonished Harry as he feigned sleep, less the officers who occasionally glanced in his direction turned their conversation to society life or sport or having a cold bird for breakfast as though the Great War was little more than an interlude in their calendar, an abrupt nuisance which would eventually be over and the old order could be restored.

Harry smiled to himself when he wondered if it was the officers who had strayed inadvertently to this elegant room, which smelt of wax polish, or whether it was him, a yokel! His most pleasant dream remained that of a cock pheasant flying across the Wolds with tails rippling before landing and disappearing into a rhododendron bush in full flush. He vowed that if he made it home he would plant a row of these bushes having torn out the roots of those that grew wild in a copse barely a quarter of a mile away from the family cottage. Of course, he also had other dreams...

Chapter 27

Corporal Harry Hardy went through another period of convalescence and declined the suggestion that he might go home for he told anyone who listened that he wouldn't set foot in England until the war was over and the Germans defeated. Many comrades thought he was mad but a few understood. Could a man, any man in England, having listened to cuckoos sitting in the woods or watching birds skimming the top of trees beyond a meadow or a moon still shining upon leafless trees or feel the grass frosted between night and dawn return with conviction to the insanity of war no matter how just that conviction had once been?

When it was time to go he had gone, the paperwork completed. He was part of a convoy returning to respective regiments along the Front. From the rear of the lorry where he sat, smoking, he could see hundreds of bell tents covering vast acreages including valleys and thousands of soldiers treading down the ground that might once have been arable or pasture. The convoy went within fifty yards of an open latrine which had thousands of blow flies busying themselves and the stench was unbearable despite buckets of chloride of lime having been poured over it.

Soldiers were dropped off at various points and eventually only four Sherwood Foresters and three Lincolns were left. When they alighted they dispersed and a rugged looking Sergeant whom Harry thought had a familiar gait walked him to his compound, "Welcome back Corporal Hardy." Those words lifted his spirits and he vigorously shook the hand of Captain Keaveney who seemed delighted to have him back and walked with him to a communal tent where hot tea and biscuits appeared to be served all day and surprisingly all ranks were permitted to go in once an officer had given the OK.

"Democracy in the British Army... I don't believe it" muttered Harry. Both men drank their tea from enamel mugs while half listening in on the conversation of senior officers who spoke about Operation orders and code names for battalions on either flanks and the armoury to be carried by N.C.O.'s and privates and the number of officers permitted to go into action.

The officers didn't pause, merely smoked their pipes and abandoned discretion. Keaveney felt somewhat embarrassed listening to their Objectives and the Formation of Battalions in battle, the time frame and advance facilitated by the building of makeshift bridges over trenches.

Sensing the Captain's unease Harry Hardy quipped "Just as well we're not Huns in disguise." It lightened the expression on the no longer youthful looking Captain's face.

"I'll say Corporal."

Before the conversation turned to Operation and Amendment Orders they departed relieved to be back outside. The Captain puffed his cheeks out and was oblivious to his senior scout's smile; he didn't know that this idiosyncrasy had been adopted by the men in the Captain's presence even though he remained blissfully unaware. It was noticeable that neither spoke about Donald Reid as they walked to a tent where the scouts were gathered having been instructed to do so by Keaveney.

Corporal Hardy felt a tinge of nervousness as he entered the tent because the patrol would be composed of new faces who might resent him despite the presence of his brother – Arthur – whom he hoped had up to date news about Sid. Captain Keaveney could only relay that he knew Sid had shrapnel wounds that weren't life threatening though it would be some time before he returned to the Front. Fortunately the first face that looked up was Bert Jeffries "Harry, at last!" He jumped to his feet and both men shared a warm handshake. It had the desired effect. All the scouts rose and came over to introduce themselves. They looked so young and Harry was bowled over by their enthusiasm and it occurred to him that maybe Bert Jeffries, hiding as best he could the anguish of losing his brother, had garnished the stories about the Lincoln Pals exploits behind enemy lines and the way they considered No Man's Land as 'their manor'. Their Captain was genuinely moved by the men's response and it wasn't lost on Harry that these youthful figures in front of him weren't possessed solely of "skull crunching aggression and nothing else".

Soon everyone was sat down drinking tea and from his pocket Captain Keaveney took out a hip flask and discreetly poured rum into each man's mug before replacing it back in his pocket. Everyone chinked enamel mugs and the Captain instructed them to rest for the next twenty-four hours because he would be back with detailed maps for they were going out the following evening. He made no pretence about the danger and suggested that the Germans were fighting for their very existence and it would be savage, more so than before, until the enemy capitulated. Not one of the men dared to even think war's end was in sight, because it was considered a bad omen as was looting from dead enemy soldiers, still considered a death wish.

When they were alone Bert and Harry talked intimately about those no longer alive and those injured and though he tried to obliterate the idea from his mind Bert wondered if Harry might eschew caution when they ventured out because the question why did he survive might nag him particularly during sleep. It certainly hadn't eaten at Bert but then for much of his young life he had been a quiet cavalier, though the death of his own brother had left questions of mortality in his own mind which he was quick to dispel.

What had characterised the Fens Pals before going out at night in operational duty was that they all had a secret corner in their lives which no friend could penetrate and yet collectively the only one outside their circle which they also allowed to stand on the threshold and listen was Captain Keaveney. Often his silence was the silence of sympathy because he feared he might be sending his men to certain death despite the number of missions completed and it was a burden he struggled to carry despite retaining the outside appearance of an officer wearing a starch collar and polished boots.

As morning turned into afternoon the mist thickened, clouds dropped and rain scattered everywhere but didn't dull the noise of battle or stock bombs going off miles away. Occasionally the distinctive buzz of a Howitzer shell had the British soldiers instinctively dropping their heads into protective shoulders even though they were well out of range.

Harry and his brother Arthur waited until the patrol group had dispersed before they greeted each other; neither had wanted a showy embrace which might have surprised the new arrivals. The flashes of guns seemed to intensify as they walked to where the horses were corralled rather than look out at vast open spaces where a world of lost and dying soldiers, many tangled in wire, could be seen through powerful binoculars. Harry instinctively patted the top of an emaciated horse's hind leg which elicited a slow movement in the animal's head and then they sat on the second wooden barrier wrapping their arms and hands round the top one for support.

Arthur thought his brother looked empty and weary. "Are you sure you're ready to be back?"

Harry dismissed the question with a smile. "Sure, besides when exactly is the right time to return?" He followed up before Arthur could respond. "The war goes on, never pausing, day or night."

Arthur asked him about Donald Reid. "We hear he's in a bad way?"

Harry didn't elaborate because he didn't have medical knowledge but he looked his brother in the eye. "That man has bravery I didn't think he had." He said it in such a thoughtful manner that his brother realised that past animosities had been buried forever.

"Captain Keaveney told us that Alfred has lost his legs." The Corporal said while watching the horses shuffling into a more comfortable position.

"We heard that too but it wasn't confirmed until we got a message from one of the nurses who'd been transferred from the hospital he was in to another near here. She made a point of finding us and said Alf had asked her to when she informed him of her pending departure."

Harry interrupted. "What else did she say?"

"That Alf was in good spirits, knew the operation had saved his life… he always had guts."

A minute's worth of distress enveloped Harry Hardy before he spoke. "His mother's a widow, Alfred is her only son."

They would have spoken longer but one of the new scouts, whose eyes had an extraordinary gentleness, a softened finesse that usually came after having witnessed suffering, strolled over to their position. He offered them a roll up each from his tobacco tin, which both Fens men noticed, had ten snouts neatly packed in a row. They accepted graciously and both were surprised when their fellow scout lit all three, "Look if you two want to talk... 'cos you haven't seen each other..."

Before he continued Harry put him at ease. "No, stay it's nice for us scouts to talk away from the turmoil of our life after dark." He smiled and the other man relaxed. Arthur felt nothing but admiration for his brother as there was no bitterness in Harry's voice as he regaled the recruit with secrets of the Lincolnshire Wolds, "Spring that's the month – the silver gold buds of the Pear trees in our garden." Arthur's face lit up and he wanted his brother to continue which he did after a long draw on his cigarette. "And if we are lucky, fruit. The other trees look great." And noting the quizzical look on the scout's face he elaborated "Chestnuts with a green tint and then there are Elm boughs purple against a blue sky... come on brother tell him about the others."

Arthur continued as if the pause had been joined up. "Beeches bronze sometimes gold and the Oaks well still dark." Both brothers laughed and the other man joined in before taking his leave and leaving any apprehension behind on the fencing.

That afternoon the unit ate together before retiring to their tent and on the Corporal's insistence examining, ruthlessly, all the equipment. No scout patrol ever needed a second reminder because something faulty... As a precaution each man examined another's after the owner was satisfied.

Harry insisted that they get some rest; he declined to say sleep for obvious reasons. Four hours passed very slowly and it was a relief for the men to hear the Corporal's voice "OK let's start getting ready." The tension was broken by one of the new scouts soaping his jaw with a soft bristled shaving brush. When the others looked at him quizzically he nonchalantly said "Want to look myself don't I?" Whether it was the soft Devonian burr or the ludicrousness of his actions or both it reduced the men to ribald laughter; and even Harry couldn't restrain himself.

Captain Keaveney could hear the laughter as he approached their tent armed with blueprints and maps. There was a pinched look to his mouth and knew he would have to talk in a precise tone and with careful deliberation because he knew this sortie was potentially more dangerous, if that was possible, than previous forays behind enemy lines. He entered the tent and the light from the lamp hanging against the central pole lit his face, highlighting his expression of concern. He threw a meaningful glance at his Corporal who shrugged his shoulders and continued laughing while pointing at the Devonian. Suddenly the Captain's posture seemed casual and he relaxed, then smiled for he knew his men were a group apart, not tamed and unsafe because of that unique atmosphere of readiness akin to a tightly wound spring but because they remained the ultimate professionals, and it was often a paradox, hard to reconcile. When Corporal and Captain moved to the small table at the far end of the tent the gears shifted in the men's heads and the wet foam was wiped away as everyone now congregated.

Captain Keaveney turned his back on the maps and addressed the scout patrol "Senior command are puzzled as to the Hun's intentions and quite surprisingly they crave information." He looked about for a reaction.

"Go on Sir" Harry said as though it was a command.

"I attended a conference at HQ and the CO took me into his confidence… I'll spell it out short and simple – they are anxious to get a prisoner."

The assembled pals nodded because they had accomplished this once before but knew only too well how fraught with danger the operation was and how lady luck had shone on them that night. The new recruits waited for the officer to continue. He did but with a greater air of seriousness. "A few stealth raids have been attempted but none have been successful."

The conversation slowly revealed that the men would not be going that night but the raid would be carried out "during our tour of the line". This was a welcome announcement and was also the signal to brew-up and the Captain accepted the invitation to stay awhile. A hubbub of smoke filled the tent as the three newcomers Bill (the Devonian), Wilf (a Bristolian) and 'Ginger' from Southampton were asked to relate their war to date and what they thought about being seconded to the Fens Pals. It was a mutual relief to everyone that no one was disgruntled with the situation and as each man spoke openly it occurred to both Captain and Corporal that these men had, too, seen horror at close range and would be able to be relied on.

The following afternoon Harry was summoned to the officers' quarters by Captain Keaveney. His instructions were clear "Find out where the German outposts are on our Front and also the condition of their defences. After that we can plan our assault."

The military men pored over the latest maps which had tiny handwriting in pencil on them, barely legible. Harry was invited to give his opinion based on previous experience. Keaveney waited expectantly with a glow of pride as the Corporal pointed out the German habit of communication trenches and those which more than likely would be manned. The officers were impressed for they knew this volunteer soldier, having spent months recovering from injuries, had declined the chance to return to England for further recuperation, "I think gentlemen we will find someone here." He prodded the exact location with his forefinger.

Without hesitation the CO stated "OK Corporal thank you. Gentlemen we will go there." He said it in such a manner that no one would offer dissent. In fact a couple of the officers congratulated Corporal Hardy though it remained unlikely they would ever invite him into their mess.

"They were impressed Corporal," said Captain Keaveney as both men left Headquarters and climbed into a military vehicle. The journey through a seamed landscape was a time for reflection as rotten carcasses both human and animal were never far from sight. It was a relief to set foot back in the compound and both men strolled lazily back to the Pals tent.

Tea was brewed up immediately and out came the smokes and the maps.

"Business as usual" said Arthur Hardy with a grin. It was what the scout patrol were itching for even though they knew in this particular part of the offensive line the Germans supplied all the artificial light for No Man's Land. The plan was to go out on the left flank almost in the corner. Captain Keaveney instructed the men to rest up and they would meet with him at 11 p.m. precisely at the front line trench.

When the scout patrol arrived Captain Keaveney, wearing an extremely large overcoat, instructed them that all the sentries had been warned that a group was going out.

"Any activity Sir?" asked Corporal Hardy gazing out into the still views, from a hand held periscope.

"Yes, those bastards keep sweeping the area with machine gun bursts... no regularity to it, just haphazard."

The patrol took off their steel helmets and pulled on woollen balaclavas. Harry waited for another burst of machine gun fire then he climbed out of the trench, over the wire and dropped into an empty trench the other side. Five silhouettes followed leaving Captain Keaveney on the safe side; he clenched his fists hoping it would relieve the tension but he couldn't relax his clenched jaw. No matter how many times these sorties occurred he remained tighter than a drum until the patrol returned. A rugged looking Sergeant, someone who made the term 'bold as brass' seem strangely inadequate, approached the officer and speaking in an unmistakeably Nottinghamshire accent said "Brave men, those bastards Sir." Keaveney who remained looking through the periscope muttered "Yes."

Harry instructed Bill and Ginger to keep a special lookout, whispering that he didn't want to be cut off by an enemy patrol getting in behind them. He released his revolver from its holster and careful not to disturb anything underfoot moved along the trench. Visibility was down to yards which increased the anxiety that he always kept under control less it affected the men with him. Tiptoeing in single file the patrol covered a couple of hundred yards but stopped dead. Voices could be heard a short distance ahead, then they were silent.

"Have they seen us?" Harry whispered to himself taking a bomb from his pocket and making sure the others did the same. He knew he would be exposed getting into a position to throw it and as he did the German ran. Suddenly explosions wrecked the night's silence and inevitably machine gun fire strafed the air. The scout patrol ran hell for leather back through the maze of trenches before scrambling back into their own where a pale faced Captain Keaveney stood. Breathing heavily Corporal Hardy gasped "Well we know the location of one of their posts!" They returned to their tent and slept like babies making sure the 'Do Not Disturb' sign had been roped to the flaps covering the entrance.

Breakfast, mid-morning, was a great treat – a fry up and the obligatory hot sugary tea. All the men slapped their lips in appreciation and all raised their heads in slow enquiry before bidding a hearty good morning to Keaveney who was smiling and passing on HQ's congratulations for a job well done. He left as soon as he had arrived. Harry was pleased with the latest arrivals and knew he could rely on them not to panic in the face of sudden danger. It was obvious Bill, having been reared in the Devonian tradition, had learnt from childhood to adapt himself to circumstances and protect himself. He was lightly built but not a man to be trifled with whereas Ginger, more introvert but none the less combative, seemed to have pin points of reflection in his eyes whenever he sat by a candle flame. Both men knew the true meaning of integrity and loyalty only too well, from previous exploits and fate's fickle hand.

When the Captain stubbed out his cigarette and left their company Arthur got out the 'boys magazines'. The near nude ladies with their combination of mascara, eye shadow and vivid lipstick seemed too much of a good thing. More heartening was the rest of the day off! Harry laughed and walked slowly to the entrance flap which occasionally was moved by a south westerly breeze. He paused and looked back at the men while leaning against the canvas, lounging easily with the strange patience of a man who is paid for his time rather than his work.

Outside he strolled to the compound containing the horses, he liked to be in their company because he could sit in the sun of a reminiscent maturity and admired the way they were cared for despite many looking emaciated. He had never forgotten his own father telling him when he was a boy "If you look long enough into a horse's big brown eyes you will see a whole lifetime." He hadn't understood what his father had said then but he did now.

The following morning Captain and Corporal decided on a daylight patrol along a communication trench. Though Harry wanted his brother, Captain Keaveney vetoed it. A coin was tossed. Ginger would accompany him.

The three of them sat in a makeshift stores hut with a map spread over their knees and each spoke. Ginger stated the obvious but it didn't seem facile "How do we avoid being seen by glasses and telescopes constantly searching for any sign of movement?" He had an idea and it was to attach a length of string from the right boot of the man in front to the right wrist of the second man and move in as straight a line as possible with the second man never having to raise his body over an inch from the ground. "Only I will raise my eyes, Sir, as the front man."

The Captain thought for a brief second that Harry might think he was playing second fiddle but was pleased with his Corporal's reaction "Very sensible Ginger."

Mid-morning the operation had begun and two exhausted scouts finally reached the other side of the wire block. They paused to rest and Harry released his revolver while Ginger took a bomb out of the pocket sewn into the back of his coat.

"This is the dangerous part" Harry muttered to himself as he took over the lead because the zigzag nature of the trench lines meant the enemy could suddenly come into view – mayhem like being suddenly caught in a thunderstorm arriving without warning. The men paused because the barbed wire was new and strewn deliberately so as to catch clothing on its angry looking points. They manoeuvred delicately over this but ahead was impassable well-constructed wire blocks and behind it sandbags propped up on top of each other.

"No way through Ginger" whispered Harry. Before Ginger could come up with a suggestion a German soldier suddenly appeared head and shoulders above the sandbags. The surprise dulled his reflexes but not Ginger who clicked the release lever on his bomb and threw it with alarming accuracy.

The explosion heralded shrieks of pains and the Pals scampered back to their own trenches. Captain Keaveney was ecstatic with his men and after sugary tea and a smoke he informed Corporal Hardy that he would accompany him to the headquarters of the battalion that would be joining with them in an assault so that preliminary details could be ironed out. Harry even found time for a joke "They're not going to make me an officer are they Sir?" His Captain laughed louder than he'd ever heard him laugh, in fact it was the only time since the visit to himself and Donald Reid in hospital.

Both left in a military truck and arrived late afternoon as the sun was going down behind the battlefields. Everywhere was pocked with shell holes and quiet, weary soldiers in greatcoats shuffling along congested roads; the wounded lay in rows, huddled together for warmth though many were dying by the hour. Captain and Corporal made no remark and finally as the last light from the dead sun fell on the low wall to the rear of the building they climbed the stone steps, every one of them cracked and now crumbling.

The most senior officer whose personality dominated the room in a pleasant way welcomed everyone and any rivalry among junior officers, their self regarding egoisms, had long gone courtesy of a war now in its fourth year and nowhere near the end despite military propaganda from both sides. Captain Keaveney and Corporal Hardy listened attentively with the former making notes on a pocket pad with a small HB2 pencil. It was arranged to have an extensive reconnaissance by joint patrols on a five hundred yard frontage – a frontal attack on a weak area of trenches with smaller parties working up old communication trenches.

"This is a step up Sir" said the Lincolnshire man to his Captain.

"Yes it is" said Keaveney in an unemotional voice for it was more than serious – large parties for the attack were to be assembled in No Man's Land and the main function of the patrol was to select assembly positions.

At midnight the operation unfolded; the scouting parties moved about undisturbed. Harry's men found themselves adjacent to a railway track which ran across No Man's Land at right angles to the British lines. Aerial reconnaissance had suggested the enemy was digging new trenches well beyond his existing line. The Corporal whispered to Ginger to follow him while Arthur and the others remained in an absurdly shaped crater. They expended much energy crawling on their stomachs until they were roughly twenty-five yards from their objective. The distant sound of men working with pick axes and shovels could be heard. "Cheeky buggers" whispered Ginger into Harry's ear, before smiling. The sudden appearance of two German soldiers from nowhere wiped away their grins. They laid like dead wood, not daring to breathe and like a light going out the Germans disappeared. The two Pals couldn't get back to the crater quick enough.

Harry had observed that one of the old communication trenches now had a machine gun post behind it; vital information for in front was where the main assault would have to cross. Through the chain of command Corporal Hardy knew he'd been given a position to attack anything that might prove an obstacle to the Allies. Again Ginger offered to go with Harry and no one dissented. Fortunately the moon had chosen not to appear that night and Harry insisted that everyone rested for fifteen minutes.

The atmosphere was electric when they rolled out of the crater and rolled into a smaller one and proceeded to crawl cautiously as specks of rain hit their faces. Both crawled through the wire looking and listening and pausing, relying on animal instinct before progressing further.

They didn't notice the shadowy outlines of half a dozen German soldiers digging until a flare went up in the distance. Another flare, much closer, lit the sky and Ginger croaked "Corp." A German soldier's rifle cocked barely twenty yards away, he had seen them. There was a blinding flash, then another as the bullets shuddered into the ground inches from the scouts. A bomb would have finished them had they not been able to wriggle back out of the wire and into a shell hole. A bomb exploded where they had been seconds earlier and machine gun fire peppered the air about them.

Ginger bared his teeth. "I've got my bombs."

Before he could take the fight to them, Harry grabbed his arm "No! We'll come back tomorrow night." He repeated it then both scarpered back to the party waiting in the crater.

The other patrols made it back safely and intelligence was updated. Once again Captain Keaveney congratulated his men but daren't show his pride in the fact that it was his men that had engaged the enemy. When he reported again to headquarters with new HB1 pencil drawings on his map and a spring in his step, he even had time to notice the blue cloudless sky. Inside the building other scout patrol officers stood attentively and they greeted Keaveney with aggressive curiosity and he refused to be pricked because he knew his men were the best and more importantly so did the two most senior officers who later praised him in the absence of the others.

More men, some with soft features others with brutish faces were detailed to join Corporal Hardy's next escapade; they clustered around as he showed them the map and sketches of the trenches that were of particular strategic value. He pointed out operations that were forty yards from the British line and then they would have to crawl thirty yards before they confronted strong wire blocks in front of the enemy bombing post.

"We meet up in the bomb craters on each side of this trench." He prodded the map with his finger and everyone's head instinctively moved forward. The 'yellow belly' allowed them to digest the information before continuing "Eight men under Arthur will rush this trench, four from each side."

"When?" One of the men asked.

Harry had anticipated the question. "Four grenades will be lobbed into this machine gun rest, here," he pointed, "thirty-five yards to the rear of the bombing post... That will be the signal that me, Ginger and the others will attack the machine gun post. The mobile charges will have to be in place because there are dug outs to be blown up." He looked around at the concentrated faces "Zero hour is one o'clock in the morning and hopefully we will be in position half an hour before that. Artillery fire will rain down on the Boches' trenches behind the ones we are going to knock out... hopefully confusion in the ranks but men SPEED is of the essence, this goes for the other scouting parties... we are all working in tandem."

There were no questions and Harry attempted to lighten the mood "Double rum after the show OK?" The men chuckled and listened to their leader telling them that they would be going up to the front line within the hour and have the posts pointed out to them.

Harry and Ginger crawled out towards the post they would make for in the early hours while the others watched. It was dangerous, more so where the terrain and its debris became familiar. The sight of a dead German soldier signalled their decision to return. Arthur was detailed to draw all the equipment, ammunition and extra bombs required and assemble the men at 11 p.m.

That night Captain Keaveney looked conspicuous as the only white face among charcoal black ones; he watched one of the men burning cork and after it had cooled applying another layer of camouflage.

Again the munitions were checked meticulously. "Twelve bombs in these two haversacks, Sir" said Corporal Hardy to his Captain. The obligatory sugary tea was drunk and cigarette smoked before Keaveney shook every man's hand in a sincere fashion even though anxiety gripped him in the pit of his stomach. He walked out the tent with the scouts and hoped that one day in life's afterglow he would remember vividly this image because it mattered to him.

Chapter 28

Everything was going to plan. The men crawled out in duos and assembled a few yards from the German wire. They split into groups as pre-arranged and waited. Harry slithered up the mound and smiled to himself when he saw the soldier he'd seen the previous night – all head and shoulders of him above the trench. He kept his chuckle inside and slowly rejoined the band.

Everything was still and the men waited as though they had temporarily been released from the silence of purgatory; it was always difficult just before battle to quell the disturbing whispers in each combatants head and each man dealt with it in his own way. The chill in the air was ignored as Harry whispered "Anytime now" while glancing at his watch.

Suddenly the world erupted and the screaming of hundreds of shells deafened everything. In front of the Pals shrapnel exploded in all directions and the roar of high explosives sent myriads of coloured light high into the sky. The enemy lines were illuminated and the bombardment continued with the hope that it would sap their morale and disorientate them while the patrols counted down the seconds to their assault.

"Get ready... Now fire off the grenades!" rasped Corporal Hardy and their operation had begun. Machine gun fire was returned amidst more blinding explosions and men in the jaws of death cried out. Harry and Ginger single-mindedly pursued their objective and clamoured over the block wire and into the German trench where they met stern opposition. The Devonian threw a couple of bombs at the barely disguised entrance within the trench while Harry emptied his revolver of bullets whilst screaming obscenities at those soldiers advancing with bayonets at the ready. Ginger scrambled towards the machine gun nest and threw two bombs; the explosion knocked him off his feet and when he came round he was shot in the head by an enemy soldier before he too died when shrapnel blew part of his head off.

The others joined their Corporal and more grenades were dispatched into the disguised openings. Several red flares went up in the rear; it was the signal to retreat back. Ginger's body was carried back to the deep shell hole they had congregated in and Arthur solemnly informed the group that he had lost two men, cut down by machine gun fire. As he relayed the details in a sombre tone, despite the enemy's continuing retaliation, the moon sailed into a patch of unclouded sky and for the last time a soft yellow glow lit up Ginger's face; this was followed by an oppressive silence. Harry Hardy felt his face flush but he said nothing for he knew his voice would flail and crack. War was a business. A nasty business.

Donald Reid had been hospitalised over a year and for the first five months he had teetered on the brink of death. Only his strength, fitness and iron will had kept him going to the surprise of his doctors. He was in constant pain because surgery had failed to remove splinters of shrapnel throughout his upper body though the surgeon who had operated had written in his notes that no vital organs had been destroyed. It was small comfort to a man with blurred sight in only one eye, a collapsed lung and legs that wouldn't work.

For three months he had been lifted from his bed wrapped in heavy blankets, placed in a wheelchair which was carried down three flights of stairs by two burly sentries and positioned by a wall which afforded shelter from the south westerly breeze that attacked the area each day. Bed sores prevented him getting comfortable in any position but he never complained. He appreciated those soldiers hobbling about on crutches who came to sit with him, hold his hand and tell him about their life back home besides helping him drink the hot sugary tea. On one occasion before the wounded men departed he whispered to one to get a nurse for him while he waited and mustered his strength. Nurse Hedger arrived with a smile and a pressed uniform spotted with occasional dried bloodstains. He was conscious of her as a cloud of pastel colours and thought the fragrance he absorbed was lavender water. He intimated for her to come closer and he could just make out a face calm and sweet and knew in an instant, inside was a radiant heart.

Nurse Hedger held his hand and Donald muttered the word "letter". She understood because nurses were only too aware that any letter long or short sent back to family or a friend provided a feast for badly wounded men's morale. She whispered "Give me five minutes and I shall return with hospital paper." Donald could feel the inner drizzle in his whole body being momentarily clear and he was buoyed. The hospital writing paper was pale blue and stamped with a Military Hospital in France where the address would have been in peace time.

"Dear Father,
By now you will have been told that I'm in hospital somewhere in France. My life has been saved unlike those, doctors could do nothing for though I am bed ridden which is extremely uncomfortable. Each day I try and remain optimistic though it is difficult and I think constantly of mother, yourself, Flora and Helen. Please don't alarm them, just say I'm getting better and hope to come home one day. My medication takes some of the pain away but leaves me exhausted, still, sometimes when I'm asleep I'm back home shepherding with Black Bob. How I long to hear his distinctive bark.

Well I will finish here as it is time to be returned indoors.
Your loving son.
Donald."

Nurse Hedger wanted to shed a tear but she didn't. Her Ward sister had repeatedly instructed her charges "never to let the men see you cry... they will think they must be dying."

Donald was carried back to his room which now had two more beds crammed into it. He couldn't see the occupants but if he could he would have seen a man with sunken eyes, pale faced and wearing a constantly worried expression. He could hear this man crying in his sleep but couldn't see that both his legs had been amputated and the fact he had no control over his bowels was obvious. The other occupant seemed in the grip of hysteria; he lay shaking most of the day despite medication and was completely lost in a maze of mental horror. Harry's bed was empty, two days earlier its occupant had died during the night.

Five days later after Donald had his dressings changed, now every three days, not the daily exercise it had been on his arrival, two doctors appeared in the room armed with clipboards and notes; it was unusual to have two making their rounds together. They stood at the foot of Donald's bed and were unanimous. The older doctor sat down and spoke quietly to his patient "You are not getting well at the pace we hoped you would, so I am sending you home to convalesce." On the chart attached to the metal frame at the foot of the bed he wrote in capital letters the word BUNK and both doctors signed and stamped it with the hospital's rubber signature.

Usually that word flooded patients like it was a narcotic fix but Donald showed no elation he merely lay there solemn and quiet for he didn't want his mother and the girl he had hoped to marry to see him in this state of helplessness. That night he simmered not with suppressed delight but with foreboding unaware that the legless man opposite him suffered a burst appendix sometime between 3 and 4 a.m.

Everything happened so quickly. Two orderlies appeared and put Donald's possessions into a small pillowcase before loading him onto a stretcher and carrying him down the flights of stairs and laying him on the large stone floored reception area. A nurse appeared and helped him drink hot milk with a dollop of honey. It made the injured man realise his taste buds were still working and he forced a smile. When the motor ambulance arrived the orderlies lifted the stretcher up into it where four other men, in various states of decay, lay silently.

The canvas door was drawn back and when the ambulance approached the coast, Donald was aware of the pungent aroma of salt air. It raised his spirits and obviously that of one of the wounded who suddenly whimpered "I'm going home" before crying, uncontrollably. The ambulance pulled up along the quay but Donald couldn't make out the large red cross painted on the side of the ship; it appeared like a large smudge. The iron doors on the side of the ship were open and he was carried in to where there were countless rows of beds with railed sides filling up the complete area.

He lay for an hour before a vibration was heard and felt which told everyone they were heading for the open sea. He slept fitfully. The images of the people and his life before the Great War raced through him at an unstoppable pace and he was fearful but this receded when he reasoned that come what may, at least Black Bob would just wonder where his master had been – the barometer of his affection would always be constant "Yes, it's true" Donald whispered with an air of salvation "a dog is a man's best friend."

Trucks, specially re-designed with shelves to take stretchers were waiting at Southampton docks. Some were detailed to take the less injured to military hospitals where after an overnight stay and medical examination they would begin their convalescence in another establishment.

The more serious cases were being transported to military hospitals nearer to their homes, by train. During moments of lucidity in the previous year Donald had thought of having his worst leg, the right one, amputated because the wounds wouldn't heal or so it seemed that way having listened as best he could to the surgeon's diagnosis but had pulled back reasoning that he would be unable to work the land, after the war. It was all he knew.

A convoy of converted trucks commissioned by the army were packed from head to toe and a shrill blast gave drivers the go ahead to transport the badly injured to Southampton stations where hospital trains, all with the carriage windows and doors opened, waited. The platforms designated had been cleared to facilitate the trucks parking alongside at various intervals and the press had not been encouraged to take endless photographs especially of those dead lying on stretchers in rows with a blanket pulled right over them. "At least they made it back to England" one of the drivers said to an ashen faced railway porter who had given up counting the bodies of the dead. Cold had come into the air as the sun lost its power and began to fall inch by inch under the horizon. Finally the last stretchers were carried into the final carriage as the train driver looked out of his cab back along the platform waiting for the station manager's wave and a long blast on his whistle. Doors were slammed shut often three at a time by porters transferred from the other platform and at last that screeching noise was heard.

It was a relief. Though the lights of France's raging battlefields were finally behind the wounded men and dusk was approaching, the drop of five degrees in temperature accompanied each one of them in his loneliness. The rhythm of the steam engine offered a balm of sorts to some of the men while nurses appeared to tiptoe through the carriages which remained in near darkness because the lights were deliberately kept low. The early twentieth century had witnessed a great development in different religions, each one professing to be the superior. In every hospital ship and on every hospital train, all religions were the same; made up from mens fears. It lived there in silence, known, avoided and understood.

When the train pulled into Waterloo Station, Donald was in a drug induced sleep. He had a vague awareness of being carried somewhere and of another train offering that distinctive rumble. When he woke from his slumber a nurse was standing over him. She held his hand when he moved it and whispered "We've arrived in Sheffield… one night here and tomorrow an ambulance will take you to Lincoln." She remained a shadow to this Fens man and he appreciated her humanity.

No sooner had Donald been carried into a military ward at Sheffield's largest hospital, his bandages were changed and he became aware of a pungent smell of iodine and of voices in the treatment room. The next thing he remembered was being helped to drink hot sugary tea at 8.00 a.m. the following morning, it gave him a burst of energy and then was it gone. A youthful doctor, hardened by over three years of attending to the war wounded, sat by his patient's bed reading the notes but showing no sign of emotion. A nurse, dutifully quiet, stood with a serene smile on her face which she hoped Donald could make out if only partially "After lunch you will be taken to Lincoln… you'll be in good hands there."

Only once did the mask drop when the patient raised, slowly, his right hand offering a handshake which the doctor, swallowing, obliged "Good luck Private Reid" he whispered into Donald's ear. Then he moved to the next patient on the right for on the left the occupant had died during the night – another who'd made it home.

John Reid had insisted he would go and see his son, alone, and then would take his wife and daughter on the second visit. He was himself, a veteran of war and unlike most military men he didn't believe in what he thought a noxious phrase – the Field of Honour. Now he was about to see his surviving son mutilated, mangled and he couldn't sleep the night before. He rode pillion on a friend's motorbike and he knew he had to be strong, for his family.

The reunion in Ward 7 was emotional and John admired his son's courage when he whispered at great effort "I'm not bitter, dad… I just wish Peter was here." John Reid fought back his own tears as much because he hadn't heard his son use the word 'dad' since he was a little boy as he pondered what if any future there lay ahead. A nurse appeared, carrying two steaming mugs of tea and placed them delicately, on the bedside cabinet. She touched her patient's forearm "I'm not far away, at all times, Donald" then she glided away. John Reid was touched. His son asked him to talk about Tunby Hill which he did having leaned closer to his son's face. Occasionally he paused to look around at the other men invalided out of this war and wasn't consumed with any envy when he could see some obviously mending quicker now they were back in their home environment and conversing confidently with their visitors but always careful not to laugh out too loud for some in this ward might never leave.

The visit had lasted an hour and both men were exhausted. It was mid-afternoon when John walked carefully down the stairs holding on to the banister and pausing at the entrance to light a cigarette. He was joined by his friend, who asked the standard questions out of politeness but was careful not to be seen prying. They sat on a bench in the hospital grounds and the motorcyclist produced his hip flask and John was touched by his friend's obvious empathy.

Back at the farm he spoke in measured tones about his son to both mother and daughter and was careful to avoid repeating what the senior doctor at Lincoln Hospital had told him about his son's chances of a recovery that would allow him to lead a semblance of an ordinary life. Mrs Reid sensed her husband's foreboding and hid it behind her own large measures of gin while her daughter topped up her father's whisky. At midnight the parents were asleep in their armchairs as the flame left the open fire and only a glow remained. When Carrie Reid woke up at 4.00 a.m. her face seemed to have aged; her husband was awake and in spite of the silence the couple seemed to draw closer to each other. She gave him a wounded smile before making a pot of tea and collecting a couple of blankets from the airing cupboard. They drank from large clay mugs before resuming sleep; no conversation passed between them.

The nurses, bright, breezy and articulate attempted to make Donald as presentable as possible for the visit from his mother and sister. He was washed, shaved and had his dressings and bed linen changed but still he spoke through a strangulated voice that required great effort and consumption of energy. His mother felt cold with the shock at seeing her eldest son while his sister was frightened at the sight of the other casualties, dead or dying especially those who had bed linen pulled right up to the top of the bed frame. They sat either side of Donald and held his hands occasionally squeezing them and this movement was reciprocated. Following John's instructions his wife talked at length of Black Bob and this provoked a warm but subdued response from her son. Flora talked about village news and how she was thinking about becoming a nurse. Occasionally the pungency of iodine blew right through the ward and though it was policy to apply morphine to those in need just before visiting hours it didn't prevent the cries of those whose pain was overwhelming; fortunately it didn't happen during this visit.

An hour flew by leaving the trio tired and before she left Donald's mother took a small fruit cake she had baked from her hessian bag and held it to her son's nose for she knew what sight remained was merely a blur "I've spoken to the nurse... did so when I arrived so maybe she will cut you a bit to have at tea-time?" The sight of one tear rolling out of her injured son's eye was almost too much for Carrie Reid before she called upon all God's strength to save her from cracking up in front of Donald. His sister quickly wiped away her tears with a lace hanky scented with Palmolive. Meanwhile Donald had fallen asleep again as though all life's sustenance had been sucked out of him. In the recess of his mind he contemplated that life might pull pieces out of him until it got tired of doing so and if that was the case could he outlive life?

In the grounds of the hospital mother and daughter sat on a bench composing themselves; there was an unwritten rule that neither would give in to hopelessness instead they would believe that Donald could only get better... They got up and started to make their way home but constant reminders were everywhere. At Lincoln Railway Station a vivid and gnarled figure in uniform and minus an arm cursed as he tried to open the door with his left hand before trying to clutch two bags with the same hand – fortunately a civilian was there to offer assistance which instantly quelled the soldier's rage.

John met them at the local station a couple of miles from their home and the three of them walked and talked about Donald's eventual homecoming and the changes the household would undertake to accommodate him. It buoyed them and hot sugary tea further bolstered their optimism. That evening the family's conversation was filled with planning, nothing escaped the microscope and only the clock striking midnight put everyone to bed. "My home has had an empty feeling recently... that ends right now" Carrie drew on her faith with these words, despite her husband's snoring, before sleep overtook her.

Helen Clements chose her wardrobe carefully for the visit to Lincoln. She wanted gaiety, no sombre colours, but she didn't want to appear as flighty. Her sister, Elizabeth, helped her with the choice of skirt and also did her hair on the morning of her visit. Like all visitors she was aware of a strong antiseptic smell patrolling the corridors leading to the wards and was thankful that a nurse of similar age to herself was escorting her to Donald's ward rather than the aggressive looking orderlies who constantly seemed to be on the move.

Her first act was to kiss Donald on his cheek and he squeezed her hand as he recognised the scent. He nodded his head slowly and Helen kept her emotions in check "The doctors say progress is slow but you are on the right tracks..." She thought about saying everyone is praying for you but stalled, instead, she talked about the Wolds and the walks they used to go on sometimes letting Elizabeth join them because her younger sister doted on them.

"Yeah." Was the injured man's response and a smile found its way onto the side of his face which elicited a wider smile from Helen. Suddenly a small, quiet man with greying hair appeared at the foot of the bed and examined the medical notes before writing something down. Noting Helen looking quizzically he said "Good afternoon I'm Doctor Gottard. Donald is in the right place." Helen acknowledged his words and then he was gone leaving her to resume small talk. After reminding Donald of the walks in the pouring rain which he had insisted upon and which had witnessed both of them laughing loudly as they got drenched, he responded though his words sounded like a wheeze "We'll do it again, one day, I promise."

She felt emotionally drained after an hour and told him she would be back as soon as possible before kissing him on his cheek and leaving alongside others; all walked with a forlorn step unlike the beginning of visiting hours when most arrived with a jaunty step and hope writ large in their eyes. Before stepping outside the front doors into the grounds many mothers smothered their tears in large handkerchiefs while fathers tried to present themselves as stoical which wasn't always successful. No visitor left unwounded.

That night Helen Clements couldn't shield her heart and hearing the sobbing, Elizabeth left her room and climbed into her sister's bed and spent the early hours there. In the morning there were still tracks that tears had made on the sides of Helen's nose and only her sister's encouragement forced her to get up and face the day.

Donald's progress over the next month could still be measured in the quarter inches then disaster struck. Pneumonia. Doctors had long feared this in many of their patients but had kept it out of conversation and instructed nurses to do likewise. Private D. Reid now patient D. Reid number 343438 was slipping away, often his heart and lungs laboured so heavily he imagined his wounds were bursting and the tissue that had slowly healed over was being torn apart. Shadows appeared under his eyes and still the nurses remained cheery; one even brought early blossoming wild flowers from her garden and a glass vase to brighten up his bedside table. Had he the energy Donald would have railed like a tormented animal with murderous impulses but unfortunately over-tiredness checked everything apart from irritability and he continued to summon up courage for he had worked out long ago that the only way to baulk the beast that was his suffering was to refuse to be broken.

Other visitors passed by his bed no doubt thinking he had the look of bored calmness and unable to comprehend that the intense self-suppression of all injured men produced levels of exhaustion, unimaginable.

John Reid's melancholy eyes reproached the young doctor, strong, fresh and unhurried when he informed him that his son may not last the month. He stood in silence, fighting his anger until the doctor excused himself and father slowly ambled to his son's bedside determined to hide this emotion and it was difficult. Some words passed between father and son and Donald instinctively knew that the damnable and cruel tormenting forces that seemed eager to break him were rapidly approaching.

"I want to go home to die" he whispered and his father squeezed his hand and replied "I promise you that." Within eighteen hours Donald's bed had been reassembled and placed downstairs by a roaring fire and he followed the licks of flames casting lines against the firewall. Helen and Elizabeth Clement came to see him and both held his hand while Black Bob assumed guard duty lying on a rug immediately in front of the fire; his eyes never left his master even when Mrs Reid fed her son soup and vegetables before retiring to the kitchen where she could cry knowing no one was watching her. She was sensitive to all beautiful things but had built an internal wall to protect herself; this way she reckoned she could lavish devotion on her son as though everything was normal despite her eyes still questioning. For Donald he could see the sadness in his mother's face.

It was about the end of March and the war was in its fifth year when Donald asked his father, summoning up great effort that he wanted to be taken out to that place in the Wolds where he had sat pre-war watching livestock and marvelling over "nature's gift to us". John quickly made the arrangements and the following morning fortified by thick porridge and honey and hot sugary tea, Donald was dressed in thick blankets and sat in an armchair, he was carried out by two friends and John and placed in an open trailer joined to a tractor. Black Bob continued to wag his tail as the tractor drove towards the deep brown plough lands and occasional Oak trees standing tall in hedgerows which contrasted splendidly with sagging stacks of hay which looked like they would take months to dry up. All this Donald absorbed through blurred eyesight. He wore a scarf over his face as thought the pure air needed filtering before his lungs could absorb rather than reject its goodness. The two friends of his father sat either side pointing out other features "Donald there will probably be wildfowl on the marshes by the coast" and the latter squeezed his hand to let him know he had heard.

At ten o'clock they reached the end of a track on an incline and the men lowered, then carried the armchair with Donald propped up against pillows to a clump of rocks that had been there since the beginning of time. Everyone had warm tea from a metal container and oat biscuits especially baked by Mrs Reid that morning. Now the men retreated to a large Ash tree and sat against its trunk smoking while Donald with Black Bob's jaw resting on his knee could be alone as he had requested.

His surroundings gave Donald strength and he was able to reflect that the crowning cup of his life was to have had the love from his parents, his late brother and Helen Clements whom he knew he would have married, someday. He was aware that the sun had mounted high enough to touch the hills opposite and casual shafts of light in a row of Poplars leaning on an incline to his right. What he was blissfully unaware of was a lone bird perched on the bough of an Oak tree nearby who watched over everything going on beneath him and while others flew in and quickly out he remained, still.

He thought about his youth and happiness spread through his veins; the crises and climaxes when he was a boy and smiled for the peace and everlastingness of his boyhood had come to him again as did the memory of summer and all its exquisite colours formed by centuries of imagination. He looked down at his faithful friend's dewy eyes and hoped that the wild roses that sprang up, often, throughout the year, still had wild clusters of colour.

The moment narrowed and Donald looking at Black Bob's eyes, sensing eternity, moved his fingers over the collie's head then the movement stopped as a cloud finally moved away exposing the whole sun. Everything was still before Black Bob pulled back a yard and barked twice before lying at the foot of his master.

John and his two pals looked over, before resuming their conversation. Suddenly a howling, associated with coyotes in the American west shattered the tranquillity and because it was repeated again and again it seemed to echo across the Lincolnshire countryside. The men rose to their feet and Bill, a life-long friend of John put his hand on his shoulder. There was a pause before they softly moved forward only to be met by Black Bob, back arched and snarling in their direction. Mr Reid took another step forward alone, then knelt down on one knee before summoning the dog who started howling in anguish. Now they knew and now everyone else would have to be told.

The service was packed and the Reverend Mitchell spoke briefly before Donald was laid to rest in a plot which the sun would hit every midday during the summer months. Helen Clements would never marry and when she died in 1950, having spent her life working on the family farm, would be buried next to him.

When news finally arrived on the Western Front, broken to the men by Captain Keaveney, a bleakness tore at the fibres of the Scout Patrol. Even the new recruits, all aware of the Pals' history, were stumped by depression made worse by the fact memories of peace time had in many cases all but evaporated. Europe was only associated with war – callous and unyielding.

It was the end of the Reid name. After generations no more would this sturdy family till the arable land of the second largest county in England. Nevertheless the war would go on even if the Reid progeny was no more. It had vanished into the night.

Chapter 29

No one knew it, least of all the infantry, but the Great War was entering its final stages. Despite the sobering experience of the Somme, a name forever associated with disaster and the misgivings of many politicians, Douglas Haig Commander-in-Chief of the British Army in France launched a renewed assault on the Ypres salient. From July to November 1917 the Allies gained over four miles at the Battle of Passchendaele. Though British casualties were less than those of the Somme offensive half a million soldiers on both sides lost their lives. Even the Prime Minister, Lloyd George, in moments of disquiet asked "if the appalling casualty list was worth such great victories?"

Optimism was rife in military circles as the first large scale deployment of tanks was seen at the Battle of Cambrai and a Supreme War Council was created to co-ordinate Allied military affairs. Dismay quickly set in though when Austro-German forces made a breakthrough on the Italian Front at Caporetto in the autumn of 1917. Worse still for the Allies was the Bolshevik revolution which ended Germany's war on two fronts and Soviet Russia's subsequent signing of an armistice with the Central Powers in December of that year finally ratified in the Treaty of Brest-Litovsk, three months later.

The final year witnessed a renewed German assault on the Western Front in January forcing the Allies into desperate defensive measures including the appointment of General Foch as Commander-in-Chief of the Allies Army. The unspoken truth was that the best the Allies could hope for was to withstand the German onslaught and pray the protracted entry of American forces would tilt the balance back in their favour.

Unsurprisingly war weariness manifested itself on both sides with labour unrest in Britain and mutiny in the French Army and German Navy; all this was conveniently played down by military leaders who had come to the conclusion that what lay before them was all or nothing and subsequently events moved at pace.

By the middle of March, Germany had transferred 400,000 men from the Eastern to the Western Front and another 80,000 from Italy. It was a terrifying prospect for the Allies since it was the first time since September 1914 the Germans had superior numbers on the Western Front. Ludendorff chose to attack the sector around Saint Quentin and the second battle of the Somme commenced on March 21st with an intense bombardment of British positions using high explosive and gas shells. Unfortunately for the Allies the effect of gas was intensified by heavy fog which trapped it close to the ground causing much confusion. The result was a withdrawal of the British forces to the west side of the Somme; this created a huge gap in the Allied line through which the enemy poured, advancing in open fields for the first time since 1914.

The newly formed Supreme War Council was at first ineffective merely because its personnel was a committee of political not military leaders until Foch 'put his foot down'. Both military leaders knew the British were in disarray having been driven back twenty miles. Ludendorff sensed victory if he could cut the British and French off from each other by attacking at Amiens. His assault was checked and fighting died down on April 6th. Though the Germans had gained a tactical victory having advanced forty miles in eight days and inflicting close on 20,000 casualties it had not been decisive; even a key range bombardment of Paris using 'Paris guns' only stiffened the French public's morale. There followed the Battle of Lys, a diversionary engagement while the Germans mustered their reserves for a second assault on Amiens. This was called off due to fierce resistance by the Allies and increasing German casualties.

Ludendorff was aware that every day more American troops were arriving in France and though the spring rain made the terrain difficult he knew he couldn't wait for the summer and subsequently attacked the Allies at the Aisne River on May 27th. A hole was forged in the Allies line and the German army rushed through occupying a salient thirty miles deep and thirty-five miles wide at the base. The German military were only too aware that the narrowness of the salient left it susceptible to the danger that simultaneous attacks at each end would cut off the main assault force from its support. Time was of the essence and Ludendorff intended to widen the salient, break through the Allies line and advance to Marne. From there he reasoned he could march on Paris.

Foch was prepared and despite the Germans throwing in fifteen diversions on June 9th in an attempt to eliminate the Allied salient from Chateau Thierry to Montdidier it held. It was another blow to the German High Command as they had also failed to take Reims, at the close of May.

After the first attempt at Marne had failed, a battle where the Americans removed any doubt about their combat ability, the Germans made a fourth and final lunge for victory on July 15th. The Germans crossed the Marne but failed to break through allowing Foch to seize the initiative, with a million American troops in France and 300,000 arriving daily the balance in numbers was back in the Allies favour, decidedly. A sudden attack exposed a German flank between the Aisne and Chateau Thierry forcing the Central Powers to retreat across the Marne. The assault continued and the main German force was cut off from its support. The threat to Paris was over and Ludendorff began a withdrawal to the Hindenburg. The wounded hobbled, the officers in torn mud soaked uniforms no longer bore themselves upright, the infantry no longer marched with brutal pride. All they had in common was the size and shape of faces fixed in exhaustion, perhaps they knew it was over.

The Battle of Amiens was all important. General Haig was in command of an attack on a thirty mile sector between Amiens and Montdidier. Four hundred tanks provided the fire power and the enemy was completely taken by surprise as the Allies moved forward on August 8th gaining seven miles. Many Germans threw their weapons down and surrendered in what Ludendorff referred to as 'a black day'. Desertion was rife as the Allies attacked on the line from Noyon to Soissons on the 20th August; the British were attacking again on the old Somme front.

It was familiar territory for the original Pals – of which only the Hardy brothers, Harry and Arthur remained. Their brother Sid was still in hospital while Alfred had been repatriated, minus both legs. Captain Keaveney looked ragged as he addressed the scout patrol while the sun going down behind the battlefield resembled a raw wound. He was grateful that his Corporal eschewed tiredness or thoughts about what he might be doing if he was home in Lincolnshire. For Harry's part he knew that entertaining any melancholy sunset thoughts he might never see another sunset or sunrise for that matter – caution and animal instinct he hoped would never desert him while he remained in France. The sky, he thought was never empty of shells whether in the distance or nearby exploding and peppering everywhere with red spots of shrapnel. The marching of Allied divisions could still be heard after several hours making their way to the Front in readiness and this rhythmic sound still continued as the last light drained out of a rapidly dying sky.

Chapter 30

"The intelligence people are very anxious for us to get a prisoner." Captain Keaveney watched for any look of dismay but none was forthcoming and relieved he continued allowing adrenaline to hide him in his own dust cloud of energy. "Recently a few stealth raids have failed to bag anyone, now we have received orders." He looked deliberately at Corporal Hardy. "We are to co-operate with a battalion on our flank, though this is a preliminary announcement of our intention, secrecy is essential. We will execute it during our tour of the line."

"When Sir?" asked one of the Pals, handing an enamel mug of hot sugary tea to his officer.

The Captain paused to slurp his tea which elicited a chuckle among the men, relieving any tension and this wasn't lost of Keaveney. "Tomorrow night, at midnight we settle down to the routine of a trench tour." He explained the confidence British High Command had in the momentum that would "surely propel the Allies to victory" and pointed out on a military map of the Western Front the gains over the last year.

Everyone gathered around him and the scene became reminiscent of a confident history teacher in public school instructing his small class of pupils, even if half the pupils were smoking and occasionally slurping their tea!

Before leaving their quarters he told them to get a good night's rest and "tomorrow I've arranged a solid meal for you early evening."

"Hurrah!" Was the jovial response from one of the newer recruits.

Corporal Hardy walked with the Captain across the compound so he could hear his specific orders in private "It's important that you locate the German outposts on our front and also how strong the German wire is, it's essential we know before any plans for the raid can be activated." Keaveney looked rather embarrassed "God, how many times have we had this conversation Corporal?" Their conversation stalled as both watched huts of wood and asbestos going up, around the clock for miles.

"Bloody outbreak of dysentery in the north west region... What we don't want before the big push." Keaveney had said this while looking at the night sky before the Corporal brought him back down to earth.

"We can engage the enemy at will, Sir?"

"Yes, tomorrow you and I will go over the scouts' day out and discuss where we might get quick results." Both men stopped and bid each other good night before the Captain walked in an easterly direction to his quarters leaving Harry to speculate about the word audacity which his officer often inveigled into his conversation pertaining to military matters. He looked up into the dark sky and there was dead silence for half a minute before he uttered "Are you an audacious sky?" Then he chuckled and walked back to the ramshackle hut. He got under his blankets and slept solidly for seven hours, utterly oblivious to the vibrations caused by other men's snoring. It was a strong ray of sunlight that shot through the window and settled on his face that eventually brought Harry from his slumbers and he was surprised to find the hut empty before realising the others were at breakfast.

That evening Harry ran over the map with his fingers while the other scouts, having assembled, prepared and double checked each other's weapons and listened intently. "Running out from our line here, to the Boche line are some old communication trenches... we will try our luck here."

Captain Keaveney studied the map. "You believe you will find someone at home here, Corporal?"

"It seems a likely place, Sir."

"OK."

The other scouts were aware that their Captain trusted their Corporal's judgment without reservation. No Man's Land was lit up with the usual shells and Arthur quipped "artificial light".

All the sentries were warned that the Pals were going out and the small group hastily made their way to a trench thirty yards out from the front line. They were greeted by dense barbed wire and a Sergeant telling them to "keep you heads down." As he uttered the words machine gun fire swept over the top of the patrol, "every ten minutes they let us know they are here." Harry could sense the strain in the Sergeant's voice despite his muscular frame and a square jaw that shrieked resilience.

The scouts removed their steel helmets and put on balaclavas. "Seven of us are going out Sergeant and we will be gone somewhere between one and three hours," Harry indicated their direction and waited for another burst of machine gun fire before sliding out of the trench and rolling into another yards ahead. Suddenly the silence of the night hit each one of the men. Despite having done this again and again during the war the eeriness always gripped them like a wrench. Fortunately it never lasted longer than half a minute.

Corporal Hardy whispered to Arthur and the latest seconded scout to stay and watch for any movement that might suggest the Germans were attempting to get in behind them.

"Don't worry." Was his brother's clipped response.

Harry drew his hand gun from its holster and gingerly crept along the trench careful not to kick any lose stones lying redundant on the soil. Because the trench zigzagged, visibility was down to four yards and Harry could hear his heart beating an incongruous sound with war all around him. He stopped suddenly when he heard voices and drew out two bombs from his haversack with an air of gentlemanly reserve; now he needed every fibre of concentration, all the vigour of a steam engine for his life depended on it.

A Hun patrol, he reasoned and pulled the pin out of his bomb and let fly just as an enemy soldier came into sight. The explosion splintered the patrol and Harry ran in their direction firing his revolver until an enemy bomb exploded above him knocking him to the ground. He scrambled to safety and quickly made his way back; the objective had been achieved.

Back in the British compound, intelligence was overjoyed with the location and in the afternoon Corporal Hardy talked at length with Captain Keaveney about going out the following morning along an old communication trench. "The difficulty, Sir, will be getting out of our trench and through the wire without being seen by their telescopes."

His Captain wasn't that keen and he surmised if his Corporal wasn't consumed with survivor guilt. He also knew that dissuading his patrol leader would be futile nevertheless he was relieved that Harry didn't name his brother to accompany him.

The clock raced overnight to the following day and it was left to Arthur to double check his brother's and Richard's, the third Devonian to join the expanding patrol, weaponry. The duo squeezed and wriggled their way to the other side of the wire block, barely raising their torsos off the ground. It left them exhausted but jubilant and this jubilation carried on when Harry came across new barbed wire fifteen yards ahead; it was usually a sign that a post wouldn't be that far beyond. Unfortunately they hit an impassable wire block further ahead and before frustration could gnaw at the two Englishmen a German appeared out of nowhere, albeit his head and soldiers; the surprise was mutual but the no nonsense Devonian who would never be a healthy young man with impeccable table manners pulled the switch on a bomb and let fly followed by another. The sound of the explosion and cries of pain joined together and the duo scarpered.

Later that day Keaveney came to the patrol quarters for Harry was wanted by the CO. Despite the salute and effected bonhomie the CO had a wolfish grimace and an artificial voice that belonged more in an elocution lesson than on a battlefield and even the Captain suspected what his Corporal was thinking for he was thinking it too!

"We need reconnaissance over most of the front on which the raid will take place and the purpose of the patrol parties is to select assembly positions for the later attack."

They pored over the most recent maps which had new pencil marks on them and were satisfied they had what they wanted, after Captain Keaveney had drawn in on his own copy. They were about to leave when, surprisingly, the CO invited them to stay and have a hot drink and smoke. He immediately re-lit his pipe which had been resting on a bone china saucer inviting the men to sit down. Later Captain Keaveney told his Corporal "Everything has to be black or white with that CO, he has no feeling for grey areas." Both chuckled for it promised to be an eventful night with so many patrols investigating No Man's Land.

Keaveney was on tenterhooks as he'd insisted on going out because the parties required larger numbers for such an exercise; burnt cork completely eradicated his obvious Anglo-Saxon features and it was a sense of amusement that cheered everyone. An aerial photograph had revealed the presence of a railway line and closer scrutiny had revealed it was barely seventy-five yards from where the Germans were digging new trenches for their front line.

Once the group reached the track a greenish light seemed to filter down from the sky; everyone was on red alert and conversation amounted to muted whispers between separate personalities.

"Sir, both of us will go up the track to the new trench." Harry signalled slowly, deliberately and the others all understood what was about to happen. He unknowingly, had over the last couple of years revealed his physical idiosyncrasies which were sometimes mimicked behind his back at camp. Both Captain and Corporal crawled up the outside of the track and slowed barely twenty-five yards from the new trench; both could hear the sound of pick axes and shovels at work. They returned to the group and more reconnaissance was carried out and details noted on small maps.

All intelligence was assimilated back in the British compound and the scouts including their Captain, Keaveney, now sat around a smouldering brazier drinking more hot sugary tea; the officer, at last, felt he was one of the men.

Once again Harry insisted on going out with Richard the following night to investigate a locality he suspected was vital to the enemy – a bombing post. Both men worked cautiously around a heavy block of barbed wire to where it was noticeably thinner. They rested and just as the Corporal was about to move, Richard put his hand on his shoulder; Harry froze and turned toward the Devonian for he had seen the shadowy outlines of half a dozen of the enemy digging. Suddenly a flare lit up the sky and a dozen yards in front of them stood a German infantryman, rifle at the ready. Two shots, two close misses and the scouts scurried away as machine gun fire zipped the air above them.

"We must have been seen... the bastards." Richard's Devonian accent sounded so rich, so creamy that Harry despite the mortal danger began laughing. He was still laughing back at camp as Richard was still fermenting with rage, until a bout of hiccups distracted him.

The decision not to engage the enemy, Corporal Hardy told the Captain, was so as not to alarm him "But we intend to go back there after midnight and give him what for." After a few hours sleep Keaveney joined his men in their quarters; all were clustered around Harry who showed them his map and sketches of the trench that they were interested in. "Right here is our own post and forty or so yards along this CT from our own line. Here," he pointed with his new pencil, "is the German bombing post about forty-five yards along this CT – we saw the German sentry here last night." He paused and everyone laughed because he made no mention of being shot at from almost point blank range. "We assemble in shell holes on each side – eight men with Arthur will rush this post, four on each side. Four rifle grenades will be fired, here" he pointed out a machine gun post. "Then the other eight, myself included, will rush it. Two to stay in the background because your job is to blow up two dug outs with the mobile charges. Speed... That will determine the success or failure of this operation. We don't want to get our tails caught in the wringer."

The men responded with an affectionate chuckle including Captain Keaveney whose stomach still burned sourly from the whisky he'd consumed earlier to ensure unbroken sleep. When invited to speak he complimented his Corporal on the attention to detail reminding the men "Let's not forget the Germans are tricky bastards... they know 1918 is make or break time especially with over a million Americans joining the fray." On a more sombre note he told the men no unnecessary heroism, for the end might soon be in sight and he didn't want to have to write any more letters....

The men rose from their chairs and walked about rolling their cigarettes while Archie the newest member of the team, ten days short of his twenty-second birthday and long since departed from youthful idealism, was detailed to make the tea which he did with infectious enthusiasm. After little more than fifteen minutes and fortified they sat back down in the same seats; it was a ritual but no one could remember when it started.

Corporal Hardy stubbed his cigarette out in a tin, doubling as an ashtray on the table and cleared his throat; only his brother smirked.

"Zero hour is 2 a.m. and we want to be in position fifteen minutes before then. First an artillery barrage from our boys to soften their rear and make no mistake because these posts are close to our own and the artillery daren't risk it – there will be a fight. We have to get this machine gun post." He tapped its exact location on the map and waited before continuing.

"How soon do we...?" Asked someone.

Harry anticipated the question. "We wait ten minutes from the end of the gun fire and move forward as all the other parties will do." The quips and fond remarks which had often characterised earlier briefings were absent.

Harry looked at Richard and nodded before commencing, "Richard and I are going to take you up to the front line to show you exactly where their posts are. The first one is adjacent to a British cemetery you'll see the little crosses."

In the afternoon the men were taken out in twos to the British bombing posts and the two posts that were their objective were pointed out to them. The 'yellow belly' and the Devonian were keen to see in daylight the place they had engaged the enemy the previous night. It was a calculated risk but they knew and hoped the scouts in the rear watching them would be familiar with the place come darkness. A burst of machine gun fire told the two they were unwelcome as they approached the chosen location so they scurried back.

Back in the compound it was decided they would draw all the equipment and ammunition at 6 p.m. and assemble in their quarters at 8.30 p.m. for a final briefing. Without warning a storm broke, peals of thunder reverberated through the air and flashes of forked lightening danced in the sky. The fine morning had changed to a rainy, misty afternoon which in turn had changed to a clear bright evening and that evening had now become overcast with portentous clouds...

The country boys were oblivious to this. Weather was neither good nor bad, it was weather and this type was often welcomed as it was dramatic and relieved the boredom when they worked at night back home, but Corporal Hardy was aware that many experienced a dread of thunderstorms as if they might be on the threshold of the next world and he momentarily wondered if his Captain might be affected. Fortunately the storm abated half an hour before the reconnaissance unit assembled, though each man was only too aware that No Man's Land would be wet, soggy, slippery and muddy terrain which would add additional exhaustion.

Corporal Hardy held up two haversacks "Twelve bombs in each, right each man to check his chum's equipment." This was carried out meticulously and after a mug of the inevitable hot sugary tea it was time to get the show on the road. Richard was instructed to take the first two men out to the agreed rendezvous with Harry bringing the rest out two at a time. It was slow and difficult with the men crawling thirty yards on their stomachs and dragging equipment. Finally they were stationary only a few feet from the German wire, men stationed on either side. The rifle grenades were prepared for shooting. It was approaching ten minutes to 2 a.m.

The two men who'd disturbed the German the previous night decided to crawl up and see if anyone was there. It was a surprise to see who they thought was the same German they'd encountered earlier, they stifled their amusement and when they returned whispered "He's going to get an almighty surprise soon!"

Occasionally a flare light went up but stillness was the order of the day but that was about to change. Suddenly and without warning the quiet was violently broken. Shells of all calibres passed over the scout patrols in a ceaseless screeching roar; shrapnel was bursting ahead shattering the air and rocking the ground. Myriads of coloured lights filled the night sky and a storm hidden in smoke and dust was raining down on the Germans. Harry reassured his men, one or two he knew had never experienced anything exactly like this before. "It's all ours, this will have them cringing in fear." He noticed Richard fingering his revolver in anticipation and breathing evenly and then he looked at his watch – less than four minutes to go. Surprisingly, the leader retreated into himself and he found himself thinking about what he had heard an army chaplain say to a group of men; it was the first and last religious service he had attended since war began. "If a soldier is aware of his soul and understands ultimately it is God's property then with the help of God he will withstand the terrors of the abyss which suddenly opens to him."

"We shall see, Father," he whispered to himself. Then the moment arrived.

"Fire your rifle grenades!" he ordered. They did and he shouted "Forward!" Several blinding explosions were all around as the enemy fought to defend their position; rasping machine gun fire could be heard and cries of pain. Harry saw Richard fall and one glance told him it was fatal. The wire defences on each side were impenetrable but when Arthur leapt over the top into the unknown he was quickly followed by others. Fierce fighting followed, no quarter asked or given. Corporal Hardy dispatched three Germans to eternity and all he heard was a gurgling sound as his enemy collapsed to the ground.

Two other scouts behind the Corporal quickly dispatched their bombs at the entrance of the partially boarded-up trench. They wanted to throw another but Harry stopped them "No, save them, quickly follow me." He now carried his spare pistol and began shooting at shadowy figures taking shape through the dust. Beside him Johnny West, a morbid youth from Gosport, took great delight in throwing two more bombs until he realised that was the last of them. "Bastard!" was all he muttered as he cocked his revolver and waited for the inevitable retaliation, "I'm going to be nice to her from now on" he muttered.

"Not too nice I hope?" Offered Harry and as an aside muttered, "they're bloody strange creatures those chaps." As though to relieve the tension both men laughed in unison and shot three more Germans who emerged out of the entrance in quick succession. They looked at the fallen enemy and the laughter dried up.

On the other side, Arthur's team had enjoyed similar success. A mobile charge had eradicated the machine gun nest and blown up the German in it. Three of Arthur's men lay dead and it had taken all his resolve not to kill the young German he'd taken prisoner following his surrender.

The sky began filling up with red flares, the signal for the scout patrols to return. The prisoner was made to carry Richard's body back as covering fire was initiated by the British to enable the patrols to retreat relatively safely. Captain Keaveney took the news of fatalities badly when the Fens Pals finally got back to their quarters and Harry gave him a blow by blow account. A Lieutenant new to this theatre of war and a man caged in his own weak character had accompanied the Captain to meet the patrol; fortunately he said nothing other than to thank them for their unyielding bravery. When he took his leave Captain Keaveney remained and took a bottle of whisky from his briefcase and poured measures into more mugs of hot sugary tea and toasted 'absent friends'.

After most operations the Captain had found time to see and help his men, each in a separate loneliness, for such dangerous missions, despite the outward bravado, took their toll. Fate awaited each one of them and the constant rolling grind of steel and marching boots with hooves and infantry divisions in the background could be seen as the descent of the dead which they might be a whisper away from joining.

Harry more than the other scouts had the habit of settling his mind, maybe because he was the leader and knew that if he let it, fear would tear then break him down and that was a horror far worse than joining the underworld in pieces, having been blown apart by a 9.2-inch howitzer shell.

Captain Keaveney who now saw the same sunsets as the rural men under his immediate command had long given up wondering where God fitted into the scheme of things; his fresh faced optimism had dried up like a shallow stream under fierce unrelenting sun. He may have been obliged with other officers, some senior in rank, to attend religious services in the field but he was no longer convinced. He didn't dislike the clergy, merely questioned quietly why they peddled a fairy story. "Still, summer's nearly here men" he said and received a tired, collective smile. Perhaps he hoped the men, for one night, might dream about their roots: several white cottages scattered among a small nucleus of civilization and nearby the bank of a stream where anyone watching its patient flow would be mesmerised before staring up and looking on an enchanting hillside. Gorges, purple with shadow, cornfields, bristling yellow, and small clumps of woodland offering all shades of green and wild flowers in many colours. "It's not a lot to ask for" he said to himself. He had the angry eyes of a heavy drinker but hadn't drunk that much, instead he retreated into introspection as he made his way back to his own quarters and that evening found a quiet corner away from any bustling activity where he could reflect on his war now that the end, he hoped, was in sight. He felt blurs of redness on each of his cheeks as he recalled the service of the 6th, 7th and 8th Battalions of the Lincolnshire Regiment he'd been seconded to.

The last two had been raised at Lincoln in September 1914 as part of Kitchener's second New Army. The 7th had been selected for Home Defence duties in southern England but this was reversed and they'd found themselves in France in July 1915 near Omer.

Following trench familiarisation in the southern Ypres salient they took over the front lines and saw action at the Bluff, south east of Ypres on the Comins canal then moved south to the Somme where they captured Fricourt during the Battle of Albert. In 1917 they were moved to Arras and saw action in both battles of the Scarpe. Later that summer they had moved to Flanders and fought at Passchendaele, where British casualties were high. Keaveney sighed at this sad memory before smiling and thinking of the Fens Pals, his men in the 8th though not all had joined up on the day or the month after the declaration of war.

They had landed at Boulogne and endured much suffering at Loos in late September. They were in action at the Somme and fought in the Battle of Ancire and in 1917 had distinguished themselves during the third battle of Ypres. Now they were back in action on the Somme. "The Hindenburg Line... that is the prize we must break them there." As the Captain muttered these words he was only too acutely aware more lives would be lost and he shivered when he thought that according to statistics about life expectancy for junior officers on the Western Front, he should have been dead long ago. No memory for all combatants was complete without the misery of persistent rain and the digging of assembly trenches, knee deep in slimy water, feet trapped in clogging mud and the irony that the wounded who'd rolled into craters for protection often drowned knowing they were doomed because they hadn't the strength to drag themselves up slippery mud once the skies opened. Despite his rank he too had dug trenches with the men and every day he examined, cleaned and cleaned again his standard issue Webley Mark 6 Officer's revolver for he'd heard stories of those whose weapon had failed them because it had not been serviced regularly and for this laxness many had paid the ultimate price.

Chapter 31

Momentum was with the Allies. The second battle of the Somme was part of a strategy destined to push parts of the German line back behind his own supply line thus making it impossible for the efficient maintenance of German forces on the front. The battle had begun on 21st August around Baupalme which fell a week later.

To aid confusion the Allies maintained equal artillery and air fire along the various fronts, moving troops only at night and feigning movements during the day to disguise their actual intent.

After participating in a record advance the Lincolnshire men were hustled north with long night marches and little rest during the day. They travelled by train and bus and fatigue was apparent despite a few hours sleep. Once again Captain Keaveney came to his men with instructions from command. The scouts were to proceed forward for a reconnaissance of the area they were to move up that night.

The area had only been captured the previous day and an all too familiar sight prescribed itself: a long string of ambulances and walking wounded and bedraggled prisoners.

Captain Keaveney and Corporal Hardy studied route maps that hundreds of men would later use; it was a huge responsibility.

When night fell so did the rain. Everywhere was packed with traffic – guns going forward, ammunition columns dashing up with shells, engineers and infantrymen crowding out roads, medical and food supplies on the march. The Fens Pals accommodation in the trenches was a return to the bad old days.

The following morning the Commanding Officer summoned Keaveney and Hardy. He handed the Corporal the most recent map instructing him to take a couple of men and to make contact with the HQ of the brigade in the line and return with any necessary information as they were expecting to go into the line that night.

Despite shelling and disorientating smoke Harry, with two scouts, arrived at brigade headquarters where he was met by other scouts each on a quest for information. The CO invited him to hang around as an attack early afternoon would determine their new position which the brigade, holding back, would relieve that night.

Tension and speculation fuelled a strange excitement as the minutes ticked down. The CO was staunch, loved and hated in equal measure by his men for he believed fighting mattered; the satisfaction lay in accomplishment and as he told Keaveney "when a struggle ceases, men cease to be men." Harry wasn't sure of this career soldier. He'd never heard a man talk with such eloquence about death which might be the opening of a door 'for those who'd lived a life of stubborn effort'. The fact that the Colonel was minus his left arm was impressive he thought, before capturing his Captain's eye.

The battle raged and conflicting reports came back to HQ. There was no authentic news and both 8th Lincoln scurried back to their own line as it was imperative the battalion was brought up that night to relieve the attacking force. Information filtering back was patchy and just before midnight the CO decided to press forward when a report arrived that one battalion had lost all its officers. The scouts would lead the way.

An hour later they reached a supporting battalion and were informed that other battalions had gone into the fray but nothing had been heard since. Corporal Hardy took it upon himself to go in search with another scout for it was inconceivable that three battalions had been wiped out; his was an emulous curiosity but without arrogance.

In darkness and rain they eventually stumbled across half a dozen Bristol soldiers in a trench.

"What happened?" asked Harry.

The answer was bleak and uttered by a croaking voice. "Machine gun fire ripped us apart, methinks the Officers are dead."

"What about the others?" Harry offered quickly.

"Scattered, probably like us in shell holes."

The Corporal gave them a smidgen of hope. "Stay here, when we've located the others we'll bring some men to relieve you." Suddenly the scouts were gone. Nevertheless the information was relayed to the Reserve Company Commander who decided on the spot to bring his men forward, though it was daylight before this was completed.

Because the left flank was exposed, due to lack of information about the other battalions whereabouts, Corporal Hardy set out on his own despite his Captain's misgivings especially as German snipers were the most patient of all enemy soldiers.

The prodigious muscular power that nature had bestowed on the scout's upper body and which had been exercised in recent years allowed him to move at speed and with great dexterity. No sooner had Harry moved through a trench in the direction of the enemy line he paused to assess the situation; inevitable gunfire would ring out, nevertheless, he pressed on; instinct warned him not to proceed too far lest he was ensnared. He sat on the edge of his suspense before deciding it was time to return.

Captain Keaveney was exuberant and quickly the intelligence was relayed up the chain of command resulting in the Allied forces advancing several hundred yards without casualties followed by preparation to root out the Germans from occupation of a village. Heavy artillery drove them into a narrow salient in front of the British forces.

Intelligence was required as to whether the Kaiser's forces had evacuated their trenches or were waiting for further Allies advancement. Once again it fell to the scouts and instructions were issued at 11 o'clock that evening.

Memories of uplift and endeavour propelled Arthur to insist that he carry out the mission and before his brother could protest, Captain Keaveney said he would accompany the younger brother. "Thanks friend" he said with a glow in his eyes that suggested mischievous tenderness. The Corporal insisted on going over the latest maps with them before they slurped yet more sugary hot tea.

After some deliberation it was agreed that four not two would go out into what was becoming an extremely dark night. An advantage. The other was the burning village to the right, behind enemy lines, which lit up parts of their prospective trail. The party slowed and checked, once again, their weaponry as they realised the trench they now moved along had recently been used. In the distance they could hear shells whistling their way towards the German lines before exploding and lighting up the sky for a few seconds.

Arthur slowed; the darkness hampered visibility and the scouts felt their way along the walls of the latest trench. Suddenly he stumbled, having come into contact with a wire drawn taught a foot off the ground. He managed to steady himself with the immediate help of his Captain. Each man passed the message to the one behind him and having mounted the wire they crawled under the next one slightly higher then climbed over the next one. Above them the sky grew more spacious and within them so did fear for they knew the enemy might be inches away.

When another shell lit up a huge mound of earth directly in front, Arthur indicated for everyone to remain still while he investigated. In crouching movements he pedalled his way along the inner wall of the trench, then a blinding flash followed by a flare-light lit everything up and he moved himself into a crude ball shape before darkness enshrouded everything once more.

The waiting troops were whittling away at the teak of their collective patience, each man primed for action – life or death. No one thought a word not even the articulate Captain whose steady finger leaned against his revolver's trigger while the rest of his hand sweated.

The need to get back to the Allies lines permeated Arthur's whole consciousness and he conveyed this to everyone, careful not to betray his rising emotions less it made him appear jerky and impulsive. He led the way back with Keaveney at his side and it was almost 3 a.m. when they entered the British compound unscathed. Captain Keaveney immediately wired the latest intelligence to brigade using the camouflage language HQ demanded.

Three hours later the assault commenced and the scouts went with the second wave of support. A dozen Fokkers riddled the ground with machine gun fire but casualties were minimal. Finally, when the scouts reached the mound, all around was evidence of fierce combat. Keaveney felt his legs tremble when he was informed that a dozen machine guns and a score of prisoners had been taken. The ground was littered with bodies blotched, sore and rottingness which would eventually eat away their identity leaving the underworld to claim more ugly lives and ugly souls and he realised only too well that hours earlier one of them might have resembled him.

Unknown to the infantry was the political and military squabbles going on between Haig and Foch and Pershing whose American army had distinguished themselves but were reluctant to be pawns in any French military strategy. The American General wanted his forces to operate independently and surprisingly Petain sympathised with Pershing while Haig was convinced that victory lay within his grasp and they should pursue it with all means necessary by sending all reserves immediately to France. The French President Clemenceau complained bitterly to Foch that "Those Americans will lose us our chance of a big victory before winter... you have to make Pershing see. Put it to President Wilson."

Despite the rival egoism Haig's First and Third armies launched an all out attack on the most formidable defence system on the Western Front, the Hindenburg Line. Fifty-seven German divisions waited and each knew success against them would have a crushing effect for the Allies had pushed them back twenty-five miles on a forty mile front.

The British Field Marshal could smell victory and was delighted that the advance had been achieved with fifty per cent of his infantry under nineteen years of age lead by junior officers. Perhaps the biggest surprise was that for a military tactician known for his inflexibility and stubborn rigidity he was embracing inventiveness urging Corps Commanders to show initiative and knock the enemy off balance when opportunity arose.

When Keaveney and Harry attended a meeting the CO was in a bullish mood. "Now chaps things are a bit mixed up." Before either could respond the Colonel continued, "your unit will have to relieve elements of three battalions... the fighting was hard and we're not sure of development through a lack of information." In the patchwork of life's emotion thought Corporal Hardy this CO had put the incompleteness of passion out to grass nevertheless it was Harry's job to listen and he did. The CO pointed out on the map the plan for attack the following morning. "We need to remove the Hun from this hillock."

At midnight the guides from the front line battalion arrived at the rendezvous and Keaveney enquired of their Officer in charge how long it would take to get to the front line. "Fifty-five minutes" was the brusque answer.

Keaveney seized the initiative. "One company into the line, the second one will have to get into shell holes behind."

Corporal Hardy spoke firmly. "The second company need to keep in touch with the first and we'll do it with guides."

Keaveney insisted on spelling out the time for the attack "5.20 a.m. it all kicks off."

"The general idea," retorted the other officer, "is that we advance about twelve hundred yards and dig in."

A stillness crept over the conversation, the silence broken only by this officer muttering "St George for England." Keaveney and Hardy exchanged glances and the latter wondered if he was looking into the soul of Peter Pan...

On the morning of September 27th 1918 at precisely 5.20 a.m. came the whispered order "Fix bayonets". The scream of shells flew over the Allies heads and crashed on the German line. It appeared to many infantrymen that the power of hell had been let loose and chaos reigned along the Hindenburg Line for lights of every colour shot into the sky before order was restored and German machine gunners swept the ground.

Once again the British army, including the rural boys of the 8th Battalion, Lincolnshire Regiment, were required to reach for that invaluable asset – victory over oneself in the next days of hurried movement and ceaseless attacks.

Chapter 32

For now the thorough and methodical gathering in of information which had given scope to the scouts was abandoned as every success was exploited to the utmost degree.

"What direction Corporal?" asked Captain Keaveney.

"North east." Was the authoritative reply. Word was passed down the line to close up. They hurried across a road, through an old shelter in a partially collapsed trench aware that machine gun fire could erupt anytime.

Harry glanced at his watch and nodded to his Captain "Time's with us Sir." The relief was almost in position and a company guide said he would bring the Company Commander up from the rear.

"Christ we cleared this yesterday, Boche didn't know what hit him" said the Commander arriving twenty minutes later. The hillock was in sight.

"It's just possible they don't know we've come this far, again" offered Harry quietly confident.

Keaveney was more cautious. "Corporal, those three trenches by the side might be machine gun nests." He then showed the map with scribbled notes on it to the Commander and his Corporal. Watching them pore over it he encouraged suggestions from each as to how to proceed. Keaveney realised both men had an enviable personality, a young dignity, well built bodies and probably more wisdom than could be found in books on military strategy.

The semi-darkness had lifted and the enemy trenches were clearly visible now the smoke from the barrage had cleared. Two machine guns were being set up and the Commander seized the opportunity knowing that any delay would prove fatal. Bayonets had already been fixed and his Sergeant blew on the whistle.

The enemy were momentarily stunned and offered piecemeal resistance but to no avail. Several were shot and bayoneted and all in less than half an hour because the bomb throwers among the Pals had nullified two of the enemy's 'nests'. British soldiers ran amok through the labyrinth of trenches behind the nests shooting anything that moved. The support had arrived and now orders were given to dig in and consolidate. The Lincoln Scouts returned to the British Camp, one had sustained a flesh wound which the others derided as an excuse to go home early. Even their Captain joined in the badinage and dared to think but refused to say, "When it's all over the drinks are on me in the first bar we hit in England."

A spirit of confidence prevailed at British and Commonwealth Headquarters all over France for the momentum was irresistible and confidence never higher after years of hard slog and the Fens Pals were in the middle of it. An ambitious plan was unveiled by senior ranking officers which involved a collective sweep forward, over-running villages and trench systems – Battalion was to 'leap-frog' battalion, brigade to 'leap-frog' brigade and finally division to 'leap-frog' division. Post war a song would enter the annals of military history causing much hilarity.

Behind the attacking infantry, cavalry and motor machine guns would be propelled forward in support of tanks while low flying aircraft would strafe the enemy lines.

"What time's kick off Sir?" asked an eager Arthur with a grin on his face. It was the subsequent smile that disarmed his Captain who realised long ago that these men were his true comrades, their voices more comforting than his parents had ever been, their words often saving him from the despair of fear no matter how justified it was. He felt he belonged to them and knew it was essential he retain a heightened caution for he didn't think he could bear the loss of another one, particularly those who'd been in at the beginning when he'd taken charge.

"OK men," he looked at his group drinking hot sugary tea and he chuckled. "Don't I get an enamel mug of that swamp-like, festering, parasitic liquid you Fens Pals call tea?" The assembly erupted and even Captain Keaveney collapsed with laughter before bringing full circle once again the conversation about orders from HQ.

"The main assault commences at 4 o'clock or just after, then we join the fray at 7.30. The CO explained the details of the attack to me and the others. Our battalion is to secure a village here." He pointed with a ruler on the map already fixed to a crumbling wooden post. "Then sweep through this wood beyond it." Again he pointed. "We, the scout patrol, then go ahead and send back messages... a dozen of us."

"Sir." Piped up Corporal Hardy, having rolled a cigarette and lit it with a match drawn from a scruffy book of them. "Will we split into two groups?"

"Depends what's out there Corporal... I take your point." He looked at the men fully attentive. "I will lead one group and Corporal Hardy will take charge of the other if needs be... Corporal you decide who goes with who."

"Sir." Came Harry's quick response.

"Get as much rest as you can, we leave 6.15 tomorrow morning." The Captain put his enamel mug back down on a box and turned to leave and the men immediately rose to their feet.

"Gentlemen as you were," was Keaveney's final words as he and his Corporal left the hut and walked together across the compound discussing what might lay in wait the following day. It had given both men an intimacy that not all junior officers shared with their respective troops.

The barrage began on time and as the dozen Lincoln men moved forward in single file they could see artillery being prepared to follow at a later stage. The Pals were amazed at the sheer volume of wire protecting the German line – fifty feet of dense entanglement and yet the forward troops had broken through it. Even Captain Keaveney was awed at the sophisticated trenches and the abundance of concrete machine gun nests that had finally been overrun. Again the spectre of dead bodies stiffened the men who were reluctant to look into the open eyes of their dead enemy for it heralded years of nightmares according to legend, the same as looting was considered a curse that had consequences...

Ahead tanks continued to flatten large areas of vicious wire methodically laid out between the enemy's front and support line. It all resembled a leisurely Sunday afternoon stroll. The Germans had retreated to the support line and awaited the inevitable.

The scout patrol moved into position - ahead was the village. Corporal Hardy looked at his watch and nodded to his Captain. "Fifteen minutes Sir, then you can count the shells whizzing overhead." It happened and on time, the noise momentarily deafening and of increasing worry to the men of the battalion was their own artillery shells exploding too close for comfort; many huddled together in ditches and offered silent prayers. Not all were heard as a shell exploded among one group killing all but two instantly.

When the barrage went silent the scout patrol moved forward, one carried a Lewis gun while another was weighed down with belts of ammunition. Resistance here, was spasmodic as though the Germans really knew, despite propaganda to the contrary, that not only had the second offensive failed but the much vaunted Hindenburg Line wasn't impregnable.

The Allies high command was jubilant. Marshal Foch was witnessing his grand co-ordinated attack – everyone was fighting from Flanders to Verdun. In the north, the Belgians were attacking at Ypres, British forces under General Rawlinson were either through or approaching the Hindenburg Line and to their right the Americans with energy and enthusiasm were concentrating on a major push in the Meuse-Argonne. Maybe Haig was right – victory would come in 1918 not that that was of any interest to Captain Keaveney and his men who still had work to do despite war weariness and a longing which engulfed Europe – for the fires of Hell to be finally put out.

One of the scouts was wounded by a German officer firing his Luger as he ran before being cut down by machine gun fire. Harry shot two Germans who climbed out of their trench brandishing weapons and Captain Keaveney shot a third from close range before a white flag was waved above a trench. "Careful it's not a trap!" barked the Captain but the throwing out of rifles and revolvers was followed by German soldiers, their hands clasped together above their heads. Soldiers from the battalion swarmed into the village and Corporal Hardy quipped, "The game's up for them."

"Well it ain't over yet brother, remember that" said his brother with suspicious eyes darting from one building to another.

The following day the scout patrol moved into the countryside behind at first light as a soft broodiness fell over the terrain. Rain drops began to fall. "This will help the plants, if there's any of them still left" said Paul Briggs who'd finally joined the Pals in September 1917 having previously lied about his age. It was his sombre tone which gave the others food for thought and no one replied. They knew his experiences had changed him from boy to man and his Captain hoped that the nightmares he'd recently experienced would not plague him in peace time. Suddenly 'The Beast' as he'd become affectionately known, cocked his rifle as a German officer in impeccable uniform walked out of a copse, smoking and heading in their direction. Corporal Hardy quickly put his hand on the barrel lowering it, as the scout took aim.

Unabashed he walked towards the Captain and in impeccable English offered his surrender, taking his revolver from his holster and giving it to the Englishman much to the bemusement of the men. He offered everyone a cigarette from a shiny silver cigarette case and apologised for having no matches before slumping against the rocks the Pals had congregated by. The sun was bursting through white clouds and ending the rain drops; it had mounted high enough to touch the horizon of hills in the distance leaving a network of dewy gossamer under foot.

Maybe the spirits of dead men lurked in the late autumn air but for now everything stood still, previous anguish passed and in the silence perhaps these men realised the utter futility of war. It also occurred to Captain Keaveney, and he was able to chuckle inside, that if his fellow officers enquired how they had been relentlessly able to breach the Hindenburg Line he might be called up to ask his men to demonstrate the art of leap-frogging - but then it might seem disrespectful to all those men who had sacrificed their lives. Instead he gazed at his men, individually then collectively and he could see and it moved him, that for the first time since leaving England's second largest county they could inhale a natural living landscape.

Chapter 33

THE GERMAN GOVERNMENT ACCEPTS THE ARMISTICE CONDITIONS OFFERED ON NOVEMBER 9. They had wanted less harsh conditions fearing that famine would engulf Germany, followed by anarchy. It was agreed that the Allies would supply food during the armistice and finally on November 11th all the signatures required were complete with not one handshake passed between the two delegations. Cessation of hostilities would come into effect at 11.00 a.m.

Along the Western Front miserable drizzle greeted both armies yet that didn't dampen the Americans enthusiasm for more battle, they were just getting used to war unlike the weary enemy they faced.

News spread quicker than a tidal wave and it was greeted with bewilderment, shock and suspicion which amounted to disbelief. At 10.45 a.m. British troops who had taken Mons were east of the city when a messenger galloped by yelling "The War is over, the war is over!" "Don't listen to him boys... the poor blighter's probably suffering from shell shock" said a gruff Sergeant wearing an oversized balaclava that allowed for shrinkage. Anxiety gnawed the men as more shelling of the German lines continued as if the sole intention was to obliterate any notion the enemy might have of changing his mind at eleven o'clock.

The bells suddenly rang out throughout France's churches and while the Americans and the British strolled into No Man's Land the vanquished Germans remained, huddled together in their trenches. The roar of voices was the product of utter relief. Gradually the enemy filtered out into No Man's Land and it was all summed up by a correspondent in Mons who wrote "The fires of hell have, at last, been put out".

The surrender of self control began as citizens and soldiers began to celebrate and the British Prime Minister, Lloyd George, in a voice trembling with emotion addressed the House of Commons. "At eleven o'clock this morning came to an end the cruellest and most terrible war that has ever scourged mankind. I hope we may say that thus, this fateful morning came an end to all wars." All politicians cheered. Suddenly there were no political divisions, then Lloyd George in a more solemn voice continued. "Our hearts are too full of gratitude to which no tongue can give adequate expression." Thousands of German infantry believed they had been betrayed by those back home and one Corporal suffering from temporary blindness in hospital took the surrender personally and vowed he would enter politics and bring Germany back to greatness one day.

The Great War had profound effects: Gone was the gracious way of privilege, a technical revolution had taken place borne out of necessity, the emancipation of women was in full swing while a rigid class system was loosened. Nevertheless along some areas of the Front there was little celebration as the firing continued after 11.00 a.m. as though the foes wanted to give each other their own farewell to arms and many fell.

When night moved in, the quietness was viewed with suspicion and ate at many souls; they still believed the Armistice was temporary. The Lincoln Pals sat around an open log fire, the first they had ever enjoyed at the fighting front. Captain Keaveney tried to reassure them that there were no enemy batteries spying on them from distant ramparts and no German planes waiting for first light to blast them out of existence. Conversation was in low tones for some of them were nervous, understandably so. Harry probably had the most even temperament and he didn't want to die "Not on the last day, Sir."

Captain Keaveney responded "I know." He paused. "And you won't if I have any say in the matter." It crossed his mind that if one day he married and raised a family would he ever feel as close to his children as he did his men? Also, he was only too aware that after long months of intense strain facing mortal danger each day that the abrupt release from it was a different kind of agony – physical and psychological. He was aware many fighting men would suffer a nervous collapse and he gathered the Pals around him. "Men, I want you to think that someday you will return home and embrace friends, loved ones. Yes we are only too aware that everywhere is marked by the corpses of our comrades and now peace... our existence as soldiers is suddenly meaningless. This shock does have a numbing affect for we have been consumed by the immediate past and lost good men. What happens tomorrow, who cares..."

Before he had finished some had fallen into an exhausted sleep and shortly after so did Captain Keaveney, dreaming of posters telling of cricket matches and horticulture. He had evidently taken his position in the world – he was no longer a boy, but a man.

The stillness and the silence of guns that greeted the following morning was viewed with suspicion. It was unnerving. Even a moon faced cleric with sloping shoulders and an extended paunch failed to raise a laugh even when he spoke with nasal jollity. "'Ere watch out vicar, the devil yonder on hill might take a pot shot at you because you know his sins..." That garnered a faint chuckle and the cleric smiled and raised his eyebrows a few times before walking away as though he was escaping his self, for now, not every horizon registered death and men might start to think after an absence of years about the length of their days. One thing was a certainty, there would be no more gas rising up and congregating into rolling grey clouds choking the life out of men who failed to get their mask on in time and choking the will of men to go on, who had to watch this unsavoury spectacle powerless to do anything.

By midday on the 12th only the occasional explosion was heard far in the distance and before the week was through any explosion, usually faint, was ignored while magazines featuring ladies in stages of undress were passed around with new found enthusiasm and of course the ribald comments grew more coarse and more funny. However, it was a week before regulars could dismiss the standard line – 'Never believe anything once it is officially sanctioned or denied'.

Captain Keaveney had been summoned to HQ and given the news that Sid Hardy had died on Armistice Day. The commanding officer's tone was light with a tinge of regret. "Of all the days... This day."

The Captain's face began to quiver and crumble despite his remaining at attention.

"Please, at ease," said the Colonel striving to lessen the blow. "It's never easy," he continued, "poor chap was on the mend according to his medical record."

"Then?" interrupted Keaveney his eyes demanding an explanation. "Was the hospital bombed?"

"No" said the Colonel, "he succumbed to influenza as many men and citizens are... there's a pandemic but it's under reported, goodness knows when it will end. Brave men having endured everything this enemy has thrown at them, only to die from this." Unknown to either man or the world this strain would go on to claim over twenty million lives and no vaccine would ever be found for it; a time bomb waiting to be set off again in the future.

The Captain was lost for words; he knew that influenza was claiming lives, everyone did but it was considered a civilian's illness not a soldier's and because of this he felt angry inside and his manner, rare for him, became petulant. "Can't the medics find an antidote for this?"

The Colonel offered nothing; instead he lit a cigarette and waited for he understood only too well those junior officers who had a real bond with their men while others remained supercilious. Minutes later the Captain left HQ, his mind was muddled and he didn't relish telling the Hardys that their brother had died not from shrapnel wounds... The war was over but any reconnection with life pre-war was an illusion, for his had been as simple and uneventful as the life of a plough horse, despite comparative privilege, how four years had changed him, forever.

He delayed returning to his camp until evening then went straight to his quarters and drank double measures of whisky before tumbling into his crumpled bed. That night he dreamt about the Devil and all the damned in Hell, drinking up whole clouds of rain and when he woke up in a sweat he had a thunderous headache and no aspirin to relieve it. At 8 a.m. he shaved and polished his boots before putting his uniform on; it was his notion of respect when he had to do the inevitable. But not even warm water could disguise the haggard look on his face and he held back the tears for he remembered overhearing Sid Hardy telling his brothers "That Captain Keaveney may be different to us but he's a sincere man... that's OK in my book."

It was midday when Captain Keaveney finally broke the news to Harry and Arthur, and understandably shock waves reverberated through them yet despite their grief they were at pains to put the Captain at ease for they realised he, too, would share their suffering. The genuine camaraderie of army scouting patrols was second to none. For the first time since the outbreak of war the brothers together with others in the patrol attended Sunday mass conducted in Latin by a French priest and all took communion including Captain Keaveney who'd been brought up in the Protestant tradition.

A week had passed since their brother's death and details of his burial in the British cemetery had been filtered through. The brothers surmised that any time now their parents would be informed and news would spread quickly through the village and surrounding parishes. For now though, they waited for the actual date for Sid's and others burial and when it came it was a relief for all concerned and noble references and anecdotal stories abounded in the French cafe the Pals retired to for a celebration drink in honour of the youngest Hardy boy.

Captain Keaveney had begun to lift the smog that clouded his mind and took his Corporal to one side as the drink fuelled remembrance of a young life lifted the mood of unhappiness that originally clouded the room. Neither could be overheard as Captain Keaveney related a story from his school days. "We were informed that the Book of Revelation describes the four horsemen of the Apocalypse – conquest, death, famine and war as hardships that human kind must endure before the end of the world." Harry listened intently and his Captain continued in a lower voice. "This is on an equal footing – so much suffering, despair..." When his voice cracked Harry put his hand on the Captain's shoulder to support him.

"Let's hope Sir this really is the war to end all wars." He removed his hand and the Captain looked up.

"Let's hope so." Fortunately they were interrupted by one of the newer recruits who insisted on filling up their glasses with red wine. Neither objected.

The following week and after much wrangling on Captain Keaveney's part he was able to inform Corporal Hardy that despite the regiment not being disbanded until March 1919 he had arranged for Harry to go home in December, on compassionate leave. "I tried to include your brother but the authorities took a dim view... didn't want to set a precedent."

"Understandable Sir" was the Corporal's surprised answer. "And thank you."

"It's the least I can do" said Captain Keaveney in an understated manner and both men shook hands. As an afterthought Keaveney said all the travel warrants and documents would be handled by himself and HQ. When Harry informed his brother he was relieved there was not one scintilla of jealousy, on the contrary Arthur was concerned with how his brother would cope with their parents as they would still be raw. The two brothers had always known in their hearts, even if it was never brought up in conversation once the reality of trench warfare had set in, that it was unlikely all three would survive not when brothers were being lost on a daily basis in this carnage. Now both had one of those moments of absolute lucidity which happen unsought and unplanned and both realised in this flash of illumination how they carried the memory of their brother, would be determined by how they carried the rest of their respective lives. Neither had ever been particularly demonstrative with the other so they retreated into their own world of loneliness, that bereavement commenced with.

By mid afternoon the sun was dead in the sky, its last light spread over divisions of soldiers, in heavy greatcoats marching along congested roads packed with craters and by the side other men resting, smoking, playing cards and all still trying to comprehend the continuing absence of bursting shrapnel, rapid gunfire and drifting smoke. The worse time of day for infantrymen was just before dusk because superstition suggested that this was when the spirits of dead men lingered in the air waiting for the bugles to sound the Last Post which told them they hadn't been forgotten and it was OK for each to return his gift of life to humanity.

By December 1918, the days crept past with leaden slowness not helped by shivering winds, flakes of snow, leafless trees and skies that possessed more darkness than light. The men of all ranks were growing restless and they wanted to go home for having given years to the army none could see the point of remaining on European soil. "The army moves when the army wants to move" said a veteran of Mons, Loos and Passchendaele who had a habit of taking out a photo of his family and running his fingers over it, on the hour, every hour. "We are alive... be thankful for that..." and it quietened everybody down. Despite the curse in his voice he was astute. "Enjoy the luxury of boredom, some never will..."

No such boredom for Corporal Hardy, he was on his way home by mid December. When he said his goodbyes to the patrol emotion was kept to a minimum, hands were shaken in a manly fashion and the one hug was reserved for his brother. Captain Keaveney escorted him to a transport lorry already packed tight with soldiers and parked at the compound gates. "If I'm honest Corporal, I'm lost for words but there is something I must say and please don't think me sentimental," he paused and looked his Corporal in the eyes. "It's been a privilege to command the Lincoln scouts."

"It's been a privilege to serve under you, Sir." Both men saluted, then shook hands and suddenly rain drenched the compound, it fell in buckets and neither man moved for a few seconds, they waited until their smiles were over.

Harry was hauled into the back by a couple of Welsh Fusiliers. "Don't worry about him, Sir, we won't leave him behind in a brothel before we board the ship!"

shouted one and everyone laughed including Keaveney who turned his collar up and walked away. The transport vehicle was barely five minutes into its long journey to the port of Calais before the repertoire of songs began 'Pack up your troubles', 'Long way to Tipperary' and 'Glasgow belongs to me'. The hours passed until most men were asleep, but not Harry, he thought of the warmth and the light expression in his younger brother's face, always smiling. He couldn't imagine Sid, dead. The rain fell even heavier as though nature was attempting to wash away forever, the last four bloody years. Eventually Harry gave in to fatigue but not before he felt a hand, from one of the Welshmen, pat his shoulder a couple of times, confirmation once again, of a tacit understanding between men who have been through hell.

The constant whirr of the truck's engine provided a balm of sorts for the sleeping soldiers and only an occasional bump when the suspension rode over a pothole interrupted the pattern of those that snored. Harry's dreams were of the Wolds and ploughing fields in glorious sunshine and tending cabbage patches, flower beds and orchard trees laden with fruit. It was the first time in years he'd had such a dream and when he awoke he sensed a new vigour as though a new mood of optimism might be struggling, somewhere within, for recognition.

The truck rolled to a halt and stiff limbed men groaned as they pulled themselves to their feet. The walking wounded were helped down first and the party dispersed in cliques, all sucked in the fresh air enthusiastically and somewhat self-consciously. Harry noticed a starling on the roof of a bombed out building and it immediately promoted memories of home. One of the Welshmen observing him asked "Country boyo are you?"

Harry smiled. "Yes, it's a sight we regularly saw when we set off for work early morning... it would be singing its head off." Then he laughed.

"Important you never forget it" said the Welshman and when he thought Harry looked quizzically at him he expanded. "Always thought of the Mumbles, the sea rolling in, see I'm from Swansea, David Evans. It's what I concentrated on before zero hour, no matter how many shells went over us in the trench. It helped me compose myself... others would be pale, shaking... for we all knew this might be our last moment on earth. I thought of my Mam and imagined her saying 'Well if you're going to meet God I hope you have clean underwear on, I don't want him thinking I don't care for you properly!'"

It elicited a smile from Harry Hardy because the lilt in this man's voice was beguiling and innocent. "War hurts everyone," he continued, "we are the lucky ones even if we have to live with recurring images of boyos without heads, arms, legs or no top half at all." He stopped, suddenly the words had dried up and Harry moved closer to him and put an arm around his shoulder. This spontaneous gesture buoyed the Welshman and he reached into his greatcoat pocket and retrieved his tobacco tin. Both men walked and smoked roll ups before a loud booming voice yelled "Everyone back in the truck, unless you want to walk to

Tipperary!" Suddenly David Evans realised he hadn't had a leak and struggled with the buttons of his greatcoat, tunic and flies while he stood against a centuries old Oak tree with his roll up between his lips at an acute angle. Harry laughed for the first time in a long time especially when a vexed Sergeant yelled "Come on Evans, I don't want to tell your mother why we left you behind... you have chapel to go to this Sunday."

David Evans and Harry were the last two to climb in the back amidst the jovial jeering of the others. For the rest of the journey Harry imagined, then felt, the flow and cheerfulness of a coal fire with logs piled upon it; it eventually nursed him off to sleep.

Chapter 34

Chaos, sheer abandoned chaos ruled the waves at the port of Calais. At first appearances it seemed that half the British and Commonwealth army had descended there and the town was in danger of sinking, fast. Ships, some converted to floating hospitals with operating theatres were busy taking on board the severely wounded and from a vantage position Corporal Hardy realised that strange as it seemed everything was under control. The soldiers were to report at a number of stations far away from the quay before moving to another part of the town and from there to embarkation areas and finally to board ships that would take them across the English Channel. Most men would have to sleep rough until their time but what hardship was that after life in the trenches?

When he reported, like all the others he was told that any theft, looting or vandalism would result in immediate imprisonment in the hastily erected stockade on the outskirts of town. Surely no man, having got this far, would jeopardise his chance of going home thought Harry eyeing an occasional quartet of MP's in near pristine uniforms. The bars were heaving, those in small groups obviously drunk were sullen rather than happy, their faces contorted with rage and bitter words were mostly spoken to themselves and he muttered to himself "I can wait 'till the Red Lion". He felt strangely lost, unsure of himself as though he'd woken up in a new world alien to his nature but because he was practical he shrugged it off as the workings of a tired man in a tired body in a tired mind that ten hours unfettered sleep in a bed with crisp white sheets would instantly cure. For the rest of the morning he walked, smiled and said 'hello' to those whose gaze he held as they passed by and it was easy to recognise those that had learned to face the hardships of war, those that had been broken temporarily by the same hardships and those who would never recover no matter how long they lived and it had nothing to do with external injuries or the smoky grey eyes most soldiers now possessed. "I wonder how many here can recall the hot summer of 1911?" he said to himself and then he smiled because to laugh might seem disrespectful to the dead, all lined up somewhere and awaiting their passes to another world.

Harry examined his documentation repeatedly. Everything was in order and looking at his wrist watch, bought second hand from a jeweller's in Lincoln, he started walking in a north easterly direction thinking how majestic it was not to be afraid. "Four, six, ten hours - who cares how long it is" he said aloud and he welcomed the sight of trees, whose bark had not been scarred by bullets or shrapnel for he hadn't seen this in what seemed almost a life-time unlike the Poplars, Ash and Silver Birch inland. Suddenly he wanted a tumbler full of Mr Haigs or Mr Bells to swill around his jowls and bolster further his spirits. Then he burst out laughing for he saw an officer, who despite his grimy uniform, was the spitting-image of one he'd met when with Captain Keaveney at HQ, who, hearing rustling up in the attic above the planning room bellowed in a cut glass English accent "Those f**king rats are getting bigger than whales with appetites to match." Then he thought of his dead brother and the other Pals who would never experience the wraith of an English winter again and then his eyes turned warm when he imagined them on the threshold of heaven. It surprised him that he felt no bitterness towards his enemy, quite the opposite, for he hoped their collective graves would be opened and a summons offered to arise and live in a new world. Despite his present introspection Harry still found time to admire the young French ladies he walked by, particularly those whose bosoms was full of eager anticipation and who had eyes only for the future, regardless of walking the streets of long-spent sorrows.

At last the hanging about was over and Corporal Hardy timed his walk down to the first embarkation point. He noticed a couple of clergy holding open prayer books occasionally reciting lines when stretcher bearers carried the severely wounded towards the gang planks. A heavy downpour engulfed Calais but would it demoralise men who were finally going home?

Harry made his way to the highest point on the ship the Navy allowed and found shelter from the rain sat against the iron starboard watching the decks flow with water as the English Channel was negotiated. The occasionally jolting caused by heavy waves was felt by the wounded lying on stretchers below decks, particularly by those with bone fractures that grated causing the men to cry out despite the supposedly numbing effect of morphine sulphate. "We will walk on English soil again" said two men holding hands, prostrate on adjoining stretchers, they said it in unison repeatedly until only one voice was heard...

Military planning and organisation shone through at Dover. A strict timetable of disembarkation was observed whilst converted hospital trains and steam engines with additional carriages waited in relays at the station to carry the soldiers to Victoria, St Pancras and Waterloo. In this close confinement of overcrowded carriages all the men could see once again the results of the brutality of war and the dehumanising effect it had on them often for the purpose of survival and the stench, something they would live with, even though the toughest would have wretched and vomited if subjected to it before 1914. Most hoped they wouldn't be imprisoned by their state of mind now the war was over; some dreaded they would be and didn't want to talk about it and all knew the regaining of souls, if the scriptures were to be believed, was a lifetime's work.

The stations were heaving with thousands of soldiers, wives and sweethearts. Tears were shed by those walking past the rows of stretchers laid out against the wall of those who didn't quite get to breathe English air again or move once again in the land of their birth. There was something squalid, obscene about laying out dead men, their whole bodies covered by a blanket and it was noticeable that conversation drew to a hush when people walked by. Certainly Harry paused for thought, ignoring the hunger pains that gnawed at him before hitching a lift in a military vehicle that dropped him on the north side of the capital where he could pick up his connection for Grantham thus avoiding the ant hill that was Kings Cross. Once again he checked his travel documentation before alighting and joining another hundred or so service men, many immunised by drink, huddled on the platform, smoking and allowing former tension to continue rolling away from their body and mind, as complete darkness engulfed the sky above, while the low murmur and pushing of London's traffic provided a constant backdrop.

The train came to a halt having smothered the whole station with steam but it was standing room only after an undignified surge for carriage doors. "All aboard!" shouted the gruff looking guard followed by multiple slamming of doors, followed by three shrill blasts on a whistle. A muffled 'Hooray!' greeted the slow juddering movement as the train pulled out of the station, two suburban stations then next stop, Grantham.

It was difficult for Harry to keep his eyes open for the next hour but he was used to steeling himself for whatever occasion and it was a stiff limbed 'yellow belly' that finally put his feet down in Lincolnshire, albeit a railway platform, after almost four years. He looked at the dozen other exhausted men who walked out of the station with him and could see behind ragged uniforms there was, no more, a collection of individual varieties, envies, greeds and competing ambition, just the habit of loyalty. An army wagon sent down the hill from Prince William of Gloucester Barracks awaited them; the Corporal and driver helped the soldiers climb into the back. "Be there in fifteen minutes and a hot meal of dumpling stew to fortify you all." Faces lit up.

Corporal Hardy had his fill then took off his greatcoat and lay down on one of the make shift camp beds provided for the men, pulled a blanket up and immediately fell asleep – ten hours worth. While he shaved at 10.00 a.m. most of his fellow travellers were still asleep, occasionally snoring in unison. More of the previous evening's stew was served up and he devoured it before taking a large mug of tea into an annexe where he joined soldiers stationed permanently there who greeted him with offers of cigarettes.

As chance would have it he surmised during the half hour conversation that a motor cycle despatch rider was taking some documents to Lincoln HQ and though it was against all army regulations the rider offered to pick up Harry outside the barracks and detour to Tunby Hill. Obviously the Corporal was overjoyed and after a late lunch shook hands with everyone and walked out of the gates with enough post office string to tie three kit bags on his back.

Despite the cold the journey was invigorating and a little sentimental as the countryside became more recognisable and he could feel a smidgen of pride rise in his chest and a faint smile rise in his eyes. The teenage dispatch rider pulled up when he felt his passenger tap his shoulder. "Are you sure? I can take you to the front door," he said with innocence and the Corporal was pleased this boy had been too young to go to The Front. They shared a cigarette and Harry watched the bike roar away in first gear changing into second as a corner approached and then it was out of sight. Harry Hardy, former farm labourer, now Corporal, Veteran of World War One wanted the last couple of miles of his journey to be on foot for marching had been a companion of his in the early years even if his mind for much of that time had been adrift.

Though he remained erect he could feel a rheumatic ache from head to toe but smiled as he moved with a gentle rhythm. "Half an hour more light then that's it" he said looking at his watch. He was pleased the family cottage was on the outskirts of Tunby Hill and hoped his own mother and father would be the first to see him.

As he approached the two centuries old Oak trees either side of the track he slowed and paused to lean against the one resting his kit bag against its trunk for he knew when he turned immediately right, his whitewashed, thatched home would come into view and he wanted to savour this moment; he was almost unrecognisable as the swine he'd once been – and he rubbed the palm of his hand against the bark, for luck, it was what an elderly farmer had told him to do when he was a boy; a Lincolnshire tradition handed down through generations of farmers and their workers; the same tradition that allowed them to think in early April that the dark wintry world will be followed by heaven.

The low sun had melted the crisp frost though there remained pockets shielded by shrubs which Harry noticed and caused him to smile. The rickety gate leading into the back garden was still in need of repair and he remembered his late brother promising their mother he would repair it before he crossed the English Channel, as he lifted it up and moved it before running the bolt back through a hole to secure its position. The back door was framed by creeper and the returning veteran opened it gently; he was immediately hit by the aroma of lifebuoy soap and beeswax polish; his mother had a daily habit of cleaning everything that could be cleaned and polishing everything that was wooden. He reacted emotionally to the scent and composed himself before gently opening the door to the kitchen where he saw his mother sat by the range knitting with layers of wool around her neck. Above the range on a shelf were china plates and photos of the Hardy boys in their army uniforms; a small black ribbon was covering the top corner of Sid's. The eldest son swallowed and at that precise moment his mother saw him and her face lit up as she struggled to get out of her chair and that same face seemed to age.

Harry immediately walked over and beckoned her to sit down before cuddling her in his arms; tears ran down her face and she mopped them with a lace handkerchief she kept under the sleeve of her cardigan. No words were spoken and the embrace was only interrupted when his father came into the kitchen having finished his work for the day.

The men shook hands and father helped son with taking his greatcoat off while mother despite her gaunt face moved one of the large copper kettles into the middle surface of the range. "Mother the boy's back...have you told him you baked a fruit cake this morning." They smiled but there was no denying the sadness that percolated throughout the room; perhaps that was why Harry Hardy gave his mother, now on her feet, a long embrace while his father watched the kettle steaming away before putting his muscular arms around both son and wife. "We have to be grateful that you and Arthur survived" said Jack. "Many families throughout the country haven't been as lucky..." Though his words seemed strangely remote and devoid of emotion as though it was a chemistry formula he was reciting they had a disguised sorrow attached to them which the trio were aware of. The range was pummelled with more coal and more iron pots and kettles full of water were placed on top. Bath time. "You don't know how much I have been looking forward to a soak" said Harry eating another slice of his mother's fruit cake and drinking his third mug of tea.

His father retrieved a bottle of whisky from a cupboard and while father and son had a large measure Mrs Hardy had a small nip. When Harry proposed a toast to Sid his mother was imprisoned by silence; the woman, understandably, had sad eyes nevertheless she took a sip...

An hour passed before there was sufficient hot water to pour into the tin bath Jack Hardy brought in from the shed. Father washed son's back with a soap ridden sponge while the latter washed his own hair. The water turned grey, the same grey that announces another dull winter's day and Harry smiled. "When we are out in the fields Harry we can talk...I don't want your mother hearing anything about the war." Now there was emotion in his voice. "Politicians never learn." He was about to extend the sentence but his wife returned to the kitchen. "I'll heat the stew and tell me when you're ready Harry." "Thanks mother" he responded affectionately and minutes later stepped out of the bath, covered by a very large white towel. As an afterthought his mother who'd resumed knitting said, without looking in his direction, "I'll wash your clothes tomorrow, son". "Thank you" was her son's immediate reply.

Harry ran up the stairs carrying his army trousers and tunic and laid on his bed was clean underwear, a plain shirt and woollen socks. "Heaven" he said to himself.

He dressed and lay on his bed despite the room being extremely cold and he reasoned, despite this, if he closed his eyes for a couple of minutes he would sleep for hours and miss out on his plan to go to his local, The Red Lion.

He, again, felt his parents' warmth as well as that of the kitchen when he sat down at the table and ate dumpling stew with crusts of fresh bread. While mother cleared the plates away Harry sat by the range and announced to his father that he wanted to sleep for an hour before walking to the pub. "Don't let me oversleep?" His father smiled. Outside the wind was picking up and the end of a branch occasionally rattled against the small sitting room window where his mother sat by the open fire; it offered several interesting notes. Harry later found out from his father that this was where his wife often retreated to, alone, in the evening to think about and pray for her sons' safety. On the mantelpiece was a framed sepia photograph of the whole family in their Sunday best taken in 1908. Jack said his wife kissed it every night before going to bed.

The noise of a rural pub in full cry on a Friday evening even half a mile away was instantly recognisable and Corporal Harry Hardy was quivering with anticipation. He felt lighter in clean clothes despite the heaviness of his army greatcoat and he wondered what sort of reception he would get and he drew enough satisfaction from the knowledge he had endured physical distresses against a background of pain, patiently and proudly and his courage had never wilted and he knew he would keep this to himself for the braggart was long gone and in its place an uncomplaining dignity. It was exactly four years to the day since he had walked into the army recruiting office to join up.

Before turning the latch key front door to the village pub he looked up at the shining star sprinkled sky – it was something rural folk felt rather than saw and Harry Hardy retained that pleasure as a cheer went up and a few hands slapped his shoulder; word often spread quickly through the parishes. As he strode to the bar he noticed a couple once attached to each other and now married whom no one ever thought were suited except nature and the instinct of their own hearts and it buoyed him when his smile was returned generously. "Long time, Bertie?" The words were smiled as much as spoken and the landlord took the fresh tea towel resting over his shoulder and wiped his hands on it before shaking his former customer's hand. "It's good to have you home son." The joy in his tone was obvious as was the hint of solemnity and both understood for this man had also served his country in war. Harry Hardy watched, mesmerised as Bertie drew strong pulls on the hand pump....three and the Batemans bitter had a frothy head. He stared at it and the recollection of the Fens Pals talking about this moment was suddenly crystal clear. "It's on the house." Harry drank the first half feverishly then put the straight glass down which surprised some of the regulars stood at the bar.

Bertie immediately topped the glass up. "Thank you Bertie." Before he went to serve another customer he suggested to Harry that he might like to go to The Red Lion out of licensing hours. "See how you feel." "Thanks Bertie, maybe in the next few days." As an afterthought he added "Still the best pint in Lincolnshire" and then he smiled and everyone around could see the former rigid, vindictive, utterly selfish behaviour had been eroded.

Harry drank another couple of pints on insistence and paid for by others who, still a month after cessation of hostilities revelled in the fact that the Hun had been given a bloody nose; only later would the full horrors be revealed and this was not the time or place to start so Harry parried questions with a politician's ease but was genuinely moved by the older men some of which were ex-combatants who quietly offered their condolences saying the whole parish had lost some fine men. In their company he was able to build up the quick edifice of confidence while dry blood splattered with French mud seemingly sown into the fabric of his army overcoat provided an invisible aroma.

Attention was drawn to a group of men who burst in to the pub on the stroke of 9 p.m. armed with domino boards; the regular pub versus pub monthly challenge would soon begin.

It enabled the oldest Hardy boy to move closer to something he noticed, on the east facing wall when he'd come in forty five minutes earlier – small framed photographs of those parish pals that had given their lives. A stonemason from Louth had carved the names into the bare wall under the inscription 'Known unto God'; a recess had been cut out and a lighted candle in a brass base covered by an open glass tube was throwing tongues across parts of the recess. This would remain a feature of 'the local' until the brewery along with others nationwide decided to modernise their pubs during the sixties when talk was about white hot technology. Corporal Harry Hardy was immensely moved and raised his glass more a gesture than deliberate action and when he finished that pint another one was brought over to him as the pub landlord placed eight pints on the bar for the domino players and the noise level rose. "Ten p.m., the singing will start soon" whispered Harry to himself as he listened to the older farmers, having joined him, talk about, as they always did this time of year, the problem of farming when the ground's like iron. He was asked about his future but Harry was non-committal. If he needed any persuasion that might tip the balance in the army's favour he saw it in a mirror image of himself pre-war – a stout looking young man, probably a poacher sat heavily ironed, sullen, fierce and ignoble next to a young woman who looked petrified. His middle name could have been grudge.

Before last orders rang on the brass bell Harry decided to go home. He surreptitiously made his way to the side of the bar and the landlord let him through a side door. "Want to go home now quietly Bertie but can I buy a bottle of Whisky off you?" A quick handshake passed between them and the landlord gave him a bottle off the shelf and declined any money. "Remember, come round one afternoon and if Arthur's home bring him." "He won't be back until next year" responded Harry. Bertie nodded and opened the back entrance for Harry to walk into a bracing wind; it certainly flushed the tobacco smoke out of his eyes and when he looked at the richness of the sky above began counting the stars but there were too many so he pulled his collar up and concentrated on not slipping on the icy track.

Quietly, he let himself through the front door, replacing the key on a saucer on the seat of the hall stand and took his boots off before gently climbing the stairs; he missed the eighth one because that always creaked like a tree about to fall.

He moved the latch slowly to let himself into his bedroom. He sat down in his coat and took the whisky from the side pocket and poured a very large measure into a glass tumbler. The full moon offered enough light to his room while the curtains remained open. He was about to take a large drink but put the glass down and stared at the moon.

Not once had Harry Hardy, farm labourer, Corporal Harry Hardy, army man ever indulged in an orgy of self pity. On the contrary he acknowledged he was the lucky one and he remembered Captain Keaveney's words. "I've had to tell myself this and I want to tell you, the others…don't feel guilty because you survived when others didn't."

Harry breathed in deeply took the glass and recited the names "Sid, Michael, David, Peter, David, Donald Rest in Peace." He drank the lot and refilled the glass to the brim. This time he stood up and stared at the moon before drinking the glass empty then stripping off, putting on his night shirt and climbing into his bed heavily weighed down with several woollen blankets.

He had one more thing to do in the morning; something he'd thought of since November 11th. Now sleep moved faster than a racing car as the moon dimmed its beam; and that sleep was heavy, aided by rather than controlled by an alcoholic haze; and it produced short memorable dreams – The angels of Mons floating outside his bedroom window followed by dull organ music that usually fills a church like a rain cloud followed by the soothing sounds of a gentle flute playing Handel's 'I know that my Redeemer liveth'. It was the clear treble notes that woke Harry Hardy up at 7.30 a.m. and in complete darkness he felt, momentarily, disorientated before gathering his wits and recounting his dreams – He couldn't name the composer or the title of the piece yet it seemed familiar to him. When he tried to concentrate his hangover wouldn't let him so he stumbled out of the bed and dunked his head, in a sink of cold water, in the kitchen before returning upstairs and getting dressed.

His mother was cooking porridge on the range and kissed him gently before offering her son a large mug of piping hot stewed tea. Before drinking it he gave his mother a large embrace for he knew the lost of just one son was a wound that could never be thoroughly healed; his thoughts travelled to Mrs Reid but he said nothing.

Jack Hardy came in from outside and bolted the front door, the sound of which prompted his wife to fill up another mug with tea before dropping dollops of honey into porridge. The oil lamps were adjusted to throw heavier light into the kitchen before everyone sat down at the table. "What's on the cards today, Harry?" asked his father. "I want to familiarise myself with everything – there are a few people I want to call on." His mother smiled with reverent affection while Jack Hardy nodded approvingly. At 8.30 a.m. while light and dark grappled with each other in the sky, Harry warmed his overcoat against the range before putting it on and stuffing a couple of apples in each pocket. He broke the silence in the room saying "I should be back before midday" and with that hurried out of the cottage.

Within half an hour he was farther into the Lincolnshire countryside and he sought an elevated position, one of several that the boys had often used as a rendezvous.

It was 9.30 a.m. when Harry sat down against the trunk of an Elm tree. Light was everywhere and the wind had fallen to a whisper and he repositioned himself to get the newly formed sun on his face.

With such a wonderful view unfolding the Hardy's eldest son began reminiscing while keeping his head erect. It was as if he was living life over again with more human insight, a more poignant understanding and of course humility that four years of attrition had eventually taught him. He didn't have the Church's belief in God but before he could speculate on how he might keep his soul erect a wild deer appeared to his right and only fifteen yards away. Maybe this was mid-winter's glimpse of the first day of spring which always brought rejoicing to the rural community for it re-opened hope for sinking hearts and the promise of change – that troubles will not last. It was common knowledge that these graceful creatures could smell human beings from fifty yards and that was as close as anyone could get, yet this one eschewed any notion of danger. Strange.

Harry remained transfixed; maybe he surmised that it was his greatcoat that still held particles of mustard gas, foreign soil and dead blood even decayed human tissue not visible to the naked eye that neutralised the humanity of its wearer. In the background, in front of a copse a dozen other deer mingled and the sight warmed Harry. When the deer moved to within twelve yards he felt awed as though a reconnection with nature had been reborn in him; neither man nor animal moved when the flute song of a blackbird was heard overhead followed by the whistling of a blue tit hunting for insects.

Harry could see the brown watery eyes of his visitor and suddenly the individual images of each of the Fens Pals as if operated by a carousel came into vision; his smile now had a roguish confidence and he asked the deer "You want to know why?" The animal scurried away over open ground towards the others and Harry Hardy stood and shouted "Why?" And mustering every last ounce of energy in his chest and lungs he shouted "You want to know why? GO ASK THE FELLOWS WHO CUT THE HAY".

It was the release he wanted for here he could look out on life and the landscape and he saw the different composition thrown up by the different seasons, the bright colours, the dull colours, the greenness of trees nearer to the eye and the diminishing height of Poplars in the distance leaning against green cushioned hills. "With this there's no need to attend church or stay at home and read St. Peter..." he said to himself and then he sat down in a repose of silent thought before eating another apple, including the core.

Again he drank everything in as more splinters of sunshine sharpened the countryside and the burr of a tractor engine could be heard albeit faintly though out of sight.

His mind retreated to the conversation he'd had with his father after he'd volunteered which the latter thought his son wasn't listening to or worse his words were going in one ear and out the other. It elicited a smile and that smile moved Harry's heart and he was aware of a tear in his eye for he knew he was fit to walk back to his own cottage and take off all the army's clothes and put his own clothes on for he realised he could enter his home justified; that was all he wanted and the future could take care of itself.

Time eventually soothed over some of the pangs and taught many a consoling lesson but the life the village had known for generations was lost forever.